A
TALON'S
WRATH

A
TALON'S
WRATH

Riftborn * Book 3

STEVE McHUGH

Podium

For Faith.

Copyright © 2023 by Steve McHugh

Cover design by Podium Publishing

978-1-0394-2524-8

Published in 2023 by Podium Publishing, ULC
www.podiumaudio.com

Podium

GLOSSARY

SPECIES:

Ancients: The oldest, but not necessarily the most powerful, members of the rift-fused. They ensure that there are checks and balances between rift-fused and humans.

eidolons: Living embodiments of rift power that reside as caretakers of a Riftborn's embers. Can change shape to most animals as needed. Are always two for every Riftborn's embers.

fiends: Animals that die on Earth close to a tear and are brought back to life from the power of the rift. Comes in three kinds: lesser, greater, and elder.

practitioners: Those born inside the rift. Can create constructs along with using the rift to imbue writing and potions with its power.

Primes: The rulers of Inaxia, the capital city of the rift.

primordials: Creatures that live inside the Tempest in the rift.

revenants: Those who died on Earth as human, close to a tear, and were brought back to life by the power of the rift. There are ten different species of Revenant.

rift-fused: Anyone or anything given power by the rift.

rift-walkers: Can create tears between the rift and Earth at will.

riftborn: Those who were mortally wounded on Earth as human but were taken into the rift and gifted incredible power. Can move between earth and the rift using their embers.

GROUPS:

Guilds: Seven groups of powerful rift-fused who ensure that humans and rift-fused live in harmony.

Investigators: Police force of Inaxia.

RCU (Rift-Crime Unit): Multi-nation agency who investigate crimes committed by and against the rift-fused.

Talon: Guild member trained in secret to remove threats to their Guild.

PLACES:

Crow's Perch: Prison city in the rift, run by the Queen of Crows.

embers: The pocket dimension used by riftborn to travel between Earth and the rift, as well as to heal any physical wounds the riftborn has sustained.

Harmony: The area surrounding the Tempest.

Inaxia: Capital city of the rift.

Lawless City: City in the rift that lives free from Inaxia rule.

Nightvale: Settlement in the rift.

rift: Dimension attached to our own that allows incredible power to flow out from it through tears between dimensions.

Tempest: The maelstrom of power at the north of the rift.

A
TALON'S
WRATH

CHAPTER ONE

The last few months had been somewhat more . . . interesting than I was particularly comfortable with.

The rift-fused are not considered to have a particularly large worldwide population. There are, at a push, about nine million of us on Earth. And while that number has steadily increased over the millennia, it would take tens of thousands of years before they're anything close to even one percent of the human population.

So, when a rift-fused is shown on TV arresting a Member of Parliament for the British government, people tend to notice. The fact that the person doing the arresting was me meant that for the last four months, I'd been far more recognisable than I was happy with.

After my brief appearance on every news channel in the UK, and quickly followed by a majority of them in the world, people had wanted to know more about me. Who was I? What was I? And where did I live? These were all questions that people online had tried to fish answers for. I *trended* . . . a word I was not happy to have occur or needed to know existed.

Thankfully, my flat in Brooklyn is under a different name, which meant no one could track me to my home. My friend Gabriel, on the other hand, and his church in Hamble, New York, received more visitors than ever before. In the end, we decided to use his church as a point of contact should anyone try to get hold of me. So far it had worked out, and after a few weeks, the media of the world decided there was something new to focus on and I was largely forgotten about.

Unfortunately, that still meant lots of people trying to contact Gabriel to find me, some friendly, some not. Gabriel was a big boy, though, and could more than handle himself.

I was putting all of that behind me for a few days as I was taken from New York and flown to London. There I was driven through the city in the back of a Range Rover to an eight-storey building near the Shard.

Ravi Gill, head of the UK Rift-Crime Unit, had told me beforehand that because the RCU were stretched thin, he'd requested a driver from the Met police.

The UK RCU branch had a real problem with people working for them who were essentially employed by MP Jacob Smythe, who'd turned out to be a crime boss. Ravi had done his best to ensure that only his people were still in the RCU, and I hoped, for everyone's sake, that was the case.

The piece of work I was visiting was that very MP. After trying to open a permanent tear to the rift, which would have turned a large portion of the Hampshire countryside into an apocalyptic nightmare, I'd made my very visible capture of Jacob Smythe. He was the type to hold a grudge, and I wasn't sure how he was going to react when he saw me for the first time since his arrest.

The building I was heading to was the front for an underground rift-fused prison. The facility had been in use since well before the rift-fused had been public knowledge. It housed a little over a hundred prisoners, although currently the number of inmates was single digits.

There were prisons like this all over the globe. Most of them out of the way, underground, or somewhere so heavily guarded that the world at large assumed it was some sort of government facility.

It was winter in England, which meant it was either windy and cold or windy and raining, or, on this particular occasion, both.

"I'm beginning to think we're going to need an ark," Ravi said as we dashed from where our cars dropped us off to the front entrance of the eight-storeys-high building.

Ravi was over six feet tall, with brown skin, a Cockney accent, and a tendency to wear exceptionally nice-looking suits. Today's choice was dark purple, which I was pretty sure I could never get away with but looked like it was made especially for him. Ravi was also human, which was a rarity for the RCU, although it had no bearing on him being good at his job.

We walked through the large foyer, where two receptionists sat behind a large semicircle table in front of a bank of monitors showing various news networks all on mute. Half a dozen armed guards stood next to a set of metal detectors, in front of four lifts and two sets of stairwells. The guards were a mixture of human and rift-fused, all armed with both rift-tempered bladed weapons and guns.

Ravi nodded to them as we walked silently through the metal detector, with me having placed my dual rift-tempered daggers and anything else that might cause a beep, on a counter to the side, pausing to put it all away when done.

"I always find it amazing that you can just walk around anywhere with those things," Ravi said after he used his security card on a reader next to the lifts.

"Things?" I asked as we entered the newly arrived lift.

"The daggers," he said.

"Ah, well, the Guild medallion gives me a lot of leeway," I said, talking about the copper-coloured medallion that hung around my neck. It was in the shape of a buckler shield with a sword and hammer crossing over each other in front, and a steel raven sat atop it. As the sole surviving remaining member of the Raven Guild, it had taken me a long time to start wearing it again.

"Can you take them on a normal flight?" he asked, selecting the button for the fourth underground floor on the panel next to the door.

I nodded. "It's weird, but whenever Guild members fly and we've got whatever bladed or blunt weapon we use with us, people appear to be calmer about the flight."

"I guess if there is trouble, having someone who can stop it makes people feel better," Ravi said.

"Never given it much thought," I said. "Normally, Guilds used private flights and cars."

"Where's your Guild's private plane, then?" Ravi asked.

"Destroyed a long time ago," I said. "Not entirely sure the Ancients would give me a new one."

"You ever thought about re-forming the Ravens?" Ravi asked.

I nodded. "I did, but then Callie Mitchell and her turn-people-into-monsters scheme fell in my lap and here we are. Ji-hyun and Nadia send their apologies for not coming."

"They okay?" Ravi asked.

"Ji-hyun is in charge of not just the RCU in New York but most of the eastern states of America's offices, so busy . . . and frustrated. And Nadia is . . ." I thought for a second. "She didn't want to come and see Jacob."

"Because?"

"She wasn't sure if her ability to see possible futures might make her see one where she's meant to rip his head off," I said. "Didn't want to risk it."

"Probably wise," Ravi agreed.

The lift stopped and the doors opened slowly, revealing a small foyer with four more armed guards. The guards were stood either side of the only exit out of the foyer, a long corridor that led to a large metal door.

There were, like at the front entrance, metal detectors to walk through, although these were built into the corridor you had to walk down to reach the door. There were one-way mirrors on either side, and more guards sat inside, watching your heat patterns and X-rays.

A guard walked with us down the corridor, making us wait for several seconds while she turned a huge wheel on the door, which made a loud beep when it was fully rotated. A second beep, this one muffled, came through from the other side of the door, and with a loud hiss of air, the door slid into the wall.

More guards were behind the door, and like every other guard so far, they wore padded armour and black masks pulled up to their eyes. Anyone working there was always at risk of an inmate escaping and going after their family. Most rift-fused prisons used a mixture of human and rift-fused workers, and usually only the rift-fused or those in high positions were unmasked.

We continued down the corridor, past several closed doors that I was pretty sure led to more corridors and deeper parts of the prison, until we reached another foyer with more guards and a second large metal door.

"This is it," Ravi said. "You ready?"

"Always," I told him.

The door opened without any input from the guards, and a middle-aged man walked out. He had long grey hair, a matching beard, and was nearly seven feet tall with a barrel chest.

"Dr. Striker," Ravi said, shaking the doctor's huge hand.

"It is good to see you, Ravi," Dr. Striker said with a Scottish accent.

"Is our guest ready for visitors?" Ravi asked.

"I think we should talk first," Dr. Striker told us. He turned to me. "Lucas Rurik."

I noticed he hadn't offered me his hand.

"Is there a problem?" I asked.

"I am curious about how you will react to my prisoner," Dr. Striker said. "I am in charge of this prison and the inmates here, which means I am also in charge of their safety. Along with the safety of my people."

"You think I'm going to try to kill Jacob now that he's had his Parliamentary status removed," I said.

"The thought crossed my mind," Dr. Striker confirmed.

"I'm not going to kill him," I said. "I just want to talk."

"Yes, that's another problem," Dr. Striker said. "Why would Jacob only talk to you?"

"I'm lucky?" I suggested.

Dr. Striker didn't smile. "I do not want him to say something that you retaliate to. I do not wish to have to clean up the mess of a Guild member. Again."

And the penny dropped. "I'm not killing him or hurting him; I just need to talk to him," I said. "Whatever issues you have with Guilds has nothing to do with me. I don't murder people in custody."

Dr. Striker stared at me for an uncomfortably long time before nodding and walking back through the open door with Ravi and me behind him.

Ravi shrugged.

The corridor behind the door had the same white walls and ceiling as everything else, but the black tiles had a green line running the length of the corridor.

"Jacob is at the end," Dr. Striker said, leading us down the eerie corridor, past a dozen doors.

"This whole place is a bit of a maze," I said.

"It's why there are coloured lines," Dr. Striker said without turning back. "Each of these doors leads to either a corridor or to cells. Jacob is the only prisoner in the Green Zone of the prison. We decided it best to keep him separate from anyone else in case his parentage was discovered and it caused . . . complications."

"You know that his father is a Prime in Inaxia?" I asked.

"He told us," Dr. Striker said as we reached the door. He turned back to me. "You swear you will not harm him."

I crossed over my heart. "Promise."

Dr. Striker removed a card key from his black suit jacket pocket and swiped it over a small card reader, which beeped. The door made a clicking noise and Dr. Striker pushed it open.

The room beyond was maybe fifteen feet wide by thirty feet long. There was a partition after six feet, dividing the visiting area from the cell. There were no doors or windows in the cell, although a lamp inside the cell and one in the visiting area were bright enough to illuminate everything.

There were three comfortable-looking leather chairs in the visiting area, and a couch that sat against one side of the room. A table on the opposite wall had various recording equipment on it, presumably for *official* visits for prisoners.

Dr. Striker walked over to the recording equipment and activated it, tapping a microphone. "Do not disable this," he said to me.

I ignored him and walked over to the partition separating me from the cell itself. The cell had two rooms, both of which were visible from where I stood. One room had a bed, seating, a table, TV on the wall, and a small stereo system, while the second room had a toilet, sink, and shower. There was no such thing as privacy in these cells.

Jacob was lying on his bed. The last time I'd seen him, he'd been wearing an expensive dark blue suit and custom-made shoes. They were now replaced with a bright blue jumpsuit and dark grey socks. He was reading a newspaper, although I couldn't see which one or what the article was about.

"Jacob," Dr. Striker said from the electronics table.

"Yes, Doctor," Jacob said without moving.

"You have visitors," Dr. Striker said.

"Thank you, Percival," Jacob said, placing his newspaper on the floor and swinging his legs off his bed. He'd grown a slight beard in the months from when I'd last seen him.

"How are you doing in there, Hannibal?" I said. "You wanted to see me?"

Jacob gave a tight smile and walked over to what passed for a kitchen sink, filling a kettle, plugging it in, and switching it on.

"Always the joker, Lucas," he said. "If you don't mind, I would like a cup of tea before we begin.

"What, no *fava beans* with a nice *Chianti*?" I said with a smirk.

Ravi stifled a laugh.

I sat down in one of the comfortable seats, with Ravi taking the seat beside me and Dr. Striker remaining by the electronics table.

"Dr. Striker, our agreement, please," Jacob said.

I looked over at Dr. Striker, who was staring at me. He nodded once and pushed a button on the far wall. The foot-thick, bulletproof glass partition between us slid down into the ground.

"Ah," Jacob said. "Thank you, Doctor."

I stayed put. "We could have just spoken with that there if you were concerned I'd hurt him," I said to Dr. Striker.

"Jacob refused to speak to anyone unless he had several demands met," Ravi said. "No partition. Speaks only when you're here. And a kettle with tea and milk delivered regularly."

"That's it?" I asked.

"He also asked for an internet connection, but funnily enough, we vetoed that," Ravi said.

The kettle finished boiling and Jacob calmly made himself a cup of tea, adding milk and sugar to the hot water and stirring it slowly without looking back at us.

"Jacob," Dr. Striker said, an almost-plea in his voice. "We really do need to begin."

Jacob let out a deep breath, turned back to us, and, cup in hand, walked out of his cell, moved the chair beside mine so that it was facing me, and sat down.

"I wish you to know that should anything occur here that jeopardises either party, I will hit the panic button," Dr. Striker said, pointing to a red button on the wall beside him.

I got up, moving my own chair so that it was facing Jacob, and retook my seat. "Could have saved us a lot of time and effort if we didn't have to do the theatrics," I told him as Ravi pushed his chair back. Far enough away to not be involved in the conversation, but close enough that he could stop me from murdering Jacob. Well, technically, he couldn't stop me if he tried, but I liked Ravi, so I wasn't going to do anything stupid.

"Lucas Rurik," Jacob said, before blowing on his hot cup of tea. "It's been a while. My beard isn't quite as full as your own, but it's getting there."

"I'd be glad to share grooming tips," I told him. "If it helps, the prison jumpsuit really looks good on you. The colour is great for your skin."

Jacob laughed. "I imagine you have many questions. Most of which I refused to answer without you being here. Do you know why?"

"Because you're a self-aggrandising dipshit?" I suggested with a shrug.

Jacob's smile didn't reach his eyes, where only hate lived.

In contrast, my smile beamed.

"We want details on where Callie Mitchell is," Ravi said. "We also want information on your work while you were a Member of Parliament, and every single other member who was aware of your status and did nothing."

"The Prime Minister," Jacob said first.

"We know about him," Ravi said. "He's currently under criminal investigation."

"He's a moron," Jacob snapped. "He used my ill-gotten funds to prop up his electoral campaign; he used my knowledge and contacts to help push through legislation. In short, he was only made Prime Minster because I couldn't be seen to have any higher profile than I did. I helped him, and he pushed through the legislation I needed. I gave you all of the intel about the Prime Minister."

"And it'll take a long time to go through," Ravi said. "There's a lot of detailed notes and journals."

"I liked notes," Jacob said. His gaze snapped around to me. "How is being famous?"

"I get better restaurant tables," I said nonchalantly.

"Where is Dr. Callie Mitchell?" Ravi asked.

"I've told you a hundred times, I don't know," Jacob said. "She contacted me using a burner phone and pinging her IP across a million different places. I don't know where she is, I don't know what she's doing, I just know that when she's done, she's going to change the world."

"What does that mean?" Ravi asked.

"It means exactly how it sounds," Jacob said. "She's going to change the world. It's what she does."

"She's a monster," I said. "She experiments on people, fiends, on anything she can get her hands on. She's a murderer and a torturer. She's closer to a war criminal than an actual doctor."

"She really got under your skin, didn't she?" Jacob asked. "She said that you were in her charge for several days. I guess she made a good impression on you. Did she show you her experiments? Did she show you the leaps she's made?"

"I saw a lot," I said softly.

"You know the suit I wear right now, the one that's designed to stop me being able to access the rift?" Jacob asked, pulling his jumpsuit collar aside to show off the dark blue second-skin suit. "Do you know how it works?"

"Yes," I said.

"You ever worn one?" Jacob asked.

"Yes," I told him. "Practitioners help make them. They create potions that can stop people accessing the rift; those suits are soaked in them. It's not quite as permanent as Callie wanted me to believe when I first met her, but it lasts long enough. Were you the practitioner who helped her?"

Jacob shrugged. "What if I was? What if I helped Callie subjugate and experiment on rift-fused? You'd consider me a monster, wouldn't you? Even though I was banished here with Callie, with the Blessed. Betrayed and banished for trying to make our lives better."

"By murdering a whole bunch of people," I pointed out. "I will give you that maybe your dad could have used a little murdering. He did betray you, after all."

"My dad is the real monster here," Jacob shouted, almost jumping up. "And you helped him."

"Jacob, please," Dr. Striker said, his voice soothing. "This isn't helping."

Jacob let out a sigh and sat down. "Fine; let's start again, shall we?"

CHAPTER TWO

The meeting went on for what felt like an age, and despite all of Jacob's posturing and general dickish behaviour, all I really discovered was that he genuinely didn't know where Callie Mitchell was and had very little to do with her "research."

Dr. Striker winced or rolled his eyes, depending on which response was better for Jacob's smugness or my sarcasm. And it eventually became clear that we were going around in circles.

"You know, this hasn't been as helpful as I was hoping it would be," Ravi said. "You've given us nothing of value. Yet you want nicer accommodation, and you want somewhere with a window."

"We both know you have aboveground prison cells in this facility," Jacob almost snapped. "I deserve to be placed in accommodation suiting me."

"Sure," Ravi said. "Give us something concrete to use, then."

Jacob's smile was almost serpent-like.

"Look, you don't know where Callie is," I said. "You have nothing to offer us about those members of the Blessed you worked with and who are still out there. And frankly, while I'm not above torturing you for the sheer joy of it, I don't think it would garner any actionable intel. Besides, I don't want to give the good doctor heart palpitations. You want something; I want Kurt."

"Who is Kurt?" Dr. Striker asked.

"He's the rat bastard who murdered Simon Wallace," I said, thinking back to how we'd found Simon's tortured and broken body. "We took Kurt at the same time we grabbed Jacob, but because Kurt was human, he was put in a human prison. Which his friends attacked, blowing up a part of it to help him escape. Five people died in that escape. I want to find him before he resurfaces and does something else horrible."

"Simon betrayed me," Jacob said with a shrug. "He was working for the RCU. He deserved what he got."

"No one deserved that," I snapped. "Where is Kurt?"

"You haven't found him?" Jacob mocked. "I thought you were good at finding people. I thought that was the point of someone in your position."

"My position?" I asked.

"You are a Talon, yes?" Jacob asked with a smirk. "Or were. Before you let your own people get murdered. Not much of a Talon, I guess. So, I understand why you need my help."

As much as I wanted to punch him in his face, I just sat there and smiled, counted to a hundred, and leaned forward. "There are other members of the Blessed out there who are probably *really* worried about you being locked up, but even more concerned about the fact that you were responsible for their cash flow. And you had someone on your staff who made meticulous notes about everyone you worked with. Some of those people have been arrested. Some publicly. How bad do you think it'll be for you if we start to leak that you were incompetent enough to have someone spying on you and your allies? You think that those other Blessed members might get an itchy neck? Might start to wonder if you need silencing once and for all, just in case?"

The smugness evaporated from Jacob's eyes, and it was fucking glorious.

"Or maybe," I said, sitting back in my seat, "we let them know that you're helping us. You're cooperating. We let the TV stations know that. We let your friends get some seriously squeaky bums as they try to figure out whether or not you've sold them out. How long do you think it would be for them to put one of their own in a guard uniform in this facility? Maybe your food gets poisoned, or maybe you get a bullet in the head. Who knows. But it will be fun to find out which one."

"My money is on the bullet," Ravi said. "Quick, clean, no chance of him coming back. He's a practitioner, so he dies here on Earth, he dies, full stop. No afterlife in the rift for you."

"You think they'll torture him first?" I asked.

"Yes, they'll want to send a message," Ravi said. "Like the ones he used to send when he had a person's family murdered in front of them and made them watch as they died. That was sort of your play for people who crossed you. Made you sound scary. Do you think he looks scary now?"

I shook my head. "I think the people he worked with and for are much scarier. Otherwise, he'd have given them up. But I also think he's going to give up Kurt, or I'm going to make sure he lives the rest of his life in fear of someone paying him a late-night visit."

"Mr. Rurik," Dr. Striker said.

I raised my hand. "Doc, I understand your protests, but I haven't hit him, I haven't tortured him. I've laid out *exactly* what is going to happen to him should his allies believe he turned on them. And I'll make it my business to ensure they *all* believe he turned on them."

"Kurt is at a safe house," Jacob said, looking part-exhausted and part-terrified.

Ravi wrote down the address as Jacob told us. "That's a Portsmouth address."

"The docks," Jacob said, clearly unhappy he'd been forced into his current position.

I got to my feet and stretched. "Thank you for your cooperation."

"You'll get me a window room?" Jacob asked, and I was happy to hear the whine in his voice.

"If this works out, yes," Ravi told him.

"How'd you know I was a Talon?" I asked.

"Callie told me when we conducted our deal a while back," Jacob said. "The last time I saw her. She said that you were a Talon and that I should not take you lightly if our paths met. She was right. As usual."

Jacob went back into his cell, the glass partition secured in place before Dr. Striker took Ravi and me back through the facility and up to the reception area. He shook Ravi's hand and, after a second of considering, offered his hand to me, too. I shook it without comment.

"You are not the man I assumed you were," Dr. Striker said, letting go of my hand.

"What were you expecting?" I asked.

"A killer," he said, looking around before whispering. "A man who would do whatever it took to get the job done. I was led to believe that was what Talons did. What Guilds did."

"Me being a Talon isn't exactly something you want to let people know," I said, hoping that the fact he wanted to whisper it meant he knew already.

"I'm aware," Dr. Striker said. "You have enemies."

"Some," I said. "Not that many these days."

"Because your Guild was destroyed?" Dr. Striker asked.

I shook my head. "No, because I've killed most of them. Have a good day, Doc."

"Can I assume you'll be joining us in Portsmouth?" Ravi asked as his phone began to ring. "I've gotta get this; I'll see you at the car."

I gave him a thumbs-up as I returned to the car, where the driver walked over to the door and opened it, allowing me inside. He closed the door and walked around to the driver's side, opened the door, and stared at me for a moment longer than what was probably considered healthy.

"Sorry, thought you'd be longer," he said, using a vapor e-cigarette.

"Take your time," I told him.

He nodded a thanks and took a puff, blowing the smoke out over the top of the car. Despite his efforts, I caught a whiff of sweet bubblegum and tried to block it out. If you're going to smoke one of those things, at least pick a scent that doesn't smell like a sugary version of wet dog.

I looked over for Ravi, who was nowhere to be seen.

While still standing in the door of the car, the police officer placed one foot on the brake and pressed the start button, the large engine coming to life. He removed a small black remote from his jacket pocket and pressed the button. He tossed the device into the car, slammed the door, and ran as fast as he could.

I tried my door, but it was locked. I immediately turned to smoke, but even so, the explosion that took place in the car rattled my brain and caused agony to shoot through my displaced body. I screamed wordlessly, only my conscious mind aware of it as the Range Rover was torn in half by the force of the device. The roof was ripped apart from the blast, giving me a thankful exit. There was a second blast as I was moving away from the car, which took out the windows, and caused a third explosion, which blew out of the front of the car.

A black BMW screeched to a halt close to where I re-formed, as Ravi and the guards in the building flooded out, ordering the Met police officer to stand down as he jumped into the BMW and it sped away.

"You okay?" Ravi asked me as I patted down a small fire on my shoulder.

Before I could answer, there was a shriek of metal in the distance and a huge bang. I sprinted in the direction of the noise, seeing the smoke in the distance. The BMW had taken the corner too quickly, spun out, and smashed into the side of a lamp pole. Smoke poured out of the engine, and I doubted it would be long before something caught fire.

There were dozens of people all around, most looking on in shock or calling the emergency services, while more than a few immediately got out their phones to film the proceeding drama. One particularly enterprising filmmaker had got a little too close to the car when the passenger door was flung open, smacking him in the chest and sending him sprawling to the ground.

I was in front of Ravi, who was leading the charge of several guards from the prison. "I've got the runner," I shouted, as the police officer who tried to blow me up practically fell out of the car and scrambled to his feet, lurching off toward a nearby park.

He was much slower than I was, and before he'd even reached the park entrance—shooing aside spectators and waving his taser around—I'd made up the distance between us.

He turned, aimed his taser, and fired it at me, the needles harmlessly sailing through my smoke form as I continued on toward him.

I re-formed directly in front of him, pushed the taser to one side, and broke his arm at the elbow.

There were thuds from somewhere behind me.

"You work for Jacob?" I asked, keeping hold of the police officer's arm as I bent it in an unnatural angle, forcing him down to one knee.

The police officer cried out in pain.

"Don't make me ask again," I told him.

"Yes," the man said. "We planned to hit you and Ravi after you'd visited Jacob. We have someone on the inside; we bugged his cell. Jacob still has a lot of people in his pocket."

"Apparently so," I said. Considering I was being filmed again, I pulled the officer to his feet and marched him over to Ravi and the others while sirens blared in the distance.

Someone had grabbed a fire extinguisher and was busy putting out the smouldering engine of what had been a perfectly nice BMW M4. The driver was flat on his face, with Ravi pointing an MP5 at the back of his head. I didn't know where the gun had come from; I assumed one of the prison guards.

There were two more men in the rear seats of the car, which couldn't have been much fun for them. Quite why they'd decided to use a coupe for their escape attempt, I wasn't entirely sure, but they'd both been knocked unconscious from the impact and were being extricated from the still smouldering vehicle.

"I get my own people cleared from this shit and we still have to deal with everyone else that Jacob has on his payroll," Ravi snapped.

"Why not hit the prison?" I asked the officer as I planted him on the ground.

"Too well guarded," he said.

"Is Kurt still in Portsmouth?" I asked.

The police officer shook his head. "He's been gone for weeks now."

"You acted rashly," I said. "You should have waited until we were on the way to Portsmouth, but you decided to jump in with both feet, and that's going to be the end of your little band of criminals. Thanks for coming to me; saves me the trouble of hunting you down once we're done."

I handcuffed the officer with his own cuffs, attaching one end to a nearby bike lock, and left him lying on ground. Unless he was going to gnaw his wrist off, he wasn't going anywhere.

An ambulance pulled up, followed quickly by a fire engine, three police cars, and, a few seconds later, a second ambulance. Ravi organised them, and soon the police were putting a cordon in place, while the fire brigade completely ruined whatever remained of the BMW with foam. I would have sworn they were smiling while they did it, too.

The majority of the prison guards who had helped were now back in the prison, and Ravi had called the RCU, who were on their way. It was turning into quite the morning.

"You think Jacob set this up?" Ravi asked me away from everyone else as they did their jobs.

I nodded. "I'm going to go ask, either way."

"Don't kill him," Ravi shouted after me, and I gave him a thumbs-up without looking back.

"I assume you wish to speak to Mr. Smythe," Dr. Striker said the moment I was back in the building.

"You'd assume correctly," I said.

To his credit, Dr. Striker didn't argue or try to calm me down—which would have almost certainly made me even angrier—and took me back along the same route I'd taken once already today, leading me into Jacob's cell.

Jacob stood up against the divider with a smile plastered on his face. "Glad to see you survived," Jacob said. "You do understand I had to try."

"They weren't even trying to get you free," I said. "Just kill me and Ravi."

"Well, yes," Jacob said, showing me the bug in his hand.

"How often do you search his room for anything like that transmitter?" I asked Dr. Striker.

"It should be done every other day," Dr. Striker said, stammering a little under the pressure.

"Then Jacob has one of your people—at least one—on his payroll," I said, turning back to Jacob. "You have quite the little enterprise going on there."

"You deal with as much money and as many people as I did, and you gain a few allies," Jacob said.

"You must have known the explosion wasn't going to kill me," I said.

"I'd hoped it would hurt," Jacob said. "You think you've won, but this is only the start. I still have friends, and we will find you. Kurt was never going to be found in Portsmouth; he's long gone by this point. You'll never find him."

"Found Eve," I told him. "Ji-hyun put a bullet through her head half a mile away from where she sat. We'll find Kurt, too."

Jacob's mask of serenity slipped, and the nasty little man behind it came out. "I have more friends in higher places than you'll ever dream of. I'll end you, one way or another. End that bitch friend of yours, too. Eve was mine to kill. She betrayed me. I had plans for her. I've got plans for you, too."

"Can you lower the divider, please?" I said to Dr. Striker.

"I don't think that's a good idea," Dr. Striker said.

"Yes, that's right, Lucas; hide behind the good doctor," Jacob teased.

"That's not what's happening," Dr. Striker said, his voice raising a little.

"Doc," I said, my eyes never leaving Jacob. "I'm not going to kill him. I want this piece of weasel shit to live a long time in here, alone, away from the finer things in life, while we systematically dismantle everything he ever worked for. But I want that damn bug."

The divider lowered, and Jacob placed the small bug on a side table before taking the smallest of steps back. I would have to be in his personal space to retrieve the bug.

"Have you ever heard of the phrase *Don't poke the bear*?" I asked Jacob as the divider finished moving.

"You're not a bear," Jacob said. "You're just a man who has no idea what I can do to him. No idea of what my allies will do should I die here. You can't kill me, Lucas. It would turn your life to ash."

"I told the doc I wasn't going to kill you, Jacob," I said, walking over to the bug and picking it up, feeling Jacob's warm breath on my neck as I was forced to move by him. "When I find Kurt, I'll send you his head in a box for posterity's sake."

"Fuck you, Lucas Rurik," Jacob said, spitting on the small amount of floor between us.

I took a step away. "Oh, I forgot." I spun and punched him in the nose, putting every bit of anger into the blow, knocking him onto the floor as his face was quickly covered in blood. "That's for a whole lot of stuff."

I walked to the cell exit as the doctor hit the panic button on the wall. "He's still alive, Doc," I said, and left the cell.

CHAPTER THREE

I was not so very politely marched out of the prison, which was fair, and told that should I return, it had better be in an official capacity with Ravi or someone of equal rank. We all knew they probably couldn't stop me coming in if I chose to.

After checking that Ravi was okay, I let the RCU deal with the fallout of what had happened, and went back to New York.

I didn't feel bad about punching Jacob in the face. He had a very punchable face, and he'd had it coming for a long time, but I did feel bad that Ravi was going to have to deal with him alone. Alongside hunting down Kurt and investigating the Prime Minster, Ravi had his hands full.

The jet—a Gulfstream something or other—touched down on a private airfield near New York City, and I stepped onto the runway to be met by Nadia, who gave me a hug. A year before, that would have been unheard-of. Chained revenants weren't known for being overly affectionate, and Nadia, in particular, preferred not to have any direct human contact if she could get away with it.

"What are you doing here?" I asked as we walked along the runway to the small terminal.

"You haven't heard?" Nadia asked.

"Heard what?" I asked.

"You're on the television," she said.

I stopped walking. "The old Jacob thing in London again?"

She shook her head.

"The BMW crash that happened about twelve hours ago?" I asked with a deep pit of unpleasantness in my stomach.

"Ding, ding, ding," Nadia said with a smile. "People filmed you, put it all over social media. News channels picked it up, started to talk about you again. There's a particular channel in America that I won't name, but they're *really* angry you broke the arm of a cop."

"He wasn't American, so I'm surprised they care," I said snidely. "Besides, he had just tried to kill me."

"Yeah, well, they're saying that if you can disarm a highly trained police officer that easily, what's to stop you walking into the White House and killing the president?" Nadia said.

"That's a bit of a leap in logic," I said as we entered the reception area of the terminal.

"I know that, and you know that," Nadia said as I passed my credentials to the gentlemen logging passengers, and he waved me through.

Once outside the terminal, Nadia led me to a nearby parking lot, where Gabriel sat in his Toyota RAV4 SUV. "Hey, it's the most famous Guild member on the planet," Gabriel mocked as I opened the passenger door.

"Why are you here?" I asked.

"Can't I just come and see my friend in his hour of need?" Gabriel asked as I put on my seatbelt.

"No," I told him. "I didn't even know this was an hour of need. I didn't know I needed anything until about sixty seconds ago. Also, you live in Hamble, which is several hours away from here. That's a long drive to come see a friend in their *hour of need*."

"Nadia was very excited to tell you," Gabriel said.

"You were trending again," Nadia told me. "I still don't really understand what that means, but it sounds really exciting. Or terrifying; I haven't decided yet."

"Am I going to have to go live in a monastery in the middle of nowhere?" I asked.

"I think you'll be okay," Gabriel said as we set off.

"Where are we going?" I asked.

"You're going to your apartment," Gabriel said.

"That makes it sound like you're going somewhere else?" I asked.

"I'm here to go to the Stag and Arrow," Gabriel told me. "Bill and George are expecting me."

Bill and George were the married couple who owned the Stag and Arrow bar in Brooklyn. It was a predominately rift-fused bar and about a ten-minute walk from where I lived, near Prospect Park. They were good people, and it was a nice place to go for a drink and chat. Like Cheers but with more people who could bench-press a car.

"There a problem?" I asked as Gabriel navigated New York traffic with almost no use of swear words and hand gestures.

"No, feel free to just drive where you like," Gabriel shouted at one impatient driver.

I stared at him.

"I wasn't allowed to drive," Nadia said sadly. "I'm never allowed to drive."

I looked back at Nadia. "Do you think driving would be a good idea?"

"Oh, no, it would be a disaster," Nadia said. "But mostly a disaster for people not in this car."

I turned back to Gabriel. "So, you didn't answer my question," I said.

"Well, you know that people contacted the church to try and get to you through me?" Gabriel asked. "Well, one of them contacted me, and I think George might need to know about it."

"Because he's a lawyer?" I asked.

George specialised in rift-fused issues, which, being a revenant himself, also meant that his clients tended to trust him a little bit more than they might a human. Despite existence of the rift-fused being public knowledge for decades now, there's still some mistrust.

"Yes," Gabriel said. "At least partially. Also because he knows cops, knows how they think, and has worked with the RCU, FBI, and human police for a number of years."

"Can I assume that I also need to speak to George?" I asked.

"Almost certainly," Gabriel said. "I figured it better to talk to George in person and collect you on the way. I also thought you might want to go home to get a shower and change before having anything else dumped on you."

"Just take me to the bar," I said. "I'd rather know now."

Gabriel shrugged.

We reached the Stag and Arrow bar, and the three of us got out of the car. Gabriel entered the bar first, with Nadia and me close behind.

The interior of the bar was divided into three parts. The counter where people ordered drinks was in a horseshoe shape, with dozens of bottles of various spirits hanging in front of gleaming mirrors. Fridges sat below the mirrors, each full, while several craft ales and beers were available from one of the three taps.

Tables sat around the counter with booths on either side of the main entrance we'd just walked through.

To the left of the entrance were more booths and tables where people usually sat and ordered food. And the third and final part was on the right of the entrance, where there were steps leading up to pool tables, arcade machines, and a few dartboards.

The entire bar was empty. That did not bode well for two in the afternoon.

George Hawkins entered the bar first, using the staff exit. He was black with a bald head, dark moustache, and, like usual, wore an expensive suit—this one charcoal. It didn't seem to matter what time of the day, or what he'd been doing before I'd seen him; he always looked like he'd just stepped out of a magazine photo shoot. George was originally from Edinburgh, although I had no idea when or where he'd been turned into a revenant.

His husband, Bill, was right behind him, wearing his usual jeans and black T-shirt. He was white and had short-cut dark hair and the beginnings of a beard. He was about the same height as his husband, although he would be the first to admit he couldn't quite pull off a suit like George could. He was originally from Philadelphia, and I'd recently discovered that he'd been turned into a revenant during the Vietnam War. Sometimes, you knew people a long time before they were conformable telling their story of coming back. I didn't know all of the details, and Bill hadn't seen any reason to share them.

George and Bill were good people who not only offered the rift-fused a refuge from their lives but, with George's legal work, offered rift-fused a way to deal with any legal matters that might arise from someone who was dead waking up.

"Lucas," Bill said, hugging me. "You're getting quite the TV portfolio at the moment."

"I'll be sure to put the new film into consideration at the next Oscars," I said as George smiled.

"I thought I'd just be talking to Gabriel," George said, and there was a slight nervous edge to his voice.

"Lucas decided he didn't want to wait," Gabriel said. He'd grabbed a blue shoulder bag from the car before coming into the bar. I had no idea what was in it but assumed it was important.

"You want something to eat?" Bill asked. "We've given the staff the day off, but I can make a mean sandwich."

Nadia raised her hand. "Food, please."

"BLT and fries, please," I said. "Also coffee. Lots of coffee."

"Coming up," Bill told us.

"I'll go play," Nadia said, moving over to the arcade games, which had been rigged to no longer need coins to play. The sounds of *Street Fighter 2* being started fell over the bar.

"Let's talk," George said, motioning toward one of the booths on the other side of the bar, away from where Nadia had gone.

I sat on one side of the booth, with Gabriel beside me and George opposite us. "I have a question," I said when everyone was comfortable. "Why couldn't you do this over the phone?"

"The person who contacted us didn't want to risk it," Gabriel told me. "You'll find out why when they arrive."

"They're coming here?" I asked.

"That was the agreed-upon plan, yes," Gabriel said. "However, there is one more thing. No RCU, no cops. Not even Ji-hyun or Emily. Before you say anything, Lucas, it's not about who I trust; it's about who our contact trusts."

"And when will they be arriving?" I asked.

"Shortly, I hope," Gabriel said.

"I'm going to need more information," I said. "You're both nervous, which means whoever we're meeting is someone I either don't like or you don't trust, maybe both. Or you think I'm going to storm out this place the second they arrive."

"Yes, well, the person we're meeting is Noah Kaya," Gabriel said.

I stared at Gabriel for several seconds. "Are you taking the fucking piss?"

"I am not," Gabriel said.

"Noah. Kaya," I said.

"Yes," Gabriel said with a slight nod.

"Noah Kaya *the Ancient*," I said.

"You don't mess about with Ancient issues," George said. "That's why I was hesitant to have him come here."

"Noah is coming here?" I asked, realising my voice was getting louder.

"Is that a problem?" George asked.

I shook my head. "No, I just . . . Oh, damn it, it's been a long time since I've had anything to do with Ancient business. Not since the Ravens stopped being . . . well, anything."

"You've met Noah before?" George asked.

"A few times," I said. "The Noah I met was a good man. One of the few Ancients I've ever met who I don't think is a colossal asshole. He's still an

Ancient, though. Still got power and wealth; still got influence over powerful and dangerous people. He's old, like thousands of years old. Older than me by a significant amount. I'm pretty sure he was born in Babylon, back when Babylon was the biggest city on earth. Rumours are he was right there when Babylon became an empire. He saw it rise and fall and probably had a hand in both."

"You trust him?" George asked.

I shrugged. "Don't trust any Ancient. Not totally. They always have their own agendas. Noah can be calculated, cold, and he doesn't mess about. You know all Ancients have their bodyguards—the Silver Phalanx—well, Noah's are the best. Ex–Guild members mostly, quite a few ex-Talons."

"He ever asked you to work for him?" Gabriel asked.

I nodded. "I told him I'd never work for any Ancient. He accepted that."

"So, what you're saying is that Noah is a man of wealth, influence, and power," George said. "But you don't think he's likely to come here to set us up?"

"No," I said. "Although I still don't know what he's here for."

"He wouldn't say," Gabriel said. "Something to do with a missing-persons case."

That was an even bigger surprise than having Noah involved at all. "Seriously?" I asked. "Why would an Ancient need to come to me to be involved in a missing-persons case? He has people who work for him. Lots of people. Seems weird."

The screen on Gabriel's phone flicked on. "I guess we'll find out soon enough," he said after looking at it.

While I didn't think that Noah was coming there to murder us all in the bar or anything quite so dramatic, I found myself to be quietly preparing. I had no idea what he could possibly want me to do that his own army of hangers-on and security personnel couldn't do for him quietly, and at considerably less cost to his time and finances. And make no mistake: if he wanted to hire me, he was going to pay for it.

The door to the bar opened and Noah stepped inside. He was a tall, broad man with bald head, dark skin, and black beard that was perfectly maintained. That pretty much summed Noah up. His midnight-blue suit probably cost more than a car, his black boots polished to an almost mirror sheen. He wore a Cartier Moon Phases watch, which had been a gift to him from some member of royalty. He had a hundred watches, most of which were more expensive than that, but the Cartier was the one he always wore. He once told me it was because it reminded him of someone.

"Lucas," Noah said with a warm smile that appeared to be genuine. He offered me his hand, which I shook. "It has been a long time."

"Still wearing the Cartier," I said.

Noah looked at his watch, and a little sadness entered his expression. Sadness that was quickly quashed in favour of a broad smile. "You're still a watch man, I see."

He pointed to the blue and white-faced Breitling Navitimer on my wrist. It had been one of the few topics of conversation we'd had in common, and after having spent time with him and seeing the passion and love in his voice as he spoke about his watches, I had warmed to him. We were never going to be friends, but I respected Noah and on occasion thought that I might even have liked him. He was an intelligent man with a good sense of humour who was loyal to his people and expected that loyalty in return. He was also capable of exceptional levels of violence on those who crossed him. So, while yes, I respected and liked him, I didn't trust him.

"Thank you for arranging this, Gabriel," Noah said. "I appreciate it."

Gabriel smiled. "It was my pleasure," he said. Gabriel had always been someone who had respected authority in the Ancients and wanted to see the best in people. In some ways, I envied that.

"You must be George," Noah said, shaking George's hand. "Thank you for accommodating this meeting. If you're losing custom for this, I will arrange recompense."

"Thank you, Lord Kaya," George said.

"Just *Noah* is fine," he said with a smile. "Is there somewhere I can go to wash up and maybe get a coffee?"

"I'll show you the washrooms," Gabriel said. "And I'm sure Bill will be happy to get you refreshments."

"Thank you," Noah replied, and walked away with Gabriel while George stood like a statue beside me.

"You okay?" I asked him.

"I've never actually met an Ancient before," he said. "I didn't know what to say to him. Also, considering we were meant to meet before you arrived, I've been thrown off."

"You're a big-shot lawyer," I reminded him.

"Yes," George said, and he appeared to stand straighter. "I . . . I don't get flustered often, but if Noah decided he wants my firm to be involved in his request, that could be a massive deal."

Bill arrived with a plate of food and two large mugs of coffee as well as a pot of tea.

"You, sir, are a god amongst men," I told Bill as George retook his seat beside me.

Bill sat opposite me as I inhaled the aroma of the BLT. Bill had even toasted the bread. I took a bite and was very happy that I had friends who could cook. "I may love you," I told Bill after taking a mouthful.

Bill laughed. "So, an Ancient is involved?"

I nodded, tucking into my food.

"You going to be okay?" he asked.

I took a long swig of beautiful coffee and made a little contented noise. "Yes," I told him.

"Are *you* going to be okay?" Bill asked George, placing his hand on his husband's.

George nodded and smiled as Noah and Gabriel returned.

"Bill, I assume," Noah said as Bill got to his feet and the pair shook hands. Bill showed no signs that Noah was anything more than a normal customer.

"Coffee is there," Bill said. "If you want more, just shout."

"You are too kind," Noah said, and Bill walked away to leave the four of us to talk as the sounds of Nadia playing *Street Fighter 2* continued in the background.

CHAPTER FOUR

How have you been?" Noah asked me as I finished the last bit of coffee.

"Busier than I'd expected," I said. "The last few years especially. You? No guards?"

"They took their own car and followed," Noah said. "They're parked around the corner, waiting for my orders. I didn't want anyone to be concerned when I walked in with an armed escort. I wanted to show that I trusted you."

"Don't let them sit in the car," I said.

Noah smiled and sent a message on his phone.

A short time later, an old friend of mine walked through the door of the bar, saw me and smiled. "Lucas Rurik," he said.

"Hiroyuki Matsuno," I said with a smile of my own, and got to my feet.

Hiroyuki hugged me tightly. He had been born during the Sengoku period of Japan's history and had served Tokugawa Ieyasu as one of his samurai before being killed early in the fifteenth century, although he'd never shared how. Hiroyuki was maybe five and a half feet tall, and had long hair on top of his head that was in a ponytail, with his hair shaved around the back and sides. He carried a wakizashi and a tanto, both of which he'd had for several centuries and sat in sheaths against his hips. Hiroyuki wore a dark grey suit and black shoes; you didn't get to be a member of the Silver Phalanx unless you were willing to look the part. A silver pendant hung around his neck, it was in the shape of an Ancient Greek helmet.

"It's good to see you," Hiroyuki said.

"You're Silver Phalanx now?" I asked. "Congratulations." I'd known Hiroyuki when he'd been a member of the Eagle Guild, but he'd always wanted to make his way up toward working for the Ancients.

"For about forty years now," Hiroyuki said.

"I'm happy for you," I said.

"I'm sorry about your Ravens," Hiroyuki said. "I . . . should have contacted you. I didn't know what to say, and then you went missing and no one knew how to contact you."

"It's a long story," I said. "But thank you."

"Do you know who carried out the attack on your own Guild?" Hiroyuki asked.

"I got some of them," I said. "There are others I don't know about, but I'll find them one day, too."

"Of that I have no doubt," Noah said, interrupting our conversation. "I believe we should get to the matter at hand now."

"Yes, my lord," Hiroyuki said.

"I'll get him some coffee or tea," Bill said from the bar.

Hiroyuki thanked him and followed Bill to the other side of the bar as I retook my seat.

"So, what's going on?" I asked Noah.

"I require your help," Noah said. "But before I tell you what it is I want, I should tell you why."

I pushed my plate aside so I didn't feel the urge to finish my fries. "Go ahead."

"I cannot go to the RCU," Noah said. "I understand that Ji-hyun is working for them, leading them. She will be a great asset to their number, but they are too new and do not really need to be involved in Ancient issues. I could go to one of the Guilds, but frankly, I don't feel that they would best serve to deal with this issue. I need someone who can be discreet, and if you had a full Guild I would not be talking to you."

"Anything else?" I asked.

"I wish to discuss payment," Noah said. "I will pay you for your time; I believe half a million dollars will suffice."

"That's going to get you something big, isn't it?" I asked.

"You pick your team," Noah said. "But Hiroyuki will be a part of it. He will report only to me. If you agree to undertake this matter, I will explain why I am here. If not, I will leave and we'll go about our business."

"I don't even know what you're asking me to do yet," I told him.

"You ever heard of Eastfield in Massachusetts?" Noah asked.

I shook my head.

"It's a small-enough town of about twenty thousand people, a short distance south of Boston," Noah said. "It's quite the tourist trap, so I've been told. It's also the residence of someone who has done work for me in the past. His name is Anthony Sosa. He's missing. No trace. I sent people there to check on him, and they found nothing but the dead body of a neighbour."

"Okay, so, what am I meant to do?" I asked. "I get that you're searching for your friend, but you've already sent people to search. Why not have them keep looking?"

"The neighbour who was found dead in their home," Noah said. "They had been stabbed in the throat twice. Police arrived, cordoned off the whole street. Those who work for me are not Guild members, and I could not send members of the Phalanx. They obeyed the police but were unable to continue searching without revealing my involvement. Something is going on, and I cannot be seen to be officially investigating. I have, however, arranged for no police to be at either address for a few hours. Should give you time alone. That's one of the reasons why Hiroyuki will be aiding you. Also, considering you are friends, it could be seen as him just helping out a fellow Guild member."

"Is Anthony a suspect?" I asked.

"To the police?" Noah asked. "Almost certainly. He's someone who is uncontactable after the murder of his neighbour. They'd be stupid to discount him. I would rather it not reach the point where he *officially* becomes a suspect though."

"What is Anthony to you?" I asked.

"He is . . . family," Noah said. "Of a sort."

"Family?" I asked. "What does that mean?"

"We are not blood-related," Noah said. "He's someone I have helped over the years, and I have come to think of him as family. Anthony is a good man."

"I can see why you'd want a lawyer here," George said. "Has Anthony officially been labelled a person of interest? Are the police looking for him?"

"Yes to both counts," Noah said. "The RCU have not been, though. I do not wish to see the human police find Anthony before we figure out what is really going on."

"Any chance he did it?" I asked just as Gabriel took a drink of tea, causing him to almost spit it out.

"No," Noah said with complete conviction.

"Okay," I said tentatively. "Where does Anthony work?"

"He works for an organisation in Boston called Reclaimed Lives," Noah said.

"That rings a bell," I said.

"I've worked with them several times," George said. "They help people who have just either come back from the rift as a riftborn or just woken up as a revenant. They're good people."

"And Anthony works there?" I turned to George and asked. "You ever met him?"

"No," George said. "I've only ever met their legal counsel, a woman by the name of Isabelle Nadal. She's human."

"For the sake of openness," Noah said, "I should tell you that I am the sole owner of Reclaimed Lives."

I turned to look at Noah. "So, you own an organisation that helps new rift-fused. Isn't that a conflict of interests? You're an Ancient; it could be shown that you'd be using that organisation to keep tabs on new rift-fused."

"I have no dealings with them on a day-to-day basis," Noah said. "I wanted to give back to the community. Reclaimed Lives felt like the best way to do that."

"Does this Isabelle know where Anthony is?" I asked. "Have you spoken to her? To anyone he works with?"

Noah nodded. "Isabelle knows I own the charity; she contacted me to say that Anthony hadn't been to work for two days. I sent people to look at his home."

"Hiroyuki?" I asked.

Noah shook his head. "No, I didn't think it warranted sending Silver Phalanx members. My people went to his home the night before last and found it swarming with police. Didn't want to get my name involved, so they came back. I made a few calls, discovered the neighbour's murder and Anthony's disappearance. I contacted Gabriel, who told me that you were on a jet from London."

"Police still at the house?" I asked.

"I made a few more calls to friends I have in Boston PD," Noah said. "Only to get information. If I start exerting pressure on the human police to stop their investigation, there's always a chance that either the RCU will become involved or one of them will go to the human press. Ancients are meant to involve the RCU in crimes like this. Also . . ."

"You don't want your relationship with Anthony to come out," I said.

Noah stared at me for a moment before nodding.

"Why?" I asked him.

"For a number of reasons," Noah said. "He would be hounded by people wanting to know why we were close. He would be targeted by people wanting to get to me. I've known him since he was a teenager, since before he became a revenant, and I always promised him he would be able to live his life as he saw fit. I don't plan to change that now."

"He got any family?" George asked.

"A sister," Noah said. "Although that's complicated."

"How?" Gabriel asked.

"Anthony and his sister, Dani, were in a car accident," Noah said. "Anthony was killed outright at the age of twenty-seven. His sister was sixteen. She was taken into the rift."

"She's a riftborn?" I asked. "Because she's got a long wait before she comes back."

"Not a riftborn," Noah said.

"Oh, fuck," I said with a sigh. "Rift-walker."

Noah nodded.

I'd seen the aftermath of a few humans who had walked through a tear. I'd heard the screams, the pleading to be allowed to die. The fact that it had happened to a sixteen-year-old girl was . . . No one should go through what she'd gone through.

"Where is she?" I asked.

"Don't know," Noah said. "We got word from the rift that she'd survived the transformation from human to rift-walker but that she wasn't powerful enough to return. And that was the last thing I heard."

"Did you know Dani before she vanished?" I asked.

Noah nodded. "I knew their parents," he said. "They died when Anthony was sixteen, and Dani was little. His parents worked for me, and I made sure that Anthony and Dani were well looked after."

"Any ideas where Anthony could have gone?" Gabriel asked. "He's a revenant, yes?"

"Elemental," Noah said. "He can manipulate water."

"Okay, so we've got a missing elemental revenant, who the human police would like to discuss a murder with," George said. "I can get in touch with the police, find out exactly what they know. Hopefully, we can get some leads that way."

"We'll go to Eastfield and check out his home," I said. "Nadia, you up for a road trip?"

"Already packed," Nadia called out before shouting obscenities.

I turned to look at her.

"I lost," she said by way of explanation.

"She knows?" I asked Gabriel.

"Not told her a thing," Gabriel assured me. "I wasn't even going to bring her, but I went out to the car and she was already in the passenger seat, with a bag ready to go. She said the chains told her."

"That ever worry you?" George whispered. "That she lives her life based on how she deciphers a bunch of visions that may or may not show her an accurate depiction of a future that may or may not come to pass?"

"Not really," I said with a shrug. "If Nadia can deal with it, it stands to reason that I should be able to."

"Where can I send your payment?" Noah asked me.

"Talk to Gabriel," I said. "You can sort it out that way. I'd rather not take money from an Ancient. No offence."

"None taken," Noah said with a knowing smile. "And, of course, George, I will pay any bill for your services. If Anthony needs a lawyer . . ."

"That's why I'm here, right?" George said. "He's innocent, but just in case an innocent man needs a lawyer?"

"Innocence doesn't always mean much," Noah said.

George nodded in agreement.

"One thing," I said as Noah got to his feet.

"Of course," Noah said.

"If I find out that this goes way beyond just finding your friend, I will notify the RCU," I explained. "I can't keep them out of it if we find Anthony and there's more to it than a dead neighbour."

"Just please try to find him first," Noah said. "Hiroyuki, can we talk in private?"

"Of course, Lord Kaya," Hiroyuki said from across the bar.

I got to my feet and Noah offered me his hand, which I shook. "Thank you for doing this, Lucas," Noah said. "I know you don't trust the Ancients; I know they didn't always do right by you. After the Ravens were murdered, they . . . well, we sat on our hands, unsure what to do next. Normally, when a Guild is attacked, it's usually known why. A Guild gets too many members who are more interested in their own wealth and power, or they overstep their marks, but those Guild members aren't simply murdered but arrested and questioned. To have an entire Guild slaughtered and only one survivor, it . . . scared people. It's not an excuse, but I wanted you to know. I want to help you find those responsible. My resources are yours."

"Thank you," I said. "Let's get one thing at a time sorted, though. We'll find Anthony, figure out what's going on, and let you know. I do have a question, though. Why me?"

"I trust you," Noah said. "It's as simple as that. You're capable, certainly, and I have no doubt you'll do the job, but I trust you. I know you'll come into the job with open eyes; I know you won't stop until it's done. I know you'll find the truth because I know it'll gnaw at you until you find it. That's why I wanted you to look into this."

"You know that's the same even if you don't like what I find out."

"I do," Noah said. "That's also why I hired you."

"Just so we're on the same page," I said.

Hiroyuki walked across the bar to Noah, removed his Phalanx pendant, and gave it to Noah. "For when I return," Hiroyuki said.

Noah nodded once before turning to me. "Hiroyuki will have no authority," Noah said. "You are in charge here. You are the only one with a Guild medallion. I hope that's enough, because you can't count on the backing of an Ancient. There are murmurs of troubles in Inaxia with the Primes, and more murmurs of some of those Primes being unhappy with Ancient involvement in the running of the city."

"You think some of those murmurs might spill out into Earth?" I asked.

"The Ancients on Earth are not here to police the populace unless necessary, but sometimes we have had to take a heavy hand," Noah said. "Humans are concerned about the power of rift-fused, I would not give them more reasons to be concerned. It is a fine balancing act to govern the rift-fused and allow the Guild to do what they need to while also not appearing to have any direct influence over any human policing or policy. What happened in England has changed that. A practitioner posing as a human for years, taking part in their democratic process. It doesn't take much to make humans afraid, and I do not wish to stoke that particular fire."

And now the truth of it was coming out. "You think this might stoke that particular fire?" I asked. "That's why you can't be involved. You're concerned that unscrupulous humans would use it to their advantage should Ancient involvement in the matter come out."

"Yes," Noah admitted before turning and leaving the bar with Hiroyuki following behind.

"How much of that did you know?" I asked Gabriel once we were no longer in the company of an Ancient.

"You mean beforehand?" Gabriel asked. "Only that he wanted to talk to you."

"You okay?" George asked.

"I'm not sure," I said.

"So, you're going to do this?" Bill asked from behind the bar. "You're sure it's not a setup?"

"Noah is a man of wealth, influence, and power," I said. "And if he wanted to set me up for something, there are easier ways to do it. If he's behind the disappearance, he never would have asked me to look into it. Not even as some kind of frankly bizarre cover story."

"Nothing good comes from getting involved in Ancient business," Nadia said. "I believe you once told me that."

"And that is still true," I told her.

"So, you're going to do this?" Gabriel asked.

"Whatever else is going on, Anthony is either running scared, dead, or a murderer on the run," I said. "Scared rift-fused are dangerous, and I'd rather not have human politicians given more reasons to spread nonsense about us."

"And if Noah is somehow involved?" George asked. "Just out of curiosity."

"You mean, he's hired me to find Anthony because he can't?" I asked. "Then I contact Ji-hyun and ask her very nicely to arrest him. Which she'll happily do."

"She'll arrest an Ancient?" Bill asked. "She didn't strike me as the death-wish type."

"She's done it before," I said. "Long time ago."

George and Gabriel walked away to discuss law stuff, and I asked Bill for a second cup of coffee. I sat alone for a while, finished the second cup, and finally felt a little closer to being alive. I really didn't want to get involved in Ancient politics. They were murky and annoying, and often left you with either someone swearing vengeance on you for centuries or being stabbed. Or both.

Since I'd been a part of the team that had arrested Jacob, I'd felt a little like treading water. I wasn't really sure what to do with myself apart from hiding away from humanity until they forgot about me. But that probably wasn't possible in the world we lived in. Maybe helping Anthony was slightly selfish on my part, as I really didn't want to give human lawmakers any more excuses to be assholes to us, but I also didn't want to leave a potentially scared revenant alone out there to be hunted for something he hadn't done.

Hiroyuki walked back into the bar. "I am parked around the rear of the building," he said. "Red Mercedes GLA AMG. I wish I could say I'm looking forward to working with you, Lucas, but . . . I am concerned for Anthony's whereabouts. I would like to start the search as soon as possible."

"I'd like to get a shower and change of clothes first," I said. "You may as well take a seat and get something to eat. And Hiroyuki, it really is good to see you again."

Hiroyuki's smile looked genuine. "You too, old friend."

Saying my goodbyes, I left the bar and went back to my flat, where I had a long-overdue shower and got changed into a comfortable pair of jeans, a plain light-blue T-shirt, a black hoodie, and dark grey raincoat. I grabbed a small black rucksack and put in a few pairs of clean underwear, socks, some toiletries, and a few T-shirts. Anything else, I could just buy.

A voice deep inside my brain told me to be wary. It's not that I didn't trust Hiroyuki—I'd known him a long time; we'd fought alongside one another multiple times—it's that I didn't trust Ancients. Even ones I liked.

Picking up my rift-tempered knuckleduster, I put it in my hoodie pocket and kept my two daggers in their sheaths against my hips. A long time ago, I used to carry a falcata and dagger, but I'd lost the sword and never gotten around to replacing it.

I waited for a moment as the memories of my time in Carthage came back to me. I didn't really think about my time before I was reborn, or at least I tried not to think about it too often. But occasionally, I'd wonder what had happened to so many of my friends who had fought the Romans by my side. They'd probably died in battle, the Romans were very good at making sure that happened, but I'd always hoped that a few of us had survived and gone on to do something good in the world.

I kept my medallion on, although every time I went home and saw the bag where the rest of the Raven Guild's medallions were kept, it reiterated that the responsibility of bringing the Raven Guild back to full strength rested on my shoulders. It was a responsibility I wasn't ready for. I didn't even know where to start. On the plus side, that was a problem for future Lucas. Future Lucas was not going to be thrilled about that.

Melancholy settled, as it did sometimes when the length of my life weighed on me. It would leave as quickly as it came, especially when I kept myself busy and my mind occupied, but for now, I walked through the empty halls of my apartment building, feeling ill at ease.

It was a nice walk through Prospect Park, and by the time I'd reached the other side, my melancholy was just a simmering memory. Bill and George were outside their bar and waved me over.

"Everyone is waiting in the parking lot at the rear of the bar," Bill said.

"Good," I replied.

"Be careful on this one," George said. "I don't like working with the Ancients. Even ones we might mostly trust."

"I'll be fine," I said, leaving out the word *probably.* "A quick check for where Anthony might be, hopefully find him in one piece, and job's done. I can go back to trying to avoid the gaze of the human race. Which, considering how often I'm apparently on the TV these days, is proving harder and harder."

"Ah, the price of fame," Bill said with a laugh.

"There are more and more people coming to the bar," George said. "Maybe we should put a picture of you with *This man drinks here* under it."

"Your bar, it has insurance, right?" I asked.

Bill pointed a finger at me. "No," he said sternly.

"Does he think I'm a dog?" I asked George.

"He's taken few hits to the head over the years, so it's possible," George said, and gave Bill a kiss when his partner glared at him.

I left them to it and walked around to the rear of the bar where Gabriel and Nadia were waiting next to a dark green Audi R8. Or, as George said every single time he mentioned it; an Audi R8 V10 Spyder Performance Carbon Black. Apparently, the full name was important.

Hiroyuki stood beside his car and stared at the Audi, admiring it.

"Maybe Noah can get you one as a well-done gift," I told Hiroyuki.

"I will keep it in mind," Hiroyuki said with a smile, and got into his car.

I turned to see George and Bill walking toward me. "You're lending me your car again?" I asked.

"You returned it unbroken last time," George said. "So, I trust you. Besides, it's quicker than renting a car, and you have a long drive."

I'd had a Mercedes E53 AMG coupe, but it was still at Gabriel's church, where I'd left it several months earlier.

George tossed me the keys, and I popped the bonnet, which was where the boot of the car was. The actual amount of storage space in an Audi R8 was tiny, and by the time I'd put my rucksack in there and Nadia had deposited her own bag, there was very little space left. I guessed you didn't buy a sports car for luggage space.

Nadia climbed into the passenger seat and belted up, looking excited. She'd always enjoyed fast cars, even if driving them herself would have been out of the question.

"I'll let you know when I'm there," I told Gabriel.

"You sure about this?" he asked. "I got you involved, but I just want to make sure that you're okay."

I smiled. "I've been back in the field just over a year now, and in that year, I've hunted bad people and kicked a lot of ass. But when the Raven Guild was at full strength, we *helped* those who needed it. We didn't turn them away because it was inconvenient or difficult, or because it would put us up against an Ancient. Helping Anthony feels like something I *used* to do and should do more of."

"How long have you had that speech in your head?" Gabriel asked.

"A few minutes," I said with a smirk.

"Take care," Gabriel told me, and looked over at Nadia. "Both of you."

Nadia gave a thumbs-up and we set off.

CHAPTER FIVE

Once we got out of New York City, we were able to open up the car a little, which made Nadia giggle with joy.

"If I get pulled over, I'm blaming you," I told her.

"It's all my fault, officer," Nadia said in a tiny voice. "I'm just a meek, humble woman, and I used my feminine wiles on him."

I laughed. "A meek, humble woman?" I asked her.

"And my feminine wiles," she said. "Don't forget those."

"I wouldn't dream of it," I told her.

She was quiet for a few minutes and started to play with the radio until she found a station playing *Come Get to This* by Marvin Gaye.

"Can I ask you something?" Nadia asked as the song finished and was replaced with *Sir Duke* by Stevie Wonder.

"Of course," I said as it started to rain.

"This last year has been the best of probably my entire life," Nadia said. "It feels like I found a family. Like I found a home. And while I know that you're in my chains and therefore I need to keep you close enough that my brain doesn't start to flounce around, I have been able to make friends with Gabriel and Ji-hyun. It feels like I've been accepted for who . . . and what I am."

"Of course," I said paying extra attention to the suddenly slick road.

"I just—I want to know if I'm a burden," Nadia said softly. "If all of this is just because you feel like you all need to keep me around. My brain isn't always the best, and sometimes it makes me feel like I'm just being tolerated."

I slowed down the car, pulled off I-95 at the next junction, and found a nearby area to park next to a small independent supermarket. I switched off the engine and turned to Nadia as Hiroyuki pulled in behind us.

I got out of the car as Hiroyuki called over, "You want anything?"

"Get two bottles of water," I called back, just trying to think of something.

Hiroyuki gave me a thumbs-up and walked into the shop, leaving me to get back into the car.

I put my belt on and prepared for what I was going to say.

"Okay, so, whatever your brain is telling you is nonsense," I said. "You are a *major* part of this team. But not only that, you're my friend. You're a friend to all of us. You've come out of your shell, and we've accepted you for who you are. That's why we mock you. We don't mock people we don't like."

"I know," Nadia said. "It's just sometimes my brain doesn't always agree with what I know is true. If that makes sense. It's been a long time since I had anything close to a family. To having people who rely on me, and who I can rely on. It feels good but also scary. I don't want to lose that. I don't want to be the one who screws it up."

"I promise you," I told her. "You are a part of our group. Gabriel loves having you at the church; Bill and George adore having you around. You've helped Ji-hyun and Emily. You've helped me. Whatever your brain is telling you, Nadia, it's talking bullshit. You're a goddamned treasure and I can't imagine not having you around."

Nadia surprised me by hugging me, partly because she was not a hugger at all, and partly because I was still wearing my seatbelt and had to hurriedly release it so I didn't get strangled.

Nadia pulled away and looked out of the window. She took a deep breath and let it out slowly. "Thank you," she said softly.

"If your brain ever starts talking nonsense again, come see me or Gabriel, or Bill and George, or any of us," I said. "Please. Whatever you're going through, we want to help. Even if we can't help, we still want to be there should you need us. You are not alone."

Nadia looked back at me and smiled. "I am not alone," she said. "I haven't had that for a long time, too. Even when I worked for people, and some of them were bad people, I was always alone. I was always following the chains, trying to figure out where I needed to be. My chains haven't told me I need to leave. They've made it clear that *this* is where I need to be. But my chains also screw around with my brain, and sometimes it's all a jumble and I don't know which way is up. I just wanted to talk to you about it. We haven't spent much time just the two of us, especially since the whole thing in England. This means a lot."

"Any time, Nadia," I assured her. "We okay to go?"

Nadia nodded enthusiastically. "Yes, please. Thank you."

Hiroyuki left the shop, came over to the car, and passed the bottles of water and several chocolate bars through the now-open window.

"You okay?" he asked.

"Just needed to do a little catch-up," Nadia said.

"I'll wait for you to get in and start up before I head out," I told Hiroyuki.

After Hiroyuki got back into his car and switched on his engine, I turned on the Audi's and waited for him to flash his headlights before I pulled out of the parking lot. We were soon back on the interstate as the weather began to clear a little. A short shower. A hopefully apt metaphor for how Nadia was doing.

The rest of the drive was done with Nadia singing along to the occasional song but without much in the way of meaningful conversation.

We reached our destination just as the rain thankfully appeared to have stopped for good.

Eastfield, Massachusetts, was a perfectly pleasant-looking suburban town. As we drove through it, I got the impression that it was pretty much the same as a thousand other small towns in a hundred different countries. People going about their lives, just doing their own thing.

I drove past Anthony's house on Wood Lane, where a car was parked outside, two people in the front. Hiroyuki stopped his car beside them and I parked just around the corner. I got out of the Audi and looked around at the identical-looking houses, with their perfectly manicured lawns and occasional flower beds.

"Anyone else find this creepy?" Nadia asked from inside the car.

"Little bit," I agreed.

"Where are we staying tonight?" Nadia asked.

I took my phone out of my pocket and checked for messages. Gabriel had sent me the details of a hotel called the Plaza, near Boston Public Library. It was a short drive to where Anthony worked in Cambridge.

I pinged a quick thank you to him and let Nadia know where we were staying. It had been a long day, and after several hours of driving and having flown from the other side of the planet, all I wanted was a good long sleep.

The smell of fresh rain was one I always enjoyed, although the dark clouds overhead promised a lot more rain to come. I wasn't such a big fan of that part. Hopefully, we'd be out of Eastfield before there was a downpour.

"Can you do me a favour?" I asked Nadia as she joined me on the sidewalk.

"Sure," she said as Hiroyuki walked up to meet us.

"You see the woodland," I said, bringing up a map of the whole area on my phone. "That's Anthony's house there. The woodland is right behind it. Any chance you can go through the woods to get to the house. Keep an eye out for anything bad, just in case Anthony ran off through them or someone came to pay him a visit and used them for cover."

"Can do," Nadia said, and took off at a run, darting down the slight alleyway between two houses.

"Well, this is nice," Hiroyuki said, looking around.

"They were cops, yes?" I asked.

"Noah pulled strings," Hiroyuki said. "Just like he told you he would. Gives us a few hours to look around without human police interference. The body of the murder victim has been taken, no cleaning started yet. Anthony's house has not been searched, as one of the detectives knew that he worked for Noah and called it in. They've gone through the neighbour's house, though."

"You been here before?" I asked.

Hiroyuki shook his head. "I've met Anthony a few times, but we were never friends."

"What's he like?" I asked.

"Smart kid," Hiroyuki said. "Although I guess he's not much of a kid now. He lost pretty much everyone he loved in a fairly short space of time, and it made him closed off, not always open to new people. I think Noah might be one of the few who got through that outer shell."

"Any chance he's run off?" I asked.

"Because of the murder?" Hiroyuki asked. "No, none. He's not a killer."

"No, not the murder, but because he just wanted out?" I clarified.

"Ah, well, I can't say for sure," Hiroyuki said looking around the neighbourhood. "Something rings wrong about all of this. Can't quite put my finger on it, though."

"You got a key for the house?" I asked as we walked the short distance to Anthony's place.

Hiroyuki brandished a key from his pocket. "You want it?"

"I'll go through the back garden and check it out," I said.

"I'll meet you inside," Hiroyuki said, pushing open the wooden gate and walking up the path toward the front door.

I stayed where I was and took in the image of Anthony's house.

The garden was well maintained, a neat lawn, some flower beds along the side next to a literal white picket fence. The flowers weren't in bloom in November, but I was pretty sure it looked very nice in spring and summer. The garden fence ran the perimeter of the entire garden, with a gate entrance onto the stone footpath. There was a driveway in front of a garage, the door of which had been painted red.

Some of the neighbours had more shrubs in their garden, and some had trees, or more flower beds, but everything was very neat. I wondered if they had a neighbour who went around and left passive-aggressive notes for those who didn't maintain their lawn to an arbitrary standard.

I pushed open the gate and walked up the pathway, stopping at the wooden-and-glass front door. I tried the handle, because you never know, but it was locked.

"Can I help you?" someone asked from behind me as I peered through the downstairs front windows in the hope of spotting something useful.

I turned back to where the voice had come from and found a middle-aged man standing on the sidewalk. He wore dark grey trousers, white trainers, and a light blue shirt, with a charcoal cardigan and black raincoat over it. His short, greying hair was meticulously trimmed and matched his salt-and-pepper beard. He wore sunglasses despite the fact that it wasn't sunny. I didn't have high hopes about him.

He carried a clipboard in one hand. Then and there, I would have put money on him being the lawn-maintenance enforcer for the neighbourhood.

"Hello," I said with a wave and a beaming smile. I walked down the path as the man opened the gate and stood there like Cerberus as an anal-retentive middle-aged man with a clipboard.

"I asked if I could help," the man said.

"My name is Lucas," I told him, offering him my hand. He had a handshake like he was flopping a fish onto my palm.

"Tobias Lord," he said with a smile, which started to falter the longer he stared at me. "I know you."

"I'm pretty sure I'd remember you," I said.

"You're that riftborn on the news," Tobias exclaimed. "You arrested that politician in England. Well, I can tell you that we need more people like that in America. Too many politicians don't know that they work for the people."

I got the feeling that this was going to be the start of a long, drawn-out speech.

"I must ask," I said, hoping to steer Tobias away from the conversation he clearly wanted to have, "did you know Anthony?"

"Are you investigating him?" Tobias asked. "I saw that man walk into the house just now; is he a cop?"

"Did you hear anything on the night of the murder?" I asked, not wanting to give Tobias anything to latch on to and decide to tell his social-media followers that he was helping with a murder investigation.

"There was no noise. Nothing. Didn't even know he'd gone until the next morning when poor old Mrs. Walters was found."

"Mrs. Walters the lady who lives there?" I asked, pointing to Anthony's neighbour.

"Yes, she was a lovely lady," Tobias said. "Fifty-nine years old but looked a decade younger. Never married. Beautiful woman. Truly."

"You and she were an item?" I asked, more out of wanting to push his buttons than anything else. I got the feeling no one in this neighbourhood was particularly fond of Mr. Lord. If that was even his real name.

"Ah, we had a thing once," Tobias said, wistfully. "But it never worked out. I'm too much of a workaholic, and she needed more of my time than I was willing to give."

Translation: he didn't get within ten feet of a second date.

"The police still there?" I asked.

"No, they left about a short time ago," Tobias said. "Apart from the detectives who were waiting for your friend just then."

"Any cleaning staff arrived?"

Tobias shook his head. "Not seen any. Maybe they're busy. You know, I spoke to the police and gave them my details in case they needed me for more information. I see a lot that happens in this neighbourhood. A lot of people might not want some of that information given to the police. A lot of people might be happy that the police have gone."

"Meaning?" I asked.

"Nothing, just saying I see a lot, I know a lot," Tobias said with an ingratiating smile.

"So, Anthony," I said. Talking to Tobias was like pushing around a shopping trolley where both front wheels went in opposite directions. Endlessly annoying.

"He was quiet," Tobias told me. "Kept to himself mostly, although he was very friendly with Mrs. Walters and a few of the younger couples that live in the neighbourhood. Was dating a lady in Boston. A single mother, so I hear."

There was a lot of disdain in that last sentence. Tobias was letting his discrimination show.

"Thank you for your time," I said. "I'm going to carry out an examination of the house now."

Tobias shook my hand again, although I wish he hadn't bothered. "It's a joy and a privilege to meet someone who also works in law enforcement."

"You're a cop?" I asked before I could stop myself.

"Neighbourhood watch," he said, moving his cardigan aside to show me his homemade badge on the lapel of his shirt.

"You get a lot of trouble here in Eastfield?" I asked.

"No, sir," Tobias said. "And that is how I like it."

"Carry on, then," I said, and for a second I thought he might salute me.

The back garden was as meticulous as the front, although there were several small sheds and storage places dotted around the small lawn. The nine-foot wooden fence at the rear of the garden had a gate in it, although it was both padlocked shut and had bolt locks on the top and bottom. I turned to smoke and moved through the cracks in the gate, re-forming on the other side and hoping that Tobias didn't see it and decide to call the local news or something.

Nadia was just down a slight hill; she looked up at me and waved.

"Found anything?" I asked.

"Still looking," she said. "I think someone used this tree as a shelter. Cigarette butts on the ground here. It's not so wet here, so they've mostly stayed intact."

"Okay, I'll check out the house," I told her.

Nadia gave me a thumbs-up, and I left the gate open as I walked across the lawn and stepped up onto the decking. I peered through the patio doors into the kitchen-diner. Nothing looked out of place. I tried the handle and it was unlocked. Bit weird.

I pulled the patio door open and stepped into the cool house, remaining still for a moment to listen out for anything that might be moving around. The patio door hadn't been quiet, and the squeak would have been easy to hear if you were inside the house.

The front door was bolted top and bottom, like the gate in the rear of the garden, and trying the handle told me it was locked there, too. Anthony hadn't left through the front door unless he could bolt it and move through the gate like I had. Elemental revenants couldn't turn into their element, though, so the idea was quickly tossed aside.

I opened the door and found that while Tobias had moved across the street, he continued to stare at the house. I closed the door before he could do something like wave at me. I did not need him looking over my shoulder as I searched the house.

"He hasn't moved," Hiroyuki said as he entered the room from the hallway. "It's quite unnerving. What was your impression of him?"

"Something off about him," I said. "Could just be that he's an annoying asshole, or it could be that he's a stalker. But it's something."

"I'll go make a call, see if we can get more information on our neighbourhood watchman," Hiroyuki said, and walked back into the hallway.

"You checked upstairs?" I asked before he could dial his phone.

"Only a little; feel free to take a look," Hiroyuki told me.

I decided to start upstairs, going through the three bedrooms, en-suite bathroom, and separate bathroom, but finding nothing of interest. In fact, apart from some clothes in a dresser and a TV in the master bedroom, I never would have guessed anyone lived there. It looked like a show house. Everything was neat and tidy, everything in its place, and none of it looking lived in.

I went back downstairs and found that there was a similar story in the rooms there. The living room had a TV and random pieces of artwork on the walls, but none of it looked personal. There were no photos, no books lying on the coffee table, no board games, no video games, or movies, or even music. Nothing said that this place was anything more than a shell. I wondered why anyone would want to live in a place so sterile, or maybe that was the point. Anthony just used the place as a cover for wherever he was actually staying.

I was in the kitchen when Nadia came through the rear door. "It's started to rain again," she said. "Not much in the way of evidence out there. No signs of a struggle, although it's possible the rain washed anything away. Honestly, apart from a few cigarette butts, there's nothing out there to suggest anyone was even there."

"But?" I asked.

"My chains went nuts when they touched the tree," Nadia said. "Something of power was stood out there. Not the smoker; I got nothing from the cigarettes when I picked them up. Something stood out in that woods and radiated power."

"More than a riftborn?" I asked.

"More than anything I've ever encountered," Nadia said. "It felt like someone who was pure rift energy. Not even sure how that's possible. Even the oldest and most powerful riftborn and revenants aren't linked to the rift all the time. Rift-walkers aren't, either. Fiends are a one-and-done kind of thing. You know of anything that's always linked to the rift?"

"Primordials," I said. "But they can't come through into Earth." Technically, that was because no tear to the rift stayed open long enough or was big enough. Primordials live in the Tempest, the maelstrom of power at the far north of the rift. They're the only thing I've ever encountered with a constant link to the power of the rift.

"What're the chances that was a primordial?" Nadia asked.

"Zero," I said. "It would still be rampaging through the town, for one. But for two, they can't leave the area surrounding the Tempest—Harmony—that constant link of power comes with a downside."

The area surrounding the maelstrom of power known as the Tempest was called Harmony, I assumed because someone thought it was really funny.

"So, something new," Nadia said.

"Potentially new," I suggested.

Nadia sighed. "Either way, it isn't good. You found anything useful?"

"Nope," I said. "Only that if this was Anthony's home, he wasn't exactly what I would call *living*."

"I'll go have another search upstairs," Nadia said. "Maybe the chains will tell me something your eyes couldn't see."

I continued to search the dining room and removed a painting from the wall, revealing a safe. It had a number pad and required a combination of digits to open.

I took out my phone and texted Gabriel to send me a digital copy of the breakdown of Anthony's life: date of birth, date of the car crash, date of rebirth, that kind of thing. Anthony wasn't very old, so he might know more about passwords and privacy than most, but if I'd ever needed to find a four-, six-, or eight-digit code for something, it was almost always a person's date of birth or date of rebirth. One time, it had been their date of death because they'd come back twenty minutes later and it was a new day. Sometimes, it takes hours to come back, but usually, it's the day or day after they died.

Gabriel texted back almost immediately with several photos of the documents I'd seen in the bar earlier. *Anything yet?* the accompanying text asked.

Maybe, I replied. *You know of anything that is pure rift energy?*

While I waited for a reply, I input Anthony's date of birth into the keypad. Nothing happened. I tried his date of rebirth and there was an audible click.

I pulled open the safe door, but it was empty. I tapped the walls, ceiling, and floor of the safe, just to make sure there weren't any hidden compartments.

My phone vibrated.

A primordial, Gabriel said.

Can't be one of them, I replied. *Anything else?*

I put my phone on the table and took a seat. There was no national register for rift-fused, but there had been discussions in various governments about having *rift-fused* written on the passports of those of us who came under that particular category. It had originally been shot down as draconian, fascist, and various other words but had started to come back into the public discussion again over the last few years.

My phone vibrated.

Nothing good, Gabriel wrote.

Yeah, that's what I figured, I replied.

Hiroyuki reentered the room as I sat back and stared at the empty safe.

"Anything about Tobias I need to know?" I asked.

Hiroyuki shook his head. "They're going to look into him. You find anything?"

"An empty safe," I told him. "A tree out back that is loaded with pure rift energy."

"Like a primordial?" Hiroyuki asked. "At least we know it isn't one of those."

"I don't think he lives here," I said. "It's too . . ."

"Sterile," Hiroyuki said, looking around. "I agree."

"I think we need to go talk to his work," I said.

Nadia entered the room. "Nothing of interest," she said. "I mean literally nothing. Every rift-fused leaves a trace, and while there is one, it's faint; it's only the kind you'd get from staying a few hours in one place."

"So, he hasn't been here for a while," I said.

"Not for any length of time," Nadia explained.

"So, Reclaimed Lives next, then," Hiroyuki said. "I'll contact Noah and update him, and we can leave."

Hiroyuki left the house via the back door, and I sighed.

"You think we can trust him?" Nadia asked.

I nodded. "The Hiroyuki I knew was incredibly forthright and honest."

"Good," Nadia said. "What can he do?"

"Hiroyuki is a riftborn," I said. "He can make things cold, essentially. But he can also create a small frozen grenade in his hand that explodes and causes spikes to erupt out of the cold. It's quite spectacular."

"You worked for Noah before?" Nadia asked after glancing outside to check where Hiroyuki was.

"Not exactly. I've met him a few times, did some work with the Ravens alongside his Silver Phalanx members."

"I've never come across any of them before," Nadia said. "Heard they're pretty good, though."

"They're well trained, ex-Guild for the most part," I said. "You don't mess around with the Silver Phalanx unless you want to vanish. Every Ancient has between six and ten members, and Noah's are better than most. He was only ever interested in the best."

The door opened, and Hiroyuki stepped back inside, looking somewhat wetter than when he'd left. "It's raining," he said by way of explaining.

"What did Noah say?" I asked.

"To keep him updated," Hiroyuki said. "I think we should check out next door before leaving."

"Okay, let's go look at the murder scene," I said. I turned around and found that Nadia was no longer in the room with us.

CHAPTER SIX

W e should take the rear door and use the woodland to gain entry to the neighbour's house," Nadia said, reentering the kitchen.

"Where'd you go?" I asked.

"To check if our resident nosey neighbour is still there," Nadia said. "He's on the phone, still across the street. Still watching."

"What are the chances he's on the phone to the cops?" Hiroyuki asked.

"That shouldn't be a problem, since Noah owns them," I said before I could stop myself.

Hiroyuki's expression hardened. "That is not what is happening here, and you know it."

I raised my hands in apology. "You're right; that was a low blow. But if Noah does have cops who help him out, maybe he could give them a call and find out what's going on? He certainly knew enough of them to have them not be here when we turned up."

"That's not a terrible idea," Hiroyuki said as Nadia left the room again. "Although I don't need to ask Noah; I can just contact the police officer myself."

Hiroyuki dialled a number on his phone but hung up as Nadia shouted, "Too late," from further in the house.

We found Nadia in the living room, looking out of the large front windows at a police cruiser that had pulled up outside.

"Ah, excellent," Hiroyuki said, making it sound like anything but.

"We could go through the gardens," Nadia said.

"I'll go speak to them," Hiroyuki said, making sure his pendant was visible. "They will listen to me. You two go to the neighbours and look around. What they don't know won't hurt them."

"You rebel," I said.

"I've known you too long," Hiroyuki said with a smile.

"You know I have a Guild medallion that means I'm legally allowed here," I said.

"True," Hiroyuki agreed. "But do you want the police involved, too? Do you want to be questioned about your involvement? You might be allowed to be here, but you're already in the public eye. Let's not make you any more famous than you already are. I should say your form has suffered since we last met. It took you longer than I'd expected to break that policeman's arm."

"Thank you for the tip," I said with a chuckle.

"You know that the Minister who you had arrested is a member of the Blessed, yes?" Hiroyuki asked.

"It came up once or twice," I said.

"We've been hearing chatter about them for a while now," Hiroyuki said. "On Earth, I mean, not in Inaxia and the rift. A group of practitioners exiled from the rift. Apparently, one of them is a congressman or a senator. The story changes every time you hear it."

"Are you thinking that Anthony is involved with Blessed members?" I asked.

Hiroyuki shook his head. "I doubt that very much. But something really strange is going on here, and right now, there's nothing I won't rule out."

I really hated that he had a point.

"Go," Hiroyuki said. "Before the cops decide to kick in the door."

Nadia and I rushed out the back door, and I turned to smoke, billowing over the fence into the neighbour's garden and pulling myself back together. Something that is usually fairly straightforward but is considerably more difficult in the rain. One wrong move, and I get put back together utterly saturated or coughing up water.

Nadia scaled the fence the old-fashioned way, although I was sure the use of her chains helped, and landed in a flowerbed just behind me. She cursed and followed me onto the decking and to the back door, which led into a conservatory. There was just a wooden frame with a mesh over the door, and the mesh had been cut through, so it was easy enough to get into the conservatory.

The door beyond was of the sliding-glass variety, and while it was locked, there was a small window that was ajar. I turned to smoke again and moved through the gap in the window, re-forming in a large kitchen.

Once I'd unlocked the latch in the sliding door, I pulled it open and let Nadia in.

"This is very nice," Nadia said, looking around the large kitchen-diner, which was the same style as Anthony's but finished to a much more impressive standard.

"It looks more lived-in," I said, motioning around me. There was food on the counter, an open bread bin, a dishwasher that was ajar and half-full. I wondered if maybe Abigail had been in the middle of cleaning up when she'd been attacked.

I walked through to the hallway and found bloodstains on the wall and remains of the rug on the wooden floor. "She was stabbed repeatedly after her throat was slit. Who cleaned up the blood?"

"Blood spray," Nadia said, ignoring my question. "The attack was from behind as they walked through the door."

"So, Abigail Walters is doing something in the kitchen, it's quite late, maybe she's having a snack," I said. "Knock on the door. She answers it, sees it's someone she knows, invites them in, turns away, and is killed a second later. How does that sound?"

"I think she definitely knew her attacker," Nadia said. "It happened just inside the doorway, at night. She opened that door to them. There's a spyhole, so she knew who it was before she opened it. She wasn't scared or concerned. She didn't think she was in any danger."

"So, who was it?" I asked. "And why did she have to die?"

There was a knock at the door, and I opened it to find Hiroyuki, who stepped inside, giving me a view of two police officers talking to an exceptionally irate-looking Tobias.

"How'd that go?" I asked.

"Not well for Tobias," Hiroyuki said. "Turns out the police don't like being told that there's something going on just because you don't like the look of someone. Also, Noah got me what I wanted about the crime-scene photos; I've sent them to you."

My phone vibrated, and I flicked through the photos until I found one of the crime scene as it was originally found. "There's not enough blood here," I said, enlarging the photo of Abigail Walters' body and showing it to Hiroyuki and Nadia.

"Someone took her blood?" Hiroyuki asked. "So, we're dealing with what, a vampire?"

"Wait, I get to hunt down a vampire?" Nadia asked. "Oh, this is going to be awesome."

"It's not a vampire," I said.

"Could be," Nadia almost whispered, sounding a little dejected.

"If it helps, when we find who did this, if they give us any trouble, you can still stab them in the heart," I said.

"Deal," Nadia said, perking up.

"You're disturbingly happy about being allowed to stab someone," Hiroyuki said.

"They'll almost certainly deserve it," Nadia pointed out. "So, what took her blood? There's still some here. It's on the walls. Arterial spray, for one."

"I don't know," I said.

"No one feasted on her," Hiroyuki said, reading something on his phone. "She was stabbed in the throat, which was the killing blow, and then repeatedly under the ribs. Why do the latter if you're doing the former?"

"They wanted to make sure she was dead," I said.

"Or they liked it," Nadia finished for me.

"Anything taken, according to the report?" I asked Hiroyuki.

"The upstairs was turned over," Hiroyuki said. "No one knows what was taken, although there was a safe that was open and empty."

"Where?" I asked.

"Master bedroom," Hiroyuki said. "It overlooks the front of the house."

Nadia was already heading up the stairs as I stepped over the blood on the floor and followed her, with Hiroyuki following behind.

There were four doors upstairs; two were open, revealing empty bedrooms, one was a bathroom, and the final was where Nadia stood.

"What did you find?" I asked her as I peered into the room.

"Just look at it," Nadia said with a wave of her hands.

The entire room had actually been turned over, with even the bed being flipped onto its side and pushed to the side of the room. Drawers were spilled over, the cupboards had their contents thrown about, and one of them had its back completely torn off.

The safe was in the corner of the room, next to where the bed lay. It had been set into the floor of the room, with a piece of carpet covering it to make it look like nothing was there. The carpet was off to one side, the door to the safe open just like Hiroyuki said.

"Empty," Nadia said. "You think this was what they were looking for? Why they killed her?"

I shrugged, surveying the destruction of the room. "We've got a missing man and a dead woman who was his neighbour. Coincidences happen all the time, but not like this."

Hiroyuki appeared in the doorway. "So, any luck?"

I shook my head.

I left the room and walked along the hallway to the bedroom that overlooked the front of the house. The police cruiser was still outside, although there were no police or Tobias around.

"They must be really giving him a talking-to," I said, looking around the mostly empty room.

Someone had killed Abigail, searched her home, found a safe, and removed the contents. And I was pretty sure it was linked to Anthony. Somehow.

I made my way back to Nadia and Hiroyuki. "I think we should get going."

No one disagreed, so we left the house, returned to our cars, and took off, but the whole time, I got the feeling that something bad had happened. That I was missing something important. Hopefully something that wasn't going to come back and bite me in the ass.

The drive took a little under forty-five minutes, which, considering the build-up of traffic as it started to become rush hour, was making good time.

I pulled up in a car park close to Reclaimed Lives, which had a building at the end of the block.

Hiroyuki parked his car beside mine, got out, opened the boot, and removed a katana in a black-and-red sheath.

"Working for Noah has perks, then," Nadia said as she got out of the Audi.

Hiroyuki looked back at the Mercedes. "I can't complain," he said with a smile. "I think yours might be a little ostentatious for you."

"I think you're just jealous," I said with a smile of my own.

We walked the short distance to Reclaimed Lives, which was still open, and the three of us stepped inside.

The reception area to the building was spacious and decorated with a variety of styles of colourful artwork on the bare-brick walls. There were wooden chairs sat at one side of the area, surrounding a glass coffee table. A door next to the reception desk had a numerical keypad next to the handle.

"Can I help you?" a young man asked from behind the reception desk. He was white with long pink-, blue-, and green-streaked hair, and several piercings in his ears and a hoop in his lip. He wore a plain black T-shirt, his arms showing a variety of tattoos from a number of influences.

"I'm Hiroyuki," he said, offering his hand, which the young man shook. "This is Lucas and Nadia."

"Nice tats," Nadia said.

"Thank you," the man replied. "I'm Austin."

"We'd like to see Isabelle Nadal," I said.

"Oh," Austin said. "Let me just make a call and I'll get someone out to see you. Please, take a seat."

We thanked him and sat down around the coffee table. "I like the art on the walls," I said as Austin's tapping on the keyboard filled the room.

"All of the art here is done by rift-fused." Hiroyuki said "Or those with rift-fused relations. We need to remember that while we have been touched by the rift, our loved ones have to learn how to deal with our newfound abilities. It's not easy for them, either."

"Not something I had to worry about," I said. "Everyone I knew was dead when I returned."

"Me too," Hiroyuki said. "But for revenants, it's a very different matter."

"Everyone I knew was dead," Nadia said putting her hand up. "To be fair, that was mostly because I killed a lot of them for murdering my parents."

"Seriously?" Hiroyuki asked.

"She's been through some stuff," I said.

"Lots of stuff," Nadia said with a smile.

The door opened and a woman stepped through. She had chestnut hair and wore a dark grey suit with a light blue shirt and white sneakers, she had multiple bracelets adorning both wrists and wore several rings. She had several ear piercings in each ear, with a dangling blue-and-gold hoop being the most prominent.

"You're here about Anthony?" the lady asked.

"Yes," I said, getting to my feet and introducing us all.

"My name is Isabelle Nadal," she said, her accent placing her from the Bronx.

"Pleasure to meet you," I said.

"Please, come with me to my office and we'll discuss more," Isabelle said.

The three of us followed Isabelle through to the large open room beyond the reception; branching off were a half dozen rooms on either side, some of which were occupied.

We followed Isabelle up a metal spiral staircase to the balcony above and continued to a door at the far end, which had Isabelle's name on the wall beside it.

The room had bookshelves that probably groaned under the weight of dozens upon dozens of books, awards, and several toy Teenage Mutant Ninja Turtles. The opposite wall had a large, bright, and colourful mural of a map of Boston.

Isabelle sat behind a large wooden desk, her back to the equally large window that stretched the width of the office.

"Please, have a seat." She indicated several chairs placed opposite her desk. "Anthony is in trouble, isn't he?"

"That's what we're trying to find out," Hiroyuki said.

"You spoke to Noah Kaya?" I asked.

Isabelle nodded. "When Anthony didn't come in to work and no one could get hold of him."

"We've been asked to look into it," I said. "But when we got to his home in Eastfield, we found his house empty. I'm not sure he's ever lived there, and his neighbour is dead. We're hoping it's a coincidence, but I doubt it."

"You think Anthony killed her?" Isabelle asked. "You don't know Anthony."

"No," Nadia said. "That's sort of why we're here."

"We're hoping he didn't kill anyone," I said. "We're worried about what he might have gotten involved in. Like, for example, why he had a house he clearly didn't live in."

"Anthony never liked the place," Isabelle said. "I think Noah gave it to him, but he preferred to stay in Boston. He said he didn't like one of the neighbours there."

"We met him," I said. "Neighbourhood watch. Anthony ever say anything else about him?"

"His name is Tobias," Isabelle said. "It's weird because Anthony always used to say how nice he was, and about a year ago, he just changed. Anthony thought he might have gone down some conspiracy-theory rabbit hole and been seduced by some dark side. Not sure why. Just a vibe he gave off."

"Did you know the neighbour who was killed?" I asked. "Abigail Walters?"

"Oh, no, not Abigail?" Isabelle asked. "No, not well. I met her once or twice and she was always cordial. I think she got the impression that Anthony and I were dating, which couldn't be further from the truth, but it meant it was easy for me to come and go as needed. And without awkward questions."

"People came and went a lot there?" I asked.

"Not for about four months," Isabelle said. "We used the place as a sort of halfway house. Anthony would crash here on one of the sofas and let his house be used by whoever needed it."

"Funny how Tobias never mentioned people coming and going," Hiroyuki said.

"Would he have noticed?" Nadia asked.

"Oh, yes," Isabelle said. "That man didn't miss a thing."

"What is Anthony like as an employee?" Hiroyuki asked. "Noah said he was a good man, but I want to hear from you."

"He's not my employee," Isabelle said. "We are co-owners. I assume Noah told you that already."

"Maybe," Hiroyuki said. "Just want to check that everyone is on the same page."

"So, he helped run this place?" Nadia asked. "Anyone new who might be a problem?"

"He helped set this place up from scratch," Isabelle said. "As for the other question, I'm not sure if it's a problem, but there was an odd man here last week."

"An odd man?" I asked.

"White, maybe late forties, although as you know, it's hard to tell with rift-fused," Isabelle said. "He wasn't newly reborn; he had an old power about him. He had a Guild medallion."

"What Guild?" I asked.

"Hawk," Isabelle said. "He kept it tucked under his shirt, though; only showed us when we were alone. Never met a Guild member who doesn't wear their medallion openly. Like you."

I looked down at the Raven Guild medallion. Sometimes, keeping it hidden was necessary, usually because you didn't want people to freak out that you were a Guild member, and some rift-fused equate Guild and police, which isn't really what we do, but I couldn't blame people for being concerned.

"Did this Guild member give a name?" I asked.

"Matty," Isabelle said.

Hiroyuki looked over at me, "Do you know a Matty in the Hawk Guild?" he asked.

I shook my head. "I'm not really up to date on who is in what Guild. What did he want?"

"He was looking for a rift-walker runaway," Isabelle said.

"A rift-walker?" Nadia asked. "For a group of people who are meant to be rare, we sure do seem to be running into a few of them."

"They're not that rare," Isabelle said. "They're secretive."

Hiroyuki and I shared a look.

"What do you mean, *they're secretive*?" I asked.

"Well, rift-walkers are not really rare, according to our data," Isabelle said. "They're much more common than some species of revenant, like blood or arcane. They learn pretty quickly that there are bad people out there who want to use their power for their own ends. They either go into the rift and don't return, or they keep their power hidden and don't use it, or they die. Almost seventy-five percent of all rift-walkers fall into one of those three categories."

"I had no idea," I said. "I always thought they were just a rare group."

"They're rare in terms of less than one percent of the rift-fused population as a whole, but not as rare as they've tried to make out," Isabelle said. "Rift-walkers aren't big powerhouses; they don't have an attacking or defensive power, unless you consider opening a tear and running away a power."

"Unless they're forced to keep their power on," I said. "Or they lose control of it. And then you've got an exceptionally offensive power."

"Unfortunately, yes," Isabelle said. "But how often does that happen?"

"Not very," I said. "I've only encountered it a handful of times."

"And how old are you?" Isabelle asked.

"A bit over two thousand years," I said. "So, why would some Guild member be looking for a rift-walker runaway?"

"I don't know," Isabelle said. "I wish I did. I do know that it upset Anthony. He was unhappy about the line of questioning and asked the Guild member to go. He said that those who come through the doors of this building are given complete anonymity, which is true, and that he wouldn't reveal the names of anyone that we help."

"Can I assume that also extends to us?" Hiroyuki said.

"Yes," Isabelle said. "I won't give you the names of those who came here looking for help. However, in this instance, I couldn't even if I wanted to; we've had zero rift-walkers come through these doors in the last five months, at least. And they definitely weren't a runaway; they were just the unlucky man who was in the wrong place when a tear opened and he stepped inside. Human to rift-walker in an instant. After the screaming agony, anyway."

The transformation for a fit and healthy human who walked through a tear, into a rift-walker, was not a fun one. I'd found a newly changed rift-walker once, and she had been a physical mess for weeks after. She could barely move for several days. It wasn't a process I envied.

"What happened after this *Matty* left?" I asked.

"Anthony left soon after," Isabelle said.

"Any chance of seeing the CCTV footage?" Hiroyuki asked.

"It was disabled," Isabelle said. "The entire system was down all day."

"So, someone arranged it beforehand," Nadia said. "It's what I'd do if I didn't want anyone to see my face."

"So, this *Matty* comes, asks about someone who doesn't exist as far as you know, and leaves," I said. "Soon after, Anthony leaves too. How many days before Anthony left did that happen?"

"Four," Isabelle said. "Anthony came to work as normal for four days after the visit. Then he just stopped."

I looked over at Nadia. "Can you look around Anthony's office? Get a feel for him, see if we can find out anywhere he might have gone?"

Nadia stood. "On it," she said as she left the office.

"Do you have any safe houses nearby?" Hiroyuki asked.

"Several," Isabelle said. "I've called them all; Anthony isn't there. I'm uncomfortable with giving out their addresses. They're safe for a reason."

"Any chance he has a safe house you don't know about?" I asked.

Isabelle looked between Hiroyuki and me. "Yes, I think that's likely."

"Why do you think that?" I asked.

"Because of his sister," Isabelle said.

CHAPTER SEVEN

W hat does Dani have to do with any of this?" Hiroyuki asked.
"You know Anthony's sister?" Isabelle asked us both.

"No," Hiroyuki and I said in unison.

"We've been told about her," I continued. "She was taken into the rift after a car accident, she's a rift-walker, but that's about it."

"Anthony always wanted to prepare for the day she came back," Isabelle said. "But he was worried that once she did come back, there might be people wanting to use a rift-walker to their own ends. I believe he has an apartment off the books somewhere. If Dani came back, he'd put her there so she could reacclimatise herself to a world she has no knowledge about. A lot has happened in the short time she's been gone."

"You received any threats from pro-humanity groups?" I asked. "Anything that might make Anthony even more concerned about this Matty turning up?"

"Of course," Isabelle said. "We get stuff from random nutcases on a regular basis. Had a lot from a group calling themselves Sovereign Humanity."

"Ah, crap," I said.

"You've met them?" Isabelle asked.

"A while back," I said. "They were involved in some shady stuff, including murder. But I assumed their entire organisation collapsed when the man in charge of it was . . . removed from the situation."

"Removed?" Isabelle asked.

"He's dead," I said bluntly. "Super-duper dead."

"Well, apparently, the group survived," Isabelle said.

"Are they harassing those who come here?" Hiroyuki asked, a hint of anger in his voice.

"They have demonstrations in the morning," Isabelle said as Nadia returned to the office and shook her head to say she hadn't found anything. "They stand on the sidewalk across the entrance and shout nonsense at people. Sometimes, we come here in the morning and there's graffiti on the shutters. *Human Thieves* was the most recent."

"They think you kidnap humans?" Nadia asked.

"You haven't heard?" Isabelle asked. "There was a congressman who suggested that the rift-fused kidnap people to take them into the rift so that they can be brought up as a sympathiser and sent back to Earth to spread propaganda about us."

"Why?" I asked.

Isabelle shrugged. "You don't need rational thinking, or logic, when you're an asshole with a megaphone."

I looked to Hiroyuki. "You heard about this?"

"Bits and pieces," he said. "They're just loudmouthed assholes. But the congressman in question is definitely the loudest and most asshole-like of them all. He goes on these conspiracy podcasts where they think that people are from pods, or aliens are infesting our brains, and he spouts off whatever nonsense his addled brain comes up with that day. I tend to ignore it all, and I'm not sure that Noah gives it any thought, either."

"Does it need looking into, though?" I asked. "We've got a missing rift-fused, a mystery man who turned up asking about rift-walkers, and a hate group who might well be looking for a specific someone to aim that hate at. Maybe we should go have a chat with them."

"How likely do you think that would end well?" Isabelle asked.

"For us or them?" I asked her.

Isabelle's eyes narrowed in irritation.

"Fair point," I said. "So, we have Anthony out there somewhere, we don't know where, we don't know why he ran, but we do know that there are groups making rift-fused lives harder, and someone claiming to be from a Guild checking up on you."

Nadia opened the door to the office. "Got something," she said as her chains flicked around her arms. "I went into the chains. There's a building nearby, five storeys, roof garden. Lots of links lead me there. Lots of chaos, lots of . . . something bad. I can't make out if it's Anthony or someone else, but there's a picture in his office of him and a young girl."

"Dani, his sister," Isabelle said.

"I stared at it, and my chains went crazy," Nadia said. "Whatever path I'm meant to take, she's involved somewhere."

"Not to doubt you," Hiroyuki said, "but chained revenants aren't always reliable with their visions."

"Thank you for not doubting me and then doing exactly that," Nadia said with a smile. "The chains aren't always reliable. Sometimes, they show me things I won't need or will never actually see in real life, but when they go crazy, I pay attention. They went crazy when I first got wind of Lucas, and it took me years to actually track him down. That picture of Dani had a similar response."

"So, we need to find this building?" I asked.

Nadia nodded. "Don't know what we'll find, but it's a good direction."

"You know of anywhere like that?" I asked Isabelle.

Isabelle thought for a while. "We looked at a building a few blocks from here. The top floor was empty. Five apartments, leading to a roof garden. We dismissed it simply because it was so close to here that we didn't want anyone to be in a safe house close to those Sovereign Humanity morons, but Anthony loved the area, so he purchased one of the apartments. I've been there; it's empty. The work hasn't even finished to make it habitable."

"Would Anthony have been able to afford the entire top floor of an apartment building without using money tied up in this place?" I asked.

"You're thinking he went ahead and bought it all anyway," Isabelle asked.

I nodded. "It's a case of whether or not he can afford to do that without making it known by you and the people who work here."

"Anthony has a trust fund," Hiroyuki said.

"A trust fund?" I asked.

"Noah considers him family, so yes," Hiroyuki explained. "No one has access to his account, but there's enough in it to buy up whatever he likes."

"He could flee the country, then?" I asked.

"It's possible," Hiroyuki said.

"He would never leave until Dani was back," Isabelle said, getting up and grabbing her jacket from the coatrack beside her. "I'll show you to this apartment building."

"You don't have to come," I said.

"If Anthony is there and you all turn up, how do you think that'll go?" Isabelle asked.

"I work for Noah," Hiroyuki said as if that was going to be the deciding factor in Anthony trusting us.

Isabelle shrugged and we all followed her out of her office, through the building, to the outside. There were people on the opposite side of the road with various placards and signs, none of which were pleasant and in most cases not even spelt correctly.

We were already hurrying down the sidewalk when the chorus of chants and boos reached us.

"How long have they been coming?" I asked Isabelle as we crossed the road.

"Few months," Isabelle said. "Told the police, told Noah, but unless they actually do something to one of us physically, no one wants to get involved."

"You want me to get involved?" Nadia asked.

"Gods, no," Isabelle said. "We don't need deaths on our hands."

"Who said anything about death?" Nadia asked.

"No maiming, either," I said.

Nadia sighed. "Yeah, okay."

Isabelle stopped walking outside of a five-storey red-brick building.

"That's the one," Nadia said.

The building had a well-manicured lawn out the front, next to a solitary brick wall that appeared to exist solely for people to do exceptional graffiti on it.

"Anthony was part of a committee that got that wall put up in front of the building," Isabelle said, as she caught me staring at the artwork. "There are another four around here."

"He loves this neighbourhood," I said.

"He does," Isabelle agreed. "Always has."

"Did you know him before he became a revenant?" I asked her as we walked through a set of automatic glass doors and into the apartment building foyer.

"No," she admitted, pressing the button to call the lift. There was a small shelving unit on one side of the foyer, stacked full of books, above which someone had written *Take a book, leave a book.*

"I'm going to need to stop by here on the way out," Nadia whispered to me, pointing at the books.

"Do you have one to leave?" I asked.

"This is why I need to start carrying books around everywhere I go," Nadia said as the lift doors opened, and we all entered and Isabelle pressed the button for the fifth floor.

The journey up was quick, and the lift doors opened into a hallway, which smelled of fresh flowers. It took me a moment to realise that it came from a plug-in scent. There were five apartments on the floor, with one almost directly in front of the elevator, and three on one side, and one on the other, next to a large sign that said EXIT with a green arrow pointing to the left.

"The roof?" I asked.

Isabelle nodded. "It's open to the whole building; they have barbecues, parties, and even grow plants up there. It's a communal thing. I think it's the reason that Anthony liked this place; it's a very social neighbourhood. Everyone's friendly; very little crime."

"How many are rift-fused?" Hiroyuki asked.

"About half in this building," Isabelle said. "The fourth floor has a few apartments that are used as sort of halfway homes for the newly returned, but they're through another organisation. It's partly why when this floor came up, we wanted to look into it."

"Any chance you have a key?" I asked.

"Sorry," Isabelle said.

I turned to smoke and moved around the door frame, re-forming on the other side and opening the door for everyone.

The apartment was a shell. There were walls and a wooden floor, but the plumbing and electrics were still exposed inside the wall cavities, and there was no way anyone would be able to live there in anything close to comfort, let alone safety.

"You guys smell that?" Nadia asked as we reached the windows at the rear of the apartment.

I took in a long, deep breath through my nose. There was a scent in the air . . . cinnamon, and something else . . . something . . . spicy.

"Chilli," Nadia said. "Herbs, spices."

"The roof, maybe?" Hiroyuki asked.

"There are a lot of herbs and spices grown on the roof," Isabelle said.

"Bit odd that you'd be able to smell them through the ceiling, even if it's not finished," I said. "There's concrete, brick, steel, and a variety of materials between us and the roof. It's closer than that."

Nadia opened the balcony door and stepped outside, the scents I'd been able to smell allowed to rush into the apartment at once.

"Neighbour," Hiroyuki said.

"None of these apartments are being used," Isabelle said.

"Then the workers next door *really* like cinnamon in their coffee," Nadia said as she left the balcony; I stopped her before she could close the door behind her.

"You go to the hallway and around; I'll go the balcony way," I said, stepping outside.

I waited for Isabelle, Hiroyuki, and Nadia to leave the apartment before I turned to smoke and billowed across to the balcony adjacent to the one I was on, re-forming and peering through the glass sliding door. I tried the handle and found it unlocked, the door sliding open to reveal . . . a very-much-lived-in apartment.

There was a large open-plan living area with pictures on the walls, photos of various people with drinks and easy smiles, paintings of ships, of landscapes. Books, video games, and Blu-ray films in one of the many cabinets that surrounded the large flat-screen TV up against the wall.

I placed my hand against the games console that sat on the wooden furniture beneath the TV. Still warm. The room smelled of cinnamon due to a wax melt that sat in the top of a plug-in vase next to the sliding door.

The room was open-plan with a dining area and kitchen beside it. There was the sound of sizzling and I walked over to the kitchen, by a centre table with chopping boards on it with herbs, chillies, and a variety of vegetables, and switched off the cooker hob.

I left the room and walked through a small hallway with a door on one side and a coat rack next to the wooden door. I pushed open the door, which led to a second hallway with two doors on one side and a third at the far end. The hallway, like the one I was in, was wooden, and I was suddenly aware of how much noise my footsteps were making. I walked back to the coat rack, which had coats, shoes, and the like already there, and opened the front door and let everyone in.

Nadia walked by me, down the hallway into the living area. "Someone is cooking," she called back. "Pan's on the stove. Chopping board with onion, chilli, and spices on it."

"Anthony," Isabelle shouted.

The sound of footsteps on the wooden floor took my attention, and I turned to see a young woman walk barefoot out of the hallway that presumably led to where the bedrooms were. She had olive skin, long dark hair that fell over her shoulders, and several noticeable scars on her forearms. She wore a vest and some jean shorts, and held a dagger in one hand. The look on her face suggested she would be happy to use it.

"What do you want with Anthony?" the woman asked.

"Okay, no one is here to hurt you or Anthony," I said.

"The Guild medallion suggests otherwise," the woman said.

"Dani?" Isabelle asked, her tone confused.

"Belle?" Dani asked, and the pair practically ran into each other to hug.

"Oh, my god," Isabelle proclaimed. "It's been . . . it's been so long."

"Who are you?" Dani shouted at Hiroyuki and me. She turned back to Isabelle with hurt in her eyes. "Why are you with them?"

"I'm Lucas Rurik," I said. "Your brother's friends were worried about him. Asked me to look into it."

"Dani, no," a man shouted as the front door opened and he stepped into the apartment. He also had olive skin, with long dark hair that was tied back in a ponytail. He wore a pair of shorts, flip-flops, and a black vest, showing off the tattoos on the top of his shoulders that looked like the flesh was peeling away to reveal clockwork beneath. He wore a cord necklace with shells on it. He looked like a surfer.

"Anthony," I said. "Please tell this lady that we're not here to hurt you."

Dani placed the dagger on the floor.

I noticed that Hiroyuki's hand had settled on the hilt of his blade, and he visibly relaxed once the dagger was down.

"Hi, Anthony, Dani," I said. "Either of you want to tell us what the hell is going on?"

CHAPTER EIGHT

Dani moved over to one of the sofas and took a seat, although she never took her eyes off Hiroyuki, Nadia, or me.

"So, you're back, then," Hiroyuki said as he leant up against the nearby wall.

"You're a rift-walker," I said after no one spoke for several seconds. "You were taken into the rift after the car accident you were both in."

"My brother died from the impact," Dani said. "The car we were in spun around, right into a tear, which was big enough to take me inside. The tear closed with the rear of the car inside the rift. With me still strapped inside."

"That's a lot," I said, fully aware of what happened to humans who got stuck in the rift.

"You get it," Dani said. "I was alone, human, hurt from the accident, and trapped in a world I had no idea about. I unstrapped myself from the rear of the car, which had been sheared in half, walked over to where the tear had been, and then the agony struck me. I don't remember much else except waking up some time later in the hut of a village. They told me in a language I learned that instant that they track down humans thrown into the rift. They help heal them. Without them, I'm pretty sure I would have died."

I'd seen the aftermath of a few humans who had walked through a tear. I'd heard the screams, the pleading to be allowed to die. The fact that it had happened to a sixteen-year-old girl was . . . No one should go through what she'd gone through.

"I'm sorry," I said. "That you went through that. It must have been hard."

"It was," Dani said. "The hardest thing, though, was not being able to open a tear. I was told I was a rift-walker but couldn't leave the rift. Couldn't open a tear big enough to walk through. Took years of practice."

Opening tears is one thing; opening tears that are large and stable enough for a human to walk though was not something rift-walkers could do right away.

"I lived within the village to the north of the rift," Dani said. "For eight years. I helped farm, I helped hunt, I helped protect against marauders or creatures who got too close. But I never stopped thinking about my brother. I got word to him that I was alive but couldn't come back, and he couldn't go to the rift."

Like humans, revenants can't go into the rift, even with a rift-walker. They'd have to wear a Hazmat suit or breathing gear. I've seen revenants go into the rift, and if they can't get back out quickly, their inevitable deaths are less than pleasant.

"How long have you been back on Earth?" Nadia asked.

"Six months," Dani said. "I got to see my brother, to see how things have changed around here. But I don't have a high school diploma, I don't have any work prospects, or friends, or anything. Six months of being happy but also not knowing what I was going to do."

"And you two know each other?" I asked Isabelle.

"We went to school together," Dani said, looking over at a clearly in shock Isabelle. "We were . . . we were more than friends."

"Ah, young love," Hiroyuki said.

"Something like that," Isabelle said. "You've been back six months and haven't said anything to me."

I wasn't sure if her anger was directed at Dani or Anthony, although probably both.

"At first, we just wanted to be a family again," Anthony said. "But after a few days of Dani being back, someone came by the house."

"Wanting what?" Hiroyuki asked.

"They were looking for information on Dani. Said they were a journalist doing stories on those who disappeared into the rift. That they'd heard about what happened to her in the accident and wanted to know if she had made it back. Something didn't feel right. Couldn't quite work it out, but then I started to see him around the place. He came into Reclaimed Lives, and a few weeks ago I spotted him in Eastfield talking to Tobias."

"Ah, Tobias," I said. "The neighbourhood busybody."

"The thing about him is he used to be a nice guy," Anthony said. "But about six months ago, he just changed. Started to patrol the neighbour-hood, asking questions about people, being all . . . weird. I think he used it as an excuse to peer in windows. Abigail told him to fuck off more than once."

"Your neighbour?" I asked. "The one who was murdered?"

Anthony nodded.

"What happened?" Hiroyuki asked.

"I don't know," Anthony said. "Honestly, I had nothing to do with it."

Nadia and I exchanged a glance.

"I call bullshit," Nadia said before I could say the exact same thing.

"Are you calling my brother a liar?" Dani snapped, getting to her feet as Anthony placed a calming hand on her arm.

"She's right," Anthony said. "I had nothing to do with Abigail's murder, I promise you. She texted me at midnight, told me to come over quickly. Her front door was open, which was weird in itself. She was dead, but there was so little blood on the floor. It was across the walls and . . . I ran. I heard a siren in the distance, freaked out, and ran."

"You ran?" Hiroyuki asked. "You didn't think to call Noah, or the cops, or anyone? Not even Isabelle?"

"I saw someone," Anthony said. "On the street, watching me. I thought it was Tobias, but they ran off. I just . . . I didn't know what to do."

"Pretty much anything other than what you did would have worked out better than this," I said. "You found your dead neighbour, ran away after being seen, didn't inform the police, and your entire place looks like it was scrubbed clean."

"We do a deep clean after every resident leaves," Anthony said.

"Your safe was empty," I said.

"Never use it," Anthony told us. "I keep anything I need here."

"You're not in trouble with the law, so why run?" Hiroyuki asked. "I mean, you'd call Noah, and he'd send someone down there."

Anthony sighed. "I found something out. Something bad. A list of names of people who . . . have gone missing."

"Missing?" I asked.

Anthony pulled open a drawer in a sideboard and removed something stuck to the roof of it, passing me a manilla envelope. I opened it and removed the piece of paper inside with twenty-seven names on it. Each of them had a cross or a tick.

"The tick means I found them," Anthony said.

"Nineteen crosses," I said, passing the paper to Hiroyuki. "What do they mean?"

"They've gone missing within the last year," Anthony said. "Abigail was murdered four days after a man claiming to be from one of the Guilds comes to my place of work to talk to me. Abigail and I used to watch old movies together. I enjoyed her company."

"You're worried that your friendship with Abigail was what got her killed," Nadia said. "You two were in . . . whatever it was?"

Anthony shook his head. "No, we were just friends. Ever since someone came to the house to talk about Dani, I've been on edge. I was scared. I ran. I didn't know who to contact, who I'd put in danger. I thought if I just had a few days to figure out how to get out of the country without anyone spotting me—"

"You know Noah had to get involved," Hiroyuki said, interrupting.

"Okay, moving past all of that," I said before anyone started to argue. "What are the names for?"

"They're all rift-walkers," Anthony said.

"Nineteen rift-walkers have gone missing in a year?" I asked. "Not to be the one who asks, but are we sure they're not just in the rift?"

"Several of them are reported missing by their families," Anthony said. "At least half a dozen were spotted talking to a man who looked a lot like the one who came to the house."

"And what did he look like?" I asked.

"A killer," Dani said. "I've seen my share of them."

I wondered just what horrors Dani had seen. The rift was full of wonder, of genuine beauty, and mesmerising vistas, but it was also a place of darkness, where monsters roamed. And sometimes the only difference between the types of monster was that some came in human appearance.

"What was the impression you got?" Hiroyuki asked Anthony.

"I'm not a warrior," Anthony said. "I turned into a revenant, and I went and passed the bar. I work for a nonprofit organisation helping people. I've never even hit someone in anger."

"But," I asked.

"Something was off," Anthony said.

"And the Guild member who came to your work?" I asked. "What about him?"

"He was . . . not good," Anthony said. "I got the impression he was someone I should be concerned about."

"Your instincts are working, then," Hiroyuki said. "If they were working together, we're talking about a two-person team. At least."

"And one of them is a Guild member," Isabelle said. "The Guilds are after Dani?"

I shook my head. "I doubt it. Guilds usually have a rift-walker on retainer to help out if need be, so searching for Dani doesn't make much sense."

"That doesn't leave many nice options," Hiroyuki said.

"Are you suggesting that he killed a Guild member and took the medallion?" Isabelle asked, shocked at the very idea.

"Or it was fake," I said. "Anthony, could you spot a fake medallion?"

Anthony shrugged. "I've seen three Guild medallions my whole life. One is in front of me right now, one belonged to that *Matty* guy, and the third came to Reclaimed Lives because one of the people there was a family member. On none of those occasions have I been allowed to—or even wanted to—get really close to a Guild medallion."

"Or," Nadia said. "The badge is real, and it's his. He's a Guild member. A whole Guild might not be after Dani, but one member could go rogue."

"It does happen," I said. "Can't imagine one wanting to go into business for themselves and risk pissing off an Ancient, though."

"What I'm hearing is that there are no good reasons to why these men are looking for me," Dani said.

"That about sums it up," Nadia said.

"You should come with us," Hiroyuki said. "We can go to Noah's compound. You'll be safe there."

"I'm safe here," Dani said. "This is Anthony's home."

"If we found you, they could," Hiroyuki said. "I doubt it would be difficult to put a tail on Anthony. Your neighbour's death, and the suspicion it casts on you, is another reason why you need to come with us."

"I do wonder why Abigail would let them in like she knows them, then," Isabelle asked.

"The lady asks an excellent point," Nadia said.

"Did the man who came to your house leave a card?" I asked, not wanting to go around in circles trying to figure out who killed Abigail.

Anthony nodded. "Just a phone number on it."

"Where is it?" Hiroyuki asked.

"In the garbage," Anthony said. "Didn't trust him."

"Any chance he also asked your neighbours?" I asked.

"I don't know," Anthony said.

I looked over at Hiroyuki. "I'll make a call."

"Abigail could have been killed to make it look like you were the culprit," I said. "You spoiled the surprise and ran, but any chance we can look how quickly the cops were called? Doesn't answer why the house was ransacked, though. A question for whoever did it."

Hiroyuki nodded and left the room.

"So, you live here?" I asked Anthony. "But you don't tell anyone."

"I thought this was a good place to hide away," Anthony said. "Noah always told me to have a plan B. The house in Eastfield isn't really mine; it's just in my name. I only stay there occasionally. Most of the time, I'm sleeping at the office after working until late. Sometimes, I stay at one of the halfway houses or a safe house. It's been a long time since I've trusted myself to stay in one place, always worried about who might come looking for me."

"Why?" Nadia asked.

"Noah is like a father figure to me," Anthony said. "He put me through college; he helped me find my feet in the world. But his enemies are my enemies, and when I left his bubble to set out on my own, he was concerned that some people who might want to harm him would do that through me. No one knows this place exists. I can live here in peace."

Hiroyuki reentered the room. "Spoke to the detective in charge; no card at the neighbour's house. However, we do know that a phone call was made from that house around the time of the murder. It's . . . it's bad. Apparently, it's just her pleading to be allowed to live. Abigail's phone shows a text message sent about two minutes later."

"She was killed just moments before Anthony arrived?" I asked.

"No, the detective says someone recorded her pleading for her life and then played that to the dispatcher after the call," Hiroyuki said. "They think she was dead a good half hour before the text was sent. Whoever killed Abigail used her own phone to do the recording. Whoever did this killed her, took his time before he phoned the cops, and told them that they saw you, Anthony, running from the scene. They then texted you telling you to come over. You did as the sirens sounded in the night. You were meant to get arrested."

"Oh, shit," Anthony said. "Abigail is dead because of me?"

"No," I said. "Abigail is dead because an asshole killed her. None of this is your fault."

"But we don't know *who* killed Abigail," Nadia said.

"We do not," Hiroyuki said. "We do know that Anthony's fingerprints were found on a glass in Abigail's kitchen. The detective who works for

Noah contacted him, and Noah squashed the APB for a while, but he can't do it forever. We need to take you somewhere safe."

"What if the cops are in on it?" Dani asked. "What if the person who killed her was a cop? She would trust a cop. Why wouldn't you? Until it's too late. Doesn't even have to be a real cop, just look like one."

"Someone who has a Guild medallion—fake or otherwise—might have a similar effect on people," Isabelle said. "A lot of humans equate Guild medallions with some sort of law and order."

"I really wish they wouldn't," I whispered to myself. "All we know is that Abigail was killed and it was made to look like Anthony was responsible. Or at least that you were there at the time. Everything else is just guesswork."

"So, we'll take you to Gabriel's church," Hiroyuki said. "We can meet Noah there and arrange transfer of you while Nadia, Lucas, and I investigate this further. Sound good?"

"No," Anthony said. "We're safe. I can't trust yet more people I don't know."

"Gabriel is a good man," Hiroyuki told him.

"I'm staying right here," Dani snapped. "I don't know any of you, and I'm not going anywhere. I'll deal with shit by myself because that's what I do. Deal with shit alone."

"Are you okay with staying alive?" Nadia asked. "Because right now, you're not thinking sensibly."

"Who the fuck are you?" Dani snapped.

Nadia's chains slid over the ground. "I'm the person who came with these two to find out why Anthony ran. What I see are people trying to protect you while you sit there being miserable about it. I get that you've had a shitty few years, hell, a shitty life, but a lot of us have."

"Yeah, you get stuck in another fucking realm?" Dani snapped again.

"My parents were murdered in front of me when I was fifteen," Nadia said, holding Dani's gaze. "I killed every single person involved in my parents' deaths, and it led to more and more people I cared about being murdered. I'm a chained revenant. My brain tries to force me to see multiple futures all the time; it can drive me insane if I'm not careful. So, technically, I'm stuck in another world every minute of every day."

Dani blinked, and the anger that had threatened to bubble over came out in a long sigh. "Fucking hell," she whispered.

"We are here to help," Nadia said. "If you don't want it, we'll leave. Good luck with everything; I hope when they find you, you die as quickly as your neighbour did."

Anthony stared at Nadia. "We need to go, Dani."

"How are we going to be safe anywhere we go?" Dani asked, and I saw the fear for the first time.

"You're not safe here," Nadia said, and her eyes rolled up into her head as she slumped in her seat.

"What the fuck?" Dani almost shouted.

"Have you never met a chained revenant before?" I asked her.

Dani shook her head. "No. I've met riftborn and some revenants but no one like her."

"They don't come to Reclaimed Lives," Isabelle said. "Never had a chained revenant ask for help."

"They're not big on talking to people they don't trust," I said. "Took Nadia a while to open up to me, and that's only because she sees me in the future of her chains."

"Her chains?" Dani asked.

"That's what they call it when they start to see the future," I said. "That's what she's doing right now. Seeing one or dozens of possible futures. Presumably involving all of us, maybe just involving you."

"Do they always come true?" Dani asked.

"It's not that kind of seeing the future," I explained. "They don't see black-and-white definitive answers; they see a sort of possibility of what may happen. They feel emotions, they might get a glimpse of someone, or something, they might see something play out, but it's never a hundred percent. It's not like watching a film, more like watching a film while only being able to see a fraction of the TV screen. You'll hear stuff, you'll see stuff, but you have to figure out what any of it might mean."

"That sounds awful," Dani said.

"It's not a barrel of laughs," Nadia said, returning to us. "They're coming. We don't have long."

"Who's coming?" Dani asked, getting to her feet.

"No idea," Nadia said. "I can only see something where I'm involved. It's not omniscience. But a lot of different possibilities of the future all have someone trying to kill you here. Most of them have someone dying; all of them have screaming. I assume you'd like to avoid that. We need to leave."

"Any idea how long we have?" I asked as Hiroyuki walked over to the window looking down on the street below.

"Not long," he said. "Black SUV just pulled up . . . and a dark blue high-top van too. Unmarked, but I'd rather not find out what's inside."

"How did they find us?" Dani shouted.

"The protestors outside Reclaimed Lives," I said. "They followed Isabelle. Probably been following her for days. Shit, we led them right here."

"And I'm supposed to trust you how?" Dani asked.

I looked out of the window at the two vans that pulled up as six personnel alighted from the two vehicles. All wore tactical gear and carried guns. The four men who got out of the first van looked up at the building.

"There's six of them," I said. "That it?"

"Can you deal with six of them?" Anthony asked, panic in his voice.

"Alone?" I asked.

"You think maybe we should let them call some more buddies?" Hiroyuki asked Anthony.

"Are you being flippant right now?" Isabelle yelled.

"There's six of them," I said. "It's almost unfair how badly they're about to get their asses kicked."

Hiroyuki smiled. "Almost."

CHAPTER NINE

Any way to get from the roof to the building next to this one?" I asked.

Anthony nodded as he ran over and grabbed a black jacket, putting it on but making a mess out of it and trying to put two arms in one arm hole.

"Anthony," I said slightly firmly. "Calm. It'll be fine."

"Any chance Dani can just open a rift and take us all through?" Isabelle asked.

"A few problems with that," Dani said. "One, no. I can take maybe one other person, two at a push. Two, Nadia and my brother are revenants, and the second they breathe the air in the rift, they'll go into convulsions and possibly die. Three, you're human. You will almost certainly either die or live a life of agony for months until you become a rift-walker."

"*No* would have been enough," Isabelle snapped.

It was pretty obvious that tensions were raising and tempers were becoming frayed. Being hunted does that to a person.

Anthony took a breath as his sister grabbed a jacket of her own, although hers was leather. She placed a hand on her brother's arm.

"Lucas, Nadia, and I will be with you," Hiroyuki said. "We won't let anything happen."

I turned to Nadia. "You ready?"

She nodded.

"Isabelle," I said, as she stared at me. "You okay?"

"Yes, yes, yes, I'm fine," she said in one hurried outpouring of words. "I'm just . . . you know, freaking out. I'm a lawyer, not a soldier."

"You'll be just fine," I told her, looking over at Anthony who, while a revenant, certainly didn't look like he'd ever had any kind of military training.

A large number of revenants have never fought, never used their powers in anger or even to defend themselves. Most live their lives just like anyone else. I sometimes had to remind myself of that.

I opened the front door and looked out into the hallway, motioning for everyone to take the staircase directly in front of us. I waited until everyone had gone before closing the door.

"I'll catch you up," I whispered, and let Hiroyuki and Nadia take the group out of the building.

I walked to the end of the hallway and opened the stairwell door. I crouched and moved to the banister, looking down the central shaft of the spiral stairwell. The attackers wouldn't take the lift; they'd use the stairwell, as it was only five storeys. The sound of boots on stairs was easy to hear in the echo of the stairwell. They were moving at a decent pace, although not running.

They couldn't possibly know where we were in the building . . . unless they had some way to track us. Otherwise, they'd leave at least one in the foyer to make sure we couldn't escape that way. That meant searching floor by floor from the bottom or the top. Either way, we had time.

I kept the door open for a few seconds and heard a thud far below, followed by another, then another. Heavy footsteps on the stairs.

I moved out of the stairwell and jogged down the hallway, taking the door out onto the roof, where Dani and Nadia met me.

"I assume there are people coming," Dani said.

"Up the stairwell," I said. "No idea how many, but at least five with one in the foyer, so let's say that. You didn't need to wait."

"That's what I said," Nadia told me.

"Let's get off the roof before they bring a chopper or something," I told them both.

I followed Nadia and Dani across the good-sized roof, walking through a garden where people had been growing various fruits, vegetables, and flowers. There was art painted on a wall, and several small trees around the edges of the roof. It was quite beautiful, and I hoped that whoever had been sent to get Dani wasn't going to destroy it in their search.

The six-feet-wide gap between the two buildings had a small metal bridge over it that was attached to the floor on either side. I wondered how many regulations it broke to have it there. We crossed over it into the adjoining building's similarly designed roof garden; apparently, there were plenty of people with green fingers in the neighbourhood.

Hiroyuki, Anthony, and Isabelle waited beside the roof door, with the three of them going inside once they saw us.

I was last, closing the door and making sure that the bolts on the top and bottom were locked in place before hurrying down the short set of stairs to the hallway, where everyone waited for me.

"Lift down to the bottom," I said as we reached the lift. "Hiroyuki, you bring your car around the front; Isabelle, Anthony, and Dani, get in. Nadia and I will keep an eye on everything from here and catch up with you."

There was a sound from the top of the staircase as something tried the roof door, followed immediately by the door being obliterated as something smashed its way through.

Hiroyuki placed a hand on the hilt of his katana.

"Nadia, get everyone to the ground floor," I said, staring at the end of the hallway, where the stairs to the roof ended. Heavy footsteps down the hallway showed that whoever it was was in no hurry.

"Done," Nadia told me as the lift continued to slowly rumble its way toward us.

The thing that came into view at the end of the hallway was seven feet tall and wore a black trench coat, which covered a black shirt, navy combat trousers, and black work boots. It wasn't just tall but wide, too, a massive tank of . . . whatever the hell it was. It wore a mask over its face that looked like someone had taken several Talons' masks—a mask with a dark grey hood and splashes of colour around the face—and had smashed them to pieces before re-forming them. It was a hodgepodge of dark colour across the mask, with a patchwork of colour for multiple slashes.

The mask was much larger than the head it was on, with black opaque lenses over each eye, although the lenses were each the size of my hand. It made the creature look like it had the face of a metal elephant.

The lift arrived and the doors opened as the thing stood still, its eyes hidden behind the mask.

"Run," I said to Nadia, who practically threw everyone into the lift and smashed the buttons.

The lack of immediate movement from the lift felt like a lifetime as the creature went from standing still to sprinting at us in the blink of an eye.

Hiroyuki was closer to the creature than I was, and he drew his sword, but the creature was too close, too fast, and backhanded him through the nearest door, which turned into a million splitters as Hiroyuki impacted with it.

The creature continued toward the lift, and I darted forward, drawing both daggers and plunging them into its stomach as the lift doors slowly closed behind me.

I turned to smoke to avoid its counter, but the owner of the apartment rushed out with a baseball bat in hand, only to be punched by the creature. The man's bat clattered to the ground as he careered through what remained of the door.

I stabbed the creature twice more, slashing once across the artery in its thigh. But it grabbed the back of my head and smashed me into the wall. I took hold of its hand and turned to smoke, tearing away part of its hand as I drifted through the open doorway. I re-formed in the hallway next to the homeowner, but he was clearly dead.

Turning to find Hiroyuki, I was caught in the chest by a huge boot, which sent me through a hole in the wall and into the living room. I hit a sofa, spun over it, and landed heavily on a coffee table.

The creature tore through the remains of the wall as I got back to my feet.

"What is that?" Hiroyuki asked as he stood up from behind a leather armchair.

"I have no idea," I replied. "It healed after I tore its hand apart."

There was no blood from the daggers, and I'd definitely struck home. If rift-tempered weapons didn't work on it, that was going to be a problem.

A bigger problem.

The creature picked up the sofa I'd been using and hurled it at me like a shot-put; I threw myself to the side, hitting the floor and standing up next to the TV, which was attached to the wall. The sofa crashed through the window, and I hoped no one was standing on the pavement below. The creature launched itself at me, so I tore the TV free and smashed it across the thing's head. It didn't even stop, punching me in the stomach hard enough to lift me off the ground. It grabbed me by the throat, lifting me. I stabbed one of my daggers into its forearm, but the dagger broke as it touched the skin, and he threw me across the room like I was a tennis ball.

I smashed into the wall close to Hiroyuki as he threw several small balls of ice at the creature. The balls exploded, freezing everything around them and forming five-foot-long, razor-sharp spikes of ice. They destroyed a large part of the room we were in, but any that touched the creature snapped away.

The creature stood at the opposite side of the room and looked between Hiroyuki and me before punching through the ice as Hiroyuki threw more of the balls, doing little more than slowing it down.

"Get to everyone else," Hiroyuki said. "I'll keep this thing busy."

I paused. "You sure?"

Hiroyuki nodded as he continued hammering the creature with ice missiles; he tossed me his set of car keys. "Go," he shouted.

I didn't want to leave him, but he was right: everyone else was in as much danger. I turned to smoke, moving out of the ruined window and billowing down the fire escape to the alleyway, where I continued on in smoke form, moving around the building to the front.

Nadia was stood outside of the apartment building with Isabelle, the pair of them taking point.

I re-formed and ran over to them. "Dani and Anthony?" I asked.

"Inside," Nadia said. "Where's Hiroyuki?"

"Having problems," I told her, passing her the keys.

Nadia tossed the keys to Isabelle.

"Get Hiroyuki's car and get Anthony and Dani out of here," I said. "I'll be right behind you, but I can't leave Hiroyuki to whatever the hell that thing is."

I turned to leave and Nadia stopped me. "That thing isn't on my chains. I can't see anything about whatever the hell that was that attacked us."

"What does that mean?" Isabelle asked.

"It means it's not linked to the chains," I said. "It's something else. Something that shouldn't exist."

"Or something with so much rift energy inside of it that it screws around with what I can see," Nadia said. "Like the thing that was watching Anthony's house. In the woods."

"Neither of those things sound good," I said, remembering how it wasn't wounded from either my power or the rift-tempered dagger.

I left Nadia and Isabelle to sort themselves out, hoping I wasn't going to be too late to help Hiroyuki. I'd known Hiroyuki a long time, and he was one of the best fighters I'd ever met, but if he couldn't hurt the thing we were fighting, I wasn't sure that he'd be able to get away in one piece.

I was already smoke before I'd turned the corner of the building. I moved up toward the fire escape as Hiroyuki came crashing out of the flat above. He hit the fire escape, spun over the metal railing, and bounced, smashing into the wall of the building opposite, which slowed his momentum. He dropped like a stone to the ground before I could get to him, his katana clattering beside him.

I re-formed and knelt beside Hiroyuki. "Hey," I said. "Hiro."

"Don't call me that," Hiroyuki said.

"I figured annoying you might bring you around," I told him.

"Good job," Hiroyuki said though clenched teeth. "Broken ribs, arm, dislocated knee, probably some internal bleeding. None of it feels good."

There was a crash from above and I grabbed Hiroyuki, dragging him out of the way as he cried out in pain. The creature stood on the fire escape above, staring down at us. He tore the metal railing apart and stepped off it, falling to the ground and landing on his feet on the concrete a dozen feet in front of me.

I stepped in front of Hiroyuki and picked up his katana. I wasn't well versed in fighting with the sword, but I figured it was better than nothing.

I held the katana out in front of me, holding it in a two-handed grip as I stayed in front of my barely conscious friend.

"You're not getting to him," I said, meaning every word even if I couldn't physically back it up.

The thing charged at me. I stepped to the side and chopped the sword down, cutting through the thing's shoulder and chest. Except it didn't. The sword bounced off the creature's abnormally toughened skin.

The creature kicked me in the chest, sending me spiralling down the alleyway and impacting with a concrete bollard at the end. I picked myself up off the ground, slipping on a pair of rift-tempered knuckles, and sprinted down the alleyway toward the creature, who hadn't moved an inch.

My punch caught the thing in the side of the head, just to the side of where the mask ended. The creature actually took a step back before springing forward and head-butting me.

I saw stars, darkness, and probably trumpet-playing angels as I fell to the ground. I tasted blood. The creature reached down and grabbed me around the throat, lifting me off the floor and slamming my back into the wall behind me.

Again and again, the thing smashed me into the wall, my head bouncing off the brick, my back roaring in pain. The whole time, it squeezed my throat. I lashed out with foot and fist, connecting with all of them but doing nothing to slow the monster down. If I didn't do something soon, I'd either die or return to my embers seriously injured; neither was an ideal option.

A ball of ice came between us and exploded out, directly into the creature, which had to let go of me as it stepped back, away from Hiroyuki's power.

I fell to the floor, coughing and spitting as my body tried to recall how to breathe properly. My head was still swimming as I saw the creature reach down for Hiroyuki, who spat at the monster in defiance.

I ran at the creature, jumping on its back, pouring smoke under the mask, down its throat. It thrashed and bucked, smashing me again and again into the wall in an effort to force me to stop, but I dared not.

The creature shrugged me off, grabbed me by the hair, and launched me down the alleyway. I hit the ground like a rag doll, rolling along the concrete until I eventually came to a stop.

I stumbled back to my feet. "Hey," I screamed, my voice sounding raw. "You goat-fucking son-of-a-bitch." I had no idea where the insults were coming from; I could barely stand, barely think, but apparently, my subconscious has a really big potty mouth.

The creature stepped over Hiroyuki and strolled toward me.

"That's right, you cockwomble," I screamed. "You fetid piece of donkey shit."

The thing continued unabated.

"Come and get some, you fucking limp-dick wallowing turd blossom," I shouted, just spouting words now.

The thing actually started to jog toward me.

At the last moment, I turned to smoke and raced toward the creature, re-forming and connecting with a punch that caught the monster on the mask. Half of the mask exploded, the shards impaling the flesh of the monster as the power of the punch sent it flying back down the alleyway at high speed. It hit a parked car at the end of the alley and almost flipped over it from the power. I'd put pretty much everything I'd had into that punch, and the bloody thing was still alive.

I ran over to Hiroyuki, who was awake, although I was pretty sure his jaw was broken. I dragged him upright as the creature tried to extricate itself from the rear seats of the car it had hit. The SUV pulled up at the end of the alleyway. Nadia, Dani, and Anthony ran down.

"Take Hiroyuki," I said, passing his barely conscious form to Nadia and Anthony. "Be right back."

"You know you're bleeding a lot," Nadia said.

I nodded.

"And your face is busted," she continued helpfully.

I gave her a thumbs-up and raced down the alleyway as the creature pulled itself out of the car. I turned to smoke, billowing down the alleyway, re-forming directly in front of the creature, driving my fist into the monster's shoulder as it managed to get its arm up in time to block the punch. My hand broke upon impact, but the creature was thrown back across the road forty feet, impacting with the shuttered window of a music shop. The metal shutter exploded from the force of the creature hitting it, followed by the unmistakeable sound of a window being shattered.

The SUV pulled up beside me and I climbed in, lying on whoever happened to be sat in the rear of the car. "Need to get the Audi," I said.

"You can't drive," Nadia said.

"I'll be fine," I said. "Just need to get to my embers and heal. Where's Hiroyuki?"

"He's already gone to his," Isabelle said.

"Cool," I said as the adrenaline threatened to wear off.

"Why do you need the car?" Isabelle asked. "You can't take it into the embers."

"I know," I said, and winced. The pain was beginning to overcome me. I was pretty sure I had a broken hand, wrist, at least one rib, but riftborn are a hardy group and we heal fast. However, healing multiple breaks meant days on Earth; I could probably heal it in six hours in the embers. Maybe a bit more, depending on how badly my insides were damaged.

Isabelle drove like she was auditioning to be a stunt driver, practically skidding to a stop next to the Audi. I got out of the Mercedes and fell to the ground next to the Audi. I was not in a position to drive, not unless I really wanted to total the car and have Bill hunt me down.

"We really need to go," Isabelle said, looking around.

"We will," I gasped, popping the boot of the Audi and passing her a pump-action shotgun.

"I've never used one of those," she said.

"I have," Dani said, taking it from me along with a box of spare shells.

"Just in case," I said. "Do not use it unless you have to."

"Do you know the way to this church?" Isabelle asked. "I've never been there."

"I'll get us there," Nadia said, looking out of the driver's-side window at me. "You gonna be okay?"

I nodded. "I'll come back here, take the car to the church."

"I can drive it," Anthony said.

"Good idea," I told him, tossing him the keys.

"I'll take Dani," Isabelle said.

"Nadia, you go with Anthony," I said. "Call Noah; tell him everything that happened. Get him to meet you at the church. Armed and ready for trouble. Contact Ji-hyun, too. Time to get the RCU involved in this."

I removed my Guild medallion and dropped it into the Audi's boot, slamming it shut a moment later. I can exit my embers wherever I consider to be home, but I can also use items that are important to me as waypoints of a sort. In my case, my Guild medallion and Talon's mask.

"Get to Gabriel," I said. "Don't speed, don't think about being followed, don't deviate from the satnav. Don't take the highway. Too open. Just take your time and get there without trouble. I'll be back in a few hours."

There was a concern that as people knew my friendship with Gabriel, those who tried to just kill us all might attack Gabriel, too. But with Noah, Ji-hyun, and the RCU with them, I hoped no one would be stupid or desperate enough to attack.

I remained seated for a few moments, watching the two cars disappear from view, making sure they were as safe as they could be, before I opened a tear to my embers and fell inside.

CHAPTER TEN

W ere you meant to do that?" Maria asked as I lay on the soft ground, the fog from the embers swirling over me.

"Yes," I told them, refusing to move.

Maria was one of two eidolons from my embers, the other being Casimir. Every riftborn had two eidolons, who tend to the embers, ensuring things that shouldn't be capable of entering them don't. They help protect the riftborn once they're in the embers. They're also good company. Mostly.

Eidolons can change shape at will, although they can only use animals, and the larger the animal, the more energy it takes. While Maria and Casimir had a female and male name, they weren't either. They had no gender or sex beyond the names chosen by them, which was more for the sound they liked than anything else.

Maria hopped off the log they were sat on, changed shape from a frog to a crow, and landed on my chest. They looked down at me, their beak inches from my face. Getting so close to an animal—even if it only *looked* like the animal in question—when it could do serious damage to you took some getting used to.

"You're hurt," Maria said.

"Don't mock the injured," I told them.

Maria smiled.

As much as I got used to the idea of talking animals, seeing them smile never, ever gets any less odd.

Maria jumped off me and flew over to a nearby fence post, where they perched, watching me get to my feet. My body was already in full-on heal mode, which sounds like fun but actually makes me feel like I've caught an annoying virus. My entire body ached as whatever damage done to it was healed.

"What happened?" Maria asked.

"You can just read my mind and find out," I told them.

"Where's the fun in that?" Casimir asked, landing beside Maria. Casimir had taken the form of a gigantic harpy eagle. He couldn't keep the form for long, but I knew he liked to fly around the embers in it.

Eidolons have their own personalities and traits based on, from what I understood, my own. It meant that if they were sarcastic and mocking, it was because they'd taken that trait from me. I wasn't sure if I should be proud of that or not.

"I fought something that I couldn't hurt," I said.

"Hit it harder next time," Casimir told me.

"Harpy eagles shouldn't smile," I said. "It's . . . disconcerting."

"You're avoiding the point," Maria said.

"I hit it as hard as I could," I said. "Twice. Turned to smoke, re-formed, and punched. I normally don't do it more than once because . . . well, because it breaks my hand and/or arm. And I'm left exhausted."

"It didn't do any damage?" Maria asked, a touch of concern in her voice.

"Flew back through a shop window," I explained. "Could be dead, but I doubt it. I stabbed it with a rift-tempered dagger. Didn't even cut it."

I only then realised that I'd lost one of my daggers and let out a long, protracted sigh. "Bollocks."

"You can get one reforged," Maria said. They always read my mind when it suited them.

"I can, but I liked the dagger," I said. "Getting rift-tempered weaponry made is expensive. Or it's expensive if you want the good stuff. And it's not always done with money."

"Favours are important to many," Casimir said. "Maybe Neb has one you can have."

"I'd rather cross that bridge when I come to it," I said.

"No medallion again," Casimir said. "Are we starting a trend?"

"Don't start on me," I snapped. "Seriously. No choice."

"You need to find a less-valuable third item that you have an emotional attachment to," Maria said.

"I'll add that to my to-do list," I said. "Where's the exit?" I asked. "Before you start chastising me for something else."

"Not far," Maria said. "You're going to have missed several hours with those injuries, though. It's going to be an overnight visit."

"How long?" I asked.

"On Earth, maybe six hours will pass," Maria said.

Whenever a riftborn enters his embers to heal, there's always a chance that if there's a serious injury—or many small ones—it will require spending the night in the embers. Anything longer than a few hours of time passing outside of the embers will mean night will fall inside. Nothing I could do about that.

Night-time in the embers isn't fun. The embers themselves resemble a sort of approximation of the village I was born in in England and the one I grew up in near Carthage. The shadowy visions of people going about their lives in the village are the memories of people. I couldn't tell you who any of them are; there are no features or identifying marks to recognise, just the ethereal outline of a human body.

During the day, those shadows are harmless. Memories of people long passed. But at night, they hunt rift power to consume, sort of like white blood cells attacking something that isn't meant to be there. Sometimes, the outer edges of the embers will weaken and allow creatures from the rift inside. The shadows will kill that creature while the eidolons closed the tear.

Unfortunately, I too, was a foreign body in my own embers. And the shadows didn't differentiate between me and a more-hostile threat.

Basically, it meant finding a house, closing the door, and hunkering down for the night. The shadows never entered buildings at night, no matter how much they might bang and shout. I would fall asleep soon after lying down, whether I wanted to or not, and wake up feeling refreshed. My body healed entirely.

The sky was a mismatch of blue and yellow, with smudges of purple and orange. It looked a little bit like someone had painted it up there.

Maria had transformed into a rabbit as we walked along, with Casimir hovering just above, occasionally circling, dropping down and soaring high again.

Maria stopped outside of a small hut that, judging from the size and shape and the memory of my much-younger self, had belonged to a hunter from the village. Indeed, there were three shadows outside of the embers that appeared to be crouched down, working, although I couldn't have said what they were actually doing. Cleaning fur, maybe? Washing? It was impossible to tell.

I pushed open the wooden door and stepped inside, Maria hopping in before the door closed. A small mouse ran through a hole in the door, turning into a weasel a moment later.

Walking to the rear of the hut, I sat down on the furs that lined the floor. While it technically didn't get cold or hot in the embers, there was still a chill in the air during the night.

I looked up through the open hatch high in the thatched roof of the hut. I didn't remember that being there before; I didn't remember anyone having skylights in the roof, but it's hard to tell what's a memory and what's the embers just adapting to what I wanted. And right now, I wanted to see the sky.

The colourful sky turned volcanic red and black; darkness was coming.

The first sounds of the shadows howling in the embers sent a shiver up my spine. I've heard them a thousand times, probably more, but every time, their primal screams make me nervous. I guess that's a good thing; if I wasn't concerned about one of the few parts of the embers that could certainly hurt me—if not kill me—I'd probably have been killed a long time ago.

I lay down on the fur rugs and was soon fast asleep.

I woke to the sounds of Casimir's rooster crow. It's always Casimir.

Opening my eyes, and there was Casimir, in full rooster plumage—stood atop the hole in the roof. Casimir looked down at me. "Morning," they said.

I flipped the rooster off and sat up, feeling rested and ready to get back to Earth. It took me a long time to get used to the fact that spending the night in the embers didn't mean a night would pass on Earth or in the rift, but I was always grateful for the refreshed feeling it gave me.

"How close to the tear?" I asked.

"Just outside, hut opposite," Casimir said, dropping from the roof, turning into a sparrow mid-fall, and flying to land on my shoulder.

"Show off," I said and Casimir chuckled.

I opened the hut door and stepped outside. The shadows had gone back to doing whatever it was shadows did, the sky its normal swirling mass of colour. A lynx sat in the middle of the street.

"Trying something new?" I asked Maria.

"There are a wealth of animals out there," Maria the lynx said. "Maybe it's time to spread my creative wings a little."

Power spilled out of the doorway to the hut opposite, which had become a small tear back to Earth. I walked over and placed my hand against the tear, which increased in size until it filled the doorway. I turned back to Casimir and Maria. "Take care," I said.

"We're fine," Casimir said. "Stop getting hurt."

"I'll try," I said, and stepped through the tear into the car park at the rear of Gabriel's church.

It was pouring with rain, and I took a moment to get my bearings before walking toward Gabriel's home. It was a building separate from the church, and the three-storey townhouse-styled building was home to not only Gabriel but to several newly born rift-fused.

I knocked on the door, which was opened by Gabriel, who rushed me inside, where the smell of fresh baking made my stomach rumble. "You're soaked," he said.

"It's raining," I told him. "Where's my medallion?"

"Still in the trunk of the Audi," Gabriel said. "Nadia left it there."

"Keys," I said. "Please."

"It's raining," Gabriel said.

"And I'm already drenched, so another minute isn't going to make much difference," I explained as Gabriel passed me the car keys.

I left the house and jogged over to the Audi, popping the boot and retrieving the medallion. It felt good to put it on, something I never really thought about when I wasn't wearing it.

I looked around the car park, found Hiroyuki's Mercedes parked in the corner, and felt a pang of relief. I was glad everyone had seemingly made it back in one piece. It was parked beside several large SUVs. Either Noah had arrived with his entire Silver Phalanx or the RCU were there. Either way, anyone attacking us now was going to be in for a rude awakening.

I walked back to the house and stepped inside, where I discovered that Gabriel had placed several large towels on the floor.

"Strip," he said.

"Excuse me?" I asked.

"Your clothes are wet; get out of them," he said with a slightly exasperated tone.

I stopped the several dozen retorts in my mind and pulled off my jacket and T-shirt, followed by everything else I wore until I was standing stark-bollock naked. Gabriel threw a towel at me.

"Thank you," I said as I started to dry myself.

"There are clean clothes in the room there," Gabriel said, pointing to the usually busy living room. "I'm keeping everyone upstairs while you sort yourself out."

"You, sir, are a scholar and a gentleman," I said with a smile, and checked my watch. I'd been gone just under seven hours. It could have been worse.

Gabriel's expression remained sour.

"What happened?" I asked as I walked into a reception room and grabbed my clothes, putting them on, ignoring any damp patches on my body that they came into contact with.

"We didn't know how long you were going to be out," Gabriel said. "Ji-hyun and Emily came. Noah is going to meet up with us later at the RCU headquarters on Moon Island."

"Okay; Dani and Isabelle okay?" I asked.

Gabriel nodded. "All four of them are fine," he said. "Hiroyuki hasn't come back yet, but he may well have gone straight to Noah's compound."

"Quite possibly," I said. "Why the sour expression?"

"Ji-hyun did some investigating," he said.

"Gabriel, stop beating around the bush," I said. "Where is everyone else?"

"They're in the living room," Gabriel said. "They were going to stay until morning and then head to Moon Island."

"And why do you look really pissed off about it?" I asked.

"Because I'm worried about you," Gabriel said. "You came up against something you could barely hurt. It hurt you well enough, though."

"Thanks for the pep talk," I said, raising my hands in mock surrender before Gabriel could reply. "I know; I got my ass kicked. What aren't you telling me, Gabriel?"

Before Gabriel spoke, Nadia entered the room, taking a seat beside me.

"You got back okay, then," I said.

"I drove," she said, with a beaming smile.

"You did what?" I asked.

"I drove," Nadia said, almost squeaking with joy. "I didn't break it or anything."

I looked up at Gabriel. "Seriously?"

"Isabelle was too tired to drive the whole way," Gabriel said. "She was worried she'd crash."

"I was worried we'd crash if I drove," Nadia said. "But I got here in one piece."

"I'm very proud of you," I said with a smile.

"Me too," Nadia said. "Oh, Gabriel, Ji-hyun wants you to hurry up; she has news. She said that Gabriel needs to tell you before you go in to talk to everyone. She said you need to . . . get it out of your system."

I looked over at Gabriel, genuine concern building inside of me. "You want to spit it out?"

"Pull the plaster off," Nadia said.

Gabriel sighed. "Ji-hyun's people got CCTV footage of the attack in Boston. Anthony spotted the man who came to Reclaimed Lives. Isabelle confirmed the ID. It's Matthew Pierce."

I stared at Gabriel for a few seconds. "Are you sure?"

"I've seen the picture," Gabriel said. "No doubt in my mind. Never going to forget that face."

I stood slowly, keeping my anger in check. "Fuck," I snapped.

CHAPTER ELEVEN

S o, who's Matthew Pierce?" Emily asked as I walked into the living room.

Emily and Ji-hyun had both arrived during the time I'd been in my embers. Ji-hyun was now the head of the eastern states of America RCU, and Emily was an RCU agent having transferred from the FBI after becoming a revenant. Both were people I trusted, and both were exceptionally good at their jobs.

Ji-hyun had never wanted the job as head of the RCU, but that was pretty much exactly why she was perfect for the job. Those who don't want the power and influence of a position are usually the ones who should have it. Besides, the RCU had been corrupted by several people over the years, and there needed to be a culling. No one was better at rooting out those who were going to be trouble quite like Ji-hyun.

Isabelle, Anthony, Dani, Ji-hyun, Emily, Gabriel, Nadia, and I were sat in the large living room in the house, everyone having found a space to sit on the many chairs, couches, and, in Nadia's case, the floor.

"So, do you want to start?" Gabriel asked me. "I'm afraid I might not be capable of saying his name without stopping to swear a lot."

"You both okay?" Ji-hyun asked Gabriel, placing her hand on his leg.

Gabriel patted Ji-hyun's hand and nodded. "It is a name I haven't heard for a long time and was hoping I'd never hear again."

"You and me both," I said.

"So who is he?" Dani asked.

"And why is he hunting my sister?" Anthony asked.

"He was the son of a Roman Senator," I said. "I don't know his original name, don't care. As a human, he enjoyed hunting people. For sport. Men, women, he didn't care so long as he got to kill them. Mostly slaves. Some peasants who displeased him.

"His father took him to Gaul, where he developed his taste further. Until he hunted the wrong person and got an arrow through the neck for his trouble. He became a riftborn, spent a century in Inaxia before eventually working for a Prime there. He would come back to Earth to *indulge* himself in his favourite pastime before going back to Inaxia.

"He tried to join a Guild about eight hundred years ago. The Hawks. He failed, primarily because the Guilds try really hard not to allow psychopaths amongst their number. He took that personally, murdered two of them, took their Guild badges. Hence the badge you saw.

"Eventually, the Hawks decided enough was enough and sent a Talon after him. Matthew killed the Talon, sent his head to the Guild in a box."

"How did you two get involved?" Emily asked Gabriel and me.

"Matthew vanished after killing the Talon. Kept a low profile, mostly popping up in various Lawless cities in the rift. He would come back to Earth, kill, get paid by various kings and lords to do awful things, and vanish when it became hot again. He did that for centuries. He killed a friend of Gabriel's at the beginning of the nineteenth century."

Everyone turned to Gabriel, who took a deep breath and slowly let it out. "He was the son of a local farmer. I'd grown up with his father, Christian, in the north of Spain, and we were good friends before I became a revenant and everything changed. His name was Josep. One night, he angered a drunk Matthew, who proceeded to hunt him back to his farm and slaughter Josep's entire family. Wife, two children, mother-in-law, aunt. There was some kind of gathering. My friend Christian, now an old man, was among the dead. Nine members of a family died that night. We didn't know it was Matthew until 1987."

"What happened?" Emily asked.

"Matthew likes everyone to know what he's done," I said. "He likes to brag; he likes to talk. But anyone who ever gets close to him ends up dead sooner or later. Matthew is paranoid, he's dangerous, and eventually you'll say or do something that he doesn't like, and he has no problems with removing you. Someone decided that ratting him out was a better option than waiting around to become the victim."

"I led the group to hunt Matthew, something the Hawks were less than happy about, so they sent their own second Talon. She had been unhappy about a lot of things, telling me how the Hawks alone should be given the right to hunt him. Right up until we found his little hidden bunker near the farm he lived on. He took trophies, made notes, everything you'd ever want to convict him of hundreds of murders over the centuries.

"The Talon asked me to let her hunt him, to bring him in. I stupidly allowed it. Matthew murdered her, and I found her body. I hunted Matthew myself after that."

"You didn't find him, then?" Anthony asked.

"I did," I said, remembering how I'd been stopped from killing him by Guild members from the Hawks and Raven. I'd done a lot of damage to him before they'd arrived, though. "He was taken to the Ancients to stand trial for so many murders; I'm not sure we'll ever find the correct number."

"And then?" Dani asked.

"And then nothing," I said. "He was meant to be dead. The Ancients told me that he was going to be executed for his crimes, most of which were against humanity. This was before the age of the mass use of the internet. I doubt very much they'd want the murderer of countless humans to be plastered all over the various social media."

"So, they lied," Ji-hyun said, her words cold and hard. She'd met Matthew once that I knew of, while he was in custody, and she'd left him with a broken orbital socket.

"I need to talk to Noah," I said. "About more than just Dani. Matthew isn't working alone. He's involved in whatever the hell attacked us in Boston."

"Gabriel told us about those," Emily said. "You've never seen them before?"

I shook my head. "I don't know of anything that can shrug off being stabbed with a rift-tempered weapon. One of which I lost, so that's also brilliant."

"Can I assume you have a plan?" Ji-hyun asked.

"I'm going to see Noah," I said. "I'm going to get the answers I need. Dani, Isabelle, and Anthony are going into protective custody."

"The fuck we are," Dani snapped. "They're coming for me. I can just go into the rift and hide."

"Okay, where are you going to hide?" I asked. "With the people who helped you all those years ago? You think that's going to stop Matthew Pierce? Because I doubt it. Besides, you run off into the rift, your brother and Isabelle are still here. They can't go with you. Who do you think becomes a target while you're gone?"

"So, what, I just wait around for them to find me?" Dani snapped.

"We can protect you," Emily said.

"No, you can't," Dani told her. "Hiroyuki and Lucas got their asses handed to them by one of these things. You just want to add more bodies in its way? Especially if those things are working with a murderous psychopath."

"She's not wrong," Ji-hyun said, breaking the silence that descended after Dani finished talking.

"What about Moon Island?" Dani asked. "That's what you were talking about, right?" She aimed the last question at Ji-hyun.

"It's fortified, hard to get to without a boat or by flying," Ji-hyun said. "We can protect you there. We can put you somewhere these people can't find. We can protect Anthony and Isabelle, too. With the RCU and Noah's forces, we should be able to figure out what's going on."

"People are trying to kill me or kidnap me; who knows," Dani said. "I'm going to travel with Lucas."

"Sis," Anthony started.

"No," Dani said, cutting him off. "I am the target. I don't know why, other than the possibility that they could be behind the disappearance of rift-walkers. What I do know is that they'll kill anyone I'm with. If I'm not with my brother and Isabelle, they won't try to hurt them. Just you, Lucas. And I've seen you fight."

"Thanks for the vote of confidence," I said. I didn't want to mention that Matthew would happily use Isabelle and Anthony as bait should he get a hold of them. Some things you're better off keeping to yourself and making sure they don't happen.

"I'm coming with you," Gabriel told me. "Matthew should be dead."

"I'll take Anthony and Isabelle with us," Ji-hyun said, making it sound like they really had no option.

It was a tone that Anthony either didn't get or wilfully ignored. "I'm going with my sister," he snapped, almost shouting. "She's . . . She can't."

Dani placed her hand on Anthony's. "I'm your little sister," she said softly.

Anthony looked at her and nodded. "I didn't protect you before. I didn't stop you from being taken into the rift, I couldn't get to you, I couldn't help. I can't let you go through this alone."

"I'm not alone," Dani said. "And I'm not helpless. I'm not a little girl, Anthony. I know you feel bad about what happened to me, but you don't need to. It's not your fault."

Anthony heaved a sigh and left, with Dani following. We all remained silent for a few moments while their footsteps could be heard going up the stairs to the rooms above.

"What's Matthew's power?" Emily asked. "Can he change his appearance?"

"He weakens the power in others," I said. "All but stopping revenants from accessing their power at all, and not letting riftborn access their embers properly. We can still use our powers, but it's to a much-lesser extent."

"Sounds delightful," Nadia said, speaking for the first time.

"You okay?" I asked her.

"I met Matthew Pierce," Nadia said. "When I was working for Sky-High Security before I left them and joined you. Mason introduced him to me. Didn't know who he was or why Mason was scared of him. Mason said he worked with Callie Mitchell."

"Not *for*?" I asked.

Nadia shook her head. "Definitely with. I've met a lot of creepy people in my life, but something was wrong with him. Something that made me hope I didn't see him again."

"You remember why he was there?" Gabriel asked her.

Nadia shook her head. "Lots of people came and went; most wanted to see Mason or Callie. Mason only introduced the staff to those he thought were important, though; I can tell you that much."

"So, Matthew was important?" Ji-hyun said. "Considering he's meant to be a dead man, he sure did land on his feet."

"Like cats," Nadia said. "I know he's not a cat, I like cats, they're nice. I'm just saying."

"So, when they've finished arguing, we put everything in motion," Emily said.

"He was a bit like a cat," Nadia continued. "Thinking about it. He had that same predatory look you see when a cat is stalking a mouse or a small bird. He had a hunger in his eyes. I doubt very much he's stopped killing."

"I'll look into unsolved murders involving people being hunted," Ji-hyun said. "There must be some."

"Or solved ones," Emily said. "Sometimes, people get arrested and they're innocent after all. And sometimes, you get guilty people who want to make a name for themselves. Admitting to crimes they didn't do seems to work for some people; the worse the crime the better."

"I guess you have work to do," Ji-hyun said with a smile.

"Damn it," Emily said with a smile of her own. "Actual police work; what a shame. I'll look into Abigail the neighbour, Tobias too; maybe we can get something out of him. It's possible that Matthew killed Abigail and made it look like Anthony was involved."

"Abigail opened the door to him, turned her back on him," I said. "He was wearing a Guild medallion."

"She sees the medallion, thinks he's one of the good guys," Ji-hyun said. "Humans really need to learn that medallions don't make you one of the good guys. It just means you're dangerous."

"It's feasible," Gabriel said. "Doesn't feel like Matthew's style, though. It was quick, clean, she didn't run, and there was a lack of blood."

"Could Tobias be involved?" Nadia asked. "He was creepy."

"He did seem to like talking to the police when they arrived," I said. "Very friendly with them."

"Ah, every tattletale loves a cop," Nadia said with a beaming smile as she looked at Emily, who rolled her eyes. "But so do a lot of murderers."

"I'll contact Noah," Ji-hyun said. "It'll probably be better to let him know of the RCU involvement and that Lucas is back."

"So, we've all got our jobs," I said, getting to my feet. "It's going to be a dangerous trip."

Ji-hyun stood and stretched her arms. "I brought people with me," she said. "They're waiting in front of the church. I'll go let them know that Isabelle and Anthony will be joining us. Can I assume you'll be going with Lucas, Nadia?"

Nadia nodded. "I need to know what those creatures are. I can't feel them. I can't see them in my chains. I don't like mysteries."

Dani appeared in the doorway as Ji-hyun went to leave.

"Anthony is going with you," Dani told her. "I am not."

Ji-hyun looked back at me and shrugged before leaving the room.

"I'll go get everything ready," Emily said, leaving the room a moment later.

"We're all leaving together," I said. "We'll head toward Boston and split up there; less likely to get attacked on the roads if there's a convoy of RCU agents coming with us."

"Will we be safe?" Isabelle asked.

"Yes," Emily told her. "There's a dozen heavily armed personnel in two armour-plated SUVs. We'll be fine."

"Famous last words," Nadia whispered so that only I could hear her.

"You see a problem?" I asked.

Nadia shrugged. "I see a lot of them. The thing in Boston screwed around with what I can and can't see, though. When it involves us, anyway.

When you left us in the elevator, I couldn't see anything that happened around us. The creature has to be responsible; it's almost like it overpowers my connection to the rift. I'd like that to stop."

There was genuine pain in her voice. A chained revenant *needs* to be able to see the flow of possibilities around them. While some delve too much into seeing *everything* and trying to find the optimum solution, being able to see nothing does little to help the release they need when they activate their chains.

"Are you okay?" I asked Nadia.

She looked at me, raised her palm so that it was flat and facing down, and moved it from side to side. "I can still see possibilities. I can still see myself. But it's like someone dragged an eraser through the picture. All I know is that those creatures are going to be in our future again."

"And we don't know how to kill them," I said.

"Maybe Noah does," Gabriel said. "There has to be some benefit of knowledge to being an Ancient."

"You going to be okay leaving the church?" I asked him. It was an important place for newly created rift-fused and those who had been among our number for centuries alike.

"It will be fine," Gabriel assured me. "There are people here capable of looking after it while I'm gone. And with this being Matthew Pierce, I'd like to actually be able to see for myself that he stays dead this time."

"I can't guarantee that," I said. "I want to, but I can't."

"I can," Gabriel said. "If I get the chance, I'm going to end his life. He's been living on borrowed time for centuries. That time ends now."

I knew not to argue with Gabriel when his mind was made up. He had been a formidable warrior and still was more than capable of taking care of himself. He had found a path of peace and of helping others, but I had no doubt that he'd end Matthew should the opportunity arise.

Ji-hyun entered the room wearing tactical gear and carrying a black Heckler & Koch HK416. The weapon flickered blue and purple; it had been rift-tempered. If anyone ever figured out how to ensure that guns were able to pass their charge on to the bullets or shells on anything close to a regular basis, it would change everything about rift-fused warfare.

A middle-aged-looking man with long, greying hair entered the room and passed a bulletproof vest to Isabelle, who put it on without complaint. One of her people brought in a pile of them and placed them on the sofa next to Isabelle.

"Everyone wears one," Ji-hyun said. "Even you, Lucas. Emily told me the plan."

"How badly damaged is George's car?" I asked.

"It's in mint condition," Nadia said, with mock offence. "Okay, I dinged the car door hitting the central reservation when a truck got too close. Otherwise, it's fine."

"Dinged?" I asked, wincing at the thought on George's face.

"We'll take the RAV4, too," Gabriel said. "Between all of us, we'll have enough."

"I'll be putting personnel in each vehicle," Ji-hyun said. "If anyone is waiting for us, it's not going to end well for them."

"You think they will?" Isabelle asked, clearly deer-in-the-headlights about everything that was going on. She was human, inexperienced, and scared. None of which were ideal in a combat situation.

"No," I said, hoping I sold it well enough that she believed me. I didn't think they would try anything stupid now that the RCU was with us, but I was pretty sure they'd have figured out about Gabriel's church. They appeared to be able to almost track Dani.

I looked over at Dani, who glanced around as if it might be someone else I'd thought about.

"What?" she asked.

"You got your phone on?" I asked her.

"I'm the only twenty-four-year-old in America without a cell phone," she said. "I didn't want to have to."

"You think someone is tracking her?" Ji-hyun asked.

"I think that the attackers in Boston knew where we were," I said. "Those soldiers headed up toward the top floor, but the creature that attacked us went straight across the roof."

"Isabelle," I called out. "Do you have your phone on?"

She nodded. "It was until we left Boston," she said. "I removed the battery and tossed it out the window while we were driving."

"Okay, problem solved," Ji-hyun said. "Matthew Pierce's people had probably been tracking her phone. They got a lock and figured out you'd gone across the roof. It sucks, but Isabelle didn't know Dani was being hunted by criminals until it was far too late."

I considered that for a moment; it was as good an explanation as I had, but I also had a feeling in my gut that told me we weren't out of the woods yet.

CHAPTER TWELVE

I found Gabriel in the reception room of his house, staring out of the window into the settling darkness.

"Matthew Pierce could be out there, watching us," Gabriel said.

"He'd have attacked," I said. "He won't do it here."

"So where?" Gabriel asked.

"Probably en route," I told him. "It's where I'd do it. Set up an ambush; wait until we fall into it."

"You seem very calm for a man who said he knows he's walking into an ambush," Gabriel said, looking back from the window.

"He'll think we won't take the freeway," I said. "He'll think it would be safer to go the long way around. So, he'll set up an ambush there. Or he'll hedge his bets and split his forces. Either way, we either fight a smaller group or no group."

"Is that what you would have done too?" Gabriel asked.

"Maybe," I said. "There's a lot of RCU here, some heavy hitters. They'd be out of their minds to do it, as they'd need an army. It's hard to know when you're trying to figure out if you'd do the same thing as a known psychopath."

"What about that monster?" Gabriel asked. "What if they have more of them?"

"Then we're going to have a hell of a fight," I said.

"Everyone get ready," Ji-hyun said from the doorway. "We're leaving in ten."

"We not taking choppers?" I asked.

"No," Ji-hyun said. "For a start, we don't have enough to bring loads of you across at once. Also, sticking everyone in a jet seems like a recipe for disaster, as you and I both know that Matthew Pierce will have someone watching the runway. Driving is longer but ultimately the safest option we have available to us."

"It's been a while since I've done anything like this," Gabriel said as Ji-hyun moved away. "I want to see Matthew Pierce put in the ground. I want to know why he wasn't in the first place."

"We'll find out," I told him. "First, we need to get to Moon Island. Get ready, Gabriel. Take what you need."

The ten minutes went by quickly, and I soon found myself stood outside of the church next to half a dozen SUVs with two dozen RCU agents milling around. Ji-hyun was not doing things by half, which was why she was good at her job.

Ji-hyun marshalled everyone else out of the building to the SUVs.

"I assume there's no point in me taking my own car," I said to her.

"No," Ji-hyun said. "The SUVs are safe inside and come equipped with exceptionally dangerous RCU agents as standard. Also me. No one wants to pick a fight with me."

"Fair point," I conceded.

"We all go to Moon Island; tomorrow you can go off to Noah's," Ji-hyun said. "Yes, I'm sure you find the idea of waiting to be abhorrent, but whoever Matthew is working for isn't a slouch when it comes to the money part of their scheme. Let's just get everyone in one place before we decide what to do next."

"I'm not driving," I said.

"God, no," Ji-hyun said. "You can sit in the back and have a nap. When was the last time you slept?"

"Sleep?" I asked with a shrug. "That sounds like something other people do."

Ji-hyun's eyes narrowed.

"A day ago," I said. "In my embers."

"You've been attacked, beaten to a pulp, forced into your embers, all within the last day," Ji-hyun said. "You sure a bit of sleep in your embers is going to be enough?"

I shrugged. "Guess we'll find out."

I left Ji-hyun to coordinate and joined Gabriel as he locked up. When he was done, I passed my medallion to Gabriel who stared at it. "You think there's going to be a problem?" he asked.

"Always," I said. "But if I do have to go somewhere, I'd rather not have to come all the way back to Brooklyn."

He accepted the medallion and walked off to the car he'd been assigned.

I climbed into the back seat of the nearest black Hyundai Santa Fe to find Dani sat on the opposite side, with Isabelle in the front passenger seat and an RCU agent in the driver's seat. A second RCU agent was sat behind us in the smaller space where the sixth and seventh seats were.

"Lucas," I said, offering the agent my hand.

"Mia," the agent in the back said, shaking my hand.

"Benny," the driver said. "You just all sit back and relax, and we'll have you there in no time. No windows down, please. The air conditioning is individually set, so if you need it, feel free to use it."

"Gotcha," I said with a thumbs-up. "You okay, Isabelle?"

"Nope," she said softly. "In the last twelve hours, my life has been turned upside down, people are trying to kill me, and I'm having to go into hiding. I just wanted to help people. I didn't expect to be dragged into something like this."

"I'm sorry," Dani said, her voice barely above a whisper.

Isabelle turned back in her seat. "It's not your fault. It's the fault of whoever is trying to get to you."

"When this is over," Dani said, "I'd like to catch up. It's been a long time." Isabelle smiled. "I'd like that too."

"No one's going to try to get to anyone while we're here," Mia said.

I wished I'd felt as confident as Mia did.

It wasn't long before there was a bang on the driver's door as Ji-hyun walked by. Benny opened the door, and Ji-hyun poked her head inside. "You're going to be the second from rear car," she said. "We'll be moving you around after that. Sometimes you'll be at the back, sometimes at the front. Anyone watching won't know which car is which. The windows are tinted; no one is going to be able to see anything. The glass is bulletproof, the driver is one of my best, and Mia can shoot the wings off a fly. You are as safe as anyone can ever be. Even the President of the United States would be jealous at how protected you all are."

"It's at least a six-hour drive before we get to the boat to Moon Island," Isabelle said. "Any breaks?"

"We stop twice," Ji-hyun said. "Only Benny and Mia know when, but you'll be a few hours before breaks. I already have a car gone ahead to scout out the break areas and report back.

"Be careful," I said to Ji-hyun as she went to close the door.

"Always," she said, shutting the car door and walking away to whichever car she was going to be in.

I settled back in my seat, my seat belt on, and rested my head against the cool window. I really hoped that the drive was going to be as easy going as Ji-hyun and the RCU thought.

My phone rang after five minutes of blessed silence. The number was withheld.

"If you're trying to sell me something, I'm going to be really annoyed," I said after answering the phone.

"Lucas," Hiroyuki said.

"Hey, you retuned," I said. "How were your embers?"

"Cold," Hiroyuki said.

"So, why the phone call?" I asked.

"Do you have my car?" he asked me. "Actually, first of all, are you all okay?"

I smiled. "A little banged up, but yes, we're good. Your car is here in Hamble. It looked okay from what I saw. Noah got any clue on what we fought in Boston?"

"No." Hiroyuki cursed under his breath. "Do you know who is behind this?" he asked in Japanese.

"Matthew Pierce is involved," I told him, also in Japanese. I was always grateful for my time in the rift, if, for no other reason, for the number of languages I'd become automatically fluent in since first arriving there.

"He's dead," Hiroyuki said.

"Not according to the CCTV cameras around the building," I said. "I saw the pictures, Hiroyuki. He's definitely involved."

"Noah was involved in his execution," Hiroyuki replied, his tone insistent.

"Matthew was there," I told him, in a tone that suggested he stop arguing with me. "I don't know who he's working for, but it was *definitely* him."

"This is bad," Hiroyuki said. "Where are you going?"

"Moon Island," I told him. There was no point in lying; Ji-hyun had already invited Noah there to join forces.

"I can meet you there tomorrow morning," he said.

The darkness had well and truly settled in, and everyone was exhausted. Feeling refreshed after a good night's sleep would do me a world of good if I had to keep my wits about me when I met Noah.

"Bad chat?" Dani asked from beside me. "I don't speak Japanese; never met a Japanese person in the rift."

"Hiroyuki's back," I said. "He's going to come down to Moon Island with Noah. Saves us having to go up and see him; also means we'll be in a better position when they arrive."

"You don't trust Noah," Isabelle said.

"I trust Noah about as much as any Ancient," I said. "Which means not completely. They say it's due to them being so forward-thinking, wanting to work in decades and centuries, not days and months like humans. I say it's because they want to give themselves time to see where the wind blows. He hired me to find Anthony and, I guess, by extension, you."

"I've never met an Ancient who wasn't working their own agenda," Mia said.

"That," I said, pointing a thumb in Mia's direction.

Movement out of the rear window caused me to look back as two motorbikes came into view, moving under the freeway lighting, side by side. We were the last in the formation of RCU vehicles for the moment, so they were going to reach us before anyone else.

"Trouble?" Benny asked from the driver's seat.

"Don't know," Mia told him.

"This is car six. We have a possible problem," Benny said, using the in-car radio.

"This is car five," came the response, although I didn't recognise the voice. "Go ahead, car six. Over."

"Black Suzuki Hayabusa," Mia said as the bikes pulled up alongside us.

"That's a lot of bike," Benny said.

"The bikes?" came Ji-hyun's voice. "We're two cars in front of you. We'll pull out into the next lane, move back, and have you move up. The bikes are probably going to just go around, but just to be sure."

"Wait, the bikes are gaining speed," Benny said. "|I think they're going to pass us. Over."

"Everyone keep your heads down," Mia said. "No phones. No talking. The windows are impossible to see through from the outside; no one will know you're here."

I watched intently as the bikes pulled up beside us. They looked over and waved, although there was no way they could tell that anyone was inside or, if they were, what gesture they were making, before continuing on by us, accelerating away at considerable speed.

"Problem gone," Mia said.

Everything settled again as we remained the only thing on the road. I began to think that just maybe, Matthew had set up an ambush for us further afield. Or maybe the lack of being able to track us meant he wasn't entirely sure where we were. I was happy with either option.

After a few miles, we drove past an onramp for the interstate; a short time later, I noticed Benny looking out of the rear-view mirror.

"What's going on?" I asked.

"Probably nothing," he said. "Several lights in the distance behind us. No idea how many vehicles."

I turned to look out of the rear window of the SUV. "I think they're moving quickly," I said, although the darkness made it difficult to truly judge the speed.

Mia spoke over the radio to the other cars while I kept watch on the vans as they moved to the outer lane of the interstate.

Tension filled the SUV.

The surroundings became less civilised, with more dense woodland replacing the occasional light from a building that I'd been able to see so far.

"Car six," the radio said. "This is car one, over."

"Car one," Mia said, answering.

"Do not engage unless attacked first," car one said. "I do not want to have to explain why we just destroyed a bunch of people out for a joyride."

"These aren't bikers out for fun," Dani said as the vehicles behind us came closer, letting us spot that they were three BMW X5 SUVs, with two transit vans behind.

"Benny, unlock the windows," I told him.

"I'm sorry, but my orders were—" he started.

"Benny, unlock the fucking windows," I snapped. "I only need them to be open a tiny bit; you don't want me to break them."

"Unlock the fucking windows," Mai repeated after Benny took a second longer than she deemed necessary.

"Done," Benny said.

I moved the window down a few inches and left the controls alone. It was enough to get out of, should I need to.

"You see anything out of the ordinary?" I asked Mia, who was looking through the scope on her HK416 rifle.

"What the hell is that noise?" Isabelle asked.

The vehicles behind us were slowing down, but my attention was immediately changed to the unmistakable noise of a chopper nearby.

"Support is here," Ji-hyun said on the radio.

I had no idea what kind of helicopter it was, but it followed just up from our position, several hundred feet in the air. I turned back to the BMWs, which were still moving toward us, although at a slower pace.

I glanced out of the window to my side, looking down the embankment toward the dense woodland beside, as two motorbikes came thundering alongside us again.

"Contact," someone screamed into the radio to the sounds of an explosion followed by bullets being fired.

The biker beside us removed something from the side of the bike I couldn't see and tossed it at the window next to me.

"Everyone down," I said as whatever was thrown hit the window and stuck there for a second before exploding.

The window shattered from the impact, and my ears rang as several more explosions sounded out, followed by more gunfire.

The rear window of the SUV had been blown out.

"What the fuck is happening?" Isabelle screamed.

I turned to smoke, flew out the smashed window, billowing over to the rider beside me, and positioned myself to re-form as I held on to his back. I grabbed the brake and pulled as hard as I could, yanking the steering frame toward the SUV. I turned back to smoke as the bike impacted with the vehicle I'd just left, catapulting the rider onto the ground, where he was hit by the SUV and the two directly behind us. If he was human, he was dead; if not, he might just wish he was. Either way, he was no longer my problem.

I re-formed back inside the SUV as Benny pulled out of formation and accelerated up alongside the other front vehicle, while the two behind us did the same, leaving them as two groups of three, ensuring there was only one lane for any attackers to come in.

"Everyone okay?" I asked.

"What the fuck is happening?" Isabelle shouted over the sounds of gunfire.

"Can you do that again?" Mia asked me.

"Sure, be right back," I said, turned to smoke, and moved back out of the vehicle.

It's hard to move out of a car in smoke form. The faster the car, the harder it is. It's like jumping into a fast-flowing river and trying to automatically keep your speed up so you don't fall back. I've never pushed myself to see exactly how fast I can move in smoke form, mostly because I usually use it for short bursts of speed within a few meters of where I am.

In this instance, I flew back along the freeway, the smoke flowing over the closest biker, who was trying to position themselves to take a run up alongside the SUVs next to the inside lane of the freeway.

I re-formed myself as I sat on the fuel tank, facing the biker, who, to be frank, freaked the fuck out, pulled the brakes so hard, the rear wheel skidded around, and I turned to smoke as they lost control of the bike, and spun out into the side railing of the freeway. The biker was catapulted at speed into the trees, while the bike exploded. Wherever they landed, I hoped it hurt.

CHAPTER THIRTEEN

Bullets from the rear two SUVs slammed into one of the BMWs beside me, bursting tyres and damaging the engine enough to force it off the road. The roof of the van opened up, and someone in tactical gear came out. I was already in smoke form and moved toward the van as quickly as possible, but I couldn't get there in time. They removed a rocket-propelled-grenade launcher from inside the van, aimed it at the chopper ahead, and fired.

The rocket hit the helicopter, which exploded in the sky, raining down pieces onto the interstate as the main portion of the helicopter smashed into one of the BMWs that had now taken up alongside the RCU and opened fire. The BMW slammed into one of the RCU vehicles, forcing it off the road and down the embankment. I hoped everyone inside was okay but had no time to go check.

Pieces of the BMW that had been hit bounced down the road beside me. I missed the chance to get into the van and re-formed on the top instead. One of the people in a BMW saw me and opened fire with an SMG exactly where I was, forcing me to turn back to smoke, drop behind the van, and come up under it while trying not to touch the wheels. Not a fun experience.

I billowed into the open window of the BMW and re-formed in the empty rear seats, drawing a dagger and slitting the throat of the attacker in the passenger seat, using his own SMG to shoot the driver in the head.

The driver yanked the wheel sharp enough to flip the BMW, but I was already smoke, moving back toward the RCU vehicles, avoiding gunfire from another biker who had decided to join the fray. The remaining RCU vehicles had changed formation so that the fifth car was now straddling the lanes in the rear, allowing the two in front of it to open fire on anyone who got close, with the other two cars in front of them going at speed.

The attacker who had used the RPG had dropped down into the van again once I'd arrived on the scene. He reappeared with a second RPG. I wasn't about to let this happen again.

I flew up onto the van and down into the hole in the van roof, reforming and yanking the man down from his position by his legs. He had been stood on a metal step that had been welded into the van, and I hoped that him slamming into it face-first hurt like hell.

When I thought that there might be an ambush, I was not expecting RPGs.

The rear of the van had a metal door that was shut, with a big red button beside it. The man swung a punch at me, which was easily enough avoided. I ignored my surroundings and stepped inside another punch, bringing my elbow into his throat. His eyes went wide and he gagged as I brought my knee up into his stomach, pushed him to one side, and broke his knee with my foot, causing him to make a noise akin to a wounded animal.

Out of desperation or stupidity, he pulled a rift-tempered knife, swiping up at me. I broke his wrist, removed the knife from him, and drove it into the top of his skull as he fell to the side.

I looked around the inside of the van as the sounds of gunfire and more explosions could be heard outside. There was no way to reach the driver's compartment, as the small hatch appeared to be operated by the driver themselves. Other than the hatch, the red button that clearly opened the door at the rear of the van, and a few folding-down seats, the area consisted of me, a large footlocker full of weapons, and the dead attacker.

My phone rang; it was Ji-hyun. "You're inside one of those vans, aren't you?" she asked, although I was pretty sure she already knew the answer.

"The one with the RPG-shooting guy," I said. "He's dead, although I don't see any more RPGs."

"The remaining bikes are shooting at us, and there have been a few grenades thrown, but we're down to two BMWs and a van," Ji-hyun said. "Thanks for thinning the herd."

"No problem," I said. "There's a button in here that has a sign above it which says *push to open door*. I should push it."

"No, you should get out," Ji-hyun said.

The van lurched violently to the side, throwing me up against the wall, where I hit the red button with my arm. "Too late," I said as the door silently slid open, revealing a cage with one occupant. One of the things that had attacked us in Boston. There was a flexible pipe that led from a tank above the cage and down through the bars into a large metal mask that adorned the thing's face.

"Lucas, Lucas," Ji-hyun bellowed through my phone, which I'd dropped on the floor.

I retrieved it. "What the hell happened?"

"The van tried to ram one of us," she said. "Didn't go well for them; get out."

"One of those bloody creatures is in here," I said. "I think all the vans might have one. If that's the case, we're going to have a real problem when they wake up."

"Then get out now," she snapped.

"It's in a cage with a mask on," I said. "There's a tank above, and I think it's feeding from it. I want to know what's in the tank."

"Goddamn it, Lucas," Ji-hyun said. "Now really isn't the time for scientific curiosity."

"If we know what it feeds on, we might find out how to kill it," I pointed out. "Right now, we can't even make it bleed or hurt. We need something."

Ji-hyun let out a loud sigh. "You are a giant pain in the ass."

I ended the call and climbed up the cage, making sure to move smoothly just in case the thing woke up. The gap at the top of the cage was big enough for me to squeeze in, the tank I needed to inspect running the length of the cage, with soft padding on either side. At first, I couldn't see a way to get the tank open, but after a closer look, I saw a screw cap on top. I unscrewed the cap, having to stop twice when the van jerked from side to side.

Taking the cap off was easy, but there wasn't enough room to get a look inside the tank. The van jerked again, the sound of metal on metal making me wince as I held on to the top of the metal cage. The contents of the tank splashed out onto the back of my hand, and I recoiled in shock before realising it was nothing dangerous.

I left the cap off and climbed back down. There was blood on the back of my hand, but it was almost black and had the consistency of a thick milkshake, which was a disgusting thought, but considering how cold the blood was, that's where my mind went.

I turned to smoke and flew up through the roof of the van just as the driver smashed into the rear wheel of one of the RCU vehicles, causing it to spin to the side, strike another RCU SUV, and fishtail in front of the van.

I flew through the smashed window of the van, re-forming and grabbing the steering wheel from the shocked driver, who fought with me for a second as he planted his foot on the accelerator, pushing the SUV to the side and through the barrier of the freeway at high speed.

The driver released one hand from the wheel, removed a gun from his holster, and tried to shoot at me while we struggled. I saw the gun moving in my direction, pushed his hand away, and threaded smoke through the trigger, pulling it and shooting him through the kneecap.

The driver screamed, and I unbuckled his seatbelt as we crashed through the barrier. The van hit a large tree on the driver's side, spinning us to the side as we plunged down a steep embankment into the darkness of the forest. We hit something in the rear of the van and spun once again, the driver's-side door smashing into something as we began tumbling down the embankment. I'd turned to smoke the second we'd crashed through the barrier, but we were moving so quickly and spinning around so much, it was difficult to maintain any sort of equilibrium.

The passenger-side window exploded from the impact, and I took my chance, moving out of the van and into the forest. I stayed in my smoke form for several seconds as I reacclimatised myself before re-forming and set off down the steep hill.

There were no sounds of impact from below, so I hoped the RCU vehicle had stopped moving somewhere, preferably with the inhabitants all okay. I didn't much care what happened to the van that had attacked us, nor those inside it.

It didn't take me long to see the headlights illuminating part of the forest, near a stream at the bottom of the hill. The SUV had come to a stop near a large boulder after hitting a tree, spinning around, and facing the wrong way. The front of the Hyundai was all but destroyed, the engine visible to the world as the bonnet had been partially torn off at some point. One wheel was a dozen feet away from the rest of the car, and the other was pointed in a direction that was somewhat unnatural for a wheel to point.

"Everyone okay?" I asked as I got close.

The driver's-side door was pushed open and Benny fell to the ground. He was covered in blood but gave me a thumbs-up as Isabelle climbed out of the SUV and fell to her knees.

"Isabelle," I said as I walked over to her. She looked up at me with a faraway expression on her face. "You good?"

She shook her head, then nodded, then sighed.

I gave her a moment and checked on Dani in the rear seats, who was groaning softly, still strapped in.

"You okay?" I asked her.

"I do *not* want to do that again," Dani said.

"Mia," I called out, looking through the rear of the car.

A hand came up from behind the seats. The thumb was pointing in the wrong direction.

"You need a hand?" I asked her, hoping she didn't think I was going for a pun of some kind.

"No," she said, the hand disappearing from view, followed by an unpleasant sound and a squeak of pain.

I helped Dani out of the SUV and Mia soon after, the latter pushing me away and trying to do it herself, but she'd broken her knee and possibly ankle in the crash. I collapsed the middle set of seats and helped Mia out, placing her gently on the ground next to the large boulder they'd almost hit.

"The van," I said. "Anyone see it?"

"We were a little busy," Dani said.

"That way," Benny told me, pointing off into the forest.

"Contact Ji-hyun; tell her where you are," I told them. "I'll be back soon."

"Take this," Mia said, passing me her rifle and a spare magazine. "I've got a handgun for now, and you might actually need this more."

I picked up the rifle, flicked on the torch attachment, and stalked through the woods, using the stream as a guide until I found the crumpled remains of the van. The vehicle had been sheared in half at some point, with the front half, containing the driver, impaling itself against a large tree. The driver had been thrown out of the front window but pinned there as the van tumbled. Revenant or human, I was pretty sure he wasn't going to survive being bisected and then turned to pulp. Even so, I drew my dagger and slit what was left of his throat. Better to be sure.

The lower half of the van was in the stream a few dozen feet away. There was a massive hole in the side of the van panels, and I couldn't tell if it had been done from the multiple impacts of rolling down a hundred-foot hill, or if the creature that had been inside was now somewhere else.

I moved slowly toward the remains of the van. I wasn't entirely sure what I was going to do when I got to the monster, but if it was out and about somewhere, we needed to move a lot faster than if it was still secure.

The blood on the back of my hand tingled, and I wondered what it was and where it had come from. Was it actual blood? Was it synthetic? If it was real blood, where had it come from?

I pushed the thoughts aside and carried on across the stream, stopping by the van and looking inside. Nothing. No creature, just a destroyed cell and a lot of blood from the tank that had been crushed in the fall; I touched the blood with my fingers and almost called out in pain from the freezer burn I received. What the hell was this stuff?

I found a small plastic jar in amongst the rubble of the van and scooped up some of the goop. I had no idea what it was, but someone else could hopefully figure that out.

A gunshot from somewhere behind me caught my attention, and I turned and sprinted through the dark forest. I'd turned to smoke a lot in a short period of time and didn't want to have to do it again unless necessary. Best not to pass out from exhaustion while something is trying to kill you.

There was another gunshot and a scream of pain as Dani sprinted toward me, almost colliding with me in the stream, moving just in time but stumbling to the ground anyway.

"Thing," Dani said, as she got back to her feet.

"Stay here," I said, hopefully leaving no doubt in her mind that she should do exactly what I told her to do.

Six gunshots fired in quick succession were followed by the kinds of scream you hope you never hear. Pure incandescent fear and agony, echoing all around the forest.

I pushed on and saw the massive creature next to the SUV. It threw something at me, which bounced off the tree beside me as I opened fire with the rifle, hitting it centre mass several times, before putting two more in its mask-covered face. The mask was torn apart from the impact, revealing the grey-skinned person beneath it. It had once been human, or at least looked human, but it had been stretched out, elongated and widened so that the skin looked tight over the large skull.

It raised one hand to me, and a three-foot-long spike slithered out of the skin around its wrist.

I glanced over at Benny to find that he was dead; his head had been the thing thrown at me. Mia, still lying on the ground, was also dead, her eyes open, looking up at nothing, a gaping hole in her forehead.

I opened fire again, moving toward the creature as Isabelle scrambled around the front of the SUV and ran behind me.

"Follow the stream," I said as the creature stood and watched me.

The gun clicked empty, so I removed the magazine and, without looking anywhere but at the monster before me, grabbed the replacement. My blood-covered fingertips brushed over the top of the magazine before I slammed it home. The creature continued to stare at me, as if daring me to fire.

I fired three bullets, all at its chest.

One of the bullets must have taken a charge from the rift-tempered gun, because there was a fountain of blood cascading out of the creature's chest, followed by a roar of pain. "Run," I shouted to Isabelle, who looked transfixed on the creature.

"Isabelle," I shouted again.

She didn't need telling again and was soon sprinting through the forest, with me behind her. We reached the stream and continued along, finding Dani exactly where I'd told her to stay.

"What about the others?" Dani asked.

"We go now or end up like them," I said.

"Go where?" she asked.

"Anywhere but here," I said. "We follow the stream; hopefully, we figure that out on the way."

A huge rock smashed into a nearby tree, practically tearing the tree out of its roots.

"Run now," I said.

Everyone set off at a sprint, with me taking up the rear so I could look back and aim the rifle as the creature smashed its way through the forest and into the stream like an enraged grizzly bear.

I emptied the rest of the magazine into the head and torso of the creature before the gun ran dry. I didn't have a spare magazine, but the rifle had a torch, so I kept the rifle, turned, and ran after Dani and Isabelle but only found one of them.

"Where's Isabelle?" I asked.

"That way," Dani said, pointing to the opposite side of the stream. "She went to try and get to the highway. I told her to find help."

"Why? To see if she could dodge traffic?" I asked. "Is this not enough shit to deal with?"

By the time I'd retraced my steps and tried to find Isabelle, the creature would be on us. I just had to hope that she was far enough away and that it was only interested in Dani and probably me, considering I'd shot it in the face.

We ran along the stream, accompanied by the occasional roar of anger or impact of something as it hit the ground close to us, until the stream started to get wider and wider.

"What's that?" Dani asked as we stopped for a moment to catch our breaths.

I looked off to where Dani pointed and saw the metal door to an old bunker that had been built into the side of the hill.

"Let's go find out," I said.

My phone had been vibrating on and off since the unexpected ride through the forest in an out-of-control van, but I hadn't the time to answer it.

I removed my phone from my pocket and answered as Dani and I made our way over the deepening stream.

"Lucas," Ji-hyun said, the relief in her voice palpable.

"We're here," I said. "Dani is with me. You've lost Mia and Benny; I'm sorry. Isabelle went up to the highway. There's something down here hunting us. Big creature, grey skin, spike in its wrist. It was in the back of the van that I rode down here like a toboggan. I hurt it with a rift-tempered bullet. I think."

"We've managed to disable the two BMWs, and the remaining van has pulled back, but we can't get down to you," Ji-hyun said. "We've come off the highway and are circling to the east of your position, but we're going to be several miles from you. We can't rule out the possibility of an ambush. Can you get to us?"

I looked over at Dani. "We're going to try," I said. "We need to find Isabelle first. We'll get your way, but if this thing catches up to us, Dani can't take Isabelle into the rift. Although I guess if it's a choice between certain death here and probable death in the rift, she'd rather go there."

"Be careful," Ji-hyun said.

"You too," I told her, and hung up.

"We've got a trek ahead of us, yes?" Dani asked.

"We've got to find Isabelle," I said. "We can't leave her out here with that thing."

"Let's go," Dani said, picking herself up off the ground and starting up the steep slope toward the highway.

We were about halfway up when I spotted Isabelle at the top, sat on the railing on the side of the highway, her back toward us. It was still dark out, but thankfully, the rain had stopped and the clouds had passed by enough to allow a full moon to illuminate enough to be able to see Isabelle.

I didn't want to call out and alert the giant monster of death to our location, so I trudged on with Dani behind me.

I reached Isabelle first, tapped her on the shoulder, and my heart sank. She swayed forward onto the road, a dagger in her heart, her throat cut. I stepped back into the tree line as something smashed into my shoulder from behind, spinning me around and over the barrier.

I hit the ground hard, landing on my elbows and forearms, rolling across the highway, and coming back to my feet. I was glad it was late at night so I was less likely to be flattened by an eighteen-wheeler.

The creature didn't step over the barrier, just through it, tearing apart the metal in its effort to get to me. He kicked Isabelle's body to the side, sending her tumbling back into the forest.

I turned to smoke and flew back into the trees, colliding with Dani as I reformed.

Dani opened a tear and we both tumbled though into the rift, as the creature's shouts of rage filled the air around us.

"I can't close it," Dani said, panicked as Matthew Pierce walked toward us through the woods on the opposite side of the tear.

I drew my last dagger and threw it at creature, hoping I was going to at least hit him. The creature came through the rift as if it was the easiest thing on Earth to do; it kicked me in the chest, sending me spiralling backward toward a large hill as it dragged Dani back through and the rift slammed shut.

CHAPTER FOURTEEN

I lay on the soft, cool grass for several minutes. Moaning, I opened my eyes, immediately regretted it, and moaned again.

I stayed prone for a while, waiting for the world to stop hurting. When it finally did, I sat up and found I was at the bottom of a vast mound of white stone of all shapes and sizes, and next to a huge grass hill. The mound was probably sixty feet high, with the grass hill twice that.

The sky above me crackled with turquoise lightning. I was close to the Tempest. "Bollocks," I said, got to my feet, and looked around. There was no Dani, no tear, no nothing. The creature had come through a tear without any obvious problems, which didn't bode well.

"I'm sorry, Isabelle, Mia, Benny," I said aloud. "I will find out who's behind this and stop them."

I turned to smoke, flew up the hill as quickly as possible, and re-formed on the top. The mound of stone below stretched out toward a river on one side and a gate on the other. About halfway between here and there, the mound became a wall, increasing in height with every meter, until it was close to a hundred feet high next to the gates themselves.

There was a village just beyond the gate, although *village* was probably pushing it. It was where the guards of the gate lived and worked.

Beyond the rocks were miles of tundra, the land frozen and cracked open like an egg, showing purple-and-blue earth. Beyond that to the north, stretching as far as I could see, was the Tempest. Just to prove a point, the sky lit up with lightning again.

I needed a tear stone.

I looked around again. The hill had grass, some trees off to the side, and an animal that looked a little bit like a rabbit crossed with a rat.

I didn't know its name, but it scurried off when it caught me looking at it.

"Bollocks," I repeated, louder this time. I was stuck, alone, in the rift, with no way to contact anyone outside and tell them that Dani had been taken. Not a single part of my day was turning out particularly good.

I started walking toward the gate separating the rift from the land known as Harmony and the Tempest within. The gate had an actual name, although I was damned if I could remember it.

I set off at a jog. I could have turned to smoke and moved quicker, but I didn't want to tire myself out before I reached my destination. I didn't know how long it took me to actually run all the way to the gate, but by the time I reached it, I wished I'd gone the other way. It had been relatively warm when I'd arrived in the rift, or maybe I'd been so out of it, I hadn't noticed the temperature, but by the time I'd reached the gates, it was noticeably colder.

The second I stood before the hundred-foot-high white stone walls, the name of the place came back to me: the Gates of the Maelstrom.

I wasn't sure who had named them, but apparently, they'd wanted to scare people off going anywhere near the Tempest.

The gates themselves were about half the size of the wall, big enough to bring siege weaponry through, although to the best of my knowledge, that had happened only once, and it had been an unmitigated disaster. The gates were made of dark wood with bronze trim. The lower parts were covered in graffiti, some thousands of years old. No one tried to wash it off; no one complained. Those stuck out there on guard duty were usually the kinds of people who had pissed off the wrong Prime.

I stopped outside the gates and picked up the large hammer from beside them, using it to smash against a metal shield on one gate. The sound that rang was like an out-of-tune triangle.

There was a hatch at eye height, which opened.

"Who are you?" the man demanded.

"Lucas Rurik," I said. "I need to talk to whoever is in charge."

"Guild member?" they asked.

I nodded. "Ravens," I said.

"They're all dead," the man said with a snide tone.

"Open the fucking gate or I'll show you how dead I am," I snapped back.

"Fuck off," the man said.

I turned to smoke, billowed through the hatch before he could close it, and re-formed on the other side with my hand around his throat, pushing him up against the nearest wall.

"You want to try that again?" I asked him, his eyes wide with terror.

"Lucas, enough," a man called out from behind me.

I released the terrified guard and turned around to see a soldier walk toward me. He was my height and build with brown skin, a bald head, and a thick dark beard that was plaited with small gems down the middle. The muscles in his arms and legs bulged. He wore silver armour that gleamed, a picture of a golden lion adorned his breastplate, and there were pteruges—strips of leather protecting his upper limbs and lower body—forming a protective skirt around his legs. He wore sandals primarily because he'd never quite gotten on with wearing anything that covered his feet completely.

"Seluku," I said with a smile. "It is good to see a friendly face."

Seluku returned the smile and embraced me before chastising the guard, who quickly slunk away.

"Why are you here?" Seluku asked.

"Long story," I said. "I need a tear stone."

"The closest one is a lot closer to the Tempest," he told me. "It's in Harmony. Come, we will go to the village; you can drink, eat, tell me what is going on."

Seluku had been Akkadian and several thousand years old when I first met him during the sacking of Rome in the early fifth century by the Visigoths and their king, Alaric. We'd quickly become friends as we watched the empire that had done so much harm to those we cared about fall. We had drunk wine and toasted Alaric, in between helping civilians flee from the king's anger. I had nothing against the Roman people for the most part; I just disliked those of them who were in charge.

We'd thought that the Visigoths would be the end of the Roman Empire, and although it held on for longer, seeing the destruction the Visigoths unleashed had brought a sense of closure to old wounds of mine.

The village just beyond the wall had more civilians and families than I'd remembered when last there. It had gotten bigger, too, and there were multiple carts coming and going as we walked to the entrance.

"This your doing?" I asked.

"The village of Maelstrom needed to be revitalised," Seluku said. "We have farms beyond the walls, we have hunters, we have metal work, and people who use the land of the tundra to make and sell artefacts. We have quite the little economy going. We even make our own wine."

I looked around at the cold, barren land. "Using what?" I asked.

"The earth itself," Seluku said. "We brought fruit from some of the other villages back closer to Inaxia and used the earth here to cultivate them. The land does incredible things to produce. Makes them bigger, tastier. We had pigs here foresting on the grass of the tundra, but they grew too big, too dangerous. Had to slaughter them all. Tasted good, though." Seluku laughed and slapped me on the back.

"This isn't a Lawless village," I said as we walked down stone paths, by flat-roofed white-brick buildings.

"No," Seluku said, pushing open a wooden door painted red. "We are an anomaly. After you."

I stepped into the two-storey building. The floor was bare white stone, and the lower floor consisted of one large room—a living area and a kitchen, an archway between the two—and a separate door. There were stairs set at the rear of the house, and several pairs of sandals and boots were stacked neatly at the bottom of them.

"You live here?" I asked.

"It is my home for now," Seluku said. "I am not part of an active hunt, so I stay here. When it is my turn to hunt again, I will be out in the wilderness. As it should be."

Those who lived at the Gates of the Maelstrom were required to go out and hunt down the more dangerous creatures that lived in the area. They also dealt with any primordials who left Harmony, usually by asking nicely but occasionally in a less-pleasant way . . . usually for all involved.

I sat down on one of the chairs that I discovered was considerably more comfortable than I'd expected.

Seluku tapped a panel on the inside of the front door, and small crystals illuminated on the ceiling above me, bathing me in a calming blue glow.

"The energy of this place is greater than we know," Seluku said as he went into the kitchen and returned with two tall mugs.

He passed me a mug and I took a swig of the cold wine. "Damn," I said.

"I know," he said with a knowing nod. "There's a river to the north of here that flows almost-freezing cold water; we use it to make the wine. We drink the water, too, although it had a weird taste and, depending on your species, can have odd effects from being so close to the source of the Tempest."

I took another swig of the wine.

"What is on your hand?" Seluku asked.

I put the mug on a nearby table and turned my hands over. "There's a thing on Earth. Can't be hurt by abilities, or rift-tempered weapons—although I did shoot it and hurt it, so maybe it can. Anyway, it feeds on this stuff. It's blood, I think, but it's freezing cold to the touch. Tingles too."

"Wait right here," Seluku said, getting to his feet. "I think I know what it is, but I want a second opinion."

"What do you think it is?" I asked him, feeling somewhat nervous about having the stuff on my body still.

"Wait," Seluku said. "You have not learned patience."

"No shit," I called after him as he left the building.

I sat alone in Seluku's home and studied the dried blood on my hands. It wasn't cold still, although the stuff on my fingers had a slightly tacky feel to it. I rubbed my fingertips together and I could have sworn the blood shimmered, although that might have been the light from the crystals.

I removed the beaker from my pocket and put it on the table. I'd rather anyone who might have answers used a fresher supply than having to scrape dried blood off my hands.

Seluku returned shortly after with a woman beside him. She was white, barely five feet tall, with long hair that fell over her shoulders that had been dyed a multitude of colours. She wore a black T-shirt with *Metallica* on it, a black leather jacket with a badge of a rainbow on the lapel, jeans, and a pair of old Converse high-tops.

"Lucas, this is Melody," Seluku said.

"Pleasure," Melody said, with a strong South London accent.

"She's a revenant," Seluku said. "She's also our resident medical expert."

"How'd you get that job?" I asked Melody.

"Because I was the one stupid enough to say yes," Melody said. "Also, the years I spent learning to be a doctor and the years I spent working in A&E seemed to help."

"You were a doctor on Earth?" I asked as Melody took my hand in hers, placing the other hand on top of it and breathing slowly in and out.

"Thirty years," Melody said. "Then some twat hit me with their car, made me into a flesh revenant. Went back to work, until a different twat decided I was the fucking devil and shot me in the fucking head. Point-blank range with a shotgun. I ended up here. Lucky me."

"How long have you been here?" I asked.

Melody turned my hand over. "It's not blood," she said taking my other hand. "Here in the rift? About twenty years. Here in this shithole? About two years."

I picked up the beaker. "This is a fresher sample. Be careful; it doesn't feel good to the touch."

Melody took the beaker and held it up to the light.

"So, Seluku, what did you do to get sent here?" I asked him.

"I volunteered," Seluku said.

"Why?" I asked.

"Because Neb wanted someone she trusted here, so I said yes," Seluku said.

"Wait, you worked for Neb?" I asked.

Seluku nodded. "She arranged to have this village properly manned and have the tundra properly maintained. It shouldn't be the only people who are sent here are the ones who pissed someone off."

"So, you volunteered too?" I asked Melody.

"Neb asks, and sometimes it's hard to say no," Melody said.

"Yeah, we've met," I told her.

"That's earth," Melody said pointing to the substance on my hand and the beaker. "Essentially, it's mud from the ground around Harmony. It's been altered, though."

"Altered how?" I asked.

"It's got blood in it, for a start," she said, sitting back and looking at me. "You're telling me that someone couldn't be hurt and it drank this stuff?"

I nodded.

"A husk," Melody said, looking back at Seluku.

"A what?" I asked.

"You know how humans can come through a tear and be turned into a rift-walker?" Seluku asked. "Or they die horribly?"

"Yeah, it's come up once or twice," I said.

"There's a third option," Melody said. "An enterprising psychopath discovered that if you send a human into the land of the Tempest through a tear and force them to eat the soil of Harmony, it makes them into . . ."

"Monsters," I said. "Sorry for the interruption."

"Monsters," Melody said. "We had one here about six months ago. Newborn husk, trying to murder everything in sight. A human in constant agony, its mind shattered."

"How'd you kill it?" I asked.

"Primordial did," Seluku said. "Tore it apart."

"The claws of a primordial can hurt it," I said.

"Teeth too," Melody said. "I'm thinking that the muck they're forced to drink is full of rift energy, but so are primordials, so they cancel each other out. It's not like I'm saying that's a scientific definitive, but it's my best hypothesis."

"So, this stuff on my arms is bloody mud," I said.

"Yep," Melody told me as she removed a small Petri dish from her pocket and motioned for me to give my arm back.

I did as I was instructed and she scraped off some of the muck from my hands. I chuckled.

"Ticklish?" Melody asked.

I shook my head. "I left the beaker out so I wouldn't have to have my hands scraped."

Melody looked up at me and smiled. "Shit day for you, then."

"In every way that matters," I said.

"We don't exactly have access to high-end scientific equipment," Melody told me when she was finished turning the skin on my arms and hands raw. "But I'm pretty sure I can use what we have to take a better look. You got a few hours, maybe days?"

"No," I said. "I need a tear stone."

"Closest one is on top of a ridge by the Tempest," Melody said. "You'll need to climb up the mountain there and walk across the peak."

"Great," I said.

"You going to tell him, or do I?" Seluku asked Melody.

"There's a lake up there," Melody said. "You heard of it?"

I nodded. "Lake Spirit," I said.

"So called because if you stay there long enough, someone comes along and makes sure you're dead," Melody said. "Well, there were people there."

"When?" I asked.

"Last six months, about once every few days," Seluku said. "We've kept watch but not interfered. They were just walking about up there, apparently gathering supplies."

"How are they getting there?" I asked.

"We don't know," Melody said. "At first, we thought they were riftborn, using the tear stone, but that's not possible."

"Why?" I asked.

"The tear stone is inactive," Seluku said. "It got hit by lightning about two years ago. Hasn't worked since. Or, should I say, no one has gone and activated it since. We have a hut on top of the mountain, by the tear stone, just in case. We send people up there once a month, have them stay a few weeks and come back. No one up there now, though. It's how we saw these people."

"Who'd you inform about the people coming though?" I asked.

"Neb," Seluku said. "Who wants us to keep an eye on them. There's technically no law against people being up there, but we've spoken to the garrisons nearby, and neither have had people going through. Which leaves the question of how they got up there. I informed Inaxia, too, but was told it was probably nothing. Something weird is happening, but I can't spare the people to go looking around Harmony. Mostly because the primordials would not like that one bit."

"Don't make the large, powerful creatures mad," I said.

"That about sums it up," Melody said.

"My time in the rift just gets better and better," I said. "How far is it from here?"

"Few hours' ride," Seluku said. "I'll take you to the fog, but you'll have to go on alone after that."

"I'll come with you both," Melody said. "Just in case."

"We'll take four guards, make sure we're left alone," Seluku said. "Some of the wildlife around here has been getting more volatile recently."

"Increased Tempest activity?" I asked.

"Yes," Melody said. "How'd you know?"

"The more active the Tempest, the more wound up everything here gets," I said. "I was stationed here for a long time. Hunted here more than once."

"Don't tell me you volunteered to come here?" Seluku asked.

"Not so much, no," I said.

"There's some salted boar in the kitchen," Seluku said. "Eat, drink; we'll leave as soon as I've gotten everyone ready."

"Thank you," I said.

"Don't thank me yet," Seluku told me. "There are things in the Tempest with long memories. Get a coat from the cupboard here; you'll need it."

Melody and Seluku left me alone in the house with the rest of my mug of wine and my thoughts. I knew what Seluku was saying about things in the Tempest having long memories. I'd had to kill primordials that left Harmony, their minds warping the further they got from the safety of their home. More than one primordial had killed over and over again, attacking villages, destroying lives before they'd been stopped.

I'd had to come to the Tempest to stop a primordial by the name of Prilias who had turned on the village I now sat in. Being far from the Tempest had filled the creature with an unwavering rage, the power inside of it spiralling out of control. It had gone around the wall—which only stretched for a few miles in each direction, with a garrison of soldiers at each end—all but destroyed the garrison to the west, and gone further south, killing dozens of people until it was forced back. The battle that took place just beyond the Gates of the Maelstrom was where I'd taken its eye. It was also where I'd lost my falcata.

Prilias was still alive somewhere in the Tempest, and I doubted very much that it was going to be thrilled to see me. Primordials lived long lives, usually peacefully if left alone, but held on to grudges like it kept them warm at night.

I found the salted boar in a fridge buried in the cold ground and took a handful. Seluku was right; it was delicious. I grabbed a crimson berry while I was there. They were about the size of an apple but tasted like cherry.

I found a thick, dark green coat inside the cupboard, which was behind the closed door in the downstairs portion of the house. The coat was made from the bark of an arrow tree, which grew in vast forests not far below the gates. It felt like fur and had the same warming properties, but they were easier to make and considerably more durable, able to turn away arrows and blades as if they were armour.

I left the house and found Seluku, Melody, and four guards—three men and a woman—all atop chestnut coloured oxforth. One animal had no one atop it, which I took to mean it was mine. The saddle was already in place, and Seluku tossed me another crimson berry, which I fed to the oxforth before climbing into the saddle.

Despite looking like a cross between an oxen, camel, and horse, they were considerably larger than any of them and much faster. Having the animal like me by giving it a crimson berry was one of the better ways to enjoy the ride. They were usually docile creatures but could be picky about who remained saddled and for how long.

"So," I said, looking up at the angry skies to the north. "Shall we get going?"

CHAPTER FIFTEEN

The ride was pleasant and, despite the speed at which the oxforth ran, comfortable.

None of the group of seven spoke during the two-hour journey, with Seluku and me taking point, Melody directly behind us, and the four guards taking the rear.

The closer we got to the Tempest, the more I felt my body tingle from the power that lit up the sky from the constant lightning above us.

The tundra becomes more frozen the further north you go. Although there are forests and lakes inside the Tempest itself, neither are places I would recommend someone spend time without an army.

Entering the Tempest requires going through a fog that makes my skin crawl. It's not there all the time, and it fluctuates, but it's like being bathed in power, and it takes some concentration to keep yourself from letting go. I'd seen riftborn activate the power and just keep using it, giving up all control and becoming little more than a rift-filled vessel. It eventually kills them but not before their minds are long gone.

Everyone stopped some distance back from the fog.

"You have to go alone," Seluku said. "I can't risk taking them all."

"That the ridge with the tear stone?" I asked, pointing to the burned-orange-coloured hill to the right of where we sat. It was going to be a few hours' walk to get there.

"You'll have to activate it," Seluku said.

I nodded. I didn't like that bit. Activating a dormant tear stone meant using my blood on the stone and activating my power. It always felt a bit like being pulled in different directions, and it left you open to the rift power of the Tempest.

I climbed down from the oxforth, and Seluku passed me a rift-tempered short spear. "I'm sorry I can't do more," he said. "Please be safe."

"You've done enough," I told him. "Thank you."

I understood Seluku's reluctance to go through the fog. Too many people go through once and become addicted to the power hit. Or lost in the visions it shows you. Some don't make it a second time. Hell, some don't make it the first.

"Husks can be killed," Melody said. "Maybe hunt out the claw of a primordial while you're in there."

"They tend to be attached to primordials, though," I said.

"There's a dead one at the bottom of the hill you'll need to climb," Melody told me. "The skeleton of one, anyway. We tried to excavate it about ten years ago, but some of the other inhabitants decided we weren't allowed to; had to leave it behind. Maybe you'll have better luck."

"If it's still there, it's worth a shot," I said. "Thanks for your help."

"Luck be with you," Melody said, shaking my hand and passing me the beaker I'd used to put in the husk goop. "You might need this."

I thanked my oxforth, rubbing their chin, before Melody took their reins, and I watched Melody and Seluku ride off.

I was on my own. Time to get a move on.

I strolled across the frozen tundra, my boots crunching through the soft top layer of dark soil until the fog began to swirl around my feet. I will admit to a momentary pause right then and there. It would have been barely noticeable to anyone else, but I knew.

I continued on, the fog getting higher and higher as the desire to use my power became more enticing. I wanted to let go, to lose control. To allow my smoke to move across the Tempest with ease, to be one with everything.

It took a deep breath, slowly exhaling it, watching my breath being almost snatched out of the air by the fog, for me to regain my sense.

"You let me die," a voice said to the side of me.

"Oh, good," I said. "We're at the voices part of the show."

"You let me die," the voice repeated.

I turned to look at Isaac beside me. "Hello, old friend," I said. "You do know that you're not actually dead, yes? You're in Inaxia. I saw you not that long ago."

"You let me die," the ghost of Isaac said, continuing on as if I hadn't spoken.

"Fuck off," I snapped, and hastened my pace. It was roughly a kilometre of this shite to get through before the fog disappeared.

"You let me die," Isaac said again.

I spun on the ghost. "If this is the best you have, you're losing your touch," I snapped.

The ghost of Isaac vanished and I continued walking.

"You let me die," a new voice said.

"Hi, Jez," I said to the new ghost. Jez had pale skin, with short dark brown hair, and the starts of tattooed rings that looked like blue and green water on her forearms that were going to move up her arms, across her chest and meet just below her throat. She never got to finish those tattoos. She had been the one in our group who had always been the first to suggest doing something, usually something that could get us in trouble if we got caught. She'd been a firecracker and a good friend.

Jez had been part of the same friendship group as Sidon and me. There had been a dozen of us all in total. Jez had been seventeen when she'd been murdered by a man just passing through our village. I'd been with Jez when we'd been attacked; I'd been knocked out, and when I'd woken, she'd been taken. We found her a month later in a state I'd rather not remember. Never found the killer.

"You never got me justice," Jez said as I started to jog, a dangerous decision when you can't see the ground properly, but also, I didn't want to discuss Jez with the thing that made up her ghost. It took my memories of her, of anyone I'd loved, and twisted it through a lens of self-doubt and hurt.

I knew that I wasn't responsible for what happened to Jez or Isaac, but while I hadn't been there to help Isaac—and if I had been, there was a good chance I'd have been killed alongside him—I *had* been there with Jez. Yes, I'd been sixteen, but that doesn't matter to the pain you feel in your chest when you realise your friend is dead. I fought in the Second Punic War soon after. I never saw any of my friends again.

"Don't you ever think about what happened to me?" the ghost of Jez asked. "Don't you think about how you never found the killer?

"I am your memories," Jez said. "One of many. You lived a long life. Lots of regret there. Lots of people you never helped. Or people you killed. Their deaths must way heavy."

I laughed. "Not really," I said, and stepped by Jez.

"I fought before I died," Jez said, and I stopped in my tracks, turning back.

"What did you say?" I asked.

"I fought back," the ghost said. "I died fighting."

"There was no evidence of that," I said. "That's just my wishful thinking."

Jez smiled. "I fought and fought because I believed my attacker was going to kill you. I stood over your unconscious body and fought with tooth and nail."

"Stop it," I snapped. "I searched for her killer. I had my parents' help, but we found nothing. They found nothing. I was sixteen; what was I meant to do?"

"Did they find more victims?" Jez asked. "Because I wasn't the first."

"How the fuck do you possibly know that?" I shouted, but Jez vanished from view, leaving me shaky and angry. I moved to step back into the fog, but stopped. Was this all a trick? Probably. Using my friend to fill me with doubt was something the fog always did; it made you want to give in to the power, and when that didn't work, it made you want to stay in the fog, to scream and shout at nothing but ghosts. But that was different. That was . . . too close for comfort.

I turned away from the fog and continued walking as the thunder roared above me, reverberating in my chest.

While it was cold in the Tempest, the plant life was in abundance. There were huge trees that stretched up as far as I could see and flowers the same size as me. The power of the rift fed everything it touched, and the closer to the epicentre of the Tempest, the more it gave.

Deep red grass came up to my knees, feeling soft on my hand. I kept a close eye out for any primordials. There was an unknown number of them, but last estimates put them in the hundreds, if not thousands. Most stayed in the area closest to the Tempest, feeding on the power it gave them, living a life of relaxation, but some wanted more . . . some *craved* it. Went south to find humans to rule, to subjugate, to kill.

There was a roar somewhere in the distance, and I crouched among the blood-red grass as footsteps thundered across the openness in front of me. I was hundreds of meters from anything close to safety.

I couldn't see whatever had made the noise, but the hair on my arms stood to attention and my heart rate increased. I remained motionless, my hand tightening around the shaft of the short spear. How much help it would be in a fight with a primordial was up for debate, but it was better than nothing.

The thunderous steps faded, and I took my cue and ran through the grass. No point turning to smoke; using your power in the Tempest was a gigantic beacon for any primordials that were nearby.

I reached the bottom of the mountain and ran to the side, where the slope started. It was a steep climb, and halfway up, I wished I'd just turned to smoke. Eventually, I reached the top and sat down for a moment, gathering my energy for activating the tear stone.

When I finally caught my breath, I surveyed the area. The ridge lasted for several hundred meters across the mountain, almost dividing it in two, before the mountain range became even higher further in the distance. The flat of the mountain I was on was a hundred meters wide at least, with dark green grass and moss growing all over it, mixed with more of the red grass from below.

The tear stone was at the far easterly end of it, according to Seluku's directions, just before where the mountain increased in height, so I set off again, although it was a much more pleasurable journey.

There was occasional movement through the canopy of the forest to the side of the cliff, and each time it happened, I dropped to a crouch and waited for it to pass. I hoped nothing came from below to see who I was. I did not want to have to fight a primordial on top of a mountain. I was hundreds of meters above the ground of the tundra and the wind whipped across the top of the mountain; any combat this high up would be, at best, unpleasant.

Halfway across, I saw something unusual on the ground near Lake Spirit, which was filled with midnight-blue water. There was no telling what was inside that lake, nor did I want to find out, but that wasn't what was interesting. It was the four huts that had been built back from the shore, close to the bottom of the mountain, next to a gentle-looking slope that, while much further in distance to get up to where I was, looked like an easier journey than the one I'd taken.

The huts were made of metal and placed in a horseshoe shape, facing the Lake. Each one was on stilts, with a ramp going from the floor of the forest to the door.

"How did you get here?" I asked myself.

There had been scientists come to the Tempest from Inaxia in the past, to study it and everything that lived there, and some of them had even survived the experience. And that's who I assumed the people I'd been told about were. But there was no way a group of people had carried all of that gear through one of the garrisons at the far reaches of the stone wall close to the Gates of the Maelstrom, run across the tundra and the dangers it held, walked through the fog, and then climbed a kilometre-high mountain, and not been spotted. They'd come to the area by other means.

Four people walked out of the huts, all wearing bright yellow hazmat suits. They had clipboards, and another two emerged pushing a black cart with a large, closed box on it.

What the fuck? I asked myself. Why were they in hazmat suits? Were they humans? I had a lot more questions than answers.

There were several bright lights that had been planted in the ground, and two of the six people down there had guns.

I dropped to a prone position as a tear opened in the clearing and someone walked through. They didn't have a hazmat suit, although they did have a mask covering the bottom half of their face, and manacles on their wrists, the chains catching the light as they moved.

Rift-walker, I thought as two more people came through the tear. The first was one of the husks, looming over everything around them. I'd forgotten about the primordial skeleton that I'd been told to look for. *Damn it.*

The second person wasn't wearing a hazmat suit, but they had their back to me. I willed them to turn around as those in hazmat suits filed through the still-open tear until the husk pushed the rift-walker back through, leaving one final person. They turned around to look back at the camp.

Callie Mitchell. These people responsible for the husks, for the bloody mud, for the deaths of countless people, were working with her. As much as I wanted to jump down there and kill everything that moved, it might not end whatever her long-term plan was.

Callie stepped through the tear, which snapped shut as I ran down the pathway on the side of the mountain. I wasn't interested in catching them, there was no chance for me to do so, but I did want to know what they were doing.

It took me a while to make my way to the bottom, and I was exceptionally aware of how easy it would be for another tear to open and suddenly come face-to-face with a husk.

The lights were dim now, and I wondered if they helped keep the tears open or something. They were clearly an important part of whatever the hell was going on.

I made it to the first hut and pushed open the door. It was a small laboratory with various pieces of equipment, and a generator in the corner that was powered by the soil of the Tempest. Pieces of the soil sat on the table, the bright colours a stark contrast against the sterilised steel table. What were they doing there?

I left the hut and checked the other three in turn, each one having more of the soil, except for the last one, which had arrowheads and empty bullet casings. I picked up the arrowhead and turned it over; it had the same sort of bloody soil on it that had been in the tank that the husk had been feeding on.

There was a low rumble outside the hut, and a large shadow passed by the opaque window that looked out into the clearing in between the huts.

"I can smell you," the creature said, its voice a familiar rumble.

I opened the door to the hut.

In the centre of the clearing was an animal that looked like a cross between a stag and a wolf and was twelve feet tall. It sat on its rear legs, its black-and-crimson fur flickering in the breeze. Each of its four paws was the size of my chest, it had a thick, bushy tail, and its head looked like that of a huge stag with antlers that were as large as I was. It was a creature of pure muscle and power. It licked its face with a long blue tongue and bent down to my height, its eyes the colour of blue ice. It was a magnificent creature. It was also my friend.

"Don't take this the wrong way," it said, its voice vibrating through my chest. "But why are you here?"

"Hello, Valmore," I said. "How's things?"

CHAPTER SIXTEEN

Valmore the primordial was the closest thing I'd ever had to becoming friends with one of his kind. I'd been ignored by many of them and attacked by a few, but Valmore was different. I'd met him on my first trek through the Tempest over fifteen hundred years ago, when I'd come across him, injured by another primordial. Like all primordials, he could change his size at will, so he'd shrunk down and I'd helped clean his wound. Since then, we'd been friends.

"Any chance you can shrink?" I asked. "I'm not sure that looking up your nostril is the best view for this conversation."

Valmore chuckled and quickly shrank down to a more normal stag size. "Better?" he asked.

"Appreciated," I said.

"Why are you here?" Valmore asked. There was no unkindness in his tone, just a question between friends.

I told Valmore about the last few days, leaving nothing out. If there was anyone who might be able to tell me what these science huts were for, it was the person who was living nearby.

"Callie Mitchell," Valmore said. "I have not heard that name before."

"How about Valentina Ermilova?" I asked. "It's a name we know that Callie used in the past."

Valmore shook his head. "Sorry."

"It was worth a try," I said.

"So, you were looking to use the tear stone to get home, saw Callie in the Tempest, and decided to investigate," Valmore said. "I have been watching these people come and go for the last few months. Been watching the people from the Gate spy on them, too. We primordials always pay attention to newcomers. You were spotted the second you arrived. Nice hiding in the grass, by the way."

"Why haven't any of them been attacked?" I asked.

"Very few of us venture this close to the fog," Valmore said. "And those who do are unlikely to attack without provocation. I know that you believe that primordials are to be feared and that we devour everyone who comes here, but you must know we're not monsters. We *can* be monsters, but no more than humans can be. Most of us live here, under the lightning-burned sky, and do so in peace. You don't really believe that a village, a gate, and two garrisons are going to stop us should we decide to mobilise en masse, do you?"

He had a good point. "Never thought of it like that."

"Of course not," Valmore said with a smile. "Those in power have cultivated a narrative, and people are all too eager to believe that we primordials want nothing more than to squish you all into paste. It keeps you out of the Tempest, which is fine with us."

"To be fair," I said, "there has been some paste-squishing."

"Ah, Prilias," Valmore said. "He does not speak for us all. Those who follow him don't either. You removed his eye the last time you met. He wasn't happy about that."

"I wasn't exactly in the mood to get eaten," I said.

"Well, whatever the reason, it gave the old bastard time to think about his choices." Valmore chuckled. "It was nice to see him brought down a peg or two."

"Not that I don't want to discuss this further," I said, "but any chance you know about these people working with Callie?"

"Me personally?" Valmore asked. "Not so much. I've seen them about, seen those husks with them. One of them got to the fog and was brought down by my kin. Destroyed, thankfully. They smell . . . off. But so long as they stay here, surrounded by armed guards, they're not considered a threat."

"Oh, I was told to gather some primordial claws," I said. "Apparently, they can kill these husks, and I thought about making weapons from them. There's a primordial skeleton on the other side of the ridge, but I forgot to grab some. Any chance you can help me there?"

"You want to take the bones of my kin, weaponize them, and kill your enemies?" Valmore asked, bending down closer to me.

"I don't have a lot of other ideas," I said.

"Fine with me," Valmore said. "It's not like he's using them."

"Can they be forged into weapons?" I asked.

"Of course," Valmore said. "What do you think that medallion around your neck is made from?"

I looked down at the Guild medallion. "This is primordial bone?"

Valmore laughed, a deep rumbling sound. "You didn't know."

"Why would I know that?" I asked. "I knew it was bone; I just thought it was from . . . Actually, I never considered it."

"Long before you were born, the Ancients and primordials of the time worked much closer together," Valmore said. "Before things soured between us."

I'd heard about the war in the rift. Neb said it had been devastating, but never went into it further. A lot of the Ancients from back then lived secluded lives on Earth, or the rift, or were long dead. The rumour was that at a certain age, the Ancients walked into the Tempest and continued on to the far north, vanishing forever.

"You wait here and I'll be back," Valmore said, rushing off into the trees.

I moved back to the huts and examined each one in turn again, hoping that a second look might unearth something helpful. Unfortunately, I didn't find anything more useful and was grateful to hear Valmore as he returned with several bones in his mouth, which he dropped at my feet. He'd turned back into his full size and sat back on his hind legs again.

"You sure you're okay with this?" I asked, examining the huge femur of the primordial that was easily equal to my height. "It weighs nothing at all."

"Light and hardy," Valmore said with a slight laugh. "Better to be used by you than someone looking to make a fortune. You will need a good forge, but you'll be able to make swords, shields, anything else you can think of. They'll be almost unbreakable and, on the plus side, they'll kill anything with rift power in its body, just as well as those rift-tempered weapons you're all so fond of. You should know that also means your eidolons can also be hurt and killed by them. You still want to do this?"

"I don't think I have a choice," I said.

"Then do what you need to do," Valmore said.

"I don't think you want people to know that primordial bones do a better job than rift weapons," I pointed out, removing my coat, laying it on the ground, and placing the multitude of bones inside it.

"That's a fair point," Valmore said. "Why do you need to use the tear stone?"

"How else am I meant to get back to my embers?" I asked.

"What do you think the Tempest is?" he asked, barely managing to keep the chuckle from his voice.

"If you have some wisdom to impart, just impart it," I said, neatly folding the coat over the bones, tying it at one end to form a weirdly shaped bag.

"The Tempest is the closest veil between the rift and your embers," Valmore said. "You don't need to use a tear stone, because this whole place is a tear stone. Of sorts. I thought the fog might have given that away. The ghosts you see as you walk through it. The fact that you feel a tingle just being here. Riftborn think they know everything, but there's so much kept from you by those who would not see you take your rightful place here."

"Our rightful place?" I asked.

"Tear stones are stones taken from this place," Valmore said. "Specifically from the old town in the centre."

"There's an old town?" I asked.

"So much about this place is kept secret," Valmore said. "Which Ancient taught you of the rift?"

"Neb," I told him.

Valmore laughed to himself. "Neb, never giving information away that might come back to bite her in the future."

"Are you suggesting I've been hobbled or something, that I could be more powerful?" I asked.

"Nothing so dramatic," Valmore told me. "Power isn't something to increase over time or with shiny baubles. You're as powerful as you're ever going to be, but the knowledge contained inside the Tempest is something that should be shared."

"Can the knowledge contained help me stop Callie Mitchell?" I asked.

"I don't know," Valmore said. "What does she want?"

I opened my mouth and closed it again. "Power. She was involved with a group who called themselves the Blessed. They were betrayed, exiled to Earth. Revenge is probably still on her mind."

"The Tempest cannot just *give* people power," Valmore said. "It is power. The power of creation, of life; it is what gives us this land that we call home. The power that you use. If someone comes to try and take that power . . . well, that would be short-sighted."

"Why?" I asked.

"They would die the instant they touched the Tempest itself," Valmore said. "You can get close to it, although I would not recommend it, but touching it . . . no one could do that and survive."

"Could she somehow control it?" I asked. I didn't often get a chance to discuss the Tempest and use the rift-science degree I got many years earlier. The academic in me was fascinated.

"I do not see how," Valmore said. "Many have tried. Riftborn and primordial. None have survived."

"I would dearly love to discuss that further," I said, "but I need to go help find Dani and Callie, and stop the latter from doing whatever the hell she's doing."

"Good luck, then," Valmore said.

Checking everything, I realised I still had the beaker. "Quick question," I said, removing the beaker. "This was the stuff the husks were feeding on. Apparently, humans brought through a tear and forced to eat the soil here turn into these things."

"Not the soil as such," Valmore said. "Anything that is grown from the soil."

"They bring them here and make them eat fruit and vegetables?" I asked.

"Yes," Valmore said. "But there is another way. The blood and flesh of a primordial."

"Wait, what?" I asked.

"Primordials live on the land of the Tempest," Valmore said. "We absorb the power it unleashes. Anyone drinking our blood or eating our flesh would . . . well, for riftborn and revenants, probably nothing except some mild discomfort. For humans? It would certainly hasten the transformation of the husk. They would need a steady stream of power, though. The blood is potent, so that would be the best bet. Mixing it with the soil, turning it into a drink, and forcing it into the human would do the trick. They would have to continue feasting on it, though."

"But not pure blood?" I asked.

"No idea," Valmore said. "We occasionally get humans walking through tears, almost dying, and eating something out of delirium, but that happens so rarely that it's an aberration. If this Callie is forcing humans through a tear and then forcing them to consume the soil and/or blood, that's a very different matter to what I've dealt with before."

"Any primordials gone missing or killed in recent months?" I asked.

"I'm unaware of any," Valmore said. "But . . . we are not social creatures. I can look into it for you."

"Please," I said. "It would be nice to know what I'm dealing with. There's no evidence that they used these labs as somewhere to keep prisoners.

If they killed a primordial, they'd need to have gotten its blood quickly. They'd need to freeze it, too, and to keep it almost frozen, which would explain why the mixture was so damn cold."

"They couldn't use the flesh," Valmore said. "It dissolves too quickly. This isn't a conversation I am enjoying."

"Sorry," I said. "I'm just trying to figure out how these husks are made."

"Well, you'd need a constant influx of food," Valmore said. "There was someone, a riftborn, many thousands of years ago, who used our blood to create husks. I had hoped never to hear about their existence again. I doubt that the people being forced to transform are kept here . . . although maybe they were kept here until one escaped and was killed. Callie could have moved the operation back to Earth after that."

"Which is why they're sending people here," I said. "People come here, collect samples of soil from the land. The soil was in the large crate I saw them move."

"From where, though?" Valmore asked. "I don't see any digging."

"Are there caves near here?" I asked. "Within walking distance of a human? And why near the water? Could water be a substitute for the blood?"

"It's water," Valmore said. "It could be used to water down the blood, give them more to work with before they need to find a new supply."

"Any primordials living around there?" I asked. "Any that Callie could have killed?"

Valmore nodded. "Only a few of us venture this close to the fog, like I said. I would have noticed if one of us had gone missing. There is one in the lake just here, though. She is . . . She hides a lot. Has no interest in what anyone else is doing, so long as she's left alone."

"You think she'll answer my questions?" I asked, looking over at the lake to see if I could spot any movement.

"I think that unwise," Valmore said. "You and I share a friendship. Primordials are large and powerful, but we're still cautious about your kind, much like humans are still cautious about wolves. They might be friendly, they might not bite you the first time you meet them, but can you ever truly trust one?"

I'd lived my whole life thinking that the vast majority of primordials had been things that would eat you or step on you should they feel the need to. Even when I'd spent time talking to Valmore, it was never about other primordials. Except Prilias, but that had been the exception, not the rule. To learn that actually most primordials viewed the human-shaped people in the rift as little more than a wild animal to be wary of was quite the change of perspective.

"So," I said. "A cave or caves?"

"Come, I will show you," Valmore said.

I followed him for a while, walking through thick undergrowth in a forest where I constantly felt like I was being watched, even though Valmore said nothing was there. Some distance into the forest was a large clearing next to a massive cave.

"That's a lot of footprints," Valmore said, sniffing the air. "Many scents, but no one is here now. At least, no one is close by."

Six lights had been placed outside of the cave mouth that were identical to the ones at the campsite. They were also dim, although they were interspersed with white lights that lit up the area.

"This is where Callie's people work," I said.

"You are concerned they're coming back?" Valmore asked.

"Aren't you?" I asked.

"Yes," he admitted. "I do not like the possibility of people using our bodies to create misery and pain in others."

There were two more of the lab huts directly inside of the cave mouth, which was big enough to fly a jumbo jet into and still have clearance on all sides. It was shielded from any main paths via dense vegetation all around. If you hadn't known the way, it would have been all but impossible to find it.

"I will go talk to the primordial in the lake," Valmore said. "I would like to know why she has allowed this to continue."

The anger that rumbled around Valmore's words made the hair stand up on the back of my neck.

"I will meet you back at the huts by the lake. Take care." I watched Valmore disappear into the forest like a ghost, and was suddenly very happy he was on my side. I walked off the path and moved low through the vegetation, past the lights, and into the mouth of the cave.

The mouth was empty, although there was a door at the rear of the cave, and metal walls on either side. Someone had been preparing the use of this place for a while.

I checked each hut, finding mud in each but no signs of people. Whatever Callie was doing was a big job, considering the number of people she was apparently using.

When dealing with the Croupier, I'd discovered that Callie had been a member of the Blessed, an organisation that was, at first anyway, trying to improve the lives of practitioners—people born in the rift. It hadn't been long before the organisation had been corrupted by the needs of the few, and Callie had been more than happy to go along with it.

The Blessed had tried to overthrow the city of Inaxia, failed, and either been exiled to Earth or executed. Callie had been one of the exiled and, from what I understood, wanted revenge on Prime Roberts, one of the current leaders of Inaxia and, in the past, a leading member of the Blessed who had sacrificed everyone else to save his own skin. Whatever Callie's reasons for all of what she'd been involved in, she was nothing if not determined.

I made it to the metal door at the rear of the cave and stopped. Valmore had said that no one was close by, but I was pretty sure he couldn't smell through metal doors. I considered my options, decided I *needed* answers, and pushed it open, stepping inside a large laboratory. There was a door on one side, with the word CELLS written above it in white chalk on the dark stone walls of the laboratory. Most of the rest of the room was dedicated to workstations and stank of blood, muck, and sweat. There were blue and purple lights in the ceiling, presumably powered by the same rift energy that was used throughout the rift, but the room itself was empty.

There were several whiteboards dotted around the lab stations that had clearly been wiped away, leaving traces of inky smears behind. They'd removed any evidence of what they were doing before they left. I wondered if they did that every time they left, or if they were satisfied with their research and weren't planning on coming back except to collect more soil.

I didn't want to go to the cells, because seeing the misery inflicted on others isn't much fun, but I knew I needed to. So, with a healthy amount of trepidation, I crossed the lab to the cell door and pressed the large red button sat next to the door. There was an audible click, which sounded louder than it was in the large empty room, and I pushed the door open.

It was a tunnel that snaked down and around, out of sight. There was more of the blue and purple lighting in the ceiling of the tunnel as I followed it down, one hand firmly on my spear.

I reached the cells after a minute's walk, although I could smell the blood and death before reaching them.

There were six cages all down one side of a large cave, close to the edge of a pit. A handle sat beside each cage. I pulled one handle and the cage lifted up, the door opening. Had there been anything inside, it would have fallen the ten feet into the pit.

The pit itself was full of the soil from outside, the brightness of the turquoise a stark contrast against what was almost certainly blood. There was a metal door inside the pit, which was ajar, revealing the dead body of a three-tailed shadow. Even from the distance between me and the corpse, I could tell that it had been torn apart. I didn't need to go down and check.

I walked the edge of the pit to the stairs that led up to four seats placed on a raised dais. The chairs were comfortable, and sitting on them gave me the feeling that whoever had been there last enjoyed looking down on those who fought below. Sounded like Callie Mitchell to me.

I retraced my steps out of the death pit and back up to the lab area, walking through and out into the forest beyond. It didn't take me long to get back to the clearing where I'd left Valmore.

"So?" he asked.

"So, this is really fucking bad," I said. "What did your primordial friend say?"

"*Friend* is pushing it a bit," Valmore said. "Her name is Pru. She is . . . unhelpful. She said she saw people here, but they didn't bother her, so she didn't care. She feels that humans—and when she says *humans*, she means *human-looking*—are beneath her notice. She went back to swimming. I think she is afraid of them. I think she was afraid of what they might do. She said there were many guards, and she is far away from any other primordials. She likes it that way, but . . . she does not want to be involved."

"Anything else?" I asked.

"She saw people in yellow suits," Valmore said. "Hooded with no faces."

"Hazmat suits?" I asked.

"I have no idea," Valmore said.

"The only reason someone would come here in a hazmat suit is to not breathe the air," I said. "Which means they're either human or revenants who haven't been taken to the rift. The things they've been doing in there are . . . abhorrent."

As if on cue, there was another crack of lighting high above, followed by a roar of thunder.

"Thank you for your help," I told him.

"When you are done, return here and we will talk more," Valmore told me. "Remember, you do not need a tear stone to enter and exit the Tempest. You will always arrive just after the fog, but you can leave anywhere within the borders of the Tempest."

I picked up the coat-bag of bones. "I'll come back and tell you what happened," I promised. "Thank Pru for her help."

"She can hear you," Valmore said.

I looked over the surface of the lake but saw nothing. I opened my embers and stepped inside.

CHAPTER SEVENTEEN

The area of my embers I found myself in was unlike any I'd been to before. The buildings weren't quite formed, the fog thicker. It was as if an artist hadn't entirely finished their recreation of my memories.

I walked through the swirling fog, my surroundings becoming clearer the further I went, until I reached a large forest. I had always been told to never walk through the forest. I'd stepped through once, and it had been like living through a psychedelic dream. I hadn't been sure which way was up, or if I was even alive. I'd crawled out of the woods a few hours later, vowing never to return. Frankly, it had been an unpleasant experience, although apparently, it was one I was destined to repeat.

I stepped into the trees.

I'd moved only a few paces when everything went weird. The tops of the trees melted away, showing the swirling colours in the sky, before being replaced with a shadow that crashed down onto me, exploding into an untold number of ravens, who vanished into the trees.

Continuing on was my only option, which didn't exactly fill me with happiness, but neither had the fact that information about my embers and powers had been kept from me. I wondered if Valmore had been right about Neb, if she only ever divulged information that couldn't hurt her. I'd have expected her to tell me the truth about the Tempest, although if it had been some sort of Ancient-wide conspiracy, I understood why she wouldn't have. I didn't *like* it, but I understood.

I kept thinking about the Tempest as I continued on, hoping that my brain being occupied by an important matter would mean it wasn't occupied by trees talking to me about the weather.

I was soon out the other side, although I could have done without the mushrooms doing musical numbers on the way out. Apparently, you haven't heard *Hamilton* until you've heard it sung by a shiitake.

Casimir, a large stag, ran toward me as Maria the eagle landed a few feet away.

"Where did you come from?" Maria asked.

"The forest," I said. "Or the Tempest. Did you know that I can come and go from my embers to the Tempest whenever I like?"

"Since when?" Casimir asked.

"Forever, so I've been told," I said. "Every day's a school day."

"What are you carrying?" Maria asked.

"The bones of a primordial," I told them. "I need to get back to . . . well, wherever Gabriel is, I guess." It would be much easier if I could just appear wherever I like.

"How did you get into the rift?" Maria asked as they changed into a sparrow and landed on my shoulder, while Casimir walked beside me.

"Got dragged there by a rift-walker," I said. "Went through the Tempest; met a nice primordial who gave me these. Need to get back, find Dani, save her life, and kill every bastard who stands in the way. Been a long few days. Might pass out from exhaustion at some point."

"Are you okay?" Maria asked.

"Not even a little bit," I said. "Callie Mitchell is creating husks. Never even heard of a husk before today, either."

"What's a husk?" Casimir asked.

I quickly explained as I continued to the embers version of my childhood home, although I noticed that more and more of the buildings that were either ancient British or Carthaginian in design were now an amalgamation of the two.

"None of this sounds good," Casimir said.

"That is certainly one way of looking at it," I said. "Which way to the exit?"

Maria stared at me for several seconds without answer.

"Maria," I said. "I really am okay. Just tired and angry."

"It's this way," Casimir said, trotting off ahead.

"I have always known that the woods you just walked through were dangerous," Maria said. "I didn't know you even could walk through them."

"You don't need to apologise," I told Maria. "It seems there's a lot about the Tempest that has been kept from those in the rift. It will be a conversation for later."

"With Neb?" Maria asked.

I nodded as we reached a large hut with a flat roof and terrace.

"I'll come with you," Casimir told me, turning into a hawk. "I can help."

A thought occurred to me. "You could track Dani," I said. "She's a rift-walker, so you'd be able to track any rifts she opens."

"It looks like a flare has gone off," Casimir said.

Taking Casimir out into Earth was a risk. It would mean I couldn't access my embers without taking them back with me. Casimir was smart and capable, and while he could be hurt on Earth, it would need a rift-tempered weapon to do it.

"Okay," I said eventually. "But if we run into those husk things, stay out of their way."

Casimir made a salute with their wing. "Got it."

I looked over to Maria. "You going to be okay here by yourself for a while?"

"I will somehow cope," Maria said, completely deadpan. "Bring Casimir back in one piece."

"I will," I said as Casimir hopped onto my shoulder.

"And Casimir, come back in one piece," Maria continued.

"I will do my very best," Casimir said with a beaming smile—an off-putting thing to see on a hawk that's a few inches from your face.

"Please be careful," Maria repeated.

"That is the plan," I said. The tear opened on the door of the house, and I stepped through into a bedroom I didn't recognise. The tear snapped shut behind me, leaving me with the last view of Maria. Something felt off. I shook my head to try and dislodge the sensation.

I left the bedroom, recognising the hall beyond as belonging to Gabriel's church. I removed my phone from my pocket and found that the battery was dead. Going through a tear with anything electrical tended to kill it, which was probably why everything at the lab site in the Tempest was all whiteboards and rift power.

Casimir perched on the end of the bed frame as I opened the door at the end of the hallway and stepped into the large living area, where Gabriel sat on a sofa. He was watching the TV that had been placed on the wall in front of him, next to a large window overlooking a well-maintained garden.

"I feel I have been neglecting the place," Gabriel said with a slight sigh.

"Anything good?" I asked, placing the arrow tree coat and primordial bones on the floor.

"Superhero film," Gabriel said. "Been making my way through them. Saw a few I'd never seen before."

"How long have you been here?" I asked.

"About twelve hours," he told me. "It's not going to be long before night-time comes. We figured you'd been through the rift when we couldn't find you. Dani has been taken."

I nodded. "Yeah, she shoved me through a tear and snapped it shut before I could do anything. How'd you know? Why are you here?"

"After the attack, we brought the wounded here," Gabriel said. "It was closer than having to go all the way to Moon Island. Ji-hyun and Emily conducted a search for both you and Dani, but Nadia said you weren't there, so we assumed you were in the rift."

"And Dani?" I asked.

"She opened tears all through the forest," Gabriel said. "Small ones, about the size of a pea. Dozens of them. Ji-hyun brought one of her eidolons out of her embers, big timber wolf. It would have tracked her scent, but the tears gave off an easier trail. They took her across the freeway, two miles up to a huge clearing where a helicopter was waiting. We know it was a helicopter because some enterprising young morning hiker filmed it taking off, put it online. The news has been all over it. Ji-hyun managed to stop a lot of info from getting out, but . . . well, humans."

"Looks like Ji-hyun and I had the same idea," I said, motioning to Casimir.

"Hello, Gabriel," Casimir said. "Long time."

"Casimir or Maria?" Gabriel asked.

"Do you really need me to tell you?" Casimir said, finishing with an indignant squawk.

"Casimir," Gabriel said with a smile. "Why are there bones in that coat?"

"I'll explain later," I said. "Do we know where the helicopter that has Dani went?" I asked.

"We do," Gabriel said. "Massena International Airport. From there, we have no idea. Theory is that Dani was unconscious, as we've found no further tears. Ji-hyun already sent people to the airport to look around."

"That's not great," I said. "Are the people who you helped still here?"

"No," Gabriel said. "They travelled by car a few hours ago. Apart from Benny, Mia, and Isabelle, everyone was mostly okay."

"Shit," I said, remembering their deaths.

"Yeah, I'm sorry," Gabriel said.

"So, why did you wait here?" I asked. "Why not go back with the others?"

"I had something I needed to talk to you about," Gabriel said.

"You want to do it on the way?" I asked. "It's a big old drive back to Moon Island."

"I contacted Ji-hyun when you came back," Gabriel said. "I could hear you walking around. The helicopter won't be long."

"And where is the helicopter going to land?" I asked.

"There's a baseball field a short walk from here," Gabriel said. "We're going to meet them there."

"Oh, that's going to make some people angry," I pointed out as Casimir flew over to a bookcase, perched on the edge, and started to hop along the shelves, looking at the books there.

"Oh, yes," Gabriel said. "But they can be angry at the RCU, because they're the ones who arranged clearance there. Also, it's their chopper; not my pig, not my farm. So to speak."

"Okay, so, we've got a little while," I said, walking into the kitchen and putting the kettle on to boil so I could make some coffee. "What did you want to say?"

"I'm not going with you," Gabriel said with a sigh from the kitchen entrance, like it was something that had been bothering him for a while.

I nodded, removed two mugs from the cupboard, and set about making fresh coffee. "Why?" I asked, eventually.

"My church needs me," Gabriel said. "Look, I want nothing more than to see Matthew Pierce get taken down and buried. I want him dead and gone so he can never hurt another person. But people come to my church because they need help. Because they need to see someone who can make sure they're safe. The community expects that. I've been a warrior, Lucas. I've fought in battles; I've killed for things I believe in and things other people told me I was supposed to believe in. Now I can help people and do something I *truly* believe in, without having a body count alongside it."

I brewed the coffee and let the silence linger in case Gabriel had more he wanted to say.

"Besides," Gabriel said, "I'm concerned that my anger at wanting Matthew punished will override anything else. When I heard his name again, the flash of anger I felt was more than I'd felt for anything or anyone in a long time. I'm not that man anymore, Lucas. I can't be."

I passed Gabriel a mug of coffee. "Good," I said, grabbed a chocolate bar from the fridge, and went to sit back down in the living room, where I'd found Gabriel.

"Good?" Gabriel asked, taking a seat on the sofa again. "That's it?"

"Sorry," I said. "Very good."

Gabriel looked incredulous.

"Gabriel, what do you want me to say?" I asked. "I was fully aware of how Matthew's reappearance was going to affect you. I didn't want you involved in the first place, but I knew that if I told you it was a bad idea, your . . . nature would have overridden that."

"My nature?" Gabriel asked, in a tone that suggested that his nature wasn't far from yelling something.

"You are one of my closest friends," I said, ignoring his glare. "I love you like a brother. If anyone should ever hurt you, I would hunt them down to the furthest reaches of the rift and do unspeakable things to them. But when something makes you angry, you can become stubborn. I know because I am stubborn. You are also someone who will argue not because they think they're right but because they've been told they can't do something."

"That . . ." Gabriel said, murmuring something and looking away.

"You had to come to this decision on your own," I continued. "And I knew you would. You're too smart to let your anger cloud you for long, but you still had to come to this decision."

"And if I hadn't come to this decision?" Gabriel asked.

"We would have argued," I said. "I didn't want it to come to that."

"And Ji-hyun?" Gabriel asked. "Did she know this too?"

"Of course," I said with a smile. "She's met you, Gabriel. She knew the best way to deal with your involvement was to let you be involved. I do not mean to sound callous or cold, but your church needs you more than we do."

"I'd hate to see what you said if you meant to sound callous," Gabriel snapped.

"Gabriel," I said. "You know you've come to the right decision. You are better off here, at your church, helping people in a way only you can. I can't do what you do; Ji-hyun can't. What you have is a special power that few have, especially those of us who are centuries old. You care about people with no judgement. You still believe there is a goodness in people. I envy that."

"You don't believe in a basic goodness in people?" Gabriel asked.

"I believe that the vast majority of people are good," I said, taking a drink of coffee. "I also believe that you have to weed out those who aren't before they start to infect those who are. And the easiest way to remove those weeds is to check everything around it. Just to make sure."

"You believe in a basic goodness once you've checked them out?" Gabriel asked with a laugh.

"That is why you're a better person than I am, Gabriel," I said, and unwrapped my chocolate bar, taking a bite. "That is why your church and its members need you."

"You're going to kill Matthew, though," Gabriel said.

"I'm going to make sure he doesn't get a chance to get away again," I told him. "I'm going to find out *why* he was allowed to get away the last time."

"Ji-hyun is looking into his known associates," Gabriel said. "I think that's why she sent me here. Although she made it seem like it was my idea."

"She's a smart lady," I told him.

"The word is *devious*," Gabriel said with a chuckle.

"So, Dani can no longer be tracked?" Casimir asked. "Do you still need me around?"

I nodded. "If she opens a rift again, I'd rather have as many capable of tracking as possible. If you're okay with that."

Casimir nodded.

"You do know the risks, yes?" Gabriel asked me.

I nodded.

"Does it ever feel normal, talking to animals?" Gabriel asked.

"You sort of get used to it," I said. "Depending on the animal."

Casimir let out a squawk of amusement.

When we'd finished our coffees, Gabriel and I left the church with me carrying a coat full of bones.

"You've lost your daggers," Gabriel said.

"Hence the bones," I replied as we left the building.

"I don't know how to answer that," Gabriel said.

"Primordial bones," I told him. "Going to make weapons out of them. Some weapons. Need a forge."

"Fort Andrews has one," Gabriel said. "It used to be abandoned, but after the RCU took control of it and rebuilt large parts, they stocked it full of everything you could need in a siege."

"A siege?" I asked, getting zero odd looks from the people of Hamble as I walked along the street with a hawk on one shoulder and a bag of bones over the other, all while carrying a spear. Most in the neighbourhood knew Gabriel and said hello or waved, and he returned the greeting. A few crossed the street when Gabriel nodded a hello in their direction; some just stood and stared.

It didn't take long to get to the baseball field where the helicopter was waiting, along with several irate onlookers who stood at the edge of the field with their phones.

"You're going to be famous again," Gabriel said.

"I'd really rather I wasn't," I pointed out, feeling exhausted just from the *idea* of people talking about me in public again.

I passed the coat bag to the RCU agent in the rear of the helicopter. She gave me a weird look but took the bag onboard. Followed by an extra weird look as Casimir flew onto the helicopter and sat on one of the arm-rests. I was thankful the spear was only a short one; fitting something the size of a broadsword inside a helicopter was a lot easier than fitting a full-sized spear.

"Take care, Lucas," Gabriel said. "These people aren't playing by any set of rules."

I looked back at Gabriel as he walked away and waved. "That's fine," I said, settling into my seat and strapping myself in. "Because neither am I."

CHAPTER EIGHTEEN

I'm not a big fan of helicopters. It's not the height or the noise—although the latter sucks—it's the fact that they appear to crash a lot more than airplanes do. Could I survive a helicopter crash? Yes, and I have in the past. Do I want to do it again? No, it sucked for all involved.

Thankfully, the flight was uneventful and fairly quick, taking just under an hour and a half. By car, it would have been three times that, and seeing how time was somewhat of the essence, it was good to get back to work.

It was well and truly pitch-black outside by the time we reached our destination. Time was passing by quicker than I'd liked.

The helicopter landed on a helipad at Fort Andrews, and I stepped out into cold wind and drizzle.

"What is that?" Ji-hyun asked as she met me on the helipad.

"Bones," I said. "Primordial bones, to be exact. I'm going to need a forge and a blacksmith."

Casimir landed on my shoulder.

"You brought your eidolon," Ji-hyun said as we walked across the helipad and through a set of glass double doors. "You've never been before?"

I shook my head. "No, not that I remember," I said as we continued on down a corridor with moss-green tiles and white walls. "Nice place."

"Old fort fell into disrepair," Ji-hyun said. "RCU purchased it in the 1980s, completely gutted it, and made a state-of-the-art facility. Pretty much everything that was here is gone, replaced with this five-storey building, although there are ten floors beneath the ground, too. There are about two dozen buildings in all, with large open ground between here and the rest of the buildings on the island.

We stopped at a door marked *Staff Only*, and Ji-hyun removed a key card from a holder on a lanyard around her neck, scanning it and replacing the card.

"We'll need to get you one," Ji-hyun said as she opened the door, and motioned for me and Casimir to go through into another hallway with a lift at the end and a room on either side.

"So, it's not used for sea defence anymore?" I asked, slightly in jest, looking into the open doorways on either side of the lift as we waited. One looked like a meeting room, and the other had three RCU agents sat there.

"We use it for when we don't want to bring someone through the main building," Ji-hyun said as the lift doors opened beside us." "There's an elevator in the rear of the meeting room that goes straight to the underground facility. We took the idea from the very place you went to in London, although we're not going to have people try to blow us up."

"I hope not," I said as we stepped into the lift, and Ji-hyun pressed one of the buttons on the panel next to the door, taking us to the ground floor, or first floor, depending on whether you're English or American. It was something that, even though I'd lived in America for a long time, I'd never gotten used to.

"There are a hundred RCU agents here, right now," Ji-hyun said. "Since I've been in charge, we've moved the main offices here. We've added several guard posts and lookout towers. We're in the process of turning the tiny port into a marina so that we don't have to be limited to helicopter and the occasional ship. We added a wall between the left- and right-hand sides of the island; we're on the left, by the way. The right-hand side of the island is considerably more welcoming to newcomers. The RCU were a mess when I took over. Even Isaac, and I loved Isaac, couldn't get it sorted."

"You fixed the RCU?" I asked.

"The east-coast branch, anyway," Ji-hyun said. The lift doors opened and we walked out to a small part of a much larger foyer. There were several lifts beside the one we'd just arrived on.

"Only one lift to go to the roof?" I asked.

"Yep," Ji-hyun said. "Limited entry points, and the roof is one of them."

"There's a prison here, isn't there?" I asked.

"Bottom two floors," Ji-hyun said. "Like I told you, we modelled it on the building in the UK. What's with the spear, by the way?"

"Lost my daggers," I said. "Hence the need to see a blacksmith."

"We have one on staff," Ji-hyun said. "Fresh from Inaxia, in fact. I'll get you taken to them once we're done. I assume the bones are to replace your daggers?"

"Sort of," I said. "I have some other ideas, too. The claws of a primordial killed one of those things that attacked Hiroyuki and me in Boston."

"Sounds like we might need more bones, then," Ji-hyun said.

"You're more than welcome to go ask the primordials for them," I said.

Ji-hyun stopped walking as we reached the entrance for the building, which had six armed RCU agents stood outside. "Did you ask a primordial for them?"

"Long story; I'll explain once everyone is together," I said.

Ji-hyun stared at me for a moment before nodding. "I'll get them sent to the blacksmith. You okay with that?" she asked.

I nodded. "Just let me speak to them before they do anything."

Ji-hyun took the spear and bones over to an agent, who walked away with them.

"I've never seen so many RCU agents," Casimir said as Ji-hyun rejoined us. "Are you planning to start a war?"

"No," Ji-hyun said as we entered a corridor on the opposite side of the floor to where we'd arrived.

We walked across a glass-encased bridge joining the building we'd just left to the one beside it, which was just as high and had just as many RCU agents outside. It really did look like Ji-hyun was preparing for a war. I didn't even realise there were that many agents to begin with.

"We've recruited," Ji-hyun said, as if aware I was staring at the multitude of people.

"Everyone?" I asked.

"When I took over, there were 216 RCU agents on the east coast of America. Actually, everything east of Colorado. There were six agents for the entirety of Chicago. Six. I decided that we needed more. I went to the Ancients and to the human governments, showed them the figures and facts about the increase in rift-fused activity, the increase in fiend activity, and they agreed to increase my budget."

"By how much?" I asked as we reached the end of the walkway.

"Seventeen thousand percent," Ji-hyun said. "It's not all mine; it's the RCU for all of North America. But it worked. More agents, better agents, more coming here from Inaxia. It feels like we might actually make a difference. The Guilds can't be everywhere at once. And with more attacks, more sightings, more *everything*, we need to be able to show humanity that we're here to help."

"This doesn't exactly scream *approachable*," I said.

"These aren't the RCU agents that you see normally," she said. "These are for our protection and for dealing with high-level threats."

"You've made a Guild," I said, not quite keeping the irritation from my voice.

Ji-hyun sighed. "I've done what I thought was best to keep us safe, Lucas," she said. "To keep the humans safe, too. It's a work in progress. I've pulled back fifty percent of our staff to this place. Those assholes we fought had no issues with killing RCU agents. We need to find them and stop them."

"I agree," I said, feeling silly for being concerned about Ji-hyun. If there was one person I could trust to keep the RCU in line, to build them up into something approximating a useful force, it was her. "I'm sorry if you felt I was disparaging. This is just . . . It's a lot."

"Yeah, it is," Ji-hyun said. "I don't want to lose any more Isaacs, Lucas. I want people to know we're going to help them, and I want the bad guys to fear us. We're not cops. We're not trying to be cops. But the RCU seems to work in Europe; they're better funded, given more time to train, more integration with humans. We need that here."

I followed Ji-hyun through another door into a huge room with stairs on either side and a large open space with tables and chairs in front of us. There were multiple closed doors on either side of the room, and Ji-hyun walked over to one, pushing it open to reveal a large auditorium.

We'd come through at the bottom of the auditorium, next to a large whiteboard, a table in front of it with a laptop on it, and a second door on the other side. The six rows of seats were divided into three, all looking down on where I stood. There was a door at the rear of the room, with EMERGENCY written on it in green.

Casimir flew up to the top of the whiteboard and perched there.

The first two rows of the auditorium had several people sat, some with paper and pens on the personal workstation in front of them, and some looking like they'd just woken up.

Anthony, Emily, and three RCU agents were sat in a group on one side, with Nadia beside them, and then a gap before more agents. Hiroyuki was set off by himself a row above, with a man and woman on either side.

"Good to see you back," I said to Hiroyuki.

"You too," he said with a slight nod.

"Did Gabriel decide to stay home?" Emily asked.

I nodded. "He came to the conclusion that he was better off working at his church. I told him we'd find Matthew Pierce and make sure he didn't get a third chance to be a monster."

"Noah is coming via helicopter," Hiroyuki said. "He should be here within the hour."

"So, in the meantime, what did you learn while I was away?" I asked.

"We don't know where my sister is, who has taken her, or why," Anthony said, looking around. "That about sum it up?"

"We know that Callie Mitchell is involved," I said. "I saw her in the Tempest. Also saw a rift-walker who appeared to be forced to open and close a tear. It wasn't Dani."

I went through everything I'd seen, leaving no details out, and no one interrupted while I continued. When I was done, I leaned up against the wall as Casimir, now a raven, landed on the table

"So, we know who has my sister; let's go get her," Anthony said, almost out of his seat.

"But we don't know for certain," Emily said. "We have a theory that it's Callie, but what if Callie handed her to someone else? What if Callie is only the middle . . . woman?"

"And even if Callie definitely has her, we don't know where she is," I told him. "It's impossible to track on the Tempest side, and it's probably even worse here on Earth. You'd have to be within the vicinity of a tear being opened to know where it was. Dani had been opening small tears on the way to the helicopter, but we don't know where she's gone from there."

"And once they left the airport, all we know is they were in a dark-coloured BMW," Emily said. "Not a huge amount to work with."

"Any chance your chains show you anything?" I asked Nadia.

Nadia shook her head. "A lot of voids again. Nothing useful. I'm feeling more than a little irritated by the fact that everything in my chains seems to lead to a dead end. I don't know what that means. I can try to go longer-term, to find a chain without a dead end, but that means delving into the chains more. That brings with it . . . problems."

"If it will help my sister, you should do it," Anthony almost shouted.

"You're asking Nadia to destroy herself if it doesn't work," I told him, trying to keep the irritation at his tone out of my voice. "We will find Dani but not by getting our own people hurt."

"Can any of you actually do anything?" Anthony snapped. "You couldn't even keep Isabelle safe." He stormed out of the auditorium, the door slamming shut behind him as two RCU agents followed at a respectful distance.

"Isabelle wasn't your fault," Nadia said.

"I know," I told her. "It was Callie's. There's so much blood on her hands now."

"We have to kill her," Ji-hyun said.

"Can't," I replied.

"We bloody well can," Nadia said.

"I sort of promised Neb that I would keep her alive," I said. "No, I don't know why, but I do plan to find out."

"You think that maybe Neb wants to use her for her own means?" Ji-hyun asked.

I nodded. "There's definitely a possibility in that."

"Neb might not go around calling herself an Ancient, but she is one," Hiroyuki said. "They all have their own agendas."

"Even Noah?" Nadia asked, more than a little sarcastically.

"Even Noah," Hiroyuki said, looking down at his phone. "Speaking of which, he has arrived."

"Anyone got a phone charger I can use?" I asked. "Mine died when I went to the rift."

"We have hundreds of the things," Ji-hyun said. "We'll find you one."

"I have to go," Hiroyuki said, getting to his feet along with the person on either side. "Meet me in the main reception area; it sounds like Noah has news."

"I'll be there," I told him, and watched the three of them leave.

"You trust them?" Emily asked. "Still, I mean?"

"Depends what news Noah brought," Ji-hyun said.

"I need to see the blacksmith," I said. "We're going to need some new weapons to kill the husks. Preferably before I see Noah."

"You want me to deal with the Ancient, don't you?" Ji-hyun said.

"Well, you are in charge," I pointed out.

"I'm going to regret that, I think," Ji-hyun said with a smile. "The blacksmith is a few floors down from here. Emily, can you take Lucas so he doesn't get lost and then shot?"

"Does that mean I don't have to deal with Noah?" Emily asked.

"Looks like it," Ji-hyun told her.

"I'm sorry you lost two good people," I said. "I should have opened with that when I arrived here, but sensory overload was sort of in effect.

Mia and Benny were good agents; they probably kept things from being worse. I hope they end up in Inaxia."

"Me too, Lucas," Ji-hyun said sadly. "Losing people was the reason I never wanted this job. Or part of it. Now it's the reason I'm going to find those responsible and nail them to a fucking tree by their ears."

"Interesting imagery," Nadia said. "I approve."

"Nadia gets it," Ji-hyun said, giving Nadia the thumbs-up.

"I'll take Lucas to the blacksmith," Emily said with a smile.

I chuckled and followed Emily to the door.

"One thing, Lucas," Ji-hyun said, calling after me.

I stopped and turned back from the doorway as Casimir landed on my shoulder.

"We work together here," Ji-hyun said. "I know you want to go after these guys, but we're a team. We work as a team."

"I get it," I promised.

I followed Emily out of the auditorium and across the floor to the door at the far end, which took us outside into the driving rain. I'd seen old photos of the island a while back, with the run-down buildings and overgrown mess. I remembered being told about how it was going to be reclaimed and made better, but I'd never actually seen it with my own eyes. It looked like a cross between a military base and some old-time village. Smoke rose from a single-storey building in the distance, close to the beach that ran around the outer rim of the island.

"That the blacksmith?" I asked.

Emily nodded. "We're going to need to take a car to get there."

I followed her down the increasingly wet and windy steps to a road at the bottom, where a small car park had been placed. There were several electric vehicles in an undercover charging area, and Emily removed a cable from one of them, used a set of keys I assumed she must have had on her, and motioned for me to get in.

The car was comfortable and silent as we took off. "I always thought I'd never quite get used to no engine noise," I said. "But actually, it's quite nice."

"It's not exactly the V8 my dad had when I was a kid, but sacrifices had to be made," Emily said.

"How goes being a part of the RCU?" I asked. "Different to the FBI?"

Emily smiled. "There's less paperwork," she said. "Much less oversight, although Ji-hyun is dealing with that. The previous RCU were essentially cowboys who did whatever they liked and were occasionally looked into. It's how they got so corrupt. Ji-hyun wants to change that, and she's doing a good job."

"And the day-to-day work?" I asked.

"There're a lot more fiends than I expected," she said. "It feels like there are either more fiends than anyone here has ever seen before, or it's just that more people are willing to report them."

"Or a combination of the two," I said.

"You ever experienced anything like that before?" she asked as we drove along a road with several red-brick buildings on one side, most of which appeared to be a series of shops, some with well-known names, some I'd never heard of. A small town.

"No," I said as I looked around. "There are a lot of people."

"Lots of RCU agents are human," Emily said. "Weird, isn't it? So many humans want to be a part of this. Ji-hyun has started something exciting here. There are more and more states that want her to take control of their RCU teams. Quite a few FBI agents have moved over too. It's a period of complete change. They have shops here because it's a little village. It might actually be the most harmonious human and rift-fused place I've ever been to."

"Nice," I said.

"You don't sound thrilled," she said.

"I'm always cautious about such things," I said. "Had my hopes dashed more than once in the past. But if anyone can do it, it's Ji-hyun."

Emily parked the car outside of a building separate from any others by several hundred meters. I got out of the car, the cold winds whipping up across the beach and over the embankment to where I stood. The waves were choppy in the marina below, which had several construction crews in it. Ji-hyun really was transforming the whole place.

"The blacksmith," Emily said, pointing to the metal door. "I'll wait for you out here."

"Why?" I asked.

"They're a little . . . You'll see," Emily said, getting back in the car.

I went to the metal door and knocked. It opened slowly, creaking as it went.

"Hello," I called into the small room beyond; the wooden door separating it from the rest of the building was ajar, letting in a glow of amber light.

"Come in," someone shouted from further in the house.

I stepped inside, closed the door behind me, and pushed open the wooden door, stepping into a huge forge area. The back of the building was partially open, letting cool air into what would have otherwise been an unbearable room. The forge was in the middle, and there were dozens of blades in buckets all around; most appeared to be normal, no rift-tempered. Some of the blades looked ornate, elaborate things that would be better suited to an anime or video game. There was one sword that had a blade as long as I was tall.

The blacksmith was in the middle of the room, hunched over an anvil. They hit a glowing piece of metal several times with their gloved fists, the metal showering sparks with every punch. I watched as they removed their thick gloves, dropping them on the floor, and held their hands just above the metal, which changed shape in seconds as if it had been worked on for hours. They picked the blade and plunged it into a bucket of water, the hissing sound echoing around the room as the steam filled the distance between us.

"You're the one who brought the bones?" they asked, pointing to the pile of primordial bones in the corner.

"I did," I said. "My name is Lucas Rurik."

"I've heard about you," the blacksmith said. "They say you watched Rome burn."

"More implode," I told them.

The blacksmith walked around the forge, removed their hooded mask, and dropped it on the floor. She had long dark brown hair that was plaited down her back, with pale skin that was more than a little red around the cheeks and nose. She had piercings in her lip, nose, and ears.

"We can talk outside," she said, motioning me to go through the exit to the forge on the opposite side of the room.

I was grateful for leaving the oppressive heat behind for a moment. "I've got some things I want you to make," I said, looking down the range where there were lights in the distance around archery targets.

"Okay," she said. "I'll see what I can do."

"It would be a hurried order," I said.

The blacksmith smiled. "They're all hurried orders. RCU makes my life miserable."

"Why work here, then?" I asked.

"Better than Inaxia," she said, wiping her hands on her once-white shirt. "Sorry, I didn't introduce myself. My name is Drusilla August."

"You're riftborn?" I asked.

She nodded. "Been that way since 28 AD. Took the name from my grandfather and grandmother."

"That's . . ." I paused. "You're a Roman."

Drusilla smiled. "Looks like we didn't all burn."

"Wait, you took the name from your grandparents?" I asked. "You're the granddaughter of Augustus and . . . Drusilla."

Drusilla's smile widened. "Ta-da."

CHAPTER NINETEEN

S o, do you hate all of us, or did you get over it?" Drusilla asked.
"I didn't hate Roman people," I said. "I was killed centuries before your great-grandfather was even born."

"I'm only messing with you," she said. "Ji-hyun told me you were from Carthage. Wasn't sure how you'd be with me. Some people hold a grudge so tightly, it becomes their entire personality. Can I assume Emily is outside in the car?"

"You two not get on?" I asked.

"I dislike being told what to do by newbies," Drusilla said. "To be fair, I dislike being told what to do by everyone; that's why I'm here."

"There's more to that story, I assume," I said.

"I beat the shit out of someone who said something they shouldn't have," Drusilla said. "Apparently, I have a temper. Metal doesn't talk back to me, and I get to punch it."

"You don't use a hammer," I said. "I noticed when I came in."

"Riftborn," she said. "I can manipulate metal. Mostly it's little stuff, but when it's heated, I can do all kinds of things with it. Infuse it with rift energy, break it apart, stretch it like taffy. Sort of made a rift career for me."

"Let me guess: you weren't much for smithery when you were human?" I said.

"No, I was for mostly fucking, drinking, and getting into fights with people who told me I shouldn't be fucking or drinking," Drusilla said. "Sometimes one while I was doing the other. My father disapproved, but he disapproved of absolutely everything, so I didn't care, and then I was dead and never saw any of them ever again. You know, I'm not even in any records of ever being alive. It's wild. You?"

"Born in England, moved to Carthage when I was little," I said. "Grew up there, went to fight with Hannibal, died fighting with Hannibal. Came back and everyone I knew was dead. Carthage was gone too. It took some getting used to."

"Killed a few Romans," Drusilla said in a mocking tone.

"Killed a few of whoever stood in front of me," I said. "Romans just happened to be in front of me a lot more than anything else. To be fair, there were a lot of you."

"Like rabbits," Drusilla said. "So, what am I making with these primordial bones, which by the way, I want to know more about at some point?"

"Can you work with them?" I asked.

"You mean because they're not metal?" she asked. "I'll have to infuse them with steel. Otherwise, they can't have their shape changed, but yes, it's not a difficult process. Will take a few hours, depending on what you want."

"I have a few hours," I said. "How much will it cost me?"

"Dinner," Drusilla said. "No joke. I rarely meet people from our time. Or if I do, they just lament what it was like when Rome was in charge. Never met a Carthaginian. So, that's my price. Besides, the RCU pay me to be here, so it's not like you need to actually give me money."

A laughed. "Dinner. Seriously?"

Drusilla nodded. "We can discuss watching Rome burn. Yes, I was there too. When I returned from Inaxia, Rome was still in full force; couldn't get away from it, no matter where I went."

"Deal," I said. "What do you like?"

"Not Italian," she said. "I've been on a few dates in the last decade, and every man I've met always makes that joke that I must love pizza. It's not funny and pizza sucks."

"You want to go on a date?" I asked.

"No," Drusilla said. "I want to go to dinner. I don't date people I've just met."

"We'll figure it out, then," I said, feeling a little caught off guard about how this whole conversation had gone.

"So, what do you want made?" Drusilla asked, walking back into the forge to grab the bones. She brought them outside, placed the coat on a glass table, opened the coat, and moved the bones around.

"A falcata," I said. "Half a dozen throwing knives, two daggers, and something else if possible. This is a little more . . . bespoke."

Drusilla looked through the bones, nodded to herself. "I've made those medallions before, so I can work with primordial bones. They do not like people getting hold of them, though, so you either pissed off a lot of really powerful creatures, or you're friends with them. Which one is it?"

"Friends with one," I said.

"You're a lucky man," Drusilla said. "What's the bespoke piece?

I placed the short spear on the table. "I want the blade of this replaced with the bone; it needs to be better weighted, specifically for throwing. I also want a small piece of . . . I don't really know, on the top of the hilt. Plexiglass, plastic, metal, whichever works best. About the size of the last third of my index finger."

"Why?" Drusilla asked.

"I can turn to smoke," I said. "But I don't have to turn my whole body to smoke, just parts of it. If I turn the tip of my finger to smoke while it's inside that little box on top of the spear, I can throw the spear and snap my whole body across to wherever it lands."

"Like teleporting?" Drusilla asked, an eyebrow raised in interest.

"Sort of," I said. "I've done it before, but it's hard to do with a dagger or sword; the piece of me has to stay attached to the thing I've thrown." There was also the simple fact that it tired me out quickly. Teleporting around a fight sounds awesome until you actually have to do it. But considering what we were up against, I'd take any advantage I could get.

"I can do that," Drusilla said. "I'll need a few hours to do the sword and spear, maybe a couple of daggers. What do you want me to do with the rest of the bones? There's enough here for several dozen swords."

"Bone bullets?" I asked.

Drusilla stared at the bone for a while. "I'm not sure. The problem is that bullets don't accept a charge, and I get the feeling adding something explosive to this stuff is a bad idea, but I'm willing to blow something up in the interest of science."

"See what you can do," I said. "Daggers, swords, spears, whatever works. If we're going up against husks, I'd like to be prepared."

"I don't know what that is," Drusilla said.

I explained exactly what husks were.

"That sounds like a shit way to spend your day," Drusilla said when I'd finished. "I can get some stuff working. What about the coat?"

"I'll keep the coat," I said. "It's comfortable."

"And it's better than leather armour," Drusilla said. "Hell, it's probably better than plate armour. What I meant was do you want a lining with primordial bone inside it?"

"You can do that?"

Drusilla picked up one sleeve of the coat and examined it. "It won't stop a bullet. It probably won't stop a sword if you get hit more than once in the same place, but it might work. Shouldn't be much heavier than it is, either. Same basic principle with making the weapons. The bones need to be melted down, mixed with high-grade steel, and worked into whatever shapes I need. It'll look like your medallion but with a steel colouring. Never done it before, though, not with primordial bone. I like a challenge."

"You still need a few hours?" I asked.

Drusilla nodded. "Probably less for the spear, sword, and coat. I could get those done in a couple of hours. To do everything here, yes, a day. I'll get those three bits done first, seeing how you're probably going to need them most. I'll let Ji-hyun know. I assume you'll be going after the missing woman."

"That's the plan," I said. I considered asking for the daggers and knives as well, but I didn't want to push my luck. "Just need to figure out how to find Dani first."

"Good luck," Drusilla said.

I left Drusilla to her work, with a promise to take her out for dinner when things weren't quite so hectic. I got into the car with Emily.

"And how did that go?" Emily asked as we pulled away and set off to return to the main building.

"She's Roman," I said.

"Not just Roman but the daughter of one of their most famous leaders," Emily said. "Ji-hyun didn't want to say anything in case you decided to not go."

"I think, after nearly two thousand years, I've gotten over my dislike of the Roman Empire and the people who led it," I said. "You can't be mad forever."

"So, she's going to do what you need?" Emily asked.

"Yep, in exchange for dinner," I said.

Emily laughed. "She got you to go on a date with her? Smooth."

"I'm not entirely sure it's a date," I pointed out. "And I'm not entirely sure how I managed to get talked into dinner, either, but she was entertaining to talk to."

"She's quite the . . . firecracker," Emily said.

"Ah, she doesn't like being told what to do by *newbies*," I said.

"Or anyone else," Emily said, sounding stern. "I'm not a fan of being thought of as a newbie, either."

"You hear from Ji-hyun about Noah?" I asked, wanting to change the subject.

"He brought someone with him," Emily said as we pulled up outside the front entrance of the main building.

"Someone who can help?" I asked, hopefully.

"I'm not so sure about that," Emily said. "Ji-hyun didn't say who the *someone* was, but she didn't sound thrilled."

"You coming with me?" I asked her.

"No," Emily said. "We've got people trying to find any known associates of Matthew Pierce. We're hoping to shake some trees and see what falls out."

"Good luck," I said and opened the door.

"Be careful, Lucas," Emily said just as I stepped out into the rain. "From the way Gabriel spoke, I get the feeling Matthew hates you as much as you hate him."

"I fucking hope so," I said. "It would be a shame to have broken so many of his bones for nothing."

I walked to the front of the RCU building and found Ji-hyun sat in the reception area. She motioned for me to join her. "How'd that go?" she asked.

"I'm taking Drusilla to dinner when this is all done," I said. "Also, she's going to do everything I asked. With regards to the weapons, not anything weird during dinner."

Ji-hyun cracked a smile, although it was quickly banished. "Noah is here. He brought someone."

"Who?" I asked. "And why are you angry?"

"Tobias, Anthony's neighbour," Ji-hyun said.

"The guy with the clipboard?" I asked. "What did he do?"

"He killed Abigail Walters," Ji-hyun said. "He was the second man who went to Dani's home."

"Tobias is a murderer who's working with Matthew?" I asked. "To be honest, I thought he was a creepy little dude, so sure, why not?"

"Tobias died about six weeks ago," Ji-hyun said. "The original Tobias. This one is definitely not him."

"Superb," I said, feeling like I really could do with a coffee. "Do you have a kitchen?"

"You want a hot drink?" Ji-hyun asked.

"I really do," I said. "Where's Noah."

"Down in the cellblock with our guest," Ji-hyun said. "There's a kitchen down there. Go make yourself a drink and then you can interrogate Tobias. I get the feeling that Noah's people already had a go, judging from the condition he was in when they arrived."

It didn't bode well that whoever their prisoner was had already had the shite kicked out of him. Prisoners don't tend to want to trust you when they think you're just going to torture them some more anyway.

Ji-hyun and I barely spoke as we entered one of the elevators, and she used her key card to unlock a compartment under the usual buttons inside. She pressed a button marked *C2* and we began our descent.

"How many prisoners?" I asked eventually as the doors opened.

"Just the one at the moment," Ji-hyun said. "Tobias is our first. Or whatever his name is."

We walked down a corridor with a metal floor, the noise of our footsteps echoing all around us. There were several doors that we walked by; most were empty, although one had several RCU agents and a lot of monitors.

"We're setting up to be able to hold rift-fused criminals here until they can be transferred to a larger prison," Ji-hyun said.

"How are you stopping their abilities?" I asked.

"Callie Mitchell used those suits," Ji-hyun said, and I sensed some trepidation in her tone.

"I remember," I said, keeping all emotion out of my words. I'd worn one of those skin-tight suits that shut off the rift-fused's access to their power and, in my case, access to my embers. I didn't care for them.

"It's nothing quite so hardcore," Ji-hyun said. "It's the same basic principle, but instead of making people wear them, we got Drusilla to craft the metal of the cells and then had a practitioner create a solution that limits power. In their cell, they can use their power, but once they touch those bars, or try to leave it, boom, power cut off. It has to be reapplied every few months, but it's a hell of a lot less invasive than cutting off a person's power completely."

"Does that mean us, too?" I asked.

Ji-hyun nodded. "Only once we get to the cell area. Inside the cell, you're good to go."

"We'll interview him in the cell, then," I said.

"I'd be grateful if you didn't beat him to death," Ji-hyun said.

"I wasn't planning on it," I told her.

"Just had to say," Ji-hyun explained as we reached a huge metal door that looked like the kind of thing you'd use in a bank vault. Ji-hyun removed her pass and brushed it over a small reader beside the door.

You hear me, Casimir? I thought, feeling his presence as he flew around the top of the building, enjoying the freedom of being somewhere other than the embers.

Loud and clear, Casimir said.

We might lose our connection when I step into the cell area, I explained. *Not for long, but don't freak out.*

I have never once freaked out, Casimir said, sounding hurt. *But thank you for telling me.*

I smiled, and there was a hiss of air as the door was unlocked. It moved open slowly, first toward Ji-hyun and then rotating to the side, moving into the wall beside us.

"Welcome to the cells," Ji-hyun said as I stepped through the opening to see a large room with monitors all along one wall, while the other was a window looking out into a horseshoe-shaped open area. There were six staff in the room, all sat at workstations. Next to the door at the end was a locked gun rack, and on the other side of the door was a locked weapons rack. There was nothing in the middle but a large drop, revealing four more sets of floors.

"Are they all identical to this one?" I asked.

"The floor below here isn't," Ji-hyun said. "That's where we take the prisoners for processing. This is where we monitor every cell. No camera in the cells themselves, but one on every door, the stairs, the walkways. The cameras on the doors have infrared capabilities. These things are high-end military tech."

"You've made Arkham Asylum," I said.

"I don't know what that is," Ji-hyun said.

"It's from *Batman*," one of the guards said.

"See, she gets it," I said, offering her a fist bump, which she returned.

"You are a geek, Lucas Rurik," Ji-hyun said.

"You really want to go there?" I asked with a sly smile.

"I don't know what you're talking about," she said, looking through the large window.

"Michelangelo was the best turtle," I said.

Ji-hyun took a deep breath and let it out slowly. "I will not stoop to your silliness."

I caught the smile on two of the guards in the room.

"Where are Noah and his people?" Ji-hyun asked.

"Cell block, second level," the male guard at the door said. "They're outside the cell, just like you ordered."

"You ready to go chat with an Ancient?" Ji-hyun asked me, and nodded to the guard, who opened the door.

I followed Ji-hyun out of the control centre and across the metal grate-like floor, walking by empty cells.

"Each cell has a bed and bathroom area," Ji-hyun said. "No communal showers, and no one has to sleep next to their toilet."

"Classy," I said.

"Here to see the man now known as Tobias?" Hiroyuki asked as Noah and Ji-hyun chatted.

"Got told you guys did a number on him," I said, looking across at the two bodyguards, one male, one female. Both tall and muscular, both with brown skin and intelligent eyes. Noah didn't employ idiots.

The woman smiled first.

"He hit me," she said.

"Bet he didn't do that again," I replied.

"No, he did not," she said with a nod, and I got the feeling that was the end of the conversation.

Ji-hyun placed her card against a lock on the side of the cell. "Donatello was the best turtle, and you know that," Ji-hyun said, as the door slid into the wall, revealing a good-sized room, considering it was meant to be a cell.

Tobias sat behind a small table in the middle, the bed pushed up against the wall. The whole place was designed for someone to never leave until transported to somewhere more capable of holding them. I knew that Ji-hyun hadn't actually created all of this out of thin air. A lot of the main building we were in had been around for a while, but she'd done a wonderful job of bringing it all up to date. I doubted Tobias would agree with me, though.

"Hello, Tobias," I said, taking a seat opposite him. He'd been punched in the face hard enough to leave a mark even after all the time he'd had to heal.

"We'll all watch from the control room," Ji-hyun said. "This cell door remains open at all times. Tobias, if you try anything, Lucas will kill you well before anyone else does."

"Lucas Rurik," Tobias said. He smiled. "I think I'm going to need to make a phone call."

CHAPTER TWENTY

I laughed at Tobias. "You want to order in or something?"

"I need to call Matthew Pierce," Tobias said.

I bristled slightly at the name.

"There are microphones in this cell," Tobias said. "So, I know your friends heard me. I want to talk to Matthew Pierce. I need a phone."

"I'll tell you what," I said. "You answer a few questions and you get your call."

Tobias nodded, closed his eyes, and sighed. He licked his lips. "I'm not sure you're going to want to make him wait, but okay, let's play it your way."

"So, what happened to the real Tobias?" I asked.

"He's dead," Tobias said. "I ate him. He was quite delicious."

"You're a spirit revenant, yes?" I asked.

Tobias nodded.

Spirit revenants come in a few flavours, but Tobias's was the most dangerous of them. They could take the spirit of a person and turn into them. They have some of their memories but all of their mannerisms, tone of voice, and the like. They're an exact match physically for the person; the only difference is the bright yellow eyes, which was why Tobias had been wearing sunglasses. I'd never met a spirit revenant who could do what Tobias did and not become a criminal. But then I'd never met a spirit revenant who could do what Tobias did, who hadn't been a criminal to begin with.

"How long ago?" I asked.

"Six months, maybe," Tobias said. "I was given the task of watching Anthony's home outside of Boston. We didn't know about his apartment near his work. The local busybody was a wonderful way to do what I needed to do without having to worry that I was acting out of place."

"Why kill Abigail?" I asked.

"Who?" Tobias asked me.

"The neighbour," I said, stomping down any anger I felt. It would do me no good.

"A few reasons," Tobias said with a grin. "Firstly, I was hoping to get Anthony arrested for her murder. People arrested for things they didn't do are so much easier to . . . ply into what you need. He gets arrested, I turn up and tell him I'll help him if he helps me. We knew he was looking into missing rift-walkers. We needed that list of names we hadn't gotten to yet. He'd done quite a lot of work for us."

"And secondly?" I asked.

"Ah, well, Abigail was smart," Tobias said. "She figured out what I was. Figured out what had happened to old Tobias. She had to go. I considered eating her, but I don't like to do it too much where I'm working, so I settled for a drink of blood. By then, Anthony had gone to ground, and I was about to get ready to leave and join in with tracking him when you turned up. Scared the shit out of me at first, I don't mind telling you."

"Why?" I asked.

"You're Lucas Rurik," Tobias said. "I know who you are. More importantly, I know what you are. Raven Guild. Last surviving member. Too stubborn to die, they say. I heard about all of that. Matthew said you might be involved at some point, considering you've been after Callie for a while. You're never getting to her, you do know that. She's doing work that's too important to let go."

"We'll see," I said. "So, what's your real name?"

"I don't remember," Tobias said.

"Oh, come on, don't start with games," I told him.

"Honestly, no clue," Tobias said. "My memories are of everyone I've ever taken. I don't know which one is me. Couldn't tell you my real name if you'd written it down in front of me. I couldn't even tell you where I was born or what my parents did. So many lives live in my mind."

"So, you don't know how many people you've killed?" I asked.

"Hundreds," Tobias said. "I can tell you the names of every single one of them. Just not my own name. Is that ironic? Or is that just karma?"

I shrugged. "Why do you want to speak to Matthew?"

"Because I need to," Tobias said. "You can do better than that."

"Why'd you let yourself get taken?" I asked.

"I do what I'm told to do," Tobias said. "I was told to stay where I was until you arrived; I was assured you'd arrive. And then I was to tell you that I wanted to speak to Matthew. I've been arrested before; it always goes the same way. Badly for everyone who isn't me. To be honest, this is only the second time I've been arrested by the RCU. First time I've been taken in by an Ancient. And Noah Kaya, too. What a celebrity. I do feel honoured."

There was a knock on the door and Ji-hyun opened it, bringing in a mobile phone, which she placed on the table, and left without a word.

"That your phone?" I asked.

"It is," Tobias said. "I'm so glad you all understood where you stand."

Tobias reached out for the phone, but I took it before he could place a hand on it.

"What are you doing?" Tobias snapped.

"I'm telling you that you're not getting this unless we get something in return," I said. "You've not told us anything we hadn't figured out for ourselves. Try harder."

"I promise you that this call will illuminate any questions you might have," Tobias said. "No, please, allow me to make it."

"Speaker," I said. "If you don't mind."

"Not at all," Tobias said with a sickly sweet smile.

"Just one more thing before you make the call," I said.

Tobias had already picked the phone up but calmly replaced it on the table. "Please do," he said with no hint of irritation or sarcasm. It was like he really did want to talk.

"Why Dani?" I asked. "I mean, I have a theory, but I'd like to know why."

"What's your theory?" Tobias asked.

"A few months ago, there was a man in England, called himself the Croupier," I said.

"Good man," Tobias said sadly. "Shame he got caught."

"Yes, well," I continued, "he had kidnapped a rift-walker. And was going to take her to America for Callie. He mentioned it at the time, but I thought nothing of it. Rift-walkers were rare, so I'd always been led to believe, but recently I'd discovered that maybe they're not so rare, just secretive. And you went after Dani. I think you're using, or rather Callie is using, the rift-walkers. I saw one in the Tempest; they had on a mask covering the bottom of their face and they wore manacles, but I think you're using them to create tears. You need to do experiments on humans in the rift; it's why you have those husks. I think you're taking rift-walkers so you can pass between here and there to do those experiments."

"Well, that's some interesting ideas," Tobias said. "Maybe one day you'll find out the truth of it all. Or you'll die well before then."

"My question is, how'd you find out about Dani?" I asked. "Specifically her. How did you know that Dani was a rift-walker?"

Tobias stared at me for several seconds. "I don't know," he lied.

"Are you a terrible liar as a person, or was Tobias a terrible liar and you just have that mannerism?" I asked.

Tobias's expression soured. "We are done with this conversation," he said, picking up his phone and turning it on.

"You don't like to be criticised, do you?" I asked. "Or are you angry that you can't control everything about the person you take over? Is that it?"

"You don't know anything about me," Tobias screamed.

"Neither do you," I countered.

Right there and then, I knew that if we'd been outside of the facility, he'd have tried to kill me. He let out a breath and dialled a number on his phone before placing it on the table between us.

"Tobias," Matthew said on the phone. "I assume you have Lucas or one of his lackeys with you?"

"Lucas himself," Tobias said, almost beaming with pride.

"I don't have lackeys," I pointed out. "Technically, I am a lackey."

"Now, don't sell yourself short," Matthew said. "I know how important you must be. You were so important to the Ravens the last time I saw you. Whatever happened to your friends in that Guild, oh, that's right, they were all murdered. I think the word is *slaughtered*, in fact. But you survived. Alone. You ever wonder that the person responsible might come back and finish the job?"

"They're welcome to try," I said.

Matthew laughed. "I have missed our little chats. Do you remember the last time we spoke when it wasn't so much talking as you ambushing me and beating me to a pulp? Do you remember that?"

"I do," I said. "I don't remember ambushing you. I remember waiting for you in your home. Where you kept the trophies of those you'd murdered. I remember you walking into your office, seeing me there, and trying to run away like a scolded child. I remember me walking after you, I remember me besting you quite easily, but most of all, I remember me breaking the bones. Your arms. Your fingers. Your knees and toes. Your ribs and sternum. So many bones. Not even one for every victim. I assume there are more victims now."

"I *do so* love these chats," Matthew said, although there was no longer any humour in his voice.

"If you have harmed Dani in any way," I said, "I'll forgo breaking anything, and I'll just start cutting pieces off instead."

"The little *bitch* is fine," Matthew snarled. "She broke the noses of two of my men though."

"Shame," I said. "I'll tell her to go for their throats next time, maybe break a neck or two."

"You think this is funny?" Matthew snapped.

I said nothing but felt a smile creep onto my face as Matthew's angry breathing filled the cell.

"What do you want?" I asked eventually.

"I would like you hung by your fingers while I skin you alive," Matthew said, and took a deep breath. "But Callie has other ideas."

"Why isn't Callie the one on the phone, then?" I asked.

"She's busy," Matthew said. "So, I'm here offering you a trade."

"Tobias for Dani?" I asked.

"No," Matthew said, and Tobias's expression didn't change even though he'd just been essentially ignored as a part of Callie's plan. "You."

I sat back and laughed. "Me for Dani?" I asked. "Are you all smoking crack over there or something?"

"Listen to me, you little cretin," Matthew seethed. "Not you for Dani. Just you. Alone. You're going to give yourself up and come to us."

"Absolutely not," Ji-hyun said from the doorway.

She'd been standing to the side of the cell, listening in. I assumed Noah and his people were on the other side.

"And who might you be?" Matthew asked.

"My name is Ji-hyun," she said. "I am the head of the east-coast division of the RCU."

I pushed my chair as far to the side as I could go and motioned for Ji-hyun to come into the cell.

"I figured you might say that," Matthew said. "So, Callie has informed me that I am to explain what's happening here. I do hope you're all able to keep quiet for a few minutes so I don't have to be interrupted."

Ji-hyun turned to me, and I motioned to lock my mouth with an invisible key, tossing it over my shoulder.

"Continue," Ji-hyun said.

"There are twelve cages dotted around the city of Boston," Matthew said. "Some are near apartment buildings, some are near hospitals, at least one is near a school. Each of them has a husk inside. It's midnight, and in eight hours I'm going to press a switch and open all twelve cages at once. During rush hour, in a busy city. Can you imagine the chaos?"

I knew Ji-hyun was trying to do the mental calculations to figure out if they could find all twelve in time, if there even were twelve. Matthew wasn't exactly someone I trusted to be honest.

"I know how the RCU operates," Matthew said. "You're going to get off the phone with me, and you're going to get every agent you can find to search for these fiends. You're going to be *really* busy. Too busy to come with Lucas. Too busy to do anything but stay in Boston and mind your own business.

"Lucas, on the other hand, well he's going to get to Hanscom Field, which is where the RCU keeps its private jet. He's going to get on that jet with Tobias, who will be in constant contact with me, and he's going to fly to Massena International Airport. He will get out of that airport and there will be a car waiting for him. An Audi Q7, because I'm not going to skimp on luxury just because I hate him. He's going to drive to the destination set in the satnav. He will not deviate. He will not do anything that means he takes longer than the allotted time. If he does, I open every cage. When he arrives here, with Tobias, I will give the locations for all twelve cages."

"And Dani?" I asked.

"Dani stays here," Matthew said. "Trust me when I tell you it's important."

"Trust you?" I asked, and almost laughed. "So, you get to keep Dani, Tobias, and me, and we get nothing in return."

"You know I'll open those cages," Matthew said. "You get to ensure that the people of Boston don't live through a bloodbath. I would think that would be enough."

"Why me?" I asked.

"Callie will explain it all," Matthew said. "I have been told to assure you that you will be unharmed. She needs you unharmed. Unfortunately."

"Where am I going?" I asked. "What happens if there's traffic?"

"You'll be monitored the whole way," Matthew told me. "I'll know about traffic; I'll make allowances. You'll find out where you're going when you arrive at the airport. Not before. This isn't my first time, Lucas."

Ji-hyun stared at me.

"You have a deal," I said. "But I bring two people with me. They can drive; I trust Tobias even less than you."

"Like you had a choice," Matthew said. "And that's fine. But they leave and return without causing a scene, or lots of people die. Until then, you have eight hours to find a dozen exceptionally dangerous fiends before they turn Boston into a bloodbath. Can you imagine the news stories? The RCU not protecting little kiddies on their way to school. The RCU keeping it from the human law enforcement. By the way, I don't much care if you tell the local cops or not. The more, the merrier."

"When I've found them all, I'm going to come looking for you," Ji-hyun said through clenched teeth.

Matthew laughed. "I'll be kind and give you an hour to get to the private airfield. You will get Tobias to contact me the moment you take off. Be seeing you." He hung up.

I left the cell a second later, moving up the stairs to the control room above. Ji-hyun and the others weren't far behind me.

"You do know that this is a trap," Hiroyuki said as he entered the control room with Noah and the latter's bodyguards.

"Yes, I'm aware of that," I told him.

"And yet you're going anyway?" Hiroyuki asked me, incredulous.

"Of course," I said. "I don't go, a bunch of husks get released onto Boston's unsuspecting population, and we currently have no way of stopping them. On top of that, we have no clue where Dani is, and this might be our best chance to find her. Do you have any better ideas about how to find her?"

"No," Hiroyuki said softly.

"Matthew believes he is untouchable," Noah said. "He believes he can do as he pleases. Hiroyuki is right when he says it's a trap."

"An obvious one," Ji-hyun said. "I need to make a call."

"And yet," I almost snapped as Ji-hyun left the room, "I still have to go."

"I'm going with you," Hiroyuki said, and paused, turning to Noah. "With the permission of my Ancient."

"Of course," Noah said. "You will be on your own, though. Matthew is arrogant; he believes he has you trapped."

"Oh, I know that," I said. "Look, we all know that Matthew is going to unleash those monsters anyway. The more of you to help kill them, the better. There's primordial bone with Drusilla the blacksmith; they seem to be able to kill husks, hopefully. They're untested, but honestly, seeing how everything else we throw at them just mildly irritates them, I'll take untested. She's making weapons with the bones. If she can make even a dozen swords out of the material I've given her, you all have something to kill these things."

"You sure?" Noah asked.

"Absolutely fucking not," I said. "But right now, our options are: I hand myself in, get taken to Dani, and those monsters are unleashed, or I don't, we never find Dani, and those monsters get unleashed."

"You trust Matthew to keep his word?" Noah asked.

"No," I said with a laugh. "But Callie is calling the shots, and if she needs me for something, it's going to be something big. She wouldn't want to waste time and energy to get me to go somewhere just to kill me. She'd rather stay hidden."

"She must *really* need something, then," Hiroyuki said.

"Tobias was always meant to be captured," Noah said. "This was always the plan. To get your help."

I shrugged. "Maybe, but I don't know. It seems like a pretty long-winded way to get my help, though. I can't imagine what I could possibly bring to the table that she'd want to use."

"We have precious little time," Hiroyuki said.

"I need to go find Drusilla again," I said. "Get my gear sorted."

"Also, how did they know that Dani was back?" Hiroyuki asked. "It's been bothering me since we met her. There's no way her brother told anyone. There's no asking Isabelle, but she didn't know a thing. Who put Matthew and Tobias on her trail?"

"A conversation for us on the journey," I said. "I'm going to see Drusilla. Get everyone ready."

"Who are you bringing with you?" Hiroyuki asked as I reached the door of the control room.

"Nadia," I said.

"Is that . . . wise?" Noah asked. "She is not exactly always stable."

"I trust her more than any of you," I snapped back before I could stop myself.

"I . . . apologise," Noah said. "I was not trying to offend."

"It's okay," I said. "It's been a long few days."

I found Ji-hyun further down the hallway as she left one of the rooms. "You look pissed off," she said.

"Ancients thinking they know better," I said. "I'm going to see Drusilla, get my gear. I need to find Nadia and see if she'll come along with me and Hiroyuki."

"Before you leave," Ji-hyun said, nodding toward the room she'd just left.

I followed her inside and she closed the door.

Ji-hyun passed me a small tracker. "Just in case," she said. "Put it in your shoe or something. I don't want to have to go hunting for you after we're done."

I put the tracker in my pocket for now. "Thanks. You going to be okay?"

"Dani's brother is above," Ji-hyun said. "He tried to get off the island. Was stopped. He threw a punch. It didn't end well for him."

"How much did he get his ass kicked?" I asked.

"None," Ji-hyun said. "I don't employ people who can't deal with upset relatives. He's livid, and apologetic to the man he tried to hit, and honestly just a mass of anxiety and hurt. I think he believed that Noah would arrive and it would all be magically fixed. He can't go with you, he definitely can't come with us, but I thought I'd ask if you could explain the former."

"I'll go talk to him," I promised.

"Lucas, this has a chance to go really sideways, really fast," Ji-hyun said. "Be careful."

"You too," I said. "Matthew isn't the kind of person who does as he says and leaves it at that. He's the kind of person who will try to screw you over at the first available opportunity. He says you have eight hours, but it's more likely to be six. He says there's going to be a dozen cages, look for fourteen."

"Can I ask for your counsel?" Ji-hyun asked.

I nodded. "Any time."

"You think I could call Boston PD?" she asked me.

"And the FBI," I said. "Fuck it, call the goddamned governor. Do not leave any stone unturned, because whatever's under it will come back and bite you in the ass."

"Already done," Ji-hyun. "The governor was who I was calling just now."

Ji-hyun stepped in and hugged me.

"You're concerned," I said as she pulled away.

"That obvious?" she asked.

"Keep everyone safe," I told her. "I'll be back as soon as I can. With Dani."

CHAPTER TWENTY-ONE

Anthony sat on a chair in the reception area. He had a mug of some-thing hot in his hands, the steam visible well before I got close enough to talk to him. He looked dishevelled and hurt. His looked up at me, his eyes red, and there was a flash of anger in his face, like he was getting ready for another round.

"Fuck off," he snapped.

"You want to take a swing at me, too?" I asked, standing in front of him.

Anthony put his mug down and got to his feet.

"Maybe I do," he said.

"Anthony, I really do understand where you're coming from," I told him. "I get the hurt, the anger, the frustration. I understand it all. I've been where you are right now. Waiting for answers that no one can give. I've fretted and worried about people I love, knowing I can't do a damn thing. But if you throw a punch at me, you're going to get hurt."

To my surprise, he threw a punch.

I caught it in my open hand, twisted his wrist to the side until Anthony let out a yelp, and pushed him back onto his chair.

"Ow," he said, rubbing his hand. "You could have broken my wrist."

"You want me to?" I asked him. "Would that help?"

"No, I'm just..." Anthony let out a cry of impotent rage. "She's my little sister. I lost her before; I can't lose her again. Isabelle is dead. People are dead and missing, and I can't do a goddamned fucking thing." Anthony practically screamed those last few words.

"You can stop throwing punches at people who are only trying to help," I said.

"They refused to let me leave the island," Anthony said. "They're just assholes with too much power. How is that helping?"

"Because no one wants to come searching for your stupid ass, too," I snapped, my patience finally at an end. It wasn't entirely Anthony's fault, but he was the final straw. "Seriously, what the actual fuck is wrong with you? Did you hit your fucking head or something? Your sister has been kidnapped, and people would rather an untrained man-child *not* go running around to find her. We have all been working our asses off trying to get her back, and instead of working with us, talking to us, you throw a tantrum and try to leave, causing us more work.

"I get that you're upset, I get that you're angry, but if you go out there and try to find her, you're going to get killed. For-real killed. Just like Isabelle. Just like those RCU agents who were protecting you and Dani. The best thing you can do is go find a quiet place, sit down, and keep quiet. Or you could ask Ji-hyun how you can help and then go do that. I'm going to go get Dani back, so I don't much care if you're angry at me or just pissed off at the world, but I'll be damned if I'm going to let you badmouth those people who are doing their jobs under difficult circumstances. When you threw a punch, did they kick your ass? Did they arrest you? Did they hurt you physically or emotionally in any way? No. No, they got you here, where you can't hurt yourself, and then they had their boss ask me to talk to you. Because everyone understands the stress you're under. But there's a difference between being stressed out and upset, and just being a dick. And you're trying to pole-vault over that line."

What had started at admonishment had just grown into words pouring out of my mouth without thought. I wasn't even that mad at Anthony, but combined with everything else that had happened, it had turned into a bit of a lecture.

Anthony stared at me for several seconds. "You done?"

"I'm not sure," I said, feeling a weight lift from my shoulders. "I've been keeping a lot bottled up for a while. Didn't mean to go off on you, or lecture you but goddamn it, Anthony. Don't make it more difficult than it already is. Right now, Dani is safe because they need her. If they have you, they have leverage over her. You want her to watch you get tortured until she does what they want? Because I'm a hundred percent sure that Matthew would cut off every one of your fingers and laugh while Dani watches."

Anthony looked down at his hands. "You sure he hasn't hurt her?"

"No," I said honestly. "I can't be sure of anything, but I would put money on her being fine. Angry, yes, but in one piece."

"I'll talk to Ji-hyun," Anthony said. "I'm sorry for throwing a punch at you."

"Good," I said. "Don't do it again."

"Can you really find my sister?" Antony asked.

"I've been dealing with people like Matthew for a long time," I said. "Hell, I've dealt with Matthew. I've been doing this since your great-great-grandfather seven times over wasn't even a twinkle in his parents' eyes. I know what I'm doing. I'm going to find Dani, and I'm going to ensure those who took her aren't able to do it again."

"Thank you," Anthony said, looking completely deflated.

I patted him on the shoulder and left him to his thoughts, leaving the building and setting off at a run through the island.

Are you okay? Casimir asked.

Not really, I said. *You're going to have to either sit on a plane in raven form or find something smaller to turn into.*

Smaller, Casimir said. *We can make sure that Tobias doesn't realise that I'm there.*

Good plan, I agreed.

Do you think we can find this Dani girl? Casimir asked while I enjoyed the burning in my lungs as I increased my pace, until I was flat-out sprinting along the road in the darkness.

Yes, I said.

And if we don't find her in good health? Casimir asked.

Then I will reconsider my position on torture, I replied, and Casimir went silent with that.

I reached Drusilla's forge and knocked once before opening the door and stepping inside.

"Twice in a few hours," she said with a slight mocking tone. "What in the world have I done for such an honour?"

"I have to leave the island," I said. "Might not be back for some time. I wanted to know if you'd finished anything I gave you."

"The spear and sword are done," Drusilla said. "The coat should be too. I managed to do these as well."

I caught a set of knuckledusters that Drusilla tossed across the forge to me. They were light, and dark golden in colour. I slipped them onto my hand, and they felt good.

"Thank you," I said, removing the knuckledusters and putting them in my jeans pocket.

"And this," she said, passing me a small dagger. "In case of emergencies."

The falcata was a thing of beauty, a dark steel in colour with a red wrap around the bone hilt. I practised with it for a few moments, nothing fancy due to the close quarters, but it was wonderful to hold. Lightweight, strong, and hopefully deadly against anything, including husks.

"It's stronger than pretty much anything I've ever made," Drusilla said. "Didn't have time to do a custom sheath for it, but I have a few that should fit."

I picked a black leather sheath from the wall that Drusilla pointed at, sliding the sword home. "It's exquisite," I told her.

"The spear to your requirements?" Drusilla asked, turning back to the forge.

I picked up the short spear, which was weighted perfectly. I took it outside, stood at one side of the long range, gripped the spear in one hand, and placed my fingertip inside the small compartment on the side of the spear. I turned my finger to smoke, leaving the fingertip where it was when I threw the spear with everything I had. It landed somewhere between where I was and the archery target a hundred meters away. The tip of my finger was missing, smoke trailing around from where it had been, as if trying to seek it out. I snapped my hand shut and moved in an instant, turned to smoke, and re-formed where the spear had landed in the darkness, my finger now whole again.

I walked back over to Drusilla. "Thank you; it works perfectly."

"Of course it does," Drusilla said, passing me a custom sheath for the spear. "But you're welcome."

I put the spear sheath on so that it sat against my back, with the tip coming up over my left shoulder. It had a quick-release mechanism on it, for easy removal and replacement, which was something I hadn't even thought of. With the spear against my back and the sword against my hip, I was ready for battle.

"I see why you're so highly regarded," I told Drusilla.

"Your coat is done too," she said. "It might feel a little stiff to wear, like it's been left out overnight on the washing line, but you'll get used to it and it should become more supple."

I picked up the coat and put it on. Just like Drusilla had said, it was stiff around the shoulders and under the arms, but it wasn't uncomfortable. There was a cut in the top of the shoulder so that the spear head poked through, and a catch around the seam so that it could be fastened closed when I didn't need it.

"You definitely found your calling," I said, moving my arms to get used to the added weight. It wasn't a lot, but it was still noticeable.

"So, you still want to take me for diner?" she asked.

"I do," I said. "When I get back, we'll get food. You choose. Thank you for this, and for doing it so quickly."

"I'll get the rest done as soon as I can," Drusilla said with a yawn. "It's been a long day."

I explained to her about the husks in Boston.

Drusilla's eyes narrowed in anger. "I guess sleep can wait. I'll get the weapons done for the agents out there. They might not be pretty, but they'll work. No bullets, though; not enough time to see how they work."

"Thank you," I said.

"Be careful, Lucas," Drusilla said sounding serious for the first time. "I've met Matthew Pierce before. I met him when he was the son of a Roman senator who liked to kill people for sport. He's the same spoiled little shit who likes hurting people. Doesn't matter who he works for; he'll still find a reason to do what he wants."

"I know," I said. "Last time I saw him, I left him a beaten and bloody mess. I plan on finishing the job this time, but thank you for your concern."

"You might actually be the last Carthaginian," she said. "The last Raven. You're an endangered species."

"I wasn't born there," I told her. "Just brought up there. I guess I'm Carthaginian just as much as I'm a Briton. I don't really think about it."

Car is here to pick you up, Casimir said. *Emily just got out.*

"I have to go," I said. "Take care, Drusilla. I'll see you soon."

"I look forward to it," Drusilla said, stepping toward me and hugging me.

I left the forge and intercepted Emily before she had to knock on the door. "You ready?" she asked.

I nodded.

"Helicopter will take you to the airfield, where there's a fuelled jet waiting," Emily said.

I got into the car and put on my seat belt.

"You okay?" she asked.

"I don't like putting my trust in a known psychopath," I said. "I can think of more fun things to do, no matter how necessary it might be."

Emily drove across the island in silence for a while, the rain beating down on the car roof. "Can you beat him?" she asked eventually as the lights of the helipad came into view.

"Matthew?" I asked.

"Yeah," Emily said. "Can you beat him?"

"Repeatedly and with much vigour," I said.

"I didn't mean physically," Emily said. "Can you stop him? Whatever he has planned. Whatever Callie has planned, for that matter."

"I have no idea," I said. "But I'm going to do my damndest to try."

"I spoke to Nadia; she's on board the chopper, waiting for you," Emily said as we pulled up near the landing pad. "Hiroyuki too. I've been thinking. They're going into the rift to do experiments, to create those husks . . . What if they're planning on invading the rift?"

"Invading the rift?" I asked. "They'd need *a lot* more people than we've seen. There's no way they can take Inaxia without getting into a long, drawn-out war with some of the most powerful people in the rift. The Crow's Perch is not going to be a pushover, and Neb's Nightvale is full of people who chose to live outside of Inaxia's laws and protection. You don't do that unless you can hold your own against everything the rift can throw at you."

"The husks are impervious to harm against anything that isn't a primordial," Emily said. "They could hold out with fewer numbers against a larger force."

"True," I said. "There are a lot of things we don't know. It's certainly possible that's the endgame for Callie and her people. But not Inaxia. Not the major cities. I'm pretty sure the Ancients there will know what husks are and how to kill them. At the very least, Neb does, although she appears to be holding a lot back, so who knows what she does and doesn't know."

I sat and thought for a few seconds.

"Be careful out in Boston, Emily," I said, opening the car door.

"You too, Lucas," Emily said.

I closed the door, rushed over to the heliport, and climbed onboard the chopper, where Nadia and Hiroyuki waited for me with a restrained Tobias. Casimir was currently a mouse in my pocket. I'd take any advantage I could.

We were in flight a moment later, and no one spoke the whole time. Nadia's eyes were closed, her breathing steady, relaxed. Hiroyuki was sat next to the pilot, Tobias stared out of the window at the multitude of city lights below us, and I sat back in my seat.

Emily had given me something to ponder. Something I hadn't considered. The husks must have an endgame apart from muscle. It was a lot of effort to go to just to get muscle. I knew that Callie wanted revenge on Inaxia and those who lived there, specifically Prime Roberts. He had betrayed her group, betrayed the Blessed. He had gotten them all exiled. Maybe it wasn't about taking Inaxia as a whole; maybe it was just about getting in past the guards and killing those who ran it. With the Primes dead, the city would become more chaotic, at least for a time. Long enough for . . . for what? Did Callie want to be a ruler? She didn't strike me as the type. Matthew certainly didn't.

The thoughts swirled around in my head until we touched down at Hanscom Field with a slight bump.

"Jet is ready to go," Hiroyuki said as the door was being opened by the RCU agent, and we all filed out.

You okay in there? I asked Casimir.

I will manage, Casimir said.

I jogged across the airfield, following Nadia and Hiroyuki, the latter escorting Tobias, as we boarded the jet and got comfortable on one of the eight seats inside. It was only an hour or so flight to Massena International Airport, but it was long enough to switch the lights off above me and have a snooze. I got the feeling it would be a while before I had another.

I woke with another jolt, finding Nadia playing a complicated card game on a table next to me, while Hiroyuki had his knives out on a table further down the fuselage and was busy cleaning them.

"Good game?" I asked Nadia as the jet slowed to a halt.

"Made it up as I went," she said with a smile. "Passed the time, though."

The airport exit was far from where we were. It was a mass of light in the distance, and I wondered exactly where this car was going to be waiting for us. I was also surprised to discover that Massena International Airport was in fact really small. Just from the name, I expected it to be a thriving hub of airplanes, but I'd been very much mistaken.

The jet door was opened and the three of us stepped down onto the tarmac, where a man in a dark blue suit waited for us next to what looked like a large golf cart. "I am here to take you to your car," the man said. "Feel free to take your phones with you."

Hiroyuki and I exchanged a look of confusion but didn't argue.

"Madam," the man said to Nadia.

"Douchebag," Nadia replied with a similar courtesy.

"Any phone?" the man asked.

"I already left it in Boston," Nadia said.

The man nodded a thank you, although he was clearly bristly about Nadia's attitude. We all got onto the golf cart to be driven away from the exit toward a hangar in the distance. Outside of the hanger was a large black helicopter. The man stopped the golf cart outside the open hanger and motioned for us to get off.

"The pilot will be with you soon," the man said, and drove the golf cart back across the runway.

"Guess we just wait, then," Hiroyuki said.

It took a few minutes for the two pilots to leave the hangar and walk over to us. Both were men, both over six feet tall, and both already had on their flight gear.

"You know where we're going?" I asked.

"You'll find out in the air," one of the pilots said. "Climb aboard."

We all did as we were told, with Tobias sitting across from Hiroyuki and beside Nadia in the five-leather-seat configuration in the rear of the helicopter.

"Are these still necessary?" Tobias asked, raising his hands to show the cuffs. "I'm your prisoner. I have no intention of doing anything to jeopardise my life. It's quite precious to me."

"Yes," Nadia, Hiroyuki, and I said in unison.

When we get to wherever we're going, I'll let you out, I telepathically said to Casimir. *Track us as well as you can.*

I'll do what I can, Casimir replied.

I removed the tracker from my jeans pocket, activated it, and put it back. The fact that we hadn't been searched led me to believe that they weren't that concerned about us being tracked. It meant that they probably had a plan or they didn't care. Neither option was a good one.

"You ready?" one of the pilots called back to me.

"Sure," I shouted back, walking over to the helicopter and climbing aboard. The four of us all wore headsets as the pilots started the engine.

"You okay?" Hiroyuki asked me.

"As well as can be," I said as the wheels left the tarmac. "Let's go hand me over to the bad guys."

CHAPTER TWENTY-TWO

S o, you feel like telling us where we're going?" I asked the pilots after we'd been flying for a few minutes.

"Greater Sudbury Airport," one of them said, I didn't know or care which.

"Okay, and then what?" I replied.

"We drop you and Tobias off," the pilot said. "We take the other two back here. That's all we've been paid to do."

"Greater Sudbury again?" Nadia asked.

"You've been before?" Hiroyuki asked me.

I nodded. "Callie set up a science station there, murdered a bunch of people, did experiments on some more, and was generally a monster. Nothing new."

We all returned to being quiet. The lights in the rear of the helicopter were off, and while there was a small light at the headrest of each seat, it wasn't bright.

"How long have you worked for Matthew?" Nadia asked Tobias, hitting the back of his headrest when he didn't answer.

"I work for many people," Tobias said with a sigh of irritation. "Matthew has employed my talents many times over the years."

"Of killing people and becoming them," Hiroyuki said.

"Humans," Tobias said. "Only humans. I can't do it to rift-fused."

"You ever tried?" Nadia asked, sounding genuinely curious.

"Yes," Tobias said. "I thought my head might explode."

"So, you kill humans, become them, and then what?" Nadia asked him.

"Usually, I sign forms, transfer money through banks, change wills, you know, that kind of thing," Tobias said.

"So, rich assholes employ you to make sure they stay rich or get richer," Nadia said.

"That about sums it up, yes," Tobias said. "Sometimes, governments use me to start or end political strife. More than one used me to assassinate someone they didn't like, or someone who was causing problems. I had to fix an election a few years back. That was fun."

"You really like your job, don't you?" Hiroyuki said.

"Love it," Tobias said, sounding genuinely enthused.

"Who told you that Dani was back from the rift?" I asked.

"What?" Tobias replied.

We'd been quiet again for several minutes, and I decided that despite Tobias being a massive psychopath, it was now or never to get any information that might help.

"Dani came back from the rift," I said. "You turned up at her parents' house with Matthew looking for her. At Anthony's work. You knew she was back. How?"

"You really want to know?" Tobias asked. "I'm quite proud of it."

"I doubt he would have asked if he didn't want to know," Hiroyuki said.

"We knew that Dani was taken into the rift after the car accident," Tobias said. "The RCU had a file on it, and Callie's friends owned the RCU. Not officially, but they had enough friends working there. And we have people in the rift who keep an eye on such matters, so we knew it was only a matter of time before she came back to Earth."

"Why not take her back by force?" Hiroyuki asked.

"She was living in a village," Tobias said. "There was a possibility of her abduction getting . . . messy. Besides, what use is a rift-walker who can't open a tear? We have to wait for them to become . . . useful."

The way Tobias said *useful* made me want to punch him in the face.

"Anyway," Tobias continued. "We were looking for rift-walkers for . . . well, for Callie. And we used an online message board frequented by . . . shall we say anti-rift-fused, asking people to contact us if they knew of any."

"Like Sovereign Humanity?" I asked, remembering the group of anti-rift-fused assholes who had been involved in the murder of a friend of mine.

"Yeah, we helped set that group up," Tobias said. "Put people in charge who knew how to round up those hate-filled little people who wanted someone else to blame for their shit-heap of a life. Didn't take much to turn it from an idea with a few dozen planted people to something with fifty thousand people, all spewing venom online day after day, feeding one another their poison. It was fucking beautiful. A self-perpetuating machine of hate."

"And then what?" I asked.

"The message board would get tips about rift-walkers," Tobias said. "About a quarter were just made up for laughs, another quarter full of people who was sure celebrity such-and-such must be one, and the rest were genuine tips by angry people. Some were rift-fused, not rift-walkers; some were just assholes wanting revenge on their exes or boss or some shit, thinking we were going to burst through their door at three in the morning like SWAT."

"And in Dani's case?" Nadia asked.

"Just after Dani came back, she went for a run, bumped into an ex-boyfriend of hers who had been dumped just before she vanished," Tobias said. "He tried to rekindle, she told him to piss off, he took that personally. He was a nasty little one. I personally understood why Dani dumped him and why he remained single. He left a message on the board, Dani's name, address, things like that. We found out that Dani was real, that her case was real, and that she was back. Dani's ex-boyfriend made some cash on that tip."

Anger radiated off Nadia, and I glanced over at her and saw her sit back, her arms crossed over her chest, her chains snaking around her.

"Told you it was something to be proud of," Tobias said. "We got angry, hateful little troglodytes to do our hard work."

"I would be quiet now," Hiroyuki said.

"You asked," Tobias snapped.

"Yes, and now I would be quiet," Hiroyuki continued in a tone that suggested great harm would come to Tobias if he failed to follow those instructions.

Tobias snorted and looked out of the window with a shake of his head, and no one else spoke for at least an hour as we continued flying. What had started as an on-and-off drizzle was quickly turning into a downpour. Flying at night during a rainstorm was not a fun experience, but I was grateful we weren't driving. Anyone who has ever aquaplaned a car in the dark can tell you how buttock-clenchingly terrifying it is, even in a car with four-wheel drive.

Another hour passed by with very little comment, which, honestly, I got the impression that Hiroyuki and Nadia were okay with. According to my phone, the flight was about three hours, although that wasn't taking to account the make and model of the helicopter, but it was a good-enough estimate.

"Why did you ransack Abigail's house?" I asked. I hadn't wanted to hear Tobias speak, but I also wanted an answer.

"She was friends with Anthony," Tobias said. "I watched them spend time together, so I needed to know if she had been told anything of use. Found some money in her safe and figured that taking it would help show that Anthony had been caught stealing from her, or wanted the safe combination to get the money in there. But then he ran, and all of my hard work became pointless. Decided to keep the money for my time."

"So long as you weren't out of pocket," I said sarcastically.

"I got to do the two things I love," Tobias said with a smile. "Kill people and make money."

Nadia shifted in her seat and slammed the back of her elbow into Tobias's face. "Slipped," she said as Tobias held his nose.

"We'll be landing soon," one of the pilots said. "We'll refuel and take the two passengers back."

I looked out of the window at the lights from the airport and felt apprehensive about what was going to happen when we reached our destination. Matthew was clearly not going to let Dani and me leave without trouble, no matter if I agreed to help Callie or not.

"We've got some trouble in the airport," the pilot said. "We're going to land, and you all stay seated until we get this sorted."

"What kind of trouble?" I asked, trying to get a good look out of the window.

"They didn't say," the pilot replied, failing to keep the concern out of his voice.

All three of us and Tobias were now trying to get a look out of whatever window we were next to. There wasn't a lot to see, what with the darkness and rain.

"Oh, fucking hell," one of the pilots said.

"What is it?" Hiroyuki asked.

"It's a fiend," the pilot yelled. "It's a massive fucking fiend."

"Get this thing on the ground *now*," I snapped.

The helicopter banked to the right and I finally got a look down at the runway. There were dozens of people illuminated by the lights of the runway itself, and they were fighting . . . something *really* big.

"We're going to have to land a bit away from it," the pilot said, sounding shaky.

"I don't care if you land on the roof," I almost shouted. "Just get us down there."

"Maybe that thing will kill Matthew and we'll all be better off," Nadia said.

"If he dies, so does the chance of getting to the husks," I said. "Or maybe they're linked to him so they go off the second he dies. Can't take the chance."

The helicopter landed with a large bump. "Deal with him," I shouted, pointing at Tobias, before pulling open the door, turning to smoke, and billowing out across the rain-drenched airport runway, toward the sounds of fighting.

I re-formed next to a BMW SUV, identical to the ones that were used in the attack as we travelled from Hamble to Moon Island.

The thing fighting the dozen soldiers ahead looked like a lynx if the lynx was the size of the helicopter I'd just arrived in. The lynx was tan with light blue stripes running down both sides of its ribcage, where large spines jutted out. It had blood around its elongated face, where two large tusks tutted down, one dripping with something I'd rather not think about.

The soldiers had encircled the creature and were jabbing at it with swords and spears, but no one was willing to go forward and kill it.

Matthew stood to the side of the fight, with several wounded on the ground beside him.

"What happened?" I shouted at him.

"Your little friend, Dani, had been opening small tears the entire time we had her," Matthew said. "She let through some things."

There was a loud bang behind me and I turned to see another lynx creature crash into the helicopter, spinning it around and forcing it onto its side. Smoke began to pour from the side of the aircraft.

The creature looked like a tan-and-silver lynx but with pincers that jutted out of a skull too large for the creature. There were spines down its back and more on the back of its tail, making it look like a weird hybrid of a cat and stegosaurus.

The lynx slowly moved back to the helicopter, which exploded, throwing the lynx back across the runway.

"You deal with this one," I said to Matthew as the rear doors of two nearby vans opened and two hulking husks left them. The lynx used the distraction to leap over the soldiers guarding it and sprint flat out across the airport runway toward the woods at the far end.

I looked back at the lynx that had destroyed the helicopter as it stood, shook itself, and looked over at me. One side of its face was a mass of blood and bone, the explosion having torn its face apart. It turned and ran across the airport, through the fence, and into the woods surrounding the airport.

"If you run . . ." Matthew snarled, looking over at the husks and smiling.

"Go fuck yourself," I said, and sprinted over to the helicopter, hoping that my friends were both okay.

I continued on, jumping over the remains of the fence without stopping, moving on into the woods as the sounds of destruction could be heard from up ahead.

I stopped running. "Casimir," I said. "Could use your eyes here."

Casimir leapt out of my coat pocket, turned into a barn owl mid-jump, and soared high above the trees a moment later.

Two hundred meters south, Casimir said. *Hiroyuki and Nadia have engaged the fiend.*

I turned to smoke and moved as quickly as I could though the trees, re-forming a few feet away from Hiroyuki and Nadia, the latter of whom was covered in blood.

"Holy shit, what happened?" I asked.

I followed Nadia's pointing to find a headless Tobias.

"We got out of the helicopter and he was already gone into the woods," Hiroyuki said. "Nadia and I followed him, but that big bastard fiend ran past us just a second ago. We got here just as it tore Tobias's head off."

"He wasn't watching where he was going until it was far too late," Nadia said. "I tried to stop it, but . . . well."

I looked back at the jagged wound across Nadia's stomach. She was lucky not to be disembowelled.

"Fucking hell," Hiroyuki shouted. "Are you okay?"

"It's sore, but it's stopped bleeding," Nadia said. "And I didn't lose my skull, so I'm calling it a win."

The lynx ran back out of the wood and I drew my sword; I guessed there was no time the like present to see if it was going to work.

Hiroyuki drew his sword and stood his ground beside me as the lynx-fiend paced around the outside of the clearing it had created by knocking down trees.

"Go high," I said.

"Done," Nadia replied.

I turned to smoke and moved along the woodland floor, through the fiend's legs, as Nadia and Hiroyuki roared an attack and charged. The lynx-fiend let out a roar of its own and swiped at them with its enormous paws as I re-formed behind its rear legs, cutting through the tendon on one leg with the sword.

Dark, thick blood quickly covered the ground as I turned back to smoke, moved under the fiend's tail, re-formed, and sliced through the tendon in that leg, too.

The fiend was hamstrung now, it couldn't run, it could barely stand. Nadia wrapped her chains around the front left leg of the fiend and pulled. The noise was unpleasant.

Hiroyuki drove his katana up into the throat of the fiend, twisted, and removed it, then stepped aside and tossed a hand-sized ball of ice into the wound.

The fiends head exploded as huge spikes of ice erupted from inside the neck of the creature, which collapsed to the ground and immediately started to dissolve.

"You both good?" I called out.

"Grand," Nadia said. "More covered in blood than before, if that was even possible."

"I need to go stop the other one," I said. "You two need to get out of here. You've done your bit. There's a car rental place just outside the airport. You might want a shower or something first."

Nadia looked like she'd been bathing in blood.

"Already ordered a car," Hiroyuki said. "Did it on the helicopter."

"Are you going to be okay?" Nadia asked me.

I nodded even though I had no idea.

Lucas, Casimir said. *They're hunting the other lynx.*

"Be right there," I said aloud.

"You brought your eidolon," Hiroyuki said.

I nodded. "At first to track Dani, but I'll take anything I can get as an advantage. If I get taken somewhere the tracking doesn't work, or they find it, hopefully Casimir can relay where we are. Or at least tell me where I am."

"If you can get a message to us, we'll come running," Hiroyuki said, offering me his hand, which I shook.

"Wanna hug?" Nadia asked, her arms wide, her grin . . . terrifying, which made me laugh.

"You need to go heal first," I said. "And shower. Lots of showers. Did the pilots make it out?"

Hiroyuki shook his head. "I don't think so; we were already gone before the lynx attacked it."

"Get back to Moon Island," I said. "Kill those husks before they can hurt anyone. I'll be fine."

"I need you to know something," Nadia said sadly. "This is where my chains stop involving you."

"How long have you known?" I asked.

"Few days," Nadia said. "It's why I've been trying to stay away."

"I'll be fine," I told her.

"No, Lucas," Nadia said. "You won't. Whatever happens is going to be bad."

There's an exit to the west of here, takes you deeper into the forest, but then it circles around to the highway, Casimir said. *It's not going to be fun, but it'll be safe.*

I relayed the information to Hiroyuki.

"Be safe, my friend," Hiroyuki said.

"You too," I told him.

I held out a hand for Nadia, which she took, her chains snaking around my body, hugging me.

I watched the pair of them walk away through the woods, and I wasn't sure that I was going to see them again anytime soon, and sadness filled me.

It was fleeting, though, as I still had another greater fiend to deal with before dealing with an even larger monster . . . Callie Mitchell.

CHAPTER TWENTY-THREE

I sprinted through the dark woods, back toward the runway and the inferno that used to be the helicopter we'd arrived on.

I saw no evidence of either pilot, but I didn't have time to check. I moved beyond the ruined aircraft, turned to smoke, and flew across the tarmac of the runway, moving as quickly as possible.

It didn't take long to hit the trees opposite where the second lynx had gone, to hear the shouting of soldiers, the occasional gunfire. I continued on into the woods, pushing myself to stay in smoke form as much as possible. Sooner or later, I'd be too exhausted to keep it up, and I didn't want to get to that point.

I re-formed deep in the forest, to the sounds of gunshots in the distance. I took the tracker that Ji-hyun had given me and placed it in my belt between the buckle and loop of leather above it. At some point, I imagined I was going to get searched, and hoped they wouldn't find it there.

The sound of gunfire was louder now, and I continued on toward it. Hopefully, the lynx fiend had found them and was making them regret their life choices.

I unsheathed the spear from my back and moved low through the forest. Someone had opened fire with a semi-automatic weapon, having clearly decided that the shotguns weren't getting the job done. I stopped next to a large tree and watched three soldiers in formation, marching toward the lynx, firing their weapons, and reloading when empty, to continue the onslaught. The lynx roared in pain as one of the bullets from the rift-tempered guns took a charge. A second bullet removed a portion of the animal's skull, continued on, and hit the tree close to me, causing it to explode from the impact. Sometimes, a bullet took too much charge. Another reason to be wary of rift-tempered firearms.

The lynx lunged, catching the closest soldier off balance and almost cutting him in half with the creature's huge claws. All while the other two contained to unload more and more rounds into the seriously injured fiend.

Two more soldiers entered the fight from the other side, both using poles with ties on the end to try and get the lynx down to the ground. Apparently, the amount of damage the creature had been able to sustain and still function had taken it from a kill to a capture.

A quick turn to smoke, and I moved up one of the larger trees, re-forming on a branch high above, giving me an excellent view of the terrain below. I had to make myself known to Matthew at some point, but I wanted to know what I was letting myself in for, and this seemed like as good a time as any.

There was movement to the right of me, and I spotted torches being switched off as they closed in. To the far left of me were four vehicles: two Range Rovers and two vans. I moved through the trees, staying in smoke form as I did so, wanting to make sure that I wasn't spotted, until I sat over the vehicles. There was still firing and shouting from the lynx fight, as whoever had decided to make it a capture and not a kill had made it a hundred times harder.

The side-panel doors on the vans opened and two husks got out of each. They moved through the vegetation as though it wasn't there, and I followed from above. Part of me just wanted to see how they fared against a highly aggressive greater fiend. Would the claws of that animal do damage to them? Or was it just primordials?

I found a branch just far enough away to not be directly above the lynx as it fought against those who had wrapped tethers around its neck and legs. It jerked one leg so violently that it picked the soldier off the ground and threw him against a nearby tree. He vanished from view for a moment before coming back to the fight, this time having used his power as a spined revenant, firing spikes from his body at the fiend. The spines struck home along the legs and belly of the fiend, the scream of which echoed through the forest.

"Callie wants it taken alive," Matthew shouted as he strolled into the area flanked by the two husks I'd seen earlier. "What part of that don't you understand? Let go of it," Matthew commanded, although I didn't see who he was talking to.

The tethers on the lynx slackened and the creature pounced at Matthew, only to be practically caught in mid-air by a husk as it slammed one huge fist into the side of the fiend's head, sending it careering off against a nearby tree.

The greater fiend got back to its feet and rushed the husk. The animal was already missing a part of its head and was covered in a variety of bullet holes, its entire back and sides drenched in blood, but it still was not going down without a fight.

The lynx avoided another blow and clamped down with its jaws on the shoulder and neck of the husk, which made a noise like fingernails on a chalkboard. The husk started to punch the lynx in the head, but the greater fiend hung on, shaking the husk around. Greater fiends didn't normally take so much damage before stopping, or at least slowing down, and I wondered if a rift-walker tear allowed in a more potent form of rift energy. It was certainly possible, as a tear from a rift-walker that wasn't controlled could do serious damage to the world around it. My memory bounced back to the almost-destroyed house in England not long before, when a rift-walker lost all control of their power.

"Goddamn it," Matthew shouted, and dialled a phone number as the husk and greater fiend continued to fight.

"It won't go down," Matthew said. "I don't know, I don't care. It's killing our people. It's killing people I trained. That costs time and money. Neither of which we have an infinite amount of."

A pause.

"Good choice." Matthew hung up, turned to the two husks beside him, neither of whom had done anything to intervene in helping the other husk fight the greater fiend. "Kill it. Bring its head back to the van."

I looked back over at the husks, which swarmed the lynx greater fiend, and in moments, it was dead. There was a noise I'd rather not have heard, and one of the husks carried the decapitated head of the greater fiend back to the van.

Just like the other lynx greater fiend, the body of the one below me quickly started to dissolve. Judging from the amount of cold air pouring out of the open van, I figured that was a problem that Callie had managed to solve.

"What about Lucas?" one of the soldiers asked, instantly taking me away from the scene at the van as Matthew had remained by the dissolving remains of the greater fiend, the four husks motionless around it. All wore similar masks to the ones I'd seen already, although one of them still had a mask that was broken. Maybe it was the one I'd broken? It felt like a lifetime before, although in reality it had only been a few days.

Matthew looked around him. "Lucas, are you out there? Can you hear me?"

I dropped from the tree, turned to smoke, and re-formed on the ground. "I'm here," I said, raising my hands when several guns were pointed in my direction.

"Enjoy the show?" Matthew asked.

"Just wanted to see how you coped," I said, looking over at the husks to find the one with the broken mask staring at me with nothing but hatred in its one visible eye.

"It remembers you hitting it," Matthew said with a laugh. "So, are you impressed?"

"You should have just killed it and been done," I said.

"I agree," Matthew said, and sighed. "But Callie pays the bills, so what she wants, she gets."

"Tobias is dead," I said. "Sorry."

Matthew looked up at the sky. "That's annoying. Did you do it?"

"The other lynx bit his head off," I said. "Nothing to do with me."

"And your friends?" Matthew asked.

"They've gone," I said. "We both know that you were going to try to kill them."

"I wasn't," Matthew said, sounding a little affronted. "You have a very low opinion of me."

"You're a murderer," I said, looking around at the soldiers. "Never took you for a soldier, though. So, are we going via car?"

"No," Matthew said. "Let's go get ready, everyone."

Matthew escorted me back through the woods to the airport, where I was told to sit and behave while his people went about the task of preparing the Learjet as it taxied out of the hangar. The runway was cleared of debris and the helicopter dragged off to one side.

Two soldiers stood watching me the whole time, with many more close by, near the BMWs and Range Rovers they'd brought with them.

Hiroyuki and Nadia got away, Casimir said.

Thank you for letting me know, I said.

I'll track you as best I can, but you're going to be in a jet, Casimir continued. *And I can't hide on your person like before, if they have a chained revenant or someone who can sense me.*

It's okay, I said. *You'll find me.*

Good luck, Lucas, Casimir said.

Matthew returned to me as the jet taxied onto the runway. "Weapons, coat, turn it all over."

Two soldiers pointed guns at me, while two more shouted orders about me removing my weapons.

"Don't all yell at once," I said, shrugging off my coat.

One of the soldiers snapped forward to grab my arm, and I pushed his hand away, grabbing it and twisting it into a painful position.

"I wouldn't," I said.

"You'll be dead," one of the soldiers told me.

"You couldn't take down a greater fiend with that piece of shit," Matthew snapped, slapping the soldier around the back of the head. "You're not killing a riftborn with it. Especially not a Talon. You don't have your mask, Lucas."

"I haven't worn it on a regular basis for a while now," I admitted as I placed my coat on the floor and put my sword and spear on top of it.

"That all?" Matthew asked.

I turned around with my hands raised, showing that it was.

Matthew picked up the spear. "Nice craftsmanship," he said, turning it over. "What is this substance?"

"No idea," I said. "The RCU has a blacksmith who makes custom stuff. Seems to be pretty good, though." Matthew Pierce was the last person I wanted to inform about how primordial bone killed husks.

"And the little thing on the side of the spear?" Matthew asked. "This compartment?"

"Aesthetic choice," I said.

"It is rift-tempered?" he asked.

"Stab yourself with it and find out," I told him.

Matthew laughed and passed the spear to one of the soldiers, while another picked up my coat and sword, taking all of them to the jet.

"I get to keep them?" I asked.

"You get to bring them with you," Matthew said. "Callie's orders. You play nice, you get them all back. You don't . . . well, I imagine losing your weapons will be the least of your problems."

I was marched toward the jet, the door of which was down, and ordered to get on.

The jet inside had seating for eight, four seats facing one another with a table in between. There was a door at the end with a toilet sign on it next to another door. Three of the seats already had soldiers sat in them.

"What about the husks?" I asked, my question almost immediately answered as two husks entered the jet—one of which had the broken mask—and made their way to the back, through the unmarked door, and into what appeared to be a larger version of the van set-up. One of the soldiers entered the area, then closed the door before I could see more.

Matthew took the spear from the bundle of my stuff that had been placed behind the seat I sat in. He sat opposite me, still holding the spear, and placed the tip against my throat. "You know, I've always wanted a rematch."

"Anytime," I said, keeping my eyes on him, trying my best to ignore the spear. Matthew wasn't going to kill me. Not now.

Matthew stepped toward me, keeping the spear-tip against my neck. "I fucking hate you, you know that, right?"

"You're a murderer," I said. "A psychopath who likes torturing people for fun. A man who gets off on the fear in the eyes of the helpless. Do I look afraid to you, Matthew? Do I look helpless? You prey on those you deem weaker than yourself. You're just a bully and a coward."

Matthew's eyes radiated rage, and his grip tightened on the spear. "So smug and superior. So sure of yourself and your abilities. You know, I went to become a member of a Guild and they just shot me down. They might as well have laughed at me. Well, the Hawks didn't laugh when I killed one of them and took their precious medallion. That Talon didn't laugh when I gutted her. I am better than you all."

"They refused to take you because you're a psychopath," I said. "Or sociopath; I forget which one you are. You like hurting people. You like feeling someone else's life in your hands. You killed them to prove a point to yourself and just ended up proving their point."

"I would have killed you if you hadn't ambushed me," Matthew said, lowering the spear and placing it back with everything else of mine.

"Keep telling yourself that," I said. "So, what happens with the husks in Boston?"

"I'll sort those out in a few hours," Matthew said. "No point in giving the RCU a helping hand."

"Where's Dani?" I asked.

"She's where you're going," Matthew said as the door closed and was checked over by another soldier before she took a seat adjacent to mine. "Any other questions?"

I shook my head.

"I have one for you," Matthew said. "Callie told me you're from Carthage. Before it was turned to ash by my ancestors."

"Yes," I said. "I assume you've never been."

"No, before my time," Matthew said. "I do know a riftborn who enjoyed hunting around the area, though."

"Lots of animals there," I said before I caught his meaning. "You mean hunting people."

"I do," Matthew said with a smile. "He taught me everything he knew about hunting people. About making them hurt. I imagine he probably killed a few people you know."

"I imagine you should shut up before you lose some teeth," I said with a smile of my own.

I felt a sharp pain in my neck. I spun around to ask the soldier behind me what was going on and found my head swimming.

"Callie is a practitioner," Matthew said with a beaming smile as I crashed to my knees. "She conjured up something to help you enjoy the trip."

"I think we may have used too much," one of the soldiers said.

My head swam and everything blurred as I reached out to take hold of Matthew, who kicked my hand away and smashed me in the face with the butt of my spear, knocking me out cold.

CHAPTER TWENTY-FOUR

I woke up on a hospital bed in what was clearly a medical facility. I wasn't handcuffed or shackled in any way. I sat up and immediately wished I hadn't. There was an air-conditioning unit that made a rattling sound, and almost-freezing-cold air washed through the room.

My second attempt at sitting confirmed that I was the only occupant of the room that had six beds. The blinds along a set of windows next to the only door were pulled shut. I turned to look out of one of three windows behind me and saw a thick line of tall trees in the distance, with just wide-open space between me and them. No way to make that distance over flat land without someone noticing. There appeared to be marshland in the distance.

There was nothing that told me where I was. I could have been in a million cities in a dozen countries. It was raining, which wasn't exactly helpful either.

All I knew was I wasn't where I fell, and I had no idea how long I'd been out or where I'd ended up.

The door opened and two soldiers came in, both pointing guns at me, which I was sure made them feel better about their life choices.

Callie Mitchell came in behind them.

The last time I'd spoken to Callie had been just after killing the monster that Mason Barnes—a spoiled rich dickhead—had turned himself into via one of the concoctions that Callie had made. Before then, it was when I was in her company for several weeks, watching her "work." *Torture people* would be a more accurate term.

"Lucas Rurik," Callie said. Callie looked to be about forty, although her real age was at least several hundreds of years older. She had long dark hair that had red streaks through it of various shades, piercing blue eyes, and olive skin. She had a sleeve of tattoos on her arms, depicting the birds of each Guild. The raven was wrapped around the wrist on her right hand, and it made me just as angry to see it as it had the first time I'd seen it.

"Callie Mitchell," I said.

"Doctor," she admonished.

"Fuck off," I said with a smile that practically dared her to argue. "Doctors help people. When was the last time you helped someone?"

"Still got that anger in you, I see," Callie said with a smile of her own. "I have not had you harmed in any way. You are free to walk about the facility as you see fit. You are my guest here."

"Also your prisoner," I said.

"Well, I can't have you getting out of here to bring the RCU or Guilds down on my head," she said. "I'm too close now. You should know we found the tracker and destroyed it."

That was to be expected but no less bad news. "Close to what?" I asked.

"All will be revealed," she said. "In the meantime, I'm going to show you around the facility. Including your bedroom. Like I said, you are a guest here."

"Yeah, you're going to have to do better than that," I said. "I handed myself over to you in exchange for death not being unleashed on Boston. Where is Dani?"

"All will be answered," Callie said.

"Fine," I said. "So, where is *here*?"

"South-east Texas," Callie said.

"Texas?" I almost shouted. "You've taken me to Texas?"

"We're close to the Sabine National Forest," Callie said. "Near Louisiana, if you didn't know."

"Thanks for the geography lesson," I said. "Why am I in Texas?"

"That's where my facility is," Callie said as if I'd just asked something mindbogglingly stupid. "You'll see why later; come, let's look around."

"I'd like a change of clothing," I said. "Also, how long was I out?"

"Five hours or so," she said. "You woke up in the jet and had to be put back under again. You've been here about an hour, give or take. We'll stop at your room first; you can use the bathroom and get changed."

"Into one of your skinsuits?" I asked, putting as much venom into *skinsuits* as I possibly could.

"No," Callie said. "They proved unreliable. No, now we use a more simplified version. I'll show you."

"You're being awful nice, considering the last time we spoke, I told you I was going to find you and kill you," I said. "Paraphrasing."

"I believe that you and I want the same thing, Lucas," she said. "The betterment of rift-fused."

She had me there.

"You torture people," I said as we walked down a hallway with windows on one side, looking over the same view I'd had from my hospital bed. "Your betterment is to physically change things whether they want changing or not."

"My *betterment*," Callie said, "is to find a way to overcome the limits placed on us. I am a practitioner, yet I can't go back through the rift without a rift-walker to open a tear. You are a riftborn; you can come and go between Earth and the rift as you please, but when you die, you don't get to go spend your life in Inaxia. You just die. We all have weaknesses. I aim to remove them. To give us all a level playing field. To stop the Ancients from being able to rule us from afar as if deities. I assume you want the same."

"I want people to stop justifying shitty behaviour by saying they're doing it for the greater good," I said. "When you're actually doing it for your own benefit. Admit it."

We continued on in silence, allowing me to take in my surroundings. There was yellow lighting in the floors and ceilings, giving everything a warm glow that reminded me of the lights I'd found in the rift.

Most of the dozen doors we walked by were closed, and with no windows, it was impossible to know what they were, but the further along the circular hallway we walked, the more were open, revealing bedrooms and guards.

Callie stopped at the end of the hall, four doors away from a wooden door with a glass middle that said EXIT on it in big green letters.

"Your room," Callie said, pushing the door open and allowing me inside.

"So, how do you stop everyone's power?" I asked.

Callie pointed to the lighting in the ceiling. "Try to use your power."

I couldn't access it. I concentrated, and nothing.

I looked up at the lights. "The yellow lighting," I said. "It stops me from accessing my power, but it doesn't feel shut off."

Callie removed a set of keys from her pocket, with a black fob attached to it. "You need one of these," she said. "Please shower and change, and I will be back later to collect you. You're free to move about the facility, but anywhere marked *no entry* I would pay attention to. I don't want to have to bury you somewhere on the bayou."

Callie closed the door on her way out, leaving me alone in a small bedroom with a chest of drawers, a wardrobe, a TV on the wall, and air-conditioning pumping out of vents in the ceiling. A window beside the bed looked down on the centre of a huge circular structure where I was. Apparently, they'd made some kind of big doughnut-shaped building for people to live in. I wondered where the scientific facilities were.

I opened the chest of drawers and removed a T-shirt from among a dozen of them, a pair of jeans, and some clean socks and underwear. It was frightening that they'd gotten my size right, although the realization that they'd found the tracker and removed it wasn't a fun one. No cavalry coming.

The wardrobe had several shirts of a variety of colours, and I picked a black one, along with some thick-looking boots. I checked everything for bugs, seeing how they appeared to have a liking to using them, but there was nothing. I grabbed a towel from the chest of drawers and opened the nearby door, which triggered an automatic light.

The shower was good, although I felt like it shouldn't have been. Evil people shouldn't be making you feel welcome. I got out, got dried and dressed, and lay on my bed for a while, trying to figure out what I was going to do next. I had no way of contacting anyone, no way of telling them exactly where I was except *south-east Texas*. And the last time I checked, Texas was really bloody huge.

I got up, put my boots on, grabbed a small black jacket, and left my bedroom, finding two guards stood directly outside.

"Can I ask where you'd like to go?" one of the guards asked.

"Callie said I could look around," I told him. "Figured I may as well take her up on it."

"I think for now, it would be best that you wait," the guard told me. "She won't be long."

"Very welcoming," I told them both. "Good job."

I stepped back into my room and closed the door. *Casimir, any chance you can hear me?* I asked. I wasn't entirely sure what I was expecting. There was no chance that Casimir was going to be able to catch up with me after I'd been taken on a jet. Even so, it was disheartening to not hear anything back.

There was a knock on the bedroom door, and it opened a moment later, with Callie stood there. She'd put on a pair of jeans, an aqua-blue jumper, and a pair of trainers. For when you want to be a mass murderer but you want to look casual.

"I'm going to take you to get some food," she said. "I thought we could continue our discussion."

I left the room, and after walking through the facility for a while longer, we ended up on the first floor in an empty canteen.

"We have three of these," Callie said as if I should be impressed. "But I thought we could talk somewhere quieter."

"Where's my stuff?" I asked.

"Your weapons?" Callie replied. "You won't need them."

"Need isn't the reason I asked," I explained. "They have sentimental value."

Callie stopped walking and stared at me. "I guess we could eat in my office. Come."

She took off without waiting for a reply, and I hurried to catch up as she walked out into a large open room with dozens of models of airplanes and military vehicles hanging from the ceiling. I stopped and looked around. There were plinths with tiny models of Inaxia, and Harmony, and a diorama of the Tempest, complete with pulsating lights within.

"Officially, this is a military installation," Callie said. "We do work on a variety of different machines. It's what pays the bills, so to speak. After you apprehended the Croupier and ended our income, we had to think outside of the box. The art on the plinths has always been here. They help me remember."

"Remember what?" I asked, walking over to the wall at the far side of the room, where someone had painted a fairly accurate map of the rift.

"Why I do this," Callie said. "Why we all do this. Come, we'll go to one of the apartments in the complex and we'll talk more."

I tore myself away from the detailed artwork and walked with Callie out of the building. We walked across a large car park with chain-link fence all around it. There were guards atop watchtowers, and I had momentary flashbacks to my time at the "hospital" that Callie had been in charge of.

It was muggy out, the closeness of the air and the soft drizzle mixing together to create something unpleasant, oppressive.

We walked around to the side of the doughnut-shaped building and into a four-storey, red-brick building with a flat roof. Callie said nothing as we walked inside and up to the top floor, which had only one door on it and a lift.

Callie used a key card to unlock the door and opened it, welcoming me into her home as the two guards stood in the hallway and watched the door close with a less-than-happy expression.

"I'll have my chef bring the food here," Callie said as I looked around the large living space with ornate golden statues of birds, and paintings of birds, and the occasional stuffed bird mounted to the wall.

The large windows opposite the front door let in a huge amount of light and showed the landscape of bayou, trees, and grassland. There was nothing else for miles except for the dotting of buildings inside the perimeter.

"So, you like birds," I said, turning to look at a golden eagle that was actually made from gold. It had ruby eyes. It was quite possibly the most hideous thing I've ever seen. I know art is subjective, but damn.

"The Guilds fascinate me," Callie said. "Always have. The fact that they're named after birds, the fact that you wear those medallions, that you were the closest thing to law and order for the rift-fused for centuries. The fact that none of you did anything to ever try to make things better."

"Make things better?" I asked. "You mean overthrow the Primes?"

Callie paused then, possibly wondering exactly how much I knew about her involvement in the rebellion in Inaxia so many years before. "We could have done it," Callie said eventually.

"No," I told her. "No, you couldn't. You wanted to kill the Primes; in fact, you had Prime Roberts on your side to do just that. Right until he betrayed you all and got you kicked out of the rift."

Callie stared at me for several seconds while I tried to figure out if she knew about Prime Roberts, about his betrayal, about him having an illegitimate son who went by the name of Jacob Smythe—the Croupier.

"Roberts did not betray me," Callie said eventually. "I was always aware of what he was doing. We could not win. We would have been executed. He saved our lives."

"By getting you all banished?" I asked. "By hiding the fact that one of you was his son? By making people believe that someone else was responsible?"

"Yes," Callie said. "Roberts did all of those things. He was right to do them. If we'd had Guild help, maybe we would have won and Inaxia would be in a different place now. It doesn't matter. I'm not interested in vengeance."

"What are you interested in?" I asked.

"The betterment of rift-fused," Callie said. "Like I told you."

"And to do that, you're going to create husks," I said. "And fiend-human hybrids, and . . . do what exactly?"

There was a knock at the door and Callie barked at them to enter. Half a dozen staff strolled in with three carts before beginning to unload everything and set it up on the large table at the side of the room. It was more food than two people could eat; it was more than six could eat.

"Are we having guests?" I asked.

"No," Callie said, shaking the hands of the help. "I didn't know what you'd like, so I had them make a little of everything."

"Thanks," I said to everyone as they left, and looked at the mixture of burgers, sushi, various pasta dishes, rice dishes, and stews. It all smelled amazing.

"There is dessert," Callie said, pointing to a cart that had been left behind. "Please sit."

There are many things I've learned over my exceptionally long life, but one of the most valuable is *eat when you can*. It's a lesson that served me well on several occasions. If someone is offering you food and you think it's safe, eat it. You might regret not eating it later.

I sat at the table, grabbed some Mongolian lamb—according to the little card that was sat alongside it—and spooned it into my bowl along with some rice. It was delicious.

"Why aren't I dead?" I asked after eating enough food to feel content. "You can't seriously believe that I will just forget about everything you've done? About the people you've hurt? You don't think I'm just going to work with you, do you?"

"Not really," Callie said. "I'd hoped you might see that we share an aim, but we approach it from different points. You're alive because, honestly, it's better than you being dead right now."

"What does that mean?" I asked.

"For several years, we have been working on gaining as many rift-walkers as possible," Callie said, using a knife and fork to eat a burger. "At first, we paid for their help; we put out feelers to those we knew existed and asked for them to help in return for large financial payments. Which we honoured. But it became apparent that the few dozen we found were not going to be enough, so we began to take what wasn't offered freely. We currently have forty-nine rift-walkers working for us. About half of them are here under what you would consider duress."

"You kidnapped twenty-five rift-walkers?" I asked. "And no one noticed?"

"The RCU was fractured; the Ancients believe in themselves more than the greater good," Callie said. "All rift-walkers will have spent time in the rift learning about their abilities; they will have seen how they are treated as little more than a commodity. Upon returning to Earth, most keep to themselves. Rift-walkers are secretive, there's no list giving numbers or locations, there's no way of knowing who is a rift-walker unless they decide to tell you. Twenty-five rift-walkers throughout North America isn't as difficult as it sounds."

"So, Dani was what, the fiftieth?" I asked. "Is she okay?"

Callie nodded. "When Noah became involved, it became more difficult to acquire her but not impossible. When *you* became involved . . . well, at first, I was concerned. You and I have . . . history. But it turns out you have something I need, and you have a desire to protect people from harm."

"And Dani?" I asked.

"She is fine," Callie said. "We do not torture the people who work here."

"What about those masks I saw on the rift-walker in Harmony?" I asked.

"Ah, well, some people respond more to a stick than a carrot," Callie said. "The masks go on the ones who have shown to be . . . difficult. If they behave, the mask comes off."

"Speaking of protecting people," I said, feeling revolted in the way Callie and her staff thought of treating people, "what about those creatures in Boston?"

"Don't worry," Callie said. "I wouldn't let Matthew open any of the cages. Your friends found two of the husks and killed them. They appear to have a weapon that allows them to do this. Something you helped with, I assume?"

I shrugged. "Always nice to even the odds," I said. "Why am I here?"

"Ah, yes, the big question," Callie said. "You are here because I need your help in the rift," she said. "We'd placed video motion sensors in those lights at the camp in Harmony. I saw you walking around; I saw you talking to that primordial. You appeared to be friendly."

"I'm not going to get you a primordial to hurt," I said, suddenly angry at the thought of it.

"No," Callie said, waving away my concerns. "You're going to make sure the primordials stay away from us when we launch our assault."

CHAPTER TWENTY-FIVE

The last bit of talking that Callie had done had given a lot of info, and it took me a few seconds to rattle it around my brain. "Let me get this straight," I said eventually. "You want me to keep the primordials happy while you march an army through Harmony?"

"Basically," Callie said.

"I'm friends with one primordial," I said. "They're not a single organism."

"Oh, I know," Callie said. "But you're going to talk to your friend, and together you're going to keep my people protected."

"Or what?" I asked.

"There are still husks in Boston," Callie said with a smile. "And we still have Dani and others. It would be irritating to start executing them, but technically we don't *need* fifty rift-walkers."

"Have you listened to yourself?" I asked.

"I am pragmatic about what I *require* from you, Mister Rurik," Callie said, anger leaking from her words. "We're going to open a tear into the rift, march my people in, and take control of the Tempest."

"I'm sorry, what?" I asked. "You can't *control* the Tempest. It's a mass of power."

"We can and will," Callie said. "The Tempest controls the tears; it controls who gets what power levels and when. It controls who becomes rift-fused. I aim to *control* it."

"There's no way the Gates of the Maelstrom and the two garrisons at the wall are going to allow that," I said.

"Hence the army," Callie said with a smile. "We will take control of the Tempest, we will set up a defensive position around the mountain, and we will eventually be able to stop the random tears, the random power given out to those who are *unworthy*. We will be able to say who is healed, who is made riftborn, who is made revenant."

I was dumbfounded. It was one of the most insane and, frankly, monstrous ideas I'd ever heard of. To control the Tempest itself, to have power over the lives of people who might become revenants and riftborn.

"And then what?" I asked.

"What?" Callie replied.

"And. Then. What?" I repeated. "You take the Tempest; you have control over the tears, over who on Earth is given power to live. What happens next? You just live under a mountain?"

"No," Callie said with a smile. "We are going to create a city outside of the mountains. A city to rival Inaxia. A city of freedom, and the new seat of power in the rift."

"And how does Prime Roberts feel about this plan?" I asked. "You creating a power to rival Inaxia and all?"

Callie's smile was unpleasant. "This was our plan all along."

I sat back and looked at Callie as things started to slot into place. "You needed an army," I said. "You couldn't make one in the rift. You can't create husks with humans while in the rift, and you can't create your human-fiend monsters. You needed to be on Earth to get a steady supply of humans, to take rift-walkers without being easily caught. You made rift-walkers, too, didn't you? When you said you took them, some of them were human. You kidnapped humans and forced them to become husks and rift-walkers. You must have kidnapped hundreds of humans to do that."

"A few thousand over several decades," Callie said. "Most died. We didn't take anyone who would be missed. Criminals, people who no one cared about or what happened to them. It wasn't difficult."

"All of that couldn't be done in the rift," I said. "But you've been here hundreds of years. Valentina Ermilova."

Callie laughed. "I haven't heard that name in a while. Ah, I needed a new name for a while as a few people were beginning to remember Callie Mitchell. And yes, we needed to be on Earth, but we needed money and power, both of which take time to build up. It was even harder when people like Jacob weren't told the plan and just let their resentment fester. Stupid prick. All he had to do was bring me that rift-walker he'd found, and we never would have needed Dani and we'd have been done by now. The rift would have a glorious new city."

"How are you going to build a city?" I asked.

"We have people who work construction here, with the buildings being taken into the rift to be put up," Callie said. "It's a bit like how houses come in pieces these days. It's all being done underground. The facility stretches for three miles under here, and there are several floors. I'll take you to see the facility tomorrow."

"You forced humans to become rift-walkers and husks; you're going to invade the rift, kill a lot of people, all so you can give Prime Roberts his own city," I said. "Sounds like this benefits him a lot more than anyone else."

Callie walked over to the cart, lifted the lid, and removed a tub of ice cream before returning to her seat, opening the tub, and taking a big spoonful. "Does it?" she asked eventually.

"Let me guess: Prime Roberts is going to have a sudden and terrible case of being accidentally stabbed to death?" I asked.

"It depends on how it goes," Callie said. "He's really quite useful, but I have allies on Earth who care little for him. They get to decide what happens to Roberts; besides, a man with an ego that large can't be trusted to run a city well. I wouldn't trust him to run a 7-Eleven."

"On that point, we agree," I said. "Who's your backer, then?"

"Now, that's information I'm not going to give you," Callie said. "I can't. Not yet. Maybe you'll meet them. Maybe they'll decide whether you live or die."

"You need me to march you and your people through Harmony to the Tempest," I said. "You're worried the primordials who left you alone when you weren't a bother are going to become a very real threat when you are."

Callie said nothing.

Something dawned on me. "The husk the primordial killed," I said. "It ran out into Harmony away from your camp; it was torn to pieces. You sent it out there to see what would happen?"

"There's always a test run," Callie said. "I watched from atop the mountain with the broken tear stone. He made it a mile toward the Tempest. I watched the primordial tear it to bits; I saw three of them all watching from safety. The husks are an aberration; they are a threat to the primordials. That's my theory, anyway."

"Primordials aren't stupid," I said. "I don't know how you could possibly believe that my talking to Valmore is going to stop the rest of the primordials from eating you all."

"There's a device that we will be taking with us," Callie said. "It is designed to repel anything with high levels of rift power in it. I know it works, because I marched through Harmony myself with a smaller version of it. This device I have created is on a much larger scale."

"So, why do you need me?" I asked. "Why Valmore?"

"Because the husks can't be close to the device," Callie said. "They too are repelled by it. Rift-walkers too. You're coming to keep them safe while I stay with the device."

"I don't think Valmore is going to sign off on letting a fucking army march through his lands," I pointed out. "There's a good chance he's not going to be happy about that."

"I don't care," Callie said. "You will convince him, or your friend dies."

"My friend?" I asked.

Callie left the room and returned with a small Perspex cage, inside of which was Casimir, although he was now a mouse. There were tiny orange lights in the base of the cage.

"Those lights are why you can't talk to him," Callie said. "We've done *extensive* testing on them."

Callie picked up the cage and flicked a switch.

"I will claw out your evil eyes, woman," Casimir shouted.

"Casimir," I said. "What happened? Are you okay?"

"It turns out there's a limit on how far a riftborn and their eidolon can be apart," Casimir said. "And when you reach that distance, I ping to wherever you are."

"That's news to me," I said.

"News to me, too," Casimir replied.

"Was news to everyone onboard the airplane when an owl arrived in the middle of the flight," Callie said.

"Did they hurt you?" I asked Casimir.

"I am fine," Casimir said, standing on their hind legs and puffing out their chest. "This . . . harpy had her people take me. Are you okay?"

I nodded, biting down the rage and resentment I felt at seeing my friend trapped. "You will let them go," I said slowly. "Now."

"No," Callie said. "I won't. And if you try something, that floor will electrocute him. What happens to an eidolon when it's killed on Earth? Can they be killed? I think so. Never seen it happen, though. You help us, he lives."

"They," I corrected. "Casimir is a they."

Callie snorted. "I don't care. I'll leave you two alone. Try to break *them* out, and I'll rip their fucking head off myself. You can stay here tonight; I have work to do. Goodbye to the both of you; I'll be seeing you soon."

I watched Callie leave, despite wanting to go after her and end her right there and then.

"This place is probably bugged," Casimir said. "I am sorry for my capture."

"Don't be sorry, old friend," I said, retaking my seat. "I assume there's no way to get in contact with anyone and let them know where we are?"

"I wouldn't have thought so," Casimir said. "The harpy queen needs your help to get through Harmony. They can do it without you, but with the protection of a primordial, they don't need to worry about losing numbers before they get to the fog."

"And if I don't do it, you die," I said, not wanting any bugs to pick up what I needed to say next. "And Dani dies. And the people of Boston lose a lot of innocent lives." *The primordial bone weapons can hurt you in the rift, but here on Earth, you're just as easy to kill as anything else.*

I know, Casimir said. "And if I die . . . well, I am a construct of energy, but if I'm completely honest, I would rather not die. I enjoy what my life has become."

Okay, we need to get out of here, I said.

We need to go to the rift, Casimir corrected. *If we escape. Well, to begin with, I'm not sure how we'd achieve that. But if we escape, these people will invade the rift anyway. Those closest to Harmony will discover they have an army nearby and engage. They'd have no idea what they're walking into.*

If we can get to the rift, we can warn the gate and garrisons about what's happening, I said, getting to my feet and stretching. *I do not like this plan.*

Nor I, Casimir agreed. *But it's what we have to do.*

I walked to the main door, tried the handle, and found that it was locked. I knocked on the door, and it was opened by a guard in the hallway beyond. I told him I needed to talk to Callie, and he nodded before getting on the radio.

I took a seat on the sofa and waited for Callie. She took fifteen minutes, which equated to long enough to look like she wasn't rushing but no so long that I would feel like my help didn't matter. We both knew that it did. She'd admitted as much. Although, yes, she was keeping my friend hostage, and yes, I too was a different kind of hostage, I was there to make her life easier. I just had to figure out how to do the exact opposite of that without getting anyone killed.

Callie arrived with Matthew behind her. The man oozed smug superiority.

"How's your head?" Matthew asked, leaning against the door frame.

"I'm good," I said. "If Callie lets you, you can have some of the leftover food she gave me. I guess some people need to be wooed and some people are just lapdogs."

"You two done?" Callie snapped. "What do you want, Lucas?"

"You want my help, you've got it with two conditions," I said.

"Only two?" she asked. "I'm not having Matthew removed, if that's one."

"It isn't," I said. "They're both realistic and necessary. Matthew being there doesn't have any effect on my ability to get you through the rift in one piece."

"Okay, and your *conditions* are?" Callie asked, taking a seat in the single leather armchair.

"I need Casimir released," I said. "I go into the rift and you've got one of my eidolons caged up, I'm going to be useless."

"That true?" Callie asked Matthew.

"Probably," Matthew said. "I wouldn't take my eidolons out of the embers, but if I did, then yeah, I'd need them with me."

"Done," Callie said. "And point two? You want people released? You want me to promise not to hurt anyone ever again? You want me to hand myself in?"

"As much as I'd like all of those, I know you're never going to agree to any of them," I said. "I want my weapons. I *need* my weapons. My coat, too."

"No fucking way," Matthew snapped.

Callie raised her hand to silence him.

"Look, you want me to go into the rift, get a primordial to play nice, and tell them to tell their fellow primordials to leave us be," I said. "I need a weapon. One that can actually do damage to them. My dagger, sword, and spear are rift-tempered."

"Not like any I've ever seen," Callie said. "What are they made of?"

"I don't think you need to know that," I said.

"Then you don't need your weapons," Callie told me with a smile.

"The bones of an elder fiend," I lied, sounding exasperated.

"Bullshit," Callie said. "No fiend bones stay whole for long enough to work with them."

"The RCU has a smith, a riftborn," I said. "If you find an elder fiend, kill it, take the bones before they dissolve and freeze them, she can add metal to the bones and forge weapons out of them. We didn't have a lot to work with. So, I got my spear, dagger, and sword."

"And this," Callie said, sitting up and placing the knuckleduster on the table between us.

"And that," I said.

"So, this is a combination of elder fiend bone and metal?" Callie asked. "What metal?"

"I don't know," I said. "I wasn't allowed to watch her work. Look, keep the knuckles and figure it out. I'm just saying I need my weapons because there's a chance I'll need to show strength. An unarmed riftborn isn't something a primordial will be overly concerned about."

Callie considered it for several seconds. "Deal," she said eventually.

"No way," Matthew said in disbelief. "You're going to arm a Talon?"

"I love your appreciation of my abilities, but even I can't kill a whole army alone," I said snidely. "I'm not some magical John Wick, for crying out loud. You have husks and human greater fiends, I assume more stable ones than when I'd last seen them. You think I can take on an army of those all by myself?"

"No," Callie said.

"I keep the sword," Matthew said. "You get the dagger, spear, and knuckledusters. Make do."

"Fine," I said. "When do we leave?"

"First thing tomorrow," Callie said, getting to her feet. "I'll come get you. Be prepared." Callie walked over to the cage with Casimir and picked it up. "You get your friend tomorrow morning. Not before. You can stay here tonight; it's going to be the last time on Earth for a while, so make the most of it."

I nodded toward Casimir, who returned the gesture, and Matthew opened the door and left with Callie, leaving me alone.

CHAPTER TWENTY-SIX

Callie had someone come and clean away all of the food during the night. She might have called it a *guest apartment,* but in reality, it was just a fancy prison cell.

There were yellow lights in the apartment ceiling, which meant no access to my powers, no access to my embers.

I searched the apartment to find anything that might be useful, but while it was well decorated with some pleasant furniture, it was devoid of anything that might give me more information on Callie's operation. I hadn't expected to find anything, but sometimes it's best to search anyway.

Once I'd been sure that no one was going to come and try to stab me in my sleep—and jammed a chair under the bedroom doorknob—I'd managed to get some rest.

I was already awake when the door to the flat opened and Callie walked in. I'd made myself some coffee and was busy trying to figure out how I was going to get my plan to work. I had an idea of what I was going to do, but I'd long since stopped relying on ideas to actually work the way you wanted them to.

Callie placed my sword, dagger, and knuckleduster on the table in front of me, along with my arrow-wood coat. "These are yours," she said, pulling the harness for them out of a bag. "As is this."

"And Casimir?" I asked, putting the harness on and sheathing the sword, slipping the knuckleduster into my pocket.

"Your friend will meet you at the rift," Callie said. "Might I remind you what happens if you're lying or you try to cross me?"

"I die, Casimir dies, everyone dies," I said. "I got the gist yesterday."

"Let's go," Callie said.

I said nothing but followed Callie out of the flat. She took me outside and back toward the round building, which we continued past, until we reached a building that looked like nothing special. A door, a roof, no windows, red brick. It was the size of a large shed, but that was about it.

Callie opened the door and beckoned me inside as orange lights flickered on.

"No abilities, then," I said. "I was just beginning to think you trusted me."

Callie closed the door and stepped beside me. "Never think that," she said, pressing a button on the wall.

The whole floor moved down, rumbling the entire way. The hut had been big enough to park three cars side by side, so it was capable of bringing up and down a lot all at once. I wondered if there was a separate exit. That information might come in handy when I burnt the place to the ground, should I get the chance.

There was only one stop, and a set of glass doors greeted us, a handprint scanner beside them.

"Just so you know," Callie said, "if someone unauthorised uses this scanner, this whole place fills with the same toxin that was used to knock you out. Except it's about a thousand times more potent."

"You could have just said I'd die," I told her.

The doors opened. "Where's the artistry in that?" Callie asked, pushing me forward.

The hallway was essentially a giant mural of birds and trees and the sky, so it felt like you were walking into some kind of strange forest. Callie definitely had a thing about birds. Specifically Guild birds. Maybe she'd once dreamed of becoming a Guild member.

"Why employ Matthew?" I asked as we walked through a set of double doors and into a large control room, with a bank of windows that looked down over a circular room that was big enough to land a dozen helicopters in.

"Matthew likes money," Callie said.

"You probably could have gotten an actual ex-Guild member to do the job," I said. "There are more than enough of them out there who only care about money."

"Ah, but Matthew also doesn't care about having ethics," Callie said. "Or morals. He doesn't care what happens to the rift-walkers, or the husks, or the primordials, or you. Except he'd like to kill you. I think you broke his ego when you beat him."

"I broke a lot of things," I said.

Apart from Callie and me, the control room was empty.

"We've got an hour," she said. "Thought you might like to get any questions out of the way."

I looked out of the window again, down on the bare concrete floor of the room below. There were words written into the stone, although I couldn't see what they said.

"How do you get so many rift-walkers to open the same tear?" I asked.

"The writing on the floor," Callie said. "Took me thirteen years to write. I had to carve the words into the stone and then infuse them with rift energy. Almost killed me twice because I used too much power."

"What language is it in?" I asked, genuinely interested.

"Different ones," Callie said. "The words sort of flowed though me. Turns out part of the equation is using a language of the person opening a tear."

"Why are you telling me all of this?" I asked.

"I looked into you, Mr. Rurik," Callie said. "You are a scientist. Not at heart; at heart, you're a warrior, a killer. But you have a degree in rift science. You have worked with others who have similar qualifications. I do not like you, I do not trust you, but it is nice to be able to talk to someone who *cares* about these things. Mercenaries care about money."

"The husks in Boston," I said. "What happened to them?"

"Ah, they're still out there," Callie said. "The news has been informed. The city of Boston has been told to stay home; it's all very entertaining to watch. Do you want to know something? You might find this funny."

I was pretty sure I wouldn't. "Sure, why not?" I said.

"There were only ever five husks," Callie said. "And none of them were fully transformed. They were broken, useless to me. They'd die about as easily as any normal fiend would. I wasn't about to send a dozen highly expensive husks—in both time and money terms—to another city when I need them with me. Your friends are running around, terrifying a city for no reason at all."

I said nothing for several seconds until the door opened and a dozen personnel walked in, all taking a moment to stare at me before Callie nodded that it was safe, and they went to their workstations. I kept out of the way after that, watching the side of the room below open, where two dozen people were marched in. All wore shackles, and a few of them wore the same mask I'd seen on the rift-walker at the camp in Harmony. The rift-walkers who didn't play ball.

All of them were lined up around the circular room at regular intervals, before twenty-eight more were brought in. These weren't shackled or masked. They must have been the ones who agreed to cooperate. They were lined up opposite the ones in shackles. I recognised Dani from the shackled group; she looked up at where I stood.

"They can't see you," Callie said. "She just radiates hate, doesn't she?"

"All of these people taken to satisfy your craving for power," I said.

"Knowledge," Callie corrected. "I don't crave power. I crave knowledge. The knowledge of why some are chosen to be given the power of the rift and others are left to die. We are going to create something magical when we control the Tempest."

"You're going to move everyone through all at once?" I asked.

"No, we've been moving people through for a few days," Callie said. "We considered moving them all through over a period of time. I heard that the people at the Gates of the Maelstrom had notified Inaxia about our presence in Harmony. We decided it best not to leave large numbers of people there, but the last few days, it was deemed safe. Or safer, anyway."

I went back to looking out of the window as the floor beneath the room slid open, revealing a huge elevator that rose up from under the floor. There were two hundred people on the elevator at least. With at least half of them being husks, the other half being a combination of people in hazmat suits and what looked like humans, some in tactical gear, some in shorts and T-shirts. It was quite the odd sight.

"Begin procedure," the crony said into a speaker, letting those below know what was going on.

"How long can you keep the tear open for?" I asked.

"Infinitely," Callie said. "We need the twenty-five to thirty to open it but only need ten or so to maintain it on two-hour-long stretches."

"What happens if one of the rift-walkers dies or gets exhausted from opening the tear?" I asked as the fifty rift-walkers began raising their hands toward the group on the lift, and a tear started to form in front of them. The largest controlled tear I'd ever seen.

"The others take the slack," Callie said. "It's why they all wear heart monitors, which are checked here. None of them are mistreated, despite the shackles and masks. They are all fed well, kept warm, and exercised regularly. You might hate me for it, but we have given their lives purpose."

I watched the tear form until it covered the entire middle part of the room, forming a sort of bubble that enveloped those standing on the lifts.

"First set through," one of the cronies said.

"Let's keep them going," Callie said, clapping her hands.

"When is it my turn?" I asked. "Also, where is Casimir?"

"Let's go get you to your friend," Callie said, sounding far too enthusiastic, considering she was sending monsters to go to war using the energy of kidnapped people, many of whom had died in her . . . *care.*

Callie took me out of the control room, back into the hallway, and further along, down a set of stairs and into a small room that contained lockers and wooden benches. Hazmat suits hung on the front of several lockers. There was a second door at the far end of the room. Matthew stood between me and the second door, in the middle of the room, with Casimir on a bench beside him. Matthew had my sword in one hand and aimed the tip at Casimir.

"Now is not the time, Matthew," Callie chided, walking over to the cell and brushing her fingers over the top. The cage unlocked, and Casimir practically leapt out, running over to me, up my clothes, turning into a raven, and taking a seat on my shoulder.

"Amazing," Callie said, clapping her hands again. "Do you need a hazmat suit?"

"No," I said. "I'll be sick, but it doesn't usually last long."

"I'll be seeing you soon," Matthew said, picking up a Talon mask from the bench. It was more angular and mean-looking than my old one; his was made to create fear in those who crossed him. He'd always enjoyed that part.

"That's still not yours," I said.

Matthew looked down at the mask. "Finders keepers," he said, and chuckled to himself. He opened the door behind him and motioned for me to enter.

I walked through and made a mental note to make sure I took the mask back from Matthew.

"Follow it to the end," Callie called after me. "Do not fuck around with me on this, Lucas. Get into the rift; talk to your friend. Make sure we don't have a reason to come hunt you. We have more rift-walkers than we need. I will lower our numbers if you force my hand."

I did as she said and followed it to the end, pushing open the door which led into the large chamber.

"Go in," a guard in black tactical gear said as there was a rumbling sound from the lift while it descended back into the darkness.

I walked through the middle of the chamber, catching the eyes of several of the rift-walkers who were there by force, and a few by choice. None of them looked what I would have called *happy.*

I waited for the lift to ascend back to my level. It contained a lot less soldiers than I was expecting, but in the middle of it, pulled by four oxforth who were all still inside the rift, was a large orange light built onto a solid cart of steel and wood. The solid block beneath the light was surrounded by smaller yellow lights, and I assumed this was the device that Callie had mentioned.

I glanced at the light that was the size of a tank and walked onto the lift in the middle of the chamber, stepping inside the tear and into the cave that I'd seen when first arriving.

There were lots of people all milling around outside the cave, with several people in hazmat suits, barking orders. The husks were off to one side, stood silently, while those still human in shape were waiting for orders.

"You the primordial whisperer?" another man in a hazmat suit asked.

"Apparently," I told him, before running over to a nearby rock to throw up. I really hoped that I'd be done with that by now. Although the debilitation seemed to come on slower and end quicker. Thank heavens for small mercies, I guess.

"You okay?" he asked when I returned.

"Fucking grand, mate," I told him with a thumbs-up.

"Go do your thing, then," he said. "Mate." He used that word to ensure I understand that we were the very opposite of it.

"Revenant or human?" I asked.

"Why?" the soldier replied.

"Just wondering why the hazmat suit," I said.

"Get on with it," the soldier snapped.

The large orange light was pulled by the oxforth to the edge of camp. It made me nervous, mostly because I didn't understand how it worked. Callie had been forthcoming about a lot of things but not how the lights worked. It was something to look into if I ever found myself not being used by a complete psychopath.

I walked down a slight bank to a pool of crystal-clear water set away from the cave mouth. The plant life on the bottom was awash with multiple colours, and there were no fish that I could see.

I remembered being told that the water in pools with coloured plants was safe to drink because the plants in them filtered all the contaminants out. I rinsed out my mouth with the cool water, spitting it out on the bank beside me, before filling my hands again and taking a drink.

I returned to the cave mouth feeling somewhat better. The orange lights were off, and there was no one about. I looked out at the lake and was wishing to be elsewhere when something rippled just under the surface a few meters in. I walked away slowly, keeping my eyes on the water, until I was back in dense woodland.

"Casimir," I said.

"On it," Casimir replied, taking flight at speed and quickly disappearing from view.

"Valmore is a kilometre to your north," Casimir said. "He's with . . . he's with . . ."

"What is he with?" I asked.

"A really big lizard," Casimir said. "With six legs. And horns. And it's blood-red."

"Can you tell Valmore I need to speak to him?" I asked. "I do not want to surprise anything that lives out here."

I was still mindful that the lake wasn't far away from where I stood. I looked over at the water, and it rippled again. Something was following me as I continued along the line where the trees met the sandbank.

I walked for a minute or two until Casimir returned.

"He says he'll be here in a minute," Casimir told me. "He wanted to know if you were with the group who just arrived. I think the primordials are already talking about it."

"What did you say?" I asked.

"I said it was complicated but that you weren't here by choice," Casimir explained.

"Probably the best way of dealing with it," I admitted, and looked over the water, which continued to ripple out from the same place.

"There is something watching you," Casimir said.

"Yep," I replied. "I'm going to guess that Pru the Primordial won't be thrilled about the trespass on her domain."

"Nothing good," Casimir said. "I will go keep an eye on our unpleasant associates."

Casimir took off again and I stayed leaning up against a tree, hoping that something didn't fall out on me as I began to get an itch on the back of my neck that I knew was nothing but annoyed me all the same.

I had to wait for a few minutes before the ground began to vibrate with the steps of what I hoped was a friendly primordial.

Valmore appeared, walking along the bank of the lake, completely oblivious to whatever was lurking inside.

"I hear you've come with friends," Valmore said, making the word *friend* sound like anything but.

"Not friends," I said. "They want to march through Harmony toward the Tempest. I don't help them and people die. I help them and more people die."

"You are waiting to find an answer so only *they* die," Valmore said.

"Something like that," I told him.

"You need the primordials to fight for you?" Valmore asked. "Because that will never happen. Once one faction picks sides, the others will align themselves as they see fit. The primordials would go to war with one another. I assume you do not want that."

"No," I said quickly. "No one wants an apocalyptic war. The people here have got this light-machine thing that keeps primordials away, but I need to go with them because the husks are kept away too. They're going to leave a larger group outside of the fog for when the people at the gates and garrisons figure out what's going on and try to stop them."

"It is several hours' walk from here to the Tempest," Valmore said, almost to himself.

"They have to pull that light too," I said. "It'll be slow. So, if we can get the soldiers from the gates and garrison through the army parked in Harmony, we might be able to get enough people to stop Callie before she does something truly awful. Something *else* truly awful."

Valmore considered my words. "Do you have a plan?" he asked.

"Casimir," I said. "I'm going to need you to go to the gates. Find Melody or Seluku. Tell them everything. Leave nothing out. We need them moving here now, before Callie's forces are fully mobilised. I have to go with Callie and the husks toward the Tempest."

"I can't," Casimir said." I can't fly through the fog. I can't fly over it or travel under it."

"Bollocks," I said. "I imagine that Callie already knew that. I did think it weird she allowed me to have Casimir back so quickly. So, I guess we need a new plan."

My brain worked overtime to try and figure something out.

"We both know what needs to be done," Valmore said. "It's the only option."

"I'd rather it wasn't," I told him.

"Me too, if I'm honest," Valmore said. "As soon as you start to move north, it's not going to take long to discover that her idea of you placating the primordials isn't going to work. If they smell the husks, they will kill them."

"Hopefully, by then, there will be enough distance between them and the main force that she can't just order the execution of Dani and any other rift-walkers," I said.

"I will leave now and be back before I suffer any adverse reactions," Valmore said. "Hopefully."

Leaving the safety of Harmony was dangerous for primordials but more dangerous for anyone who came across one who had been away from Harmony for too long.

"Thank you," I said as Valmore changed shape into something approximating a wolf.

"I will need to move swiftly and without these people spotting me," Valmore said. "Follow the plan as this Callie wants you to. I will get help, and together we will stop them all before they lay waste to my home."

I watched Valmore bound off and hoped this was all going to work, because otherwise, a lot of people were going to die.

CHAPTER TWENTY-SEVEN

I returned to the science huts, walking by a literal horde of heavily armed soldiers, to find an impatient-looking Callie. "And?" she asked.

"Valmore has gone on to search out any primordials that are close to the march to the north," I said. "It's a bit difficult to know exactly who might or might not decide you're a problem that needs removing, but he'll check what he can. Besides, you have the light thing keeping you safe."

"I am more concerned about it being damaged," Callie said.

"What happens if it's damaged?" I asked, looking around to see if I could spot the light.

Callie's smile was not a pleasant one. "I assure you, you do not want to find out."

"Is it explosive?" I asked. "Have you brought a fucking bomb into the rift?"

Matthew punched me in the jaw. "Watch your tone," he snarled.

I rubbed the side of my face, bit down my reply, and repeatedly ran through a scenario in my mind where I got to cut his head off, until I'd calmed down.

"Not your concern," Callie said. "You just need to know that if it is damaged in any way, the consequences would be dire."

"So, when do we leave?" I asked.

"*We* don't," Callie said. "You have informed your primordial friend of our needs, and so you are now a carrot for that creature. It helps us, or you die. As does the girl."

Matthew sloped off into the cave and brought out a bound Dani, forcing her down to a kneeling position beside Callie.

"Dani will be staying here with you for a short time until we're prepared at the fog," Matthew said. "If you misbehave, you're going to watch her get her head cut off."

"I thought you needed my help," I said to Callie. "I helped, you let her go."

"I lied," Callie said. "We both know that if you come with me, you're going to try to stop me. You have done your part and gotten the primordial to assist us. If he betrays us, you die; if you betray us, she dies. You see how that works?" She gave me a sardonic wave and walked away.

I'd seen it coming, but it made what I needed to do next easier.

Find Valmore the second he gets back, I said to Casimir. *Tell him I'm going to need his help here.*

On it, Casimir replied.

Matthew confiscated my spear, dagger, and knuckleduster, and placed the dagger and knuckleduster in one of the science huts while keeping my spear on him. Once he was done, Dani and I were marched to the cave mouth and forced to sit.

Matthew helped usher more people coming through the tear, leaving Dani and me alone for long stretches while other guards kept watch.

Dani sighed. "My village was a few hours' walk to the south of the gate," she said.

"What was it called?" I asked.

"Hjem," she said.

"Norwegian for *home*," I said.

Dani nodded again. "Yep. The village elder was a woman from fifteenth-century Norway; I guess the word felt right."

"How did they treat you?" I asked. "Callie's people?"

"Not brilliantly," Dani said. "We were fed, clothed, not physically attacked, so by that standard, it was a five-star resort. There were people still undergoing transformation into husks; it was . . ." Dani closed her eyes. "The screams."

I looked across the lake, the thick forest, and spotted the snow-capped mountains in the distance. "You ever been there?"

Dani followed my gaze. "No, you?"

I nodded. "Went close to the Tempest once. Felt like I was being crushed by power."

"That sounds like somewhere Callie shouldn't be allowed to control," Dani said.

"What did you do for the people in Hjem?" I asked, wanting to change the topic while I figured out how to get away from Matthew and the guards he had with him and stop Callie.

"They taught me to hunt, to fight," Dani said. "But there were people in neighbouring villages who didn't like what I represented. They would follow me when I was hunting; they would try to hurt me. They only managed to really hurt me once . . . After that, they . . . well, they stayed far away from me."

Dani had a faraway look in her eyes. "Revenants in the rift are the same as those on Earth. Being here doesn't make you a good person if you were a shitty one on Earth."

Truer words never spoken.

"You're probably the first person I've met back on Earth who knows what it's like here. Everyone else is either human or revenant. People think that this is like some kind of beautiful, harmonious afterlife or a utopia. They don't understand what it's really like."

"That it can be beautiful, that it can be an amazing place, but it'll also kill you as quick as looking at you," I said.

Dani took a deep breath and exhaled slowly. "Anthony doesn't really understand. He tries to, but . . . he can't. He thinks this is aspirational. A lot of people told him that either he was brought back by God or the Devil. Shockingly, no middle ground there."

"And you?" I asked.

"Mostly the same," Dani said. "People attribute it to some all-powerful entity rather than the chance it was. I was in the wrong place at the exact right time. A few seconds either way, and I'd be dead or we'd never have been hit. How'd you end up here?"

"I went to war against the Roman Empire," I said. "Killed a lot of them, got betrayed by someone I thought was on my side, and ended up here. Riftborn. Went back a century later to find that everyone I knew was dead and the place I called home had been destroyed. Weird few years after that."

"I never wanted to go to war," Dani said. "My power is essentially the ability to run away. Not long after I came here, I learned that opening a small tear, just a few inches long, against a living being, does horrible things. I don't like doing it, though. It makes my skin crawl, for one. And it makes me feel like I'm taking another step away from my humanity. I don't want to feel like I can just kill and maim and go about my day like nothing happened."

"Did you open the tears in Canada?" I asked.

"I opened lots of small tears along the way," Dani said. "I figured you might be able to track them, but they knocked me out. I woke up and opened a much larger tear. I was afraid, didn't know what was going on."

"It made two lynx greater fiends," I said.

"Did it . . . hurt anyone?" Dani asked.

I looked over at Matthew. "No one innocent," I said.

"Good," Dani said with an exhale as if a weight had been lifted from her shoulders.

Several husks came through the tear and stood at the edge of the clearing outside of the cave. They were followed by four rift-walkers, who went to stand with the husks. The guards who had been watching us joined the group, and Matthew barked an order at them to move to the scientific huts and wait for further instruction, and they did as they were told.

The husks were motionless voids of humanity, and I wondered if they needed activating before they followed orders. It was explained to me that within each hut was a single rift-walker. I was told what would happen if anything went wrong and Matthew alerted them. I doubted I could get to them in time to stop their murders at the hands of the monsters that guarded them.

There was a single oxforth just outside the cave mouth, happily grazing on the grass there, seemingly oblivious to everything going on. I envied that animal.

"You don't look happy about having to stay here with me," I called to Matthew, who remained by the mouth of the cave. "You're more than welcome to go join your friends; I'm not going anywhere."

"Where's that damn bird of yours?" Matthew snapped without looking back at me.

"Probably exhausted somewhere," I said. "Casimir will be back; they always are."

"You give your eidolons too much freedom," Matthew said. "They are tools to be used, not friends to be worried over."

"It's shocking that you can't see why my way would be preferable to the other," I said. "Why aren't the husks in here with us?"

"They are where they need to be," Matthew said, leaning up against a nearby wall.

"You don't like them near you," I said.

Matthew looked over at me. "No," he admitted.

"They're just mindless things, aren't they?" I asked.

"That might make them easier to deal with," Matthew said. "They remember who they are; they remember what they've lost. They just can't do anything about it while the person that controls them is nearby, which is me," he said with a smile.

"Are they imprinted on you like ducklings?" I asked. "Or is it a practitioner thing where they give you a potion to drink or an amulet to wear?"

"Amulet," Matthew said after a short time. "You know, I haven't spoken to anyone about this. I don't know who would and wouldn't go running back to Callie and blab about how I dislike her cursed mannequins."

"So, Callie told me about the husks in Boston," I said. "It was mostly a ruse."

Matthew's laugh echoed around the clearing. "She didn't want to waste any," he said. "Shame, as I'd have liked to have seen what would have happened."

"And you're going to kill me, yes?" I asked. "That's the plan?"

Matthew nodded. "Callie gave you to me."

"She *gave* me to you?" I asked with a laugh. "What the hell does that mean?"

"It means that we know you sent your primordial friend off to warn the gates," Matthew said. "We knew you were going to try to betray us."

I chuckled. "Well, I knew you were going to betray me somehow; I just hadn't expected for Callie to figure out how I was going to betray you."

Matthew slipped the mask on over his face. "I'm going to give you something you didn't give me. A chance."

I laughed. "Are we doing this now? Seriously?"

"Your primordial friend isn't here to help you," Matthew said. "Another benefit of you sending him away."

"Matthew, you have this idea that I jumped you or something, and that's not how it happened," I said, getting to my feet.

Matthew placed my spear up against the wall beside him. "We're going to go out into that clearing, where there are lights. We will fight, no powers, no nothing. Just fight. And I will beat you. And when you're begging me to let you die, I will take your spear and I will end your life."

"You're going to wait to hear me beg for my life?" I asked. "Matthew, I don't think we have that long."

"Always the funny man," Matthew said, strolling out of the cave. He clicked his fingers at Dani, who flipped him off. "You sit over there."

I shrugged off the arrow-wood coat, throwing it over the stump of a large tree, while Matthew bounced from foot to foot. He was confident and he wanted me to know that. He had killed Guild members before; he'd killed a Talon. He was a man who people should rightly be scared of fighting, and the last time we'd fought, his overconfidence had played a part in his downfall. His power allowed him to play around with someone else's abilities, and it was a dangerous thing to be able to do, but it turned out if he couldn't concentrate due to, say, a broken collarbone, he couldn't use it. He'd relied too much on his power. Apparently, it was a lesson he'd learned.

"So, how are we going to do this?" I asked.

Matthew lunged toward my legs, trying to catch me off guard with a takedown, but I was already stepping back, out of the way, putting a little distance between us. He rolled his shoulders, put his hands up into a boxer's stance, and moved toward me.

I dodged a few jabs and pushed his hand away a few times. They were nothing serious, nothing to really test me; they were just done to get the measure of me.

Matthew snapped forward with a jab, which I blocked as before, but he quickly stepped to the side with a hook to my ribs. I stepped back, but he followed up with another jab and an elbow, which I was forced to block, leaving my ribs open for a punch.

All of the air went out of me while Matthew jumped up and down like he'd just won a heavyweight championship.

I rubbed my ribs and took a moment to reconsider what I was going to do. I was tired, I was preoccupied with getting out of the rift alive while stopping Callie's machinations, and I was concerned that Matthew would use Dani as a hostage. None of those things were something I should have been thinking about while in a fight. If I remained distracted, I was going to get killed.

I rolled my shoulders as Matthew pranced about.

He glanced back my way and did a double take before slowly turning to face me. He still wore his mask. It was cracked in several places, with metal wire holding them together.

"Did I break that last time?" I asked, pointing to the mask. "I don't remember."

Matthew charged me.

I sidestepped his advance and slammed my elbow into the side of his head as he tried to stop himself. I followed up with a kick to his knee, which sent him to the dirt. He rolled across, avoiding me stomping where his head would be, and came back to his feet, but I was already running toward him and drove a flying knee into his chest, forcing him back so I could catch him in the side of the head with a vicious kick.

I picked up his mask from the ground where it had fallen, turning it over in my hand. "This mask was meant to mean you were the protector of a Guild," I said. "You do not deserve a Talon's mask. You stole it from someone worthy. You have not earned it."

I tossed the mask into the mouth of the cave.

"You sanctimonious prick," Matthew said, spitting blood on the ground. "I *earned* that mask."

"Go fetch it, then," I told him.

Matthew got back to his feet, never taking his eyes off me. "You fetch it for me," he said, spitting on the ground again, removing a remote control from his pocket and pressing the button.

The orange light all around stayed on, but something washed over me, and before I could react, I felt my body being pulled apart.

My arms turned to smoke as I lost control of my powers, while Matthew smiled. A light blue aura surrounded his hands as more and more of me turned to smoke, pulling me apart further and further in opposite directions as I fought for control.

I screamed in pain and rage, never taking my eyes off Matthew, whose smile grew wider with every second he was in control.

"I'm going to tear you apart," Matthew said. "But first . . ."

The tearing stopped and my smoke was forced back together all at once with no care. I had no chance to stop my arms re-forming, my bones sliding against one another, as pain screamed through my entire body and I crashed to my knees.

When it was done, I lay on the ground, sweating, panting, agony rippling through me. I was lucky everything was back in the right place, lucky nothing had been broken or pieces of dirt hadn't been swept up inside of me when I re-formed. I knew I made turning to smoke and re-forming look easy, but it took a level of concentration that had taken me years to learn. And even longer to master. Having all of that taken away by someone who found it fun to see how much pain he could cause only increased how much I wanted to hurt him.

"As you can see," Matthew said, "while you can't use your power, I can use mine."

I looked up at him and he kicked me in the face. He followed up with a kick to my ribs.

"You want to know how?" Matthew asked as he stamped on my leg.

"Not really," I managed between clenched teeth.

He kicked me in the ribs again.

"Sure, be my guest," I said.

"The amulet," Matthew said, digging it out from under his jacket and showing me. "It allows me to control the husks, but it also lets me bypass these lights. So, I have control of your power and you don't."

My arm turned to smoke again, pain radiating up the limb, across the shoulder, stopping at the back of my neck. I kept my mouth shut. No matter the pain, I was determined to hold out for as long as I could. To not give him the satisfaction.

Matthew pulled on the smoke until it was a dozen feet away, and let go. My arm re-formed and he pulled it apart again, over, and over. After the fifth time, he kicked through the smoke as it reformed, causing me to yell out.

"Ah, there you are," Matthew said with a sneer. "There's no one here to save you, Lucas. You are my plaything."

He walked away and I crawled through the dirt to one of the lights, hoping that if I could get beyond their perimeter, I could take control over my own power. I had just about reached the light when my arms turned back to smoke, and I received another kick in the face.

Matthew returned, dragged me back into the middle of the clearing, and broke my arm.

"No more crawling for you," he said with a chuckle. "Now, wait right there."

He walked off again as my body re-formed, and I lay on the ground, looking up at the sky, my entire body in agony.

I looked over as he picked up my spear. "Let's see what fun we can have with this," Matthew said, turning back to me.

There was a dot high in the sky above me. For a second, I thought that I'd damaged my vision or was seeing things. I blinked a few times, but the dot was getting larger and moving at incredible speed. Casimir.

I smiled as Casimir the bird dove toward us, moving almost too fast for me to keep up with. I recognised the markings on the bird, the peregrine falcon. Nothing dove quicker.

"I expected more fight," Matthew said. "I guess taking away the one thing that makes you special just makes you ordinary."

A hundred feet above my head, the falcon changed shape.

Matthew started walking toward me, twirling the spear like a baton. "We are going to enjoy ourselves," he said.

"Stop it," Dani shouted.

Matthew stopped and looked back at his captive. "Quiet, or you're next." Then he looked back at me and up into the air, throwing himself to the side just in time to avoid the impact.

There are few things quite as memorable as a full-grown grizzly bear smashing into the ground directly next to you and immediately letting out the loudest growl you've ever heard. "You will not," Casimir the grizzly roared in defiance at Matthew, who looked like he was going to shit himself and backpedalled.

Casimir swiped at Matthew, catching him in the arm and sending him spiralling across the ground. Casimir continued on, grabbing Matthew in his jaws and tossing him around like a rag doll. Matthew might have been able to stop me using my power, but at the same time, Casimir was already in the rift; he was a part of my power that was not linked to me while there.

I got to my feet, feeling woozy, my arm broken, my head hurting, as Matthew rolled along the ground and threw my spear at Casimir. It never reached him as Dani intercepted it, the spear catching her in the back of her shoulder.

"That the best you got?" Casimir shouted as Matthew climbed onto the oxforth and rode off at speed.

"Fuck, fuck, fuck," Dani said through clenched teeth. I hadn't noticed when it had happened, but Dani had grabbed my arrow-wood coat and used it as a shield when diving in front of Casimir.

The spear had smashed into her shoulder with a lot of force, and the spear had gone through the coat a few inches, but the coat had stopped it from being a killing shot.

"You're going to be okay," I said, removing the spear and coat to get a look at the wound.

"But rift-tempered weapons kill our kind," Dani said, wincing with every word.

"You have what I believe the medical profession would call a bit of a scratch," I said. "If you were human, you might need stitches, but you'll be safe."

I looked over at Casimir. "Thank you," I said.

Casimir bowed their head.

"I'm going to take Casimir into the embers," I said. "My arm needs healing. Can you get out of here, go back to Earth? Tell everyone what's going on?"

Dani nodded. "Will you be okay alone?" she asked.

"I'll be fine," I said. I opened my embers and stepped inside, running through the forest to find Maria the deer waiting for me.

"What happened to you?" Maria asked as Casimir the grizzly changed into a falcon and perched beside me.

"Got hurt," I said. "Casimir saved my life. I need to heal."

I sat down cross-legged on the soft earth and breathed deeply as my body repaired itself.

When I opened my eyes, both Maria and Casimir were staring at me.

"You okay?" Maria asked. "A few hours will have passed. You look . . ."

"Like you're going to a battle," Casimir said.

I got to my feet and breathed out slowly. "Time to end this. Take care," I told Maria and Casimir, and took off at a sprint back through the trees, feeling better than I had in some time.

I ran until the forest ended, until I was in nothing, and I opened a tear, stepping back through into the rift. Back to where Dani had been hurt. I picked up my spear, turning it over in my hands, seeing the blood of my friend grace its blade. I picked up Matthew's Talon mask and hung it from my belt; I would not let it be used for evil intent.

Those responsible would pay for what had happened there.

Time to go to war.

CHAPTER TWENTY-EIGHT

I ran toward the science huts, expecting to have to fight the husks. Yearning to have to fight them. But I was too late. Valmore had already taken it upon himself to decimate the half dozen posted there. He tore the head off one husk, using his massive teeth, and spat it onto the ground.

The three rift-walkers remained huddled together in the corner of the area, by a hut. All watched Valmore with wide-eyed terror.

"Are you okay?" Valmore asked, looking down at me.

"Matthew hurt Dani," I said, my voice breaking with every word. "With my spear. Callie just wanted you out of the way; she was going to use me as a way to keep you placated."

Valmore bent down toward me, the tip of his nose against my chest. "I am sorry," he said, his voice reverberating through my chest. "I brought the Gates of the Maelstrom with me. It took a few hours, and Callie's forces were already prepared at the edge of the fog, but I left them to fight and come find you."

"How was it going?" I asked.

"Hard to say," Valmore told me.

I looked beyond Valmore to the rift-walkers who were stood at the mouth of one of the huts.

"Are they enemies?" Valmore asked, turning to look at them as someone might look at something they'd never considered a threat before.

"No," I said, and walked over to the rift-walkers. "My name is Lucas."

All three wore shackles and masks covering their mouths. I reached behind their heads and unclipped the masks. No locks, just a clasp that would be impossible to reach while wearing shackles.

The masks fell to the floor and all three took in big breaths.

"Are they dead?" one of them, a young man, asked.

"Yes," Valmore said. "That one has no head; he's extra dead."

"What are we meant to do?" another of the rift-walkers asked.

"My advice would be to leave this place and never return," I said. "Or pick up a weapon and fight those who imprisoned you. I would understand either way."

"How do we fight?" the oldest man asked. "Here? How do *we* fight?"

"You see all of this?" I asked. "All of this equipment, these lights? Destroy it all. Then go home."

"We can fight these people Callie brought," the third rift-walker said, a young woman with brown skin who looked no older than Dani.

"If there's nothing here that Callie and her people can use to do this again, you'll have struck a blow," I said.

The lady picked up a light and smashed it against the nearest hut. "That was actually fun," she said.

"Go nuts," I told them. I left them to their destruction as Valmore came with me.

"I have a favour," I said.

"You want me to take you to Callie," Valmore said.

"Please," I told him. "I can't get there in time to stop Callie from doing whatever the hell she really has planned."

He bent down and I clambered up onto his back, sitting on his neck. If I wasn't so full of the need to find Matthew and hurt him, to deliver justice for so many people, I'd have probably enjoyed riding a primordial through Harmony, but my focus was on not only finding Matthew and Callie but also on staying on Valmore, who moved like a sports car through the trees and only got faster when we reached open terrain.

The sounds of battle could be heard throughout Harmony. "Wait," I said. "If there are husks at the battle, Seluku's people are going to be killed. I need you to give this sword to Seluku or Melody. It's the only thing that can kill these husks, I hope; I haven't exactly tested it. If you want to lend a claw or tooth, I don't think anyone will complain."

"Well, I guess it's too late for me to not pick a side," Valmore said.

"You need help. If Callie wins, how long before primordials become hunted for sport or your bones?" I asked. "How long before whatever she has planned leads to the death of your friends?"

Valmore thought for a moment and nodded. "There are too many of those things to kill alone. Keep your sword. You may need both it and the spear."

"How are you going to get help?" I asked.

Valmore's howl went through me like a tidal wave of power. It bounced off the mountains nearby, echoing all around.

"I will do what I can," Valmore said. "Take care, Lucas Rurik. I hope to spend time with you in the future. To show you the sights of Harmony."

"You too, Valmore," I said. "Thank you."

I remained where I was as Valmore set off at a full sprint toward the fog, while a huge six-legged, red-skinned lizard—presumably the one Casimir had seen—bounded after him. Another primordial that looked like a combination of crocodile with huge skeletal wings and a spine-filled tail ran after the two of them, looking back at me. For a moment, I thought it nodded in my direction, but the primordial was soon gone.

"Be safe, my friend," I said, looking across the tundra to the forest on the opposite side, where more primordials left to see what was happening. Dozens of them watched Valmore and his friends pick a side. "And thank you."

I ran on toward the north of Harmony, toward the Tempest. I didn't know what Callie's big plan was, but I was certain that nothing good was going to come of her being anywhere near the largest concentration of energy in the rift.

Eventually, the landscape changed from plains and woodland to swamps and bogs, but that only made the tracks easier to follow as they skirted the huge swamp to the north of where I'd watched Valmore and his primordial friends run into the fog.

Trees jutted out from the waters of the swamp, midnight-blue or moss-green, sometimes both, sometimes with orange and magenta. The water shimmered as though someone had poured glitter into it, and if I looked at the water closer, I could see it wasn't clear at all but tinged indigo. As if the light show in the sky above wasn't enough of an indication that I was getting close to the Tempest.

The light repulsed primordials, but there were no bodies of husks or anything else around, either. There was more to Callie's machine than she had let on.

I picked up the pace and was soon running along the bog, jumping over anything that looked like it might try to swallow my feet whole, occasionally turning to smoke to move across unencumbered, re-forming into a flat-out sprint when my footing would be more solid.

It took an unknown amount of time to move past the swamps of Harmony and back out to the snow-covered plains ahead. Mountains jutted up in the distance, making the whole area feel hemmed in, and there was a pass under two of them that led to the Tempest itself. It was as if the mountains were a buffer for the energy that came flooding out. I had never made it beyond that pass. No one had that I knew of.

A huge creature cast in shadow sat atop one of the mountains, two wings wrapped around one of the many peaks that looked like spears trying to touch the sky. It gave the impression that the primordial was hugging the mountain, and I knew, without a doubt, that it had seen me.

I pushed on at speed, the tracks that had gone before me became more and more lost as heavy snow fell. I was grateful for the arrow-tree coat but even more so for the fact that the running kept me warm.

The air crackled with power, and lightning continuously struck the mountains, occasionally causing avalanches in the distance, accompanied by a noise that was almost like the mountain itself roaring out in pain.

It wasn't much further when I saw the statuesque figures in the snow, waiting for me. I continued on, removing the spear from its clasp on my back but leaving the sword sheathed.

There were a dozen husks, all stood motionless, their dark clothes standing out from the light blue snow that fell from the sky. Behind them was Matthew, with Dani and a second rift-walker—a young man I didn't recognise—sat on the snowy ground, up against a large boulder.

The dozen husks all took one step toward me. None of them had weapons, but then, I doubted they needed them.

"I thought you'd gone home," I called out to Dani.

"Couldn't let this prick get away with it," Dani shouted. "Turns out I was fuelled more on anger than common sense."

"You think some spear is going to help you?" Matthew shouted. "You should have stayed in your embers."

One of the husks started to walk toward me, and I saw the confusion on Matthew's face before it turned into a smile. He'd figure out why the husk wasn't obeying him later, I was sure he thought.

The husk stood a few feet away from me. It had a cracked mask, and I wondered if it was the same one from when I'd fought it in Boston.

"Did this," the husk said, removing the mask, revealing a face that looked like it had been torn apart and put back together again, over and over. It had grey-blue skin stretched thin over a skull that was no longer human. "Did this."

"The mask?" I asked. "You could get a new one."

"Did this!" the husk screamed.

"Kurt," I said noticing a flash of something I recognised on the thing's face. "I was looking for you in London. You worked for Jacob. He said you'd run away to hide; I guess Callie got you to undergo this. You think I got you turned into a husk?"

"Your fault," the husk screamed, and rushed toward me, hunched forward, his arms outstretched like some evil cosplay of Frankenstein's monster.

I stepped to the side, unsheathed the sword, and brought it up, all in one smooth, fast motion. The blade of the sword caught the throat of the husk, severing half of the neck. Blood poured from the wound as it pitched forward onto the soft snow.

I looked down at the dead husk and then back at the rest of those gathered before me. Matthew's smile had gone, replaced with one of shock and fear.

"I guess these work, then," I said. I removed Matthew's Talon mask from my belt and put it on. Time to teach Matthew what fear really was. "Shall we?" I asked.

There was a roar of anger from the husks as they all charged.

I threw the spear at the husk furthest from me, leaving my fingertip attached to it in smoke form, and snapped the rest of my body over to where the spear had hit the husk in the throat, pitching it backward.

I pulled the spear free and stabbed the nearest husk in the neck, stepping around its dying body and plunging the spear into the heart of the next husk. I ducked under a punch, cutting up with my sword, severing the limb at the elbow and plunging the spear through the back of the creature's skull a second later.

I threw the spear between the husks, teleporting each time, killing them one by one. Sometimes the strike of the spear was enough, and sometimes I needed to use the sword, but by the time all dozen of them were dead, I was breathing heavily and covered in their dark ichor.

Matthew looked genuinely terrified. His entire world view of what the husks were and how they were indestructible killing machines was shattered. Some people needed to take a moment after such a thing.

I strolled toward Matthew, who looked around, realised he was utterly fucked, and legged it back toward Dani, screaming obscenities at her to open a tear.

"Go fuck yourself," Dani said, punching him in the nose as he got closer.

Matthew looked toward me and held his hands out. I felt the tug of power as he tried the same thing he'd done back by the cave, but this time,

I was in control of my power, and while it took me a lot of concentration and willpower to keep my body together, it was harder on him to exert himself so much.

"You want to know where Callie is?" Matthew shouted.

I continued on, spinning the short spear over and over in my hand.

Matthew grabbed the male rift-walker by the throat and a tear opened up behind him. He stepped through the tear, pushing the rift-walker to the snow.

I started to run, which was hard to do in the snow, so I turned to smoke and moved toward them.

"Shut the fucking tear," Matthew screamed at the rift-walker, who had gotten back onto his feet.

"I can't," the rift-walker shouted back. "It's not that . . ."

Matthew slit the man's throat and Dani threw herself at the tear just as I reached her. I turned back to human form, threw the dagger at Matthew, and was happy to see it strike home in his neck, and I dragged Dani to the ground as the explosion of power bounced us back along the snow for a hundred feet.

Instead of the tear snapping shut, it shot straight up toward the sky, linking with the lightning as it streaked above. The lighting came down through the tear and slammed into the ground, throwing up snow, muck, and stone all across the plain.

"It's not shut," Dani said, scrambling to her feet and trying to run across the snow back to the tear, which was about the size of a dinner plate.

"What the hell?" I asked as I caught up to her and noticed that she was bleeding and hurt. There was no point in telling her to rest; I doubted she'd have paid any attention. "Can you shut it?"

"I can try," she said. "I don't know."

I looked up; at least it wasn't touching the sky anymore. "What happens if more of that lightning hits it?"

"I don't think anyone wants to find that out," Dani said.

"I'll have to leave you here," I said. The rage had left me while I killed those husks, but I didn't have time to chat. "Where did Callie go?"

Dani pointed off toward the mountains. "She had the cart and oxforth," she said. "She's going to switch on that light and push it into the Tempest."

"And what will that do?" I asked.

"She thinks it'll let her control the Tempest," Dani said.

"Yeah, that's unlikely," I said.

"She's convinced," Dani told me. "That big light thing, the cart under it has this giant bell on it."

"A bell?" I asked. "What's she doing with a bell?"

"It's made from primordial bone," Dani said. "At least, it looks like your medallion."

"I don't understand," I said.

"It's what's keeping the primordials away from her," Dani told me. "Not the light. The light just lets her switch on and off the powers of those bathed in it. The bell is the key here."

"Did she say what she's going to do with it?"

Dani shook her head. "Nothing good."

"Stay here; try to shut the tear," I said; it had shrunk to the size of a thumb. "I'll stop Callie."

"And if you can't?" Dani asked.

"Then I guess we're all in deep shit," I said.

"The oxforth were fading," Dani said. "I think using the bell means they can't run as quickly as they usually do. It seems to absorb power . . . I'm not really sure how it works. But hopefully, you can catch them up."

I handed the sword to Dani. "Just in case," I said.

"You think Matthew is dead?" she asked.

I shrugged. "Cockroaches tend to be survivors," I said. "But we can hope."

I left Dani to deal with the tear and turned to smoke, moving as quickly as possible toward Callie and whatever devastation she had planned.

CHAPTER TWENTY-NINE

I flew just above the snow, pushing myself. I hadn't wanted to admit how much teleporting around the fight with the husks had taken out of me, but after a while, I couldn't continue in smoke form and re-formed.

The snow was deep, but the tracks were clear and easy to follow, even though it continued to snow hard. The thunder and lightning became more constant, and the cold was beginning to seep through.

I reached the top of the steep hill that led to the path between the mountains. There was an actual name for it, although I had no idea what it was, and now wasn't really the time to care. I half-ran, half-skidded down the hundred-meter hill until I reached the path between the mountains, and stopped. Power flooded out of the path, making walking difficult. It felt like pushing my way through invisible treacle.

Every step took concentration, and more than once, I stepped, realised my foot had turned to smoke, and had to re-form myself. The level of power that flowed out from the Tempest under the mountains was uncontrollable. I wasn't even sure I could get to Callie, stop her, and survive myself. But if that was the case, if I was going to die, I figured I may as well die doing something good.

It took an age to walk the few hundred meters of the dark path under the mountains, with only blue and purple crystals in the walls for light. It was large enough to fly an airplane through, and while there was no snow inside, the cold air whipped through like a wind tunnel.

I found three of the four oxforth about halfway through the tunnel. All dead. None had a mark on them.

The light at the end grew larger and larger, and every step grew more difficult, until I was out in the open and it felt like a weight had been lifted off me.

The *open* was like nothing I'd ever seen.

I stood at the top of a basin that was the size of a city and hundreds, maybe thousands of feet deep. The basin was pale blue, with swirls of indigo, red, blue, and moss green at the top, and more and more purple the further down it went. It looked smooth enough to sleigh down, although I imagined it was the sort of thing you only got one go at.

The basin itself was made of primordial bone. Or, at least, it was rock that looked the exact same as the primordial bone. Was this where primordials were born? A question for a time when I didn't have to stop whatever Callie was doing.

In the centre of the basin was the Tempest. A massive swirling vortex of blue and purple power. Energy shot out of it up into the sky high above and exploded in lightning and thunder.

I was always told that coming there would kill me. That just being near the Tempest would kill me. The weirdest thing was how quiet it was. There was no sound when the power was ejected straight up. Despite the wind being ferocious, there was no noise as it passed over me. It was . . . peaceful.

"Move," Callie screamed, trying to force the remaining oxforth to get closer to the edge of the basin. She'd unhooked the cart from the animal and was trying to push the animal aside so that the cart could be moved.

"Callie," I shouted, pulling up the Talon mask I'd taken from Matthew so it sat atop my head.

Callie spun toward me, pulling a lever on the massive light, which set it glowing a bright yellow.

"You figured it out?" Callie asked.

"It's not about the light," I said walking slowly toward her. "It's about the bell hidden under the light. The light stops people from using their power. You're going to switch it on so the Tempest can't attack the bell underneath it and use the bell to somehow control the Tempest. Sound about right?"

Callie pulled a lever and the sides of the cart fell away, revealing the bell beneath. It was made, like Dani had said, from primordial bone, except . . . it wasn't.

"It's from the rock here, isn't it?" I said. "You've been here before. You mined some of the rock."

Callie pointed at me and laughed. "Been here dozens of times. The rock here is infused with the power of the Tempest itself."

Callie picked up a piece of rock from the floor beside her and flung it into the basin, against the wall. The Tempest immediately whipped against where the rock had struck, making a sound like . . . lightning. It echoed all around me as power shot up through the top of the mountain and vanished from view. The Tempest visibly calmed until the sound passed.

"The Tempest reaches out to the rock," Callie said. "The bell sound calms the Tempest. I plan on controlling that sound; therefore I control the Tempest. Every time it strikes the rock, it causes a tear somewhere in the rift. I've done the maths, Lucas."

"You can't possibly know where the tear will open," I said. "That's insane."

"Look at the basin," Callie said. "*Really* look at it."

I dared to step closer to the basin edge and looked down at . . . Oh, shit . . . It was a map. "It's the rift," I said, my voice echoing around me.

"*Exactly,*" Callie said. "The Ancients knew about it. They knew that the Tempest tore into this mountain. They knew that this basin formed a map of the rift. They knew they could find out where and when the tears would happen."

The Tempest struck the basin a dozen times in quick succession before falling calm again.

"Did the Tempest form the map?" I asked.

"I don't know," Callie said. "This bell will stop the Tempest from striking repeatedly. When activated, it will keep the Tempest calm. When switched off, I'll be able to tell where and when the tear will open. *Exactly.* I plan on, over time, working the Tempest to only open where it needs to."

"Based on your needs," I said.

"Who better than me?" Callie asked, and pulled the lever on the cart, which set the bell chiming away.

The Tempest changed, little flicks of power moving out from the centre, scorching the side of the basin with a sound like a whip crack, which echoed all around. The oxforth moved quickly to the side of the mountains that were all around us.

The Tempest calmed, almost shrinking, but it struck out again, hitting the basin just below the cart with a whip of power that shot up into the sky above the mountain again, but this time, it remained open. And it got bigger and bigger, until there was a sound like something tearing metal apart and the tear snapped shut.

The power slammed back down into the mountain, smashing into the basin and exploding outward.

I was picked up and thrown back across to the side of the mountain, tearing into the wall and dropping to the floor. The other oxforth was . . . disintegrated where it stood as the cart was pushed back into Callie, who screamed in pain as it slammed into her, throwing her back against the wall as the bright yellow light cracked, its power fading.

"No," Callie shouted, getting back to her feet and reaching for the cart. "You will not."

Was she talking to the Tempest? That was . . . actually I wasn't sure that was the most insane thing I'd seen today.

Callie grabbed hold of the cart and pulled the lever on the side again, the light shining brighter than before. She pulled a second lever and the bell rang over and over, quicker than it had, louder too.

The Tempest . . . screamed. I felt it in my very soul as it reverberated around the interior of the mountain. There was no other word for it. It was a mass of pulsating power and it . . . screamed.

"Stop it," I shouted at Callie, who was busy quite literally screaming obscenities into the mass of power that was going to kill us all.

Walking hurt, moving hurt, just thinking hurt, but I managed to get to the cart and pull the lever to stop the bell. And just as quickly as it started, the screaming stopped.

"What did you do?" Callie shouted at me, nothing but rage in her eyes.

"It was going to bring a mountain down on us," I said, sitting back. I was unsure how I knew what I'd told her, but I knew it with utter certainty.

"It needs to be tamed," Callie roared.

Callie reached for the lever and I stepped forward, grabbing her and throwing her to the side. She screamed out as she struck the ground, kicked out at me, catching my knee, and dove toward me. She changed direction at the last second and threw herself toward the cart, but a whip of energy from the Tempest smashed into the cart, destroying the brake lever and throwing both her and me back several feet. The cart began to slowly roll toward the edge of basin as Tempest energy crackled and whipped toward it, destroying the crystal light.

Power flooded over me as the light broke. I dove for the cart, leaping over Callie, who had crashed to the ground. I turned to smoke and re-formed atop the cart, pushing down the remains of the brake lever, trying to stop the cart from going over the basin edge and . . . I had no idea what would happen. I couldn't imagine it would be good, though.

There were four levers not broken, so I started to pull each of them. One started the bell up again, and before I could reverse it, there was a crack of energy from the Tempest which smashed into the cart, obliterating it and sending me flying back into the wall.

Callie crawled to the edge of the basin, toward the cart, and a whip of red energy hit her. She spiraled across the air, smashing into the mountain with a thud. Her arm was charred, a mass of blackened skin that went up to her shoulder, but she was no longer bleeding. I picked her up as the Tempest exploded, throwing us both through the mouth of the tunnel. I lost my grip on Callie, who fell a few feet from me and used the wall of the tunnel to get back to her feet.

Callie sprinted back toward the cart as it teetered over the edge of the basin, and I managed to get back to my feet and charge after her. Callie flung herself toward the cart, grabbing hold of it before it could go over.

"No," I shouted, running to the side of the basin and watching in horror as the remains of the cart went over the edge, with Callie still holding on to it.

"Let go," I shouted, managing to grab Callie as she lost her grip on the cart, which rattled down the basin toward the Tempest, the bell ringing with every rattling movement, and smashed into the side of the Tempest and vanished.

A crack of power reached out and struck Callie in the back, and she screamed in pain, slipping out of my grasp. I held on to her, dropping to my knees, and I noticed that the Tempest had wrapped a whip of power around her legs.

"I will not make you a martyr," I yelled, but there was a shockwave of power out of the Tempest, which threw me back across the interior of the mountain.

I hit the ground hard as Callie vanished over the rim of the basin.

I sprinted to the edge of the basin and watched as Callie scrambled in vain to get ahold of anything that might stop her tumble down the steep slope of the basin. Her screams of pain were lost in the roar of power that left the Tempest as it grew twice in size and Callie was engulfed.

Power exploded out of the Tempest, rocketing up into the sky and tearing the heavens above us asunder with reds and purples.

I ran back to the mouth of the tunnel as pieces of the mountain began to rain down around me. I hit the tunnel at a full sprint as it collapsed behind me. I hurried my pace; I was not going to get buried under a god-damned mountain.

I turned to smoke and moved as quickly as possible, reaching the mouth of the tunnel as a huge piece of the mountain smashed into the ground only a few feet in front of me. I had gotten a few hundred meters from the tunnel when I re-formed and looked up.

There were primordials flying in the sky above, huge things with massive wingspans who might not be thrilled to discover that someone had come into their home and decided to blow it up.

The sound of large pieces of mountain hitting the ground behind me stayed with me the entire time I sprinted up the hill and back toward where I'd left Dani. She was still sat on the ground, the small tear still open, although now energy was pouring out of it, directly up into the sky.

The sky. Oh shit, the sky.

The sky directly above the Tempest was one giant tear that spilled out in all directions, power leaking out of it. There was only darkness beyond the tear, unlike where you could usually see what part of Earth the tear linked to.

"What happened to Callie?" Dani asked.

"She was engulfed by the Tempest," I said. "Her little cart too. Turns out that's bad."

Dani looked appropriately terrified. "Can we fix this?"

I shrugged. "Not a clue. I've never seen anything like it. The power is just flowing out of that tear above the Tempest. I can't imagine the damage it's doing on Earth."

I picked up my sword and sheathed it as I looked toward the end of the snow plains. Valmore was only a short distance away, running toward us at full speed. "I think we've got a lift," I said.

Valmore stopped beside us. "Callie is dead?" he asked.

I nodded.

"Good," he said. "That woman is responsible for a lot of awful things."

"You okay?" I asked. Valmore had a nasty cut on the back of one leg and one under his jaw, but neither appeared to be dangerous.

"We managed to stop the attack," Valmore said. "Your friends, Melody and Seluku, are safe. The fighting spilled into the fog and out onto the tundra at the other side. The husks charged them before your friends were all the way through. It was like they lost all control. It was . . . messy."

"Thank you for your help," I said. "Any chance of a lift back?"

"Climb on," Valmore said, shrinking down so that Dani, who was still shackled with no key in sight, could get on his back, then he increased in size.

"I will go slow," Valmore said, and set off at what felt like a gentle speed.

We had reached the edge of the snowy plains when the top of the mountain exploded and the tear in the sky vanished.

CHAPTER THIRTY

Once we were back by the fog of Harmony, we were met by Seluku and Melody, both of whom had braved the fog to welcome us.

They helped Dani down from Valmore's back, while I climbed down myself. Dani slumped to the ground, clearly exhausted.

"What happened at the Tempest?" Seluku asked.

I looked back at it, half expecting to see the sky torn apart again, but there was nothing there. "I . . . don't . . . know," I said slowly, pausing between each word in case something might happen the second I said it.

"We saw the mountain," Melody said.

"Yeah, I did too," I told her, feeling more than a little confused. "I was literally under it at the time."

"At least the tear stopped," Valmore said.

"And Callie?" Melody asked.

"Callie was engulfed by the Tempest," I said. "It's not ideal, but honestly, she deserved it. That stays with us; I don't want her becoming a martyr to every asshole who thinks they can control a source of limitless power."

"You'll not tell Neb?" Seluku asked.

"Okay, maybe tell Neb," I said. "She might actually know what the hell happened."

"For now, just take the win," Melody told me.

"I want to stay here for a while," Dani said, getting to her feet. "I want to help deal with the aftermath of everything that happened. There are a lot of rift-walkers who have been used by Callie and her people, and they're going to be scared and unsure of who to trust."

"You are most welcome, little one," Valmore said with something approximating a smile. "I can take you both back to your gate. It would be safer for everyone."

Seluku smiled and looked over at me. "Thank you for all you've done, Lucas. And Valmore."

Melody, Seluku, and Dani climbed up onto Valmore. "I will see you soon," Valmore said.

"I'm going back to Earth," I said. "I'll be back soon enough. I need to see some people."

"You're going through the rift?" Seluku asked.

I nodded. "I want to know that whatever Callie did is *actually* done. Might as well use my rift-science degree for something other than decoration."

I watched the four of them leave, opened my embers, and stepped through, walking through the forest with a sense of ease and finding Maria and Casimir waiting at the other side, where I'd left them.

"So?" Casimir the falcon asked.

"So, I have no clue," I said, and explained everything I'd gone through.

"You just passing through, then?" Maria asked as we walked though my embers.

I nodded. "Need to let people know what happened; need to go back to the rift and . . . well, figure out if this is actually done or not."

"And if it's not?" Casimir asked.

"Then we figure out how to stop it," I said, stopping outside a Carthaginian-styled house.

"See you soon, then," Maria said.

I smiled and stepped through the tear, finding myself in Gabriel's front room. I picked up my Talon mask from the table beside me and compared it to the one I'd taken from Matthew. Mine looked nicer, but I placed them both on the table as Gabriel entered the room.

"Good to see you," he said, giving me a hug. "Long few days?"

"The longest," I said. "Any chance you can get Ji-hyun on the computer? There are some things I need to explain."

It didn't take long for Gabriel to set it up, sitting beside me on the sofa while his laptop dialled through to Ji-hyun's phone. She answered after two rings.

"Lucas," Ji-hyun said. "You're in one piece."

"Mostly," I said. "Callie is dead. Matthew is . . . hopefully dead. The husks are all but destroyed. She has a compound in Texas. Lots of people there need help." I texted her the location as I remembered it.

"We'll get on it," Ji-hyun said. "Do you know about the husks in Boston?"

"It was all a ruse," I said. "Yeah, I heard. Hope no one got hurt by whatever those things were she left for you. They used to be human."

"Not much left of them now," Ji-hyun said. "Where's Dani?"

"Staying in the rift to help," I told her. "Lots of people got hurt, lots of rift-walkers. Lots more people who worked for Callie need to be dealt with."

"And you?" she asked.

I told her my plans.

"Putting that degree to use, I see," Ji-hyun said.

"That's exactly what I told everyone," I said with a chuckle. "Thank Drusilla for me. I'll arrange our meal when I get back. Hopefully, it won't be long. How's Nadia?"

"She's good," Ji-hyun said. "Well, she's Nadia, so your mileage may vary. You know there are people out there who helped Callie do all of this."

I nodded. "I know, and we'll find them."

"We'll look into it here," Gabriel said. "If this isn't the end of Callie's machinations, I'd like to know in advance."

"It's the end of Callie," I said. "Unless being disintegrated by the Tempest isn't a permanent thing."

I recalled the fear on her face, the almost-living power of the Tempest. The desire to protect itself was unexpected. There was more there than I think anyone realised.

"Take care, Lucas," Ji-hyun said. "Thank you for your help."

"Thanks to you, too," I said. "Couldn't have done it without you."

I ended the call and immediately dialled Noah's number. He flashed up a few seconds later.

"Lucas," Noah said.

"Hiroyuki?" I asked. "He okay?"

Noah nodded. "He's all good. Thank you for your help in all this. I will arrange payment to your bank accounts."

"Send it to Gabriel's," I said, to Gabriel's obvious shock. "I don't need the money, and he can do a lot of good with it. I'm going to be in the rift for a while. Things to take care of. Did you know that the basin under the Tempest is a map of the rift?"

Noah stared at me for several seconds, and I thought that maybe the screen had frozen. "Yes," he said softly. "Ancients all know this."

"You've always known where the tears will happen in the rift," I said.

"But not where that corresponds to Earth," he said. "No way to track that."

"Callie wanted to find a way," I said. "She wanted to control where and when the tears happen. She has backing, Noah. Not just Prime Roberts and his cronies but serious backing."

"You think an Ancient is involved?" he asked.

I nodded.

"I will keep my ears open for any news," Noah said. "If someone bank-rolled Callie, there's no way of knowing if they'd bankroll someone else."

"Glad you see it my way," I said.

"Ancients should be protecting people, Lucas," Noah said, a little hurt. "Not making ourselves more powerful."

Noah ended the call, and I sat there for a moment and stared at the blank screen before getting to my feet and stretching.

"I think you offended him," Gabriel said.

"He'll get over it," I told him. "In the meantime, I'm going back to the rift. I'm going to figure out just how safe the Tempest is now, considering what happened."

"Be safe, my friend," Gabriel said, and hugged me again.

I picked up the mask I'd taken from Matthew. "I'll take this with me," I said. "I'll leave mine with you. Just in case I need to get back here."

"This is your home, too, Lucas," Gabriel said. "Feel free to come and go as you please."

"Thank you," I said, opening my embers. "See you soon."

ACKNOWLEDGEMENTS

And that's the first three Riftborn books done. I hope you've enjoyed the journey so far.

There are, as always, numerous people who have helped me get this book written, edited, and published.

My wife, Vanessa, and my daughters, Keira, Faith, and Harley. Their support can't really be measured. They're part of the reason I write; they're part of the reason I ever decided to try and get published in the first place. Thank you for everything you do.

To my parents, who have always been supportive of my writing and read every book I publish, thank you for being there all these years, and I am sorry (not really) for the amount of space the wall of my covers now takes up.

To my family, my friends, all of those people who have supported me, who have contacted me to tell me they've loved my work, who listen to me going on about ideas and complaining about how my brain won't shut up for five minutes to let me work on one thing, you're all awesome.

My agent, Paul Lucas, is a hell of a good guy and one I'm privileged to be able to call my agent and friend. Thank you for all you do.

To everyone at Podium. I've been working with Nicole, Victoria, Leah, Cole, and Kyle for a few books now. It's been a genuine pleasure to work with them all and I look forward to what the future brings.

My editor, Julie Crisp. An incredible editor who helps make my work better and who manages to translate the sometimes word salad that is an early draft of my book. Thank you for being awesome to work with.

To Pius Bak, the artist who did the incredible covers to all three Riftborn books. Thank you for your amazing work.

A big thank you to everyone at Wunderkind PR, who were brilliant to work with and put together a lot of cool stuff for the launch of *The Last Raven*.

Last, but by no means least, to everyone else who picks up my books, whether this is the first one or those who have followed my work for years, thank you.

ABOUT THE AUTHOR

Steve McHugh is the bestselling author of the Hellequin Chronicles. His novel *Scorched Shadows* was nominated for a David Gemmell Award for Fantasy in 2018. Born in Mexborough, South Yorkshire, McHugh currently lives with his wife and three daughters in Southampton.

DISCOVER
STORIES UNBOUND

PodiumAudio.com

Printed in the USA
CPSIA information can be obtained
at www.ICGtesting.com
JSHW022219140824
68134JS00018B/1140